THE RED WOMAN AND THE WHITE BEAR

FERN A. ELLIS

Copyright © 2024 by Fern A. Ellis
www.fernaellis.com
Cover art by Clella Red

All rights reserved.

No part of this publication may be reproduced, distributed, or transmitted in any form or by any means, including photocopying, recording, or other electronic or mechanical methods, without the prior written permission of the publisher, except as permitted by U.S. copyright law. For permission requests, contact Fern A. Ellis.

The story, all names, characters, and incidents portrayed in this production are fictitious. No identification with actual persons (living or deceased), places, buildings, and products is intended or should be inferred.

Identifiers: ISBN 979-8-9910523-0-6 (paperback) | ISBN 979-8-9910523-1-3 (e-book)

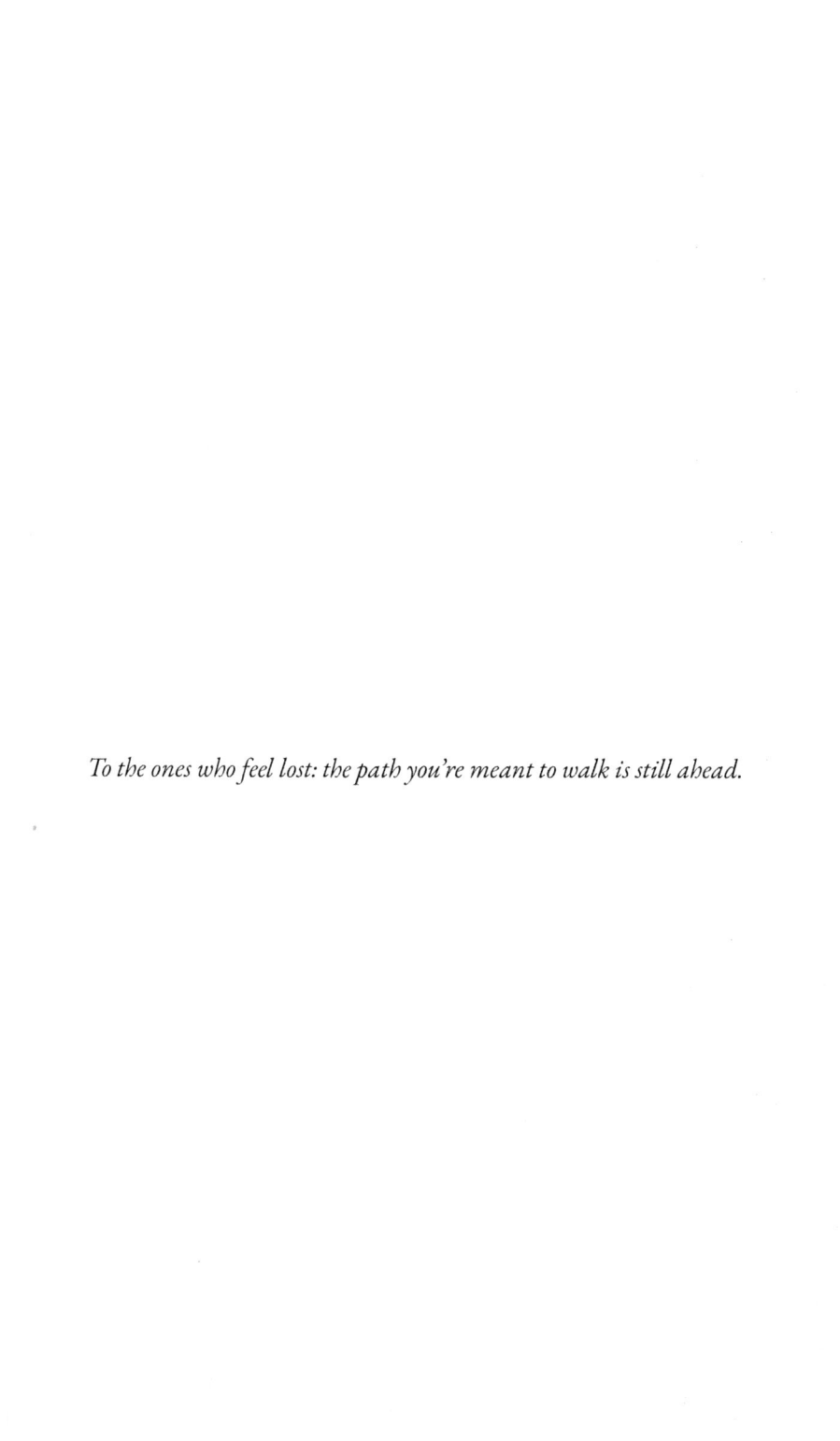

To the ones who feel lost: the path you're meant to walk is still ahead.

Contents

1. The Hunt — 3
2. The Shadowwood Mother — 19
3. Rodney — 33
4. A Plan — 45
5. Nocturne, Part I: The Invocation — 59
6. Nocturne, Part II: The Revelry — 71
7. Nocturne, Part III: The Manipulation — 83
8. The Night Garden — 95
9. To Feed the King — 109
10. Stilled — 121
11. Into Battle — 131
12. A More Comfortable Prison — 141
13. Caged Bird — 153
14. Mirrored — 165
15. Playing the Game — 177

16.	A Traitorous Heart	187
17.	Release	197
18.	Untethered	209
19.	A Small Mercy	221
20.	A Colossal, Damned Mistake	229
21.	Homecoming	241
22.	Ivran and the Dryads	251
23.	The Seelie Court	261
24.	The Breath of Life	275
25.	Shattered	285
26.	Dinner	287
27.	The Archives	303
28.	Door Number Three	317
29.	A Favor	329
30.	Too Important to Ignore	339
31.	Salve	347
32.	An Old Injury	359
33.	The White Bear	369
34.	Leverage	383
35.	Resistance	395
36.	Affinity	407

37.	A Heavy Crown	421
38.	A Study in Dichotomy	433
39.	As the Moon Draws the Tides	445
40.	Shadows and Vines	459
41.	The Red Woman	469
42.	The Silver Saints	479
43.	Elowas	487
Pronunciation Guide		493

Come away, O human child!
To the waters and the wild.
With a faery, hand in hand,
For the world's more full of weeping than you can understand.

W.B. Yeats

1

THE HUNT

AISLING

The cry was soft and distant, scarcely louder than the crunch of dry brush beneath her boots. Though it was difficult to see amidst the unchanging pines, evergreen no matter the season, the bitter-edged chill that swept through on the breeze was telling enough: fall had come hard and fast, with very little warning. Aisling stilled, straining to hear over the ambient sounds of the forest. It came again, still quiet, but closer this time. A few seconds later, the cry was followed by a trumpet blast. Its low, keening trill drew a cold sweat to bead across the back of her neck. *A warning*.

To anyone else on the island, it would have sounded similar enough to the ferry's foghorn to write off. Aisling knew better, though. She recognized this sound, if only from her mother's stories. But according to those same stories, it wasn't yet hunting season.

Either way, she didn't think she had wandered so far off the forest path as to cross into the borderlands.

Holding a bundle of firewood tight against her chest, she froze, hoping that the next sound would be muted as it moved in another direction. As she waited and listened, her mind drifted back to her mother's accounts of the creatures and beings she might encounter passing through the woods. Creatures both kind and cruel, most falling somewhere in between. Some that would lead a lost hiker home should they stray too far off the map, and some that would lure them even deeper into the forest. It was those beings of dubious morality that she feared now, far from her group and without even a pocketknife to defend herself.

Another blast of the horn, flat and haunting, set her teeth on edge. The knowledge of what it signaled, even more so. Up ahead, Briar had stopped, too. The pale fur on the dog's hackles rose slowly. A growl was building somewhere low in his chest.

"Briar, close," Aisling commanded. The large Pyrenees could almost certainly hear the anxiety in her voice; he only needed to be told once. He crept backward to his place by her side, eyes focused ahead into the deep wood. The undergrowth there was dense. It needed to be cleared and burned before winter.

Aisling shuffled to crouch in the shadow of a tall pine tree and pressed herself against its bark while she listened, eyes squeezed shut, trying to get a sense of what direction the sounds were echoing from. Whether the chase was coming towards her, or away. The woods fell still, so silent that both Aisling and Briar's breathing seemed impossibly loud.

THE RED WOMAN AND THE WHITE BEAR

That stillness was broken by something tumbling raucously through the underbrush, rapidly moving closer and closer. It sounded low to the ground—a chipmunk, maybe. *No, bigger than that. A rabbit?* But it was no rabbit. A tiny figure raced into view, emerging from a swaying bed of sword ferns. It was a woman; or, at least, something that resembled a woman. Her features were upturned, all delicate lines and sharp angles as if pinched from clay. Despite the way she'd crashed into the clearing, there was a certain lightness to her. A too-strong breeze could have swept her away.

Briar rose out of his defensive posture, more curious now than afraid. Aisling, too, was captivated by the being's appearance. She moved with frenetic energy, tripping on twigs and vaulting over stones that were nearly half her size. Her stride was both graceful and erratic as she navigated the forest terrain with a sense of urgency.

The subtle rustling of Briar's fur as he shifted drew the being's attention, and she froze at once. When their eyes locked, Aisling was gripped by a falling sensation in her stomach as though her foot had missed a step. Something shook loose deep in her mind—something she couldn't quite place, but that felt all too familiar.

Another long blast from the horn reverberated through the air. This tiny being was the target of a Fae hunt, and the riders were rapidly closing the distance between them. How many of them, Aisling hadn't a clue, but they'd without a doubt be armed. Aisling's heart raced with indecision. Something instinctual urged her to stay hidden and keep her distance from the pursuit. After all, it wasn't her problem, and getting involved could mean putting herself and Briar at the tip of an arrow or sword or whatever other weapons the hunters carried. *Do not involve yourself uninvited with matters of the Fae,* her mother had warned more than once. The logical part of Aisling's mind screamed for self-preservation.

But as she studied the figure's face, terror and desperation etched into her delicate features, a surge of empathy washed over Aisling. She wrestled with her conscience, torn between the fear of the unknown and the pull of compassion. Her mind parsed swiftly through the possibilities until, amidst the chaos of her thoughts, a resolute determination welled up within her.

She couldn't leave the being to this fate.

Of the three, Aisling was the first to move. She shrugged her backpack from her shoulders and pulled it open. The being's large black eyes darted back and forth between Aisling and the bag, once. Twice. A flicker of hope glimmered in them. Then she made her decision, scrambling forward and diving into the pack. Once she'd braced herself inside, it was Aisling's turn to run.

"Let's go, Briar!" She barked the order and spun on her heel to sprint back toward the trail she'd left an hour before. Adrenaline flooded through her veins and urged her further, faster. Her movements were far less graceful than the tiny female's had been, but her long legs could cover five times the ground in one stride. Ducking under branches and hurtling over rotting logs, her fear turned into something closer to giddy defiance.

Gradually, the sound of the horn faded into the distance and the sounds of the forest began to filter back in. Still, Aisling ran in a zig-zag pattern until she reached the trail and jogged another hundred meters for good measure before she stooped to set the bag on the ground.

Briar kept a respectful distance and eased himself into a submissive posture. His tail wagged lazily through the dirt after their run, which must have seemed like a great game. The being clamored out on shaky legs. Up close, her size seemed even more impossible. She was just as long as Aisling's forearm and her garments were sewn from leaves with delicate stitchwork only such little hands could manage.

Unsure whether such a creature could even understand her, Aisling spoke breathlessly: "You should be safe now."

She cocked her head to one side, then the other, globe-like black eyes studying Aisling and Briar with equal parts terror and fascination. They regarded each other for a beat longer before the being turned and darted off into the darkening woods on the opposite side of the trail.

"Aisling!" Her friends called out to her from the trailhead, and she rose to her feet and dusted herself off. Her hands trembled; the adrenaline was overpowering and would take hours yet to wane. The beam of a flashlight cut through the hazy dusk and found her face. Squinting against the glare, she reached up to shield her eyes.

"I was just on my way back," she called out in response. She stole one last glance back—first in the direction the being had run, then to where they'd just emerged from the trees, half-expecting to see the hunters lurking there in the shadows. She let out a sharp breath of relief when she found either side of the trail to be empty.

Briar rose to his feet and sniffed the spot where the being had stood moments before. Aisling reached out and nudged him away halfheartedly—his curiosity was one of her favorite things about him. Four years prior, Aisling had been left brokenhearted when the man she was sure she'd marry left her without so much as a goodbye. The apartment she moved into was small and lonely, and on a whim she'd stopped at a pet store after work to pick up a fish. A betta, she thought, like the blue one she had for a summer when she was young. She'd wanted something to take care of other than herself.

But when she met Briar's warm brown eyes, the decision to take him home had already been made for her. He was barely three years old then, but already weighed 130 pounds and was by far the largest dog at the adoption event. Ignoring the impracticality of bringing the colossal Pyrenees into her city apartment, Aisling had lied on the paperwork and written her old home address on Brook Isle as her permanent residence. They'd been inseparable since.

"Where's the firewood?" It was Lida rounding the corner ahead, with Jackson holding the light.

"It was all too damp," Aisling lied. "We'll have to make do with what we brought."

Jackson swore. "We've burned through a lot of it already."

She shrugged. "Send Seb back to town for more. He's the one that insisted two bundles would be enough."

Aisling sunk her hands deep into her pockets to hide the tremors and marched up the trail ahead of Lida before her friend could link their arms. On the walk back to camp, her thoughts remained consumed by the encounter with the small being and the odd sense of familiarity it had sparked in the back of her mind. Just how closely it mirrored elements of her mother's stories about the faeries she'd encountered when Aisling was a child.

Lida increased her pace to catch up and glanced at Aisling with concern. "Are you alright?"

Aisling forced a smile and attempted to push aside the lingering unease. "I'm fine," she replied, her voice betraying a hint of tension. "Just got startled by something up the trail. And I'm annoyed about our firewood situation."

Lida's brow furrowed a bit, sensing that there was more to the story, but she didn't press further. Instead, she changed the topic to the group's dinner plans—Seb had started grilling burgers. Aisling appreciated the distraction.

Seb's face, illuminated by the flames of the grill, fell when he saw Aisling and the others return without the armfuls of wood he'd clearly hoped they'd be carrying.

"What happened?"

"Poor planning," Jackson grumbled. He walked over to the fire and kicked a couple of logs off the top. They were just beginning to catch around the rough edges of the bark and would be better saved for later on as the night darkened.

Aisling crossed the campsite to unzip her tent, and Briar lumbered in past her to stretch out on her sleeping bag. Before tossing her backpack into the corner, Aisling peered inside. The little being hadn't left any trace behind, not a single hair or bit of dirt or scrap of fabric. It was almost as if she'd imagined the whole thing. Maybe she had.

Seb and Jackson were arguing over the firewood issue, both adamant the other should go back into town for more, so Aisling snagged a burger off the grill and a beer from the cooler and went to join Lida by the fire. She wasn't hungry, but it would give her something to do with her still-shaking hands.

"What do you think you heard on the trail?" Lida asked as Aisling sat down in a camp chair beside her. They pulled them up to the small fire, close enough that the pair could rest their feet on the ring of stacked rocks that encircled it. Any further back, and they wouldn't have been able to feel its heat at all.

"I don't know. A bear, most likely." The look of terror that crossed Lida's face was too serious for her to let the joke lie. "I'm teasing," Aisling amended quickly. "Probably just a deer. They're all over out here."

"Jesus, Ash," Lida sighed. "You were out there awhile. Jackson thought you'd gotten lost."

"Jackson doesn't know you're a walking compass," Seb interjected. He lowered himself onto the ground behind the girls and leaned against the log, balancing two burgers on his plate. "You know this place like the back of your hand."

"Used to," Aisling corrected. "It's changed a lot."

"Not that much. It's still in there." He flicked a bottle cap at her head and it fell into the fire when she dodged it. She rolled her eyes.

"Right before we found you earlier, I was starting to tell Jackson about that trip we all went on in high school, remember it?" A grin spread across Lida's face, her raven hair framing it in the dancing light.

Of course she did. "I don't think we need to relive it again."

Lida took a swig from her water bottle and let out a hearty laugh. "Come on, it's one of my favorites."

"This was the time we got into my brother's stash of booze, right?" Seb leaned forward so he could be a part of the conversation. Aisling nodded.

"I haven't heard this story," Jackson chimed in, joining the group. He patted Lida's knee, and when she rose, he sank into her chair and pulled her back down to sit sideways across his lap.

"Your wife doesn't come out of it looking great," Seb teased.

Lida swatted at his leg. "It was a class trip; we were supposed to be learning about...something."

"Constellations," Aisling supplied.

"Constellations, right. But Seb brought his brother's watered-down vodka, and we snuck off after Mr. Wilke went to bed. I think it was my first time drinking anything besides beer. It was your first time drinking anything at all, wasn't it?" Lida looked across at Aisling, who nodded. The memory of the alcohol's sharp burn on her tongue and its acrid aftertaste made her wrinkle her nose. Drain cleaner would have tasted better.

"And," Seb added, "all we'd had to eat was a hot dog apiece."

"We were trying to find one of the old hunting cabins to hang out in," Lida continued, her words punctuated by fits of giggles. They were infectious, as always, and laughter bubbled up in Aisling's chest as well. For the first time since her encounter off the trail, she felt she had mentally rejoined her friends. "By the time we gave up and decided to turn around, Seb could hardly see straight."

"Me?" he demanded. "Let's talk about you! You ripped a hole in your jeans trying to get over a log."

Jackson looked up at his wife for confirmation and she nodded, breathless from laughter now.

"I thought I could slide across it like the hood of a car; my entire ass was out. We were stumbling around like fawns, neither of us could walk straight. But you, Aisling," Lida pointed to her with her water bottle. "Even drunk, you led us right back to camp like you'd known where we were the entire time. I don't think you tripped once."

Aisling's face grew warm. "I'm sure I did once or twice."

"No way," Seb said. "You never do. You were practically cross-eyed but as surefooted as ever."

The forest around the group quieted for a moment, the atmosphere at the campsite stilling, before a low rumble began beneath their feet. The earth began to shake, then undulate, rolling like ocean waves. Several of the rocks stacked around the fire tumbled off. Briar ran unsteadily from Aisling's tent, tail tucked, to her side. She gripped his collar in one hand and her beer in the other, hard, so her knuckles blanched white as she attempted to brace herself against the tremors.

The earthquake lasted for only several seconds, and though Aisling's attention turned immediately to inspect the surrounding trees for leaning trunks or falling branches, her friends were unbothered. Lida stood up off of Jackson's lap to get herself a beer from the cooler.

"That was a big one," Aisling said, a little breathless, as the sounds of the forest crept back in. She'd felt a handful of tremors since returning to the island. Most of those had been so small and over so quickly that she might have thought them caused by a passing truck, had trucks that large been able to reach the island in the first place.

"We've had bigger," Seb said nonchalantly. He reached out to give Briar a reassuring pat on the head. "Remember the one around this time last year?"

Lida nodded, then settled back onto Jackson's lap. "I hate them, though."

"It's the damn fault line. One of these days, I swear it'll open up and swallow us all whole," Jackson joked. Lida elbowed him hard.

Seb shrugged and tossed his empty bottle toward the trash bag by the grill. He missed by several feet. "You laugh, but that crack in my driveway is proof enough for me."

Jackson's brows shot up. "No shit? I didn't realize that was from the quakes."

"Real glad to be back now, aren't you?" Seb's tone was sarcastic when he turned to address Aisling, but she answered honestly as her heart rate slowed and her fear of falling trees abated.

"I am, I think," she said. "Earthquakes and all."

"So…did you all get in trouble or what?" Jackson asked, drawing the group back into the memory they'd been discussing before nature's interruption.

Lida nodded, letting out a short burst of laughter that subsided into a grimace as she recalled the ending. "Not until the following morning."

"When Mr. Wilke caught me stuffing my sleeping bag into the trash," Aisling filled in the rest. "After your beautiful wife threw up in it." Lida buried her face in her hands when Jackson feigned gagging.

"I've always envied you for that, you know," Seb added and nudged Aisling's leg with his beer. "If I knew this island half as well as you, you lot would never see me again. I'd be a hermit living out here in the woods somewhere."

"Says the one who didn't bring enough firewood," Jackson nagged, still a bit annoyed. Lida nudged him playfully and Seb rolled his eyes. Aisling leaned forward to put another log atop the dying flames. There was only one left to burn once it finished, but she didn't mind much.

As the group continued to reminisce on into the night, their laughter mingled with the rustling of leaves and the crickets' melodic song. She'd missed them, missed nights like this. It was in these moments that she could hardly imagine ever returning to her life on the mainland.

Without the searing heat of the bonfire they'd all hoped for, the temperature grew to be just shy of uncomfortably cold. Once they burned the last log down to smoldering ash and each retreated to their tents for the night, Aisling took one last walk around the perimeter of the campground before settling in. However well her friends had managed to distract her, she couldn't shake the feeling of being watched from somewhere in the darkness. She imagined keen eyes peering out from the leaves, grasping arms prepared to snatch her up and spirit her away. But nothing jumped out at her. No heads poked out from behind the trees and no hands reached for her ankles from the underbrush. Even still, sleep felt a long way off as Aisling wrapped herself in her sleeping bag.

Like chasing after the tail end of a dream upon waking, she could almost recall what the tiny being reminded her of. Its pinched face was reminiscent of something blurry deep in the recesses of her memory. Her mother would have told her about something like it, maybe. Or perhaps she'd drawn a similar faerie once; it might be buried someplace in the pile of sketchbooks Aisling had found in an unlabeled box in her father's closet. She hadn't yet paged through them, but Aisling could recall sitting on the living room rug as a child watching her mother move a pencil over the page in fast, almost frantic strokes. Like she couldn't get the images out of her head fast enough. Though she would have undoubtedly referred to the being by a part of its name; Aisling hadn't even thought to ask. Not that it would have understood her either way.

She was nervous, too, that the hunters would have caught her scent. If they'd been as close behind their quarry as they sounded, it was likely. In her haste to flee, she knew she hadn't done enough to cover her tracks. There was little chance they would cross this far to seek her out, but she thought that she should avoid that part of the forest for a while in case they'd marked her. A shiver ran up her spine, imagining hunters on horseback riding her down. But Briar seemed wholly unconcerned, and she took the cue from him that they weren't in any danger for the moment. She reached down to where he was curled behind her knees and scratched the top of his head. He stirred, pressed tighter against her, then settled again. His calm was contagious and eased Aisling's lingering unease enough for her to allow her eyes to drift closed and her brain to finally quiet.

⁘

Aisling hadn't been asleep for long when she awoke to Briar's hot breath on the side of her face. She reached up to shove him away, but he panted insistently and drove his wet nose into her ear.

"Alright, I'm up," she groused. Aisling pushed herself into a seated position. Her legs were tangled in the sleeping bag and she kicked to push it down to her ankles. In the dark, she fumbled blindly until her fingers found her lantern and she switched it on. Briar was sitting now by the flap of the tent, whining softly. He looked hard at Aisling, then through the mesh door into the night. Back and forth.

She groaned. "You can hold it until morning, Bri. Lay back down."

He pawed at the flap, nearly catching his nail on the zipper. He'd have figured out how to pull it open if Aisling hadn't pushed him aside first. With another groan, she slipped on her boots. Briar seemed almost surprised when she hooked the leash onto his collar before she pulled the zipper down and nodded for him to go on. She could have let him out by himself, but she didn't trust the forest tonight.

"It's not you, it's me, buddy," she muttered. In the haze of sleep, it took her a second to realize how silent the night had become, just as it had moments before the earthquake. The crickets had hushed and the owl that had been perched above since sundown had ceased its hooting. The only sound was a breeze that rustled through the pines and wove through the brush, a dry whisper. But this time, the earth didn't tremble. Something else had drawn the silence across the campsite.

A glimmer caught Aisling's eye—a distant object up the trail was catching the silvery moonlight and reflecting it toward her in a flashing pattern. A long, low whistle accompanied it: one unbroken sound, carried on the breeze. Its pitch couldn't have been matched by the owl, nor any other bird Aisling would have recognized. She tugged on Briar's leash, but he'd heard it, too. He was rooted to the ground, immovable even when Aisling insisted he return with her to the tent. He rarely ignored her commands, if ever, but now he was so captivated by the small flickering light that he was deaf to her words. Then, he began pulling her towards it.

"Briar, *stop,*" Aisling hissed. She didn't want to wake the others, but panic was beginning to rise in her throat. *It's a trap,* she thought as she frantically tried to corral her large dog. *The hunters came back for me.* If they couldn't have their quarry, the human that had aided in its escape would be the next best thing—and certainly a much greater prize. She wrapped the leash twice around her hand to stop it from sliding through her sweaty palm and leaned her weight against it, but it was no use. Briar had a one-track mind and he was determined to drag her to that whistling light.

She hadn't thought to grab her pocketknife, or even to put on her coat before climbing out of the tent. She was grateful at least that she'd kept ahold of the lantern, but its dim light hardly made a dent. This was wilderness dark, thick and heavy as a woolen cloak and twice as strong as any light source she could throw at it.

Briar pressed forward, and as the pair neared the light, it stopped flickering. It was a still beacon now, and whatever held it a little over a foot off the ground didn't back away as they approached. Though he was bound and determined to reach his target, Briar's posture was relaxed. His tail hung down and swung loosely with each step, his soft footfall belying his size. And when they finally drew close enough to discern the figure in the middle of the trail, Aisling's breath caught in her throat. Almost as if a fragment of a dream had materialized in front of her, there stood the very same tiny being that she had rescued just hours before.

2

THE SHADOWWOOD MOTHER

AISLING

Briar, oblivious to the weight of the being's return, wagged his tail and approached her with an air of fascination. Aisling's mind raced as she tried to make sense of the situation, but there was an undeniable pull that drew her closer. With bated breath, she took a hesitant step forward, waiting for the being to make her next move. She lowered the tiny shard of mirror she'd been using to signal to Aisling and darted a few yards up the trail, stopping to turn every few steps. She wanted the pair to follow, Aisling realized. Placing the blame for her shivering on the cold instead of her fear, Aisling followed Briar's lead. He, too, continually glanced back at her as though to reassure her they were safe.

The group came upon a fork in the trail not far from where they'd parted ways earlier that evening. Rather than taking the left or the right path, the being instead continued straight, plunging into the woods. Aisling hesitated. Her raw nerves were still on edge—this was close, too close, to the path of the hunt. The party could still be nearby. When the small female stopped to wait for them, impatience obvious on her face, Briar doubled back to heel and pressed against Aisling's thigh. She relaxed; she trusted his intuition implicitly. If he was willing to forge ahead, she was too. Still, she dimmed the lantern to its lowest setting. The faint glow illuminated only just enough ground for her to see her next step and narrowly avoid the roots and rocks that dotted the ground. Navigating through the darkness, she was truly putting Seb's theory to the test.

They followed the being through the underbrush for what felt like hours, trudging ever deeper into the woods. The further they got, the more excited the tiny thing seemed to become. By the time she stopped, she was practically vibrating.

She'd led Aisling to the edge of a clearing, at the center of which stood a dense thicket—a tangle of towering trees and thorny bushes, their gnarled branches interlocking to form a web of shadowy limbs that came together as a sort of cave. Moss-covered rocks and fallen logs lay scattered on the ground, a testament to the passage of time that had long hung heavily on the island. The moonlight was different there in the glade. Brighter. Shafts of silver pierced through the clouds and diffused softly over patches of ferns and delicate wildflowers. The air carried the heady scent of damp earth and decaying leaves. To Aisling, the thicket itself seemed almost sentient, possessed by an awareness that sensed her group's approach and beckoned them closer.

Without warning, the being quickly scampered off. Aisling tracked her by the movement of the tall grass that she pushed through until she disappeared into the brush altogether. *I've come this far,* Aisling thought.

A gentle breeze at her back urged her forward, and the grass caressed her ankles almost as if to comfort her: *"You're safe here."*

She'd been right—the thicket *was* sentient. As she stood at its opening, the whole thing expanded and contracted. Breathing. A deep inhale, then a long, slow exhale. She tried to match its cadence with her own breath and found that her lungs felt more open than ever before.

"It likes you." A voice, quiet and rough like wind through dry leaves, drifted from inside the knot of branches. "Come in, girl, we haven't got all night."

Before she could talk herself out of it, Aisling tied Briar's leash to a thick branch and then ducked inside. In the light from her lantern that she held outstretched ahead of her, she found a tunnel lined with thorns and withered vines. It was long—much longer than it should have been. Aisling was forced to crouch lower and lower as she pressed forward, eventually dropping to her hands and knees to crawl the final few feet before it opened up to a small room of sorts. Here, she could at least sit up straight.

Leaning against a log, almost part of the log herself, was a small, wizened female, bent with age. The time that consumed the forest also showed on her face, which was lined with deep creases and wrinkles. Her long, gray hair was woven back in a tangled braid that she kept slung over one shoulder.

"So," she said with a grim smile. "We meet at last."

"I'm sorry, do I know you?" Nothing about her seemed at all familiar to Aisling, not even calling to mind any of her mother's tales.

"Of course not, don't be silly." The female dismissed her with a wave of her hand. When she moved, her cloak of thick, rough-spun brown wool moved stiffly with her and several leaves and twigs fell from its sleeve. "Come closer and let me have a look at you."

The tiny being that had led Aisling there was standing beside the old faerie, grinning proudly. Two rows of sharp, pointed teeth that fit together like puzzle pieces glinted in the lantern's light. When Aisling scooted closer, she made a chittering sound and hopped up into the brambles overhead.

"Thank you," Aisling called after her.

"Don't bother," the female chided. "She doesn't understand a word you're saying."

"What is she?"

"A tree sprite." She said it so matter-of-factly that Aisling nearly felt stupid for asking. She reached up with a gnarled hand to grasp Aisling's chin, turning her head this way and that. Studying her. "Tell me your name."

"Aisling."

"*Aisling.*" She tasted the name like wine. "Now, explain to me how it is you know of our kind. You appear quite undaunted by the events that led you here."

"My mother told me stories." Aisling considered her words carefully, not overly keen on delving too deep into her childhood with the faerie. "She had encounters with the Fae."

The female hummed. "Pleasant encounters?" When Aisling nodded, she posited, "She was lucky then."

"Who are you?" Of all the questions racing through Aisling's mind, this was the most pressing, and also the most dangerous. The Fae didn't often take kindly to humans asking after their identity. She was sure that's what this female was: a faerie of one sort or another.

"They call me the Shadowwood Mother." She released Aisling's chin and turned to dig through a mess of brittle papers scattered on the ground around her. "And we call *you* the Red Woman."

Aisling frowned, unsure of what to make of the statement. "I'm sorry?"

The Shadowwood Mother grumbled to herself as she searched the pile, picking up papers at random before tossing them aside again. Finally, she seemed to find what she was looking for half-buried under a clump of leaves. She shook it clean, then held it into the light of the lantern that Aisling had hung from a branch. They both leaned in close to peer at the markings on the page. The words were inked in tight black script, vertical rather than horizontal. Aisling squinted at it, but the text was hardly intelligible.

"This," the Shadowwood Mother said, "is your prophecy."

"My *what*?"

The old faerie flashed her an irritated look. "Are you going to let me read it to you or are you going to continue interrupting me with useless questions? Now, be quiet and listen."

Aisling sat back on her heels and chewed the inside of her cheek. When the Shadowwood Mother cleared her throat to speak, she listened intently as the faerie recited the words:

Across realms blackened and broken when war claims the land,

A prophecy long hidden, fate now demands:

Amidst bloodshed and darkness and winter's bitter sting, the Red Woman will rise to bring revenant spring.

Affined to another, when three signs converge, She stands a beacon of hope to quell tempest's surge.

With unwavering spirit through desolate night, She must face darkness unnamed, guided by celestial light.

When those stars align with the threads of Her fate, sacrifice begets a dormant magic innate.

Beside Her, a great White Bear shall tread, a guardian and companion through trials ahead.

THE RED WOMAN AND THE WHITE BEAR

*In a union unmatched with a bond beyond compare,
their harmony is forged by this destiny they share.*

The softly-breathing thicket quieted around them, the atmosphere becoming pensive. Reverent. The rhyme had a clear effect on the forest and the Shadowwood Mother, but its meaning was lost on Aisling. She hesitated, mulling over the couplets, searching within them for anything that might feel familiar or in any way instructive. She could tell it was important, she just didn't know why.

"I don't know what any of that means," she admitted, frustration welling slowly in her chest.

"Of course you don't," the Shadowwood Mother said. "No one does."

"That can't be the whole thing," Aisling argued. There was more, there had to be. None of those words, pretty though they were, meant anything at all. They were no more useful than a children's nursery rhyme. "Doesn't it say anything about how? Or where? Or when?"

Now they were both frustrated. "It's a prophecy, girl, not an instruction manual."

"I'm not even a redhead, and Briar..." Aisling looked back down the tunnel to where her dog was rolling on his back in a patch of mud, filthy from his nose to his tail. "Briar's hardly a bear."

"You humans," the Shadowwood Mother clicked her tongue against the roof of her mouth. "Always so literal."

"Then how can you be sure it has anything to do with me? Is it just because I helped the sprite?" Aisling was beginning to feel dizzy, as though there wasn't enough oxygen left in the small space. Despite the cold, sweat dripped from her brow. It stung her eye before she could wipe it away with the back of her hand.

"Because you were *recognized* by the sprite." The Shadowwood Mother turned back to the papers, rooting around once again. The next one she found quicker than the first. It, too, was printed vertically, and framed with illustrations so small Aisling could only imagine the hands of a sprite, or something like it, being capable of sketching such detailed markings.

"There will come three signs—a convergence—that will signal the coming of the Red Woman." The tip of the faerie's finger traced the lines down the page as she read aloud. "All will be of the natural world. The first will be sent by Aethar: the sun will rise to hang blood red in the sky. The second—"

Aisling interrupted her with a sharp laugh. "Wildfires have been burning up north for a month now; the sun has been red because of the smoke in the air. It happens nearly every year around this time. It's nothing out of the ordinary."

The Shadowwood Mother shot her a harsh glare before she continued: "*The second* will come from the Low One: there will bloom an eclipse of pale green Luna moths. And the third will be a consequence of nature, when the tides are drawn out beyond their normal reach."

Aisling's wheels were turning, rationalizing. She hadn't a clue who the entities were that the Shadowwood Mother was referring to by name. "Luna moths are rare here, but they're not unheard of," she tried. Her voice came out weaker than she would have liked.

"Sprites are far more intelligent than you might expect, and they can certainly get around quicker than a faerie with ancient bones like mine. They love few things more than shiny gifts—for a handful of new coins, I keep a number of them in my employ." The Shadowwood Mother glanced up into the tangled brambles that the sprite had disappeared into. "They are my eyes. I am the keeper of your prophecy, among others, and I have been watching for this convergence for many, many years. The red sun has risen, and the Luna moths hatched soon after. When I smelled the shifting tides here on your island, I sent my eyes out to find you."

"But how—" Aisling started.

"Sprites have an uncanny ability to sense things. There is something special about you, Aisling, and I don't doubt there is more to you than even you might understand. It is no coincidence that you and the sprite met as you did, nor is it coincidence that you are already familiar with our kind."

Suddenly overwhelmed, Aisling shifted to sit in the dirt so that she could draw up her knees and drop her head down between them. She needed the earth to stop spinning so that she could think straight.

A hand patted the top of her head. The Shadowwood Mother had reached across the space to comfort Aisling, the gesture stiff but kind. "Take a breath, girl."

"How can I be a part of something I don't understand?" Aisling pressed. "How am I supposed to know what to do?" She wished the thicket were big enough for her to stand and pace; the confines of its thorny walls were only constricting her lungs further.

"The centuries-old war between the Fae Courts has grown out of control; its devastation has reached an unprecedented magnitude. Innocents are dying. The land is dying—our forests, our rivers. Our homes. It is both the fate and the burden of the Red Woman to bring peace." When Aisling raised her head, the Shadowwood Mother was peering at her with dark eyes. They weren't looking at her, but through her. *Into* her. Scanning and parsing through whatever was inside of Aisling that tied her to this prophecy.

So she was meant to stop a war. Trepidation brought Aisling's hands to tremble and her heart to race. The significance of this moment, and the weight of the prophecy, were almost greater than she could bear. "What if I can't? Or if I refuse?" she challenged. She could crawl her way back out of the thicket now, before this went any further. And yet, she made no move to leave. Something in the Shadowwood Mother's eyes held her rapt.

"You bore witness to the answer to that question tonight when the earth moved beneath your feet." The Shadowwood Mother drew a bony hand across the dirt floor. "The tremors are echoes of war. Of magic. Of hatred. There will be more."

Aisling frowned. "More earthquakes?"

"More *echoes*—quakes, tidal shifts. The weather will change, and the land along with it. And not only here on your island, but anywhere there is a Thin Place. Soon enough, the Veil will weaken further. The echoes will spread. And then things will begin to come through." The Shadowwood Mother lowered her voice as she delivered this warning, leaning forward so the lantern's light illuminated her features. The harsh shadows it cast across her face made her wrinkled skin appear as tree bark.

"What kinds of things?" Aisling lowered her voice, too, almost whispering now.

"Things that have not been strong enough to come through for a very long time, but that have been waiting on the edges of Wyldraíocht for their turn. These are not the Fae of your mother's tales, Aisling. These will not be so friendly, and they will certainly not be confined to the borderlands. Your home will be theirs to take."

Aisling's mind strayed momentarily back to her friends, sleeping soundly not three miles away. Unguarded. Unaware. She shivered.

"That can't be all there is," she pled again. She looked around at the papers scattered around the Shadowwood Mother. Surely there must be something else amongst them that would at least guide her in the right direction.

"The prophecy will unfold as it's meant to. They always do." The Shadowwood Mother settled back against the log and folded her hands in her lap. "You'd best be on your way now; you'd do well to return before your friends wake."

There was a sense of finality to her words; Aisling knew then that there were no more answers to be found here. At least, not tonight. After several long moments of silence, Aisling retrieved her lantern and crawled back out the way she came. This time, the sharp thorns protruding from the walls of the tunnel scratched and pulled at her hair and clothes—the thicket, or whatever it was that possessed it, was reluctant to let her leave.

Briar was waiting patiently, having at some point drifted off to sleep beside the entrance. His fluffy, white fur was almost entirely brown and matted and when Aisling unhooked his leash, he pranced around her as though to show it off. It was a brief moment of levity that she desperately needed.

Retracing their steps through the woods, the words of the prophecy reverberated in Aisling's mind. She replayed them over and over, repetition etching each line deeper into her consciousness, dissecting every word for a meaning that she could understand. The imagery evoked by the lines resonated with her in a way, but she struggled to comprehend how they could be tied to her. The war, the darkness, and the destined role of the Red Woman felt at once both distant and intimately personal. She yearned for answers, but they remained elusive, teasing her with fragments of understanding that remained just beyond her grasp.

At least now, too tired to be concerned about hunters or sprites or any other manner of Fae finding her, Aisling could enjoy the hike back. Briar bounded on ahead, glad to finally be free of the leash. The early morning air was crisp and laden with dew and smelled so much sweeter than the heavy, earthy air inside the thicket. She allowed it to clear her head and quiet her racing thoughts for a time. Instead of the words of the prophecy, she tried only to hear the sounds of the forest waking up around her. The soft birdsong, slowly replacing the crickets' chirping. The steady rhythm of her footfalls.

By the time Aisling and Briar stumbled back into camp, exhausted and streaked with mud, the sun was just barely beginning to rise.

Through the haze, it still shone a muted shade of red. Aisling rolled her eyes. It felt like even the sky was taunting her.

It wasn't worth the cleanup to track all their mud back into the tent just to lay down for a couple of hours, so Aisling instead knelt outside the door and leaned in to pack up her things. Her back and shoulders ached from the tension she'd carried there all night, and shivering against the cold didn't help, either. She pulled on her heavy coat, but the chill was deeper than it could warm. The icy grip of fear squeezed her tightly, especially when she looked at the other tents where her friends were still asleep, utterly oblivious of the other side of the world around them. Ignorant of the insidious threat looming ever closer, echoing across the Veil.

Conflict surged in Aisling's stomach as she grappled with the weight of her choices. Just as she had when she saw the tree sprite, desperate and alone, she felt called to embrace her role and protect her friends. Her home. But doubt crept in like choking vines, whispering that she was ill-equipped for such a monumental task.

Sensing the swell of her emotions, Briar ambled over to Aisling from where he'd been searching for scraps around the grill. He laid down beside her and rested his chin on her thighs. He sighed a short puff of air through his nose and Aisling stopped what she was doing to scratch the top of his head. Briar's weight was an anchor that brought her back to the present and drew her away from the maddening thoughts of Fae and prophecies and world-saving. Here, they weren't the Red Woman and the White Bear. They were just Aisling and Briar.

"You'd like to think of yourself as a bear, though, wouldn't you?" Aisling teased him, finishing her own thought out loud. If he could have rolled his eyes, she was certain he would have.

"Fuck, and here I thought our mud bath wasn't scheduled until later this afternoon." Seb was the first of the others to wake and couldn't resist commenting on her appearance when he crawled out of his tent.

"Funny," she quipped. "Briar took off after a rabbit when I let him out this morning and decided to take a detour through a mud puddle the size of my car."

"And you—what? Swam in after him?" He was picking through the remains of the fire, looking for anything to burn to cook breakfast over. There was nothing left but crumbled ashes. "When Jackson and Lida wake up, we could all go back to my place to eat if you want."

"Thanks, but I think I'll head back once I'm done here and get this guy cleaned off." Aisling shooed Briar off of her lap so she could finish packing.

Though the normalcy of a morning with her friends would have undoubtedly done her some good, Aisling was critically low on patience and wanted nothing more than to sink into her bed and close her eyes and pretend that the night before had been nothing more than a bad, bad dream.

3

RODNEY

AISLING

Instead of driving back to her apartment, Aisling navigated toward the southwest side of the island. She skirted along the edge of town until she reached the trailer park that sat nestled in a grassy field just beyond. The plot of land hosted eleven mobile homes and four trailers, small and unremarkable, all peeling paint in faded pastels and weather-worn tin roofs. Apart from the trailers, each structure was the same height and the same long, shoebox shape. The lots were tight—there was little space between the buildings, yet Aisling knew that the *Lots For Sale/Lease* sign posted on the chain link fence surrounding the property would never be taken down.

Still, it was lively. Even this early in the morning, a mob of children on bikes wove in and out of the mobile homes. Their tires left tread paths through the grass and their pants were wet up to their knees from the dew that clung to the tall blades. The sound of a lawnmower competed with the children's yelling and laughter. To Aisling, the air here always smelled green.

She pulled around to park beside a blue trailer toward the back of the property. It was the rearmost home, right up against the chain link fence that had been erected a few years before when parents grew tired of their little ones running off to play in the woods beyond. Briar eagerly jumped from the back seat when she opened the door, but Aisling caught him by the collar before he could run off.

"Bath first." She led him over to the hose bib on the side of the house and turned it on. The water came out cold—freezing, almost—but Briar was unbothered by it. He wagged his tail happily while Aisling's fingers grew numb as she worked them through his fur. He'd somehow managed to get dirt all the way down to his skin.

"You look like hell." Rodney had come out when he heard the water running and was leaning against the doorframe, watching Aisling work with a bemused expression on his face.

Aisling ignored his comment, instead nodding towards him. "That's new."

"You like?" He raised a hand to tousle his hair, now a shocking shade of safety orange. It had been a rich, indigo blue when she'd last seen him a few days prior.

She shrugged, then returned her attention to Briar. "The blue looked better."

"You didn't like the blue at first, either, when I changed it from green," he reminded her. "It'll grow on you."

"Maybe. Can you grab me a towel?"

Rodney returned a moment later and tossed her a threadbare beach towel and a pair of sweatpants. "Unless you're planning on hosing off too, put those on before you come in. I don't want to clean up your mud trail."

Once Aisling had changed and toweled Briar off, she followed him inside the mobile home, rolling the waistband of the pants over several times to keep them from dragging. Rodney was in the tiny kitchen space putting a kettle on the stove to boil.

"Tea?" he asked, then held up a bag of white bread. "Toast?"

She pulled a chair out from the small table and sat and watched Briar wander into the living room to curl up on the couch. "Both, please. Everyone missed you at the campout last night."

Rodney scoffed. "Sure they did, just as much as I missed them."

"Well, *I* missed you at least," Aisling said pointedly. Rodney had never been particularly fond of her friends and didn't hesitate to make that fact known every chance he got. "How was work?"

He groaned as he slid into the chair across from her. "A nightmare. I didn't get home until two this morning."

"What happened?" Letting him sulk, Aisling got up and went to pull the shrieking kettle off the stove. She took two mugs from the cupboard—the same one her father had kept his mugs in when he'd lived there. Rodney hadn't changed much since he moved in. The place was still familiar.

"We had the schedule arranged around low tide, but it just kept pulling further and further out. It was nearly three hours late coming back in. Did the same thing last night too, apparently. Threw everything off. I was on the phone arguing with the ferry operators on the mainland half the night," he complained.

Aisling fumbled the kettle in surprise and splashed hot water onto her hand, though she could hardly feel it for the panic that seized her lungs. She cursed and moved to run it under the sink before a blister could form.

"Are you okay?" he asked, alarmed by the sudden commotion behind him.

"Fine, just slipped." Aisling's voice was thick with bile that was creeping up the back of her throat. She swallowed it down hard before speaking again. "What was going on with the tide?"

"The harbormaster said something about a spring tide and wind. Whatever it was, I hope it never happens when I'm on shift again. Massive pain in the ass."

"Has it happened before? Did he seem concerned by it?" Aisling was aware that her tone was rising, but she couldn't help it. Her heart was racing and the sound of it beating in her ears was nearly louder than her own voice. Abandoning the tea, she fell back into her chair.

"God, Ash, you've gone all pale." Rodney's thick brows pulled together with concern.

"Please just answer my question." She needed an explanation. A natural cause, something she could point to in an article or a book to rationalize the coincidence. That's all this was: a coincidence. It had to be.

"I think he said that it was lower than normal already because of a spring tide and that some offshore winds had picked up which pushed it out even further," Rodney said slowly as he tried to recall the harbormaster's description of the phenomenon. "Why are you suddenly so worried about the tide?"

Aisling propped her elbows on the table and rested her head in her hands. She couldn't speak yet, afraid that if she opened her mouth she might vomit. Rodney watched her try to compose herself for a moment before he stood and circled around the table to stand beside her. He knew something was wrong, maybe something serious, but he also knew better than to try to force an answer out of her.

"Let's go sit on the couch," he suggested. He guided her up and into the living room by her shoulders. He nudged Briar over to make room and sat Aisling down in the corner. "I'll get your tea and a piece of toast, okay?"

Aisling could only nod. Minutes later, Rodney returned and handed her a plate of buttered toast and a mug of tea. She set both down behind her on the end table; the shaking that had beset her hands made it too difficult to hold either.

"So," Rodney started. He sat against the opposite corner of the couch, his long, gangly legs splayed toward Aisling. "Are you going to tell me what happened last night?

She studied his freckled face. It wasn't his face, not really, but it was the one he'd worn as long as she'd known him. The one he'd learned how to grow and age since it was given to him twenty-nine years ago when he swapped into a newborn's crib, a changeling. He'd quickly taken to life on this side of the Veil and had integrated seamlessly into the human realm. He liked his independence—from the laws that constrained his magic, from the Courts. Here, he'd told her once, he was free to be whatever version of himself he wanted to be. And for the time being, that was Rodney Finch.

"I need to tell you something, and I need you to not interrupt me until I've finished," Aisling said cautiously once she felt she could keep her voice steady. Rodney mimed zipping his lips, locking them at the corner and tossing away the key. He was trying to lighten the mood. It wasn't working. She tucked her feet under Briar's hips and wrapped her arms around her knees before she started: "I rescued a tree sprite from a hunt a couple of miles from camp last night."

"Aisling..." Rodney's tone was one of caution, ready to lecture her. If she hadn't flashed him a look that shut him up, he'd have given Aisling her mother's same warning about the Fae.

"The sprite came back after we'd gone to bed. She took me to see the Shadowwood Mother." Aisling searched his eyes for any hint of recognition, but his expression remained neutral—whether this was purposeful or not, she couldn't be sure. Rodney was never one to lay his cards on the table right away, not even with her. "Have you ever heard of the Red Woman and the White Bear? The prophecy?"

Rodney nodded slowly. Solemnly. "Not for a very, very long time."

After drawing in a deep, steadying breath, Aisling recounted the events of the night before. Rodney, for his part, managed to keep his mouth shut and listened closely, face still holding that neutral mask that was only marred by the occasional, brief quirk of his brow. She recalled the words of the prophecy easily; she'd repeated them in her head so many times that she knew them now by heart, down to the very cadence by which the Shadowwood Mother had first recited them. Once she finished, the pair sat in silence for a long while. Aisling watched Briar's broad chest rise and fall as Rodney mentally sorted through all she'd said.

"So," he said finally, "when you asked about the tides..."

Aisling shook her head. "It has to be a coincidence."

"There are no coincidences in fate," he countered. "If the prophecy is true, then this is yours."

"If?" She looked at him hopefully. If was good—she could work with if.

Rodney offered a guilty half-smile. "I was just trying to soften the blow. Prophecies aren't a matter of if, Ash. Just a matter of when. And it seems like that's now."

"You were supposed to be helpful. You're just as cryptic as that damn old faerie." Aisling didn't try to hide the edge of bitterness in her words. He raised his hands, palms open in an apologetic gesture. "She said the Courts are at war."

"That's true."

"Okay, say more," she prompted.

"You know there's a lot I can't tell you unless you ask more specifically." Of all the rules Rodney shirked as a Veilwalker, this was the only one he was bound to adhere to, and the most frustrating one at that.

Aisling crossed her arms tightly across her chest. "Well, start with what you *can* tell me."

"The Courts are at war—they have been for a very, very long time. Centuries, I think, since the Unseelie King took the throne. His Court is bloodthirsty and power-hungry, and the Seelie Court thinks that they're better fit to rule, rather than splitting the realm as they have been. Both sides want what the other has," he explained. "But there are other fundamental differences, much older than petty land disputes and quarreling royals."

Rodney was sitting forward on the couch now, and Aisling prodded Briar out of the way so she could do the same. "Which are?"

He shook his head and she huffed in frustration. *Specific questions.*

She tried a new angle: "The prophecy mentions winter and spring—do you think that represents the Unseelie and Seelie Courts?" It made sense in her head: darkness and light, good and evil. The bitter hardness of winter representative of the cruel Unseelie Court; the brightness of spring, the benevolent Seelie Fae.

"If I were to hazard a guess, I'd say so," he posited. "But I'm not a scholar on these things."

"So 'to bring revenant spring' could mean that I'm meant to help bring the Seelie Court to power, to give them control over the Wild?" It was the first moment of clarity she'd had yet. Accurate or not, it was at least a starting point.

Rodney smirked. "You still call it that?"

Aisling rolled her eyes, annoyed by his teasing tone. "Old habits. Give them control over *Wyldraíocht*."

"Let's stick with your version," Rodney said, wincing at Aisling's poor pronunciation of the Fae realm's true title. She couldn't pronounce it as a child, either, when her mother taught her the word, so they'd settled instead on shortening it to *the Wild*. "Anyway, yeah. That's how I'd interpret it."

"And how am I supposed to do that? Where is this 'celestial light' that's meant to be guiding me?" Aisling raked her fingers roughly through her hair. They snagged hard in the knotted ends, hopelessly tangled from her night in the forest and the grasping brambles of the thicket. Her body was tired; her mind, even more so.

"I'm stuck on that part, too," Rodney admitted. "I'm sorry, Ash. I wish I could be more helpful."

She sighed heavily. "It's okay. I'm just glad I have you to talk to about it. I don't know what I'd do if I had to keep it all to myself."

"I'll keep thinking on it, alright?" He kicked Aisling's foot lightly with his own. "Put it out of your head for now. There's not a lot you can do at the moment, anyway."

"Right." There would be no setting this aside, try as she would. How could she simply forget about something such as this—something that could irrevocably change her future? She'd been consumed by thoughts of the prophecy since it was told to her; that wasn't going to change anytime soon.

"I have something for you before I forget." Rodney leaned forward and teased a slip of paper out from underneath a dirty plate he'd left on the coffee table for God knows how long. "First of the month. Rent check."

Aisling sighed and tore the check in half as soon as he handed it to her. "How many times are we going to do this? I'm not taking your money."

The mobile home had belonged to Aisling's father; he'd purchased it a number of years ago when his disability checks were no longer sufficient to cover the rising mortgage on her childhood home. He bought it outright and had willed it to Aisling, but she wanted nothing to do with it. The cramped, musty space and its patchwork furniture served only to remind her of the worst parts of the man: his laziness, his inability to care for himself. The way he'd looked when she came home those seven months ago, a skeleton, half-dead from lung cancer wrought by a decadeslong smoking habit that he never had any interest in kicking. It reminded her, too, of the way he'd treated her mother. Of the end he'd condemned her to. Though Aisling had dutifully cared for him in the final months of his life, she'd only ever got halfway to forgiving him. To forgive him entirely, she'd have to do the same for herself.

However much she disliked it, the mobile home was perfect for Rodney. He'd been living with roommates with whom he endlessly disputed the most insignificant matters. Argumentative to a fault and significantly shrewder than he looked, Rodney did best on his own.

"I have a job so I can afford a place to live," he pressed.

"You're a live-in caretaker. Consider your upkeep of the place as payment enough." Aisling eyed the dirty plate pointedly.

Rodney rolled his eyes. "I'd rather just give you cash."

Feeling the weight of exhaustion more acutely with each passing minute, as deep as her bones now, Aisling hauled herself to her feet before sleep claimed her there on the couch. She could have stayed—Briar had extra food and she had spare clothes stashed somewhere—but something about the tiredness that swept over her urged Aisling to take some time to be alone. Space was what she needed now. Space, and sleep. With one final reassuring hug from Rodney, she stepped back out into the cold morning air.

"Miss Morrow!"

Cole. She hated Cole. He was a nuisance on a good day and purported himself to be one of the island's most enterprising businessmen. But his enterprise stretched only as far as the chain-link fence that encircled the mobile home park. Despite his constant talk of expansion, he'd never buy up additional land. He enjoyed turning a profit on the lots he already owned; anything more than that would surely be too big for him to manage. Nevertheless, he'd been hounding her since just one short week after her father's funeral to buy back the lot and rent it out to plus up his own monthly income.

"Cole," Aisling acknowledged curtly as she loaded Briar into the car.

He was short—shorter than Aisling—and it seemed to take him a great deal of pulmonary effort to cross from his own mobile home to meet her. "Have you given any more thought to my offer?"

"The answer is still no." She slammed the door a bit harder than she meant to.

"I'd like you to at least consider it." His voice sounded a bit like her father's had: rough. A smoker's voice. "You know where to find me."

"I sure do," she said with sarcastic sweetness. He'd expected her to sell it off without a second thought before heading back to the mainland. She hadn't yet thought about it at all the first time he asked. Now, after this fifth time and after actually having thought about it, she still had no plans to sell—even if she did leave. It was Rodney's home now.

But as for whether Aisling would stay on Brook Isle, that remained very much undecided. Whereas her own youthful and ambitious spirit had once driven her away, now, something external was fighting to keep her here. It pulled and pulled with cold, gripping fingers that had ahold of her throat. Her heart. Her mind. She wasn't sure what it was, whether it was a physical entity or some sort of manifestation of her own guilt, but either way, she was powerless against it.

4
A PLAN

AISLING

It would be two days yet before Aisling felt ready to leave the safety of her apartment. She slept, she cleaned, she cooked. She stepped outside only a handful of times to let Briar out, but she had otherwise hidden herself away. It wasn't as though her apartment would have afforded her any degree of safety should anything come looking for her. But it was small, and there was a lock on the door, and she knew exactly how many steps it would take to reach the block of knives in the kitchen from any given room.

Amidst all the confusion and time spent parsing through the words of the prophecy, Aisling hadn't realized at first just how afraid she felt. It didn't matter what the celestial light was, or which court was spring and which was winter. What mattered was that there were beings out there who believed her to be the Red Woman.

Although to some, she'd be heralded as the last hope for their dying world, to others—likely many others—she'd be cast as the enemy. Without having done anything at all, there was a whole host of Fae that would see her dead before she could claim her fate. And that was a reality Aisling wasn't ready to confront.

So being that it was the Fae who put her in this headspace, it only stood to reason that it would take one to pull her back out of it.

Rodney turned up at Aisling's door on his way back from his early morning shift at the dock, demanding a walk and refusing to take no for an answer. The temperature had dropped significantly over those two days. Aisling tightened the thick woolen scarf around her neck and pushed her gloved hands deeper into her pockets. They'd gotten their last camping trip of the season in right under the wire.

The sky was overcast, filled with heavy, rain-laden clouds. The island wore the same somber cloak of gray that it always donned around this time of year and wouldn't shed until very late spring. At least the sun—that sickening red reminder of Aisling's alleged destiny—was hidden beneath the clouds' feathered layers.

Brook Isle was among the smallest settled islands in San Juan County; a community only 297 strong. With its limited amenities and slightly worn-down charm, it possessed a quiet sort of beauty that was kept carefully sheltered from the rest of the world. The place was almost stuck in time. For most of its residents, that was what tethered them to the island. Natives rarely left; outsiders rarely stayed.

The pair walked along the narrow street that cut through the heart of town heading south, in the direction of the harbor. The street-side dogwood trees that had been filled with white blooms all summer long were now shades of yellow and orange, bare in patches, and the damp leaves that had already fallen clung to the bottoms of their shoes.

Rodney directed Aisling toward the bakery, shoulders shrugged against the marine fog rolling off the Salish Sea that hadn't yet cleared for the day. It was early still; most of the stores wouldn't open for another hour or so. Their shiplap exteriors in nautical shades of reds and blues were faded and aged by years of salt air. While some would think them tired, Aisling was comforted by their familiarity. These buildings had been well-loved, and at this point she might even be disappointed if they were ever repainted.

As they continued their brisk walk, the sound of seagulls calling out overhead mingled with the distant crashing of waves against the island's rocky shores. The echoes of the sea breathed a calming rhythm and for the first time in days, Aisling felt better.

The bakery was already crowded with ferry commuters who would be heading out on the next boat toward Orcas Island, or San Juan Island, or even as far as Anacortes on the mainland. Rodney and Aisling wove their way up to the counter and he ordered them each a hot tea to go. Once she had the warm cup clasped between her hands, it felt almost pleasant outside.

"Was that real cash?" she asked when they were back out on the street.

Rodney smirked. "And if it wasn't?" He laughed when Aisling elbowed him in the ribs, then said, "It was, it was. I swear."

Aisling and Rodney had met close to eleven years prior, when she'd come home for the summer after her junior year of college to sulk because she hadn't landed the internship she'd applied for. Her father had sent her down to the gas station for a pack of cigarettes, and he was ahead of her in line buying two liters of bright green soda. She'd recognized him vaguely as the odd boy who'd been a couple years below her in school who only ever kept to himself. His hair had been jet black then.

His sleight of hand trick was small and had gone unnoticed by everyone but Aisling. Even then, after so many years of disbelief, she recognized Fae magic when she saw it. The cash he paid with had a certain glimmer to it, and the air a certain smell. Afterward, she cornered him outside in the parking lot before he could slip away.

"How did you do that?" she had demanded. He'd given her a stupid, goofy grin and swore he didn't know what she was talking about.

"I'm not sure just what you think you saw."

"You had playing cards in your hand. They were bills when you passed them to the cashier," Aisling accused. "You glamoured them."

No matter how much time had passed, she still wouldn't let him live it down. That was the night they became best friends. It was also the night Aisling understood, for the first time since she was young, that her mother had been telling the truth about the Fae on the island all along.

"I've been thinking," Rodney started as they sat together on a wooden bench adjacent to the docks.

"That's never a good sign."

"Funny." He rolled his eyes but was unfazed by her interruption, and started again: "I've been thinking, the only way you're going to get to the bottom of all of this is by going straight to the heart of it."

Aisling turned on the bench to face him, curling one knee to her chest so she could rest the half-empty cup on top of it. "What do you mean?"

"Well, given that it's a fairly obvious threat against the Unseelie Court's sovereignty, it stands to reason that they would have scholars or seers of some sort that would have studied the text of the prophecy. They'd probably know more about it than anyone. Better the enemy you know, and all that." His assumption made sense, but it was far from helpful.

"So, what, I'm supposed to stop by and ask them how to destroy their kingdom? Great idea, Rodney. Thanks."

"Not quite," he said, having missed the sarcasm in her voice altogether. "But if we could somehow get you into their good graces, you could at least do a little digging yourself."

"And how do you propose I do that?" Aisling asked.

He grimaced. "I'm still working on that part."

Aisling finished her tea and played with the lid of the cup, stuck inside her own mind. The two sat for a few moments in silence before she spoke again: "Maybe I should just go home."

"You are home."

"Back to the mainland, I mean. Away from all this." She gestured with her cup at the island behind them. From somewhere obscured by the mist, the sound of the ferry's foghorn reverberated around them. Its minor tone always sounded forlorn to her.

"To do what?" He was annoyed, but he wouldn't show it. Nor would he yet say out loud what they both knew: it wouldn't make a difference. He'd let her try feebly to convince herself otherwise first.

"I still have a life there. They're not going to hold my job forever," Aisling said.

He shrugged. "So quit."

"And work here at the library for the rest of my life?"

"You're happier here," he pointed out.

Aisling countered: "I'm *in danger* here."

"You'd be in more danger if you ran away, of that much I'm sure. And so would I; so would *all* your friends. So would Brook Isle." Rodney took her empty cup and stacked it inside his own, then tossed them toward the trash can a few feet away. A perfect shot. "These things have a way of getting what they want."

His words raised goosebumps down the backs of Aisling's arms. "By these things, you mean the Fae?"

"I mean fate. Prophecies. Whatever you want to call it. The Red Woman is the Red Woman, regardless of where she lives. The city won't protect you, and your distance won't protect us."

As the small boat drifted slowly into view, Rodney stood up off the bench and pulled Aisling to her feet. They'd sat in the damp air for long enough, and both of them thought better when they were in motion. Slowly, they made their way back in the direction of her apartment.

"Wouldn't it make more sense for me to try to get to the Seelie Court?" Aisling asked as they walked. "I'd imagine they'd be a bit more welcoming, given that I'm supposed to be on their side."

"Yeah, I thought about that."

"But?" she prompted.

Rodney scratched the back of his neck, self-conscious. "Well, I'm not exactly sure how to get there."

"What? You've not been?" She was surprised; she had assumed Rodney would have more answers than he seemed to. He was her only direct line to that world and he was somehow proving to be nearly less helpful than the Shadowwood Mother had been.

He reached up to swat at a leaf overhead, showering them both with tiny droplets of dew. "From their side, sure. Not through their Thin Place. I don't know where it is."

"But you've visited the Unseelie Court?" Apprehension coiled in her stomach. The more they discussed this, the more real it became. The less she'd be able to convince herself it was a bad dream. The less likely she'd be to leave Brook Isle.

"I've been to a handful of events there," he said.

She'd had just about enough of Fae talk—she was sick of trying to decipher their cryptic words and veiled subtext. "What events?"

Rodney shrugged. "A party or two. A few observances." He steered them around a family to walk in the street and lowered his voice slightly. "Religious rites."

"I didn't know you were religious." In fact, she didn't know the Fae were religious at all.

"I'm not particularly, but I identify with some of their ideas. Either way, the ceremonies are always a good show." He smirked a bit. Aisling wasn't sure whether she liked the dark look that glinted in his eyes when he thought about what he'd witnessed there.

"Do you know where to find the Unseelie Thin Place?" she asked as directly as she could this time.

"Sure do," he chirped.

She slapped his shoulder. "You've known where it was this whole time and you never told me?"

He rubbed it and looked at her sheepishly. "You never asked."

"Of course I've asked, at least a hundred times."

"Not—" he started, and Aisling finished the sentence with him: "specifically enough."

When Rodney dropped her back off at her apartment, they both agreed to think about how best to approach the problem. But Rodney was cunning and tricky, whereas Aisling was not. Though his years in the human realm had degraded much of his knowledge, he still knew far more about the workings of the Wild than she did—and probably more than he was letting on.

∴

The Brook Isle Public Library was a brick building, one of the island's oldest. It had been a hospital once, then a school, but when both of those outgrew the space, it became a library. Pony walls had been installed to separate it into sections: fiction on the left, non-fiction on the right, and children's books in the back. Two of the island's three computers were set up on a table off to the side.

From the check-out desk in the center, Aisling could see all four corners of the room if she spun around in her chair. It smelled of bookbinder's glue and old, yellowed pages. The tall, narrow windows that ran all the way up to the high ceiling let slants of light filter in that caught eddies of dust swirling lazily through the air.

It wasn't a demanding job, nor was it terribly mentally stimulating, but she loved it all the same. It gave her time to read. To think. Sometimes, to sit still and quiet and do absolutely nothing at all. Briar loved it, too. He lay under the desk at her feet for most of the day and would occasionally walk a lap or two through the shelves to stretch his legs before returning to his post. He was a favorite fixture for the kids who visited during story time when she had a weekend shift.

Today, the library was quiet. An older couple browsed the mystery section and a young boy sat at one of the computers, but she hadn't seen anyone else for several hours. When Rodney came in, he brought a blast of cool air with him. The front doors were large and unwieldy, and it took him a moment to wrestle one closed against the brisk autumn breeze. His eyes were shining with excitement as he approached.

"I have a plan," he announced loudly. Aisling shushed him harshly and eyed the other patrons, but none of them had glanced over. "I have a plan," he repeated in a whisper once he'd reached the desk.

Aisling stood and nodded for him to follow. She led him to the far corner of the non-fiction section. Briar ambled behind them. "What is it?"

"Nocturne." Rodney was smug, obviously pleased with himself.

"Keep your voice down," Aisling hissed. "I don't know what that is."

"Our talk about ceremonies and parties got me thinking about it. It's a sort of holiday in the Unseelie Court, a big one. They host a celebration every year, open to all of their dominions. Usually it's big enough that they don't mind a well-meaning Solitary or two slipping in."

"Solitary?" Her head was reeling. She'd heard the word before, from her mother, but couldn't recall its meaning.

"Like me. Fae who aren't aligned or ruled by one court or another. The Shadowwood Mother is a Solitary Fae as well. But that's not the point." He was speaking quickly. "The point is: the Nocturne celebration is our way in."

"That's *your* way in. They might not care about the Solitary, but I'm sure they won't welcome a human." They were using more Fae terms than Aisling was comfortable with throwing around in public. She poked her head around the side of the bookshelf they were positioned behind. The couple had left, and the boy was still distracted by the computer.

"I'll glamour you. You'll be one of us. A pixie, I was thinking."

She almost laughed out loud before she shook her head. "That's too risky, Rodney. For both of us."

"It isn't," he insisted. "I'm good; my glamours are stronger than most. And it's a few weeks away, so I'll have time to practice."

"*Weeks?* That's too long." Though she would have balked if he'd said he'd take her tomorrow, the thought of sitting with this anxiety that had sunken into her gut like a stone in a river was almost just as bad.

He huffed a short breath through his nose. "That prophecy has been around for at least a century, Aisling. I think a few more weeks will be fine."

"Say you've managed to weave me a flawless glamour and we've made it through the Thin Place. We're at the celebration—now what?"

He cringed. "That's the part you're not going to like."

"Rodney," she said, her tone one of warning.

"We'll need to get you in front of the king." The pair jumped when the electronic shriek of the computer's dial-up internet connecting pierced the quiet library. The boy in front of the screen ducked his head, embarrassed by his sudden disruption. Aisling rolled her eyes and the two settled back down between the shelves.

"And?" There was more to his plan; she could tell by the way he seemed to be preparing himself to deliver the rest.

"And bedding him will be the easiest way to work yourself into the Court."

This time she did laugh. But he'd meant it, his delivery sharp and pragmatic. Clinical, even. Her face fell when he didn't so much as crack a smile. "You can't be serious."

"Think about it Ash: no one just walks into the Unseelie Court, human or pixie or otherwise. The celebration will get you in the door, but from there you have to capture his attention. This will be the quickest way to do that." His thin fingers picked absentmindedly at the frayed edges of a hole in his jeans as he spoke.

"Jesus, Rodney, do you hear what you're saying?" she hissed, cheeks burning with a deep red blush. "I'm not going to fuck the Fae king!"

"I've seen him at these parties. At almost every single one, he gets drunk and leaves with one of the females there. This time, we make sure it's you."

Aisling's blood boiled with rage and shame. In the span of just several days, she'd lost all control over her future. And now, her best friend was telling her to sleep her way into a Fae court. If they hadn't been in the library, she'd be on her feet yelling at him. The best she could do here was to take a few deep breaths before speaking again in the same harsh whisper. "I won't do it."

Rodney was silent for a moment, thinking. Weighing his words before he spoke, then delivering each clearly and cautiously after a quick glance around to make sure the two were well and truly alone in their corner. "The king is a monster, Aisling. He's a cruel and wicked thing; he revels in suffering and takes pleasure in others' pain. And his appetite for power..." He shook his head, almost shuddering. "It's insatiable. You need to use him before he can use you. If you can manage to hold his attention, then you'll have a measure of control over him."

"Control?" She spat the word, still incensed, getting closer by the minute to reaching over her shoulder for a heavy book to throw at Rodney's head. "How am I meant to control a creature like that?"

"His desires are predictable. He's indulgent; he resists very few temptations. If *you* can be that temptation, if you can play into his weakness, then we can influence him." He raised a hand to stop Aisling from interrupting him and added, "At least for long enough to find the information we need."

Though hearing him include himself so naturally in the plan—referring to them as a collective rather than putting it on Aisling alone—eased her anger slightly, she still wasn't convinced. "And while I'm sleeping with the enemy, what will you be doing?"

"Working my connections," he said confidently. "I'm trying to hunt down an old acquaintance there that might be able to help. Lyre. He knows a lot—a lot of things, a lot of other Fae. And he owes me a favor."

A family spilled loudly into the library then, and Briar went to greet them. Aisling pulled herself to her feet with the shelf and Rodney did the same. She tried her best to plaster a grin on her face as she made her way back to the desk and reminded them to check the community board for upcoming reading events. When they'd disappeared back into the children's section, she turned again to Rodney.

"I'm still not agreeing to this," she warned.

He grinned, well aware that he had very nearly won her over. "Well, you have a few weeks to come up with a better plan."

5

NOCTURNE, PART I: THE INVOCATION

KAEL

"Do you feel prepared?"

Kael looked past the old hob in the mirror to meet Werryn's eyes, ignoring the feeling of her thorn-like fingernails scratching his scalp as she wove small strands of his silver hair into tight braids. Already dressed for the night in his ritual robes, long and black and exceedingly plain, the High Prelate's gaunt face was drawn as he watched from the doorway.

"Yes." After yet another unnecessarily sharp tug, Kael shooed Methild away and she scuttled out of the room quickly. He unwound the braid she'd only halfway finished.

"You say that every time," Werryn scolded the king. He was the only one that could do so without repercussion, and he took advantage of that often.

Kael worked another braid loose; the ceremonial style was too formal for his taste. He preferred to see such ornate plaits on his female courtiers, not in his own hair. "Then stop asking."

"I needn't remind you that the last three rites have ended in disaster," Werryn insisted, "and that this is one of our most important of the year."

"No, you needn't. I am well aware." Losing patience, Kael's voice came out tight and cold.

"You're backsliding. We'll bring in a tether tonight, but the longer you rely on this crutch the weaker your—"

"Enough!" Kael cut Werryn off and brought his fist down hard on the dresser in front of him. The mirror rattled against the wall. "Leave. Now."

Werryn didn't flinch, but instead held Kael's reflected gaze for a moment. He knew when to push and when to retreat, and he had pushed far enough for now. He'd served the king since even before he had the throne; had been a party to his outbursts time and again for centuries. Kael's temper burned hot as a flame that could flare at the slightest provocation. His cruelty, like smoke, was never far behind. With a resigned sigh, the High Prelate bowed his head in deference and turned to leave the room, his long robes swishing softly against the stone floor.

"As you wish, Your Grace," Werryn said as he disappeared down the hall.

Kael watched the male's retreating figure, his jaw clenched tightly. The last thing he needed tonight was to be reminded of his own vulnerability, the constant struggle to control the magic that churned and roiled within him every waking moment. His service was to his dark god, and to his court. Not to the male who called himself High Prelate. Werryn's opinions mattered very little.

Alone now in his candlelit chamber, Kael ran his fingers through his long hair, unraveling the last of the braids that had been painstakingly woven. He avoided his reflection in the mirror and rose to dress. Methild had laid his ritual robe across the foot of his bed. Similarly simple to Werryn's, but newer. His old set had become too threadbare to keep. It was a pity; after nearly a century of use, he'd finally worn them soft. The new robe was stiff and rough against his skin when he rubbed the hem between his fingers. He'd wear it to The Cut, but he couldn't stand to have it touching him during the ritual. It would be just fine to kneel on.

Despite the heavy weight on his shoulders, Nocturne had long been Kael's favorite celebration. The Low One always seemed closer to him than ever this night—almost *in* him—and to serve as his vessel was the highest honor one could hold. It was what made him king. The revelry that would follow didn't hurt, either. A smirk played on Kael's lips when he considered it: the indulgences he'd witness, the gluttony and excess of the bacchanal that would surround him and stretch into the small hours of the morning.

But he had to get through the ritual first.

Drawing in a deep breath, Kael closed his eyes and tried to steady his racing thoughts. He needed to find his center and tap into the wellspring of magic that resided there. It was a dance between control and surrender, a delicate art of wielding his power without succumbing to its dark allure. It was his fierceness that gave him his edge, but by the same token hindered him each time from maintaining proper control over himself, particularly on charged nights such as this. The very power he so craved was sometimes too much for him, its vessel, to bear.

He couldn't afford to falter again, not while his court was so deeply entrenched in its war with no end yet in sight. The Seelie Court was proving thus far to be a more formidable rival than even his most battle-hardened advisors had foreseen. Not only was it important to pay homage and receive the Low One's benedictions, but this show of power was sorely needed to build back his subjects' waning confidence.

As he prepared to leave the solitude of his chamber, now draped in the uncomfortable robe, Kael could already feel the magic building in his chest. The sensation bordered on uncomfortable; it wanted out. He took another breath, shallower this time. With a determined glint in his eyes, Kael straightened his spine. The time for hesitation had passed.

His walk to The Cut was a contemplative one, and he was glad that he'd sent Werryn on ahead so he could make it alone. The male was prone to lectures, warranted or not, and Kael's mood wouldn't allow for it tonight. Quiet as a whisper, he wound his way through the dimly-lit passages to the tall, winding staircase that spiraled up to the surface. Each of the stone steps was worn in the middle from centuries upon centuries of footfalls ascending and descending.

The Undercastle, nearly as old as the earth it was carved into, was as much a natural structure as it was hand-hewn. Most of it was underground: cut deep into the earth, its corridors wound their way through the bedrock, intertwining with the bones of the land. Its vast halls were formed of ancient caverns that had existed long before the Unseelie Court claimed them as their own. In some, vaulted ceilings dripped with glittering stalactites, sharp and wickedly beautiful. In others, the ceilings soared so high that they vanished into darkness.

The king was confident that tonight's ritual would be smooth. He let his hand drift over the railing as he climbed. He'd counted the steps once when he was young; he seemed to remember there being close to a hundred, maybe more.

Outside, the night was crisp and cool and the breeze played softly through the pines. The Cut wasn't far beyond the tree line, a clearing in the thick forest where nothing had ever grown. The trees that encircled it, though, thrived off the inhospitable soil. Their roots stretched and snaked and for the uninitiated, made the walk to the center a treacherous one. Kael knew it by heart, every bump and divot. He could navigate the whole area with his eyes closed.

He was the last to arrive. The candles were lit, and the circle of ancient runes carved into the ground dusted off. Kael moved into position just shy of its center, heart already thrumming wildly.

The tether, dressed in a white silk shift, was forced to his knees before the king. Kael glanced down at him briefly and thought he recognized the male's face, if only vaguely. One of the prisoners taken after the last surrender, more than likely. He had broad shoulders and thick arms. Though Nocturne was one of their longer ceremonies, he looked to be strong enough to withstand Kael's magic for as long as was needed to complete the invocation.

The Low One was already there waiting for them, before the ritual even began. Kael, the Prelates, and even the few higher-echelon courtiers that were invited to witness it could feel Him. He was in the air, in the trees, but most of all, He was in the darkness. He made it thick and even blacker than it would have been otherwise in that desolate clearing. The light of the candles, set up in perfect formation, barely spread more than an inch from their jumping flames.

As the Lesser Prelates took their places around the south side of the circle, Kael rolled his shoulders and his outer robe slid to the ground. He didn't miss Werryn's reproachful look when he kicked it into a ball in the dirt and knelt down on it. To the north, almost directly under the moon, Werryn stepped up to the altar. By the time he began the ritual, the moon would be aligned exactly over his head. They had several minutes yet to breathe in the electric air and gather their thoughts.

Kael shifted his weight from one knee to the other before settling back on his heels. He was uncomfortable from the inside out; if they didn't begin soon, he was afraid his ribs would crack under the pressure expanding inside his chest. Finally, Werryn raised his hands and the quiet murmuring ceased.

"Brothers and sisters of the Unseelie Court," Werryn's voice echoed as he began his sermon, resonating in the open space. "As we gather in this sacred hour, we prepare for the coming winter, and with it, the winds of change."

He raised his hands, his fingers adorned with silver rings bearing the mark of their faith. Kael had his own set that he would don after the ritual, but for this, he needed his hands unencumbered.

"Tonight, we beseech the Low One to grant us His blessings. As darkness enshrouds our Court, let us be embraced by it and draw strength from the depths of the abyss. Let us harness His gifts to weave our destiny and secure our dominion over Wyldraíocht."

Addressing the unseen forces that lay beyond the material, Werryn's words called to the dormant power within Kael. Slowly, painfully, the first tendrils of magic emerged from his skin. Kael extended his hands, palms upturned. Wisps of shadow, almost entirely translucent, curled from his fingertips like threads of smoke. Hushed, reverent whispers passed between a few of the courtiers who hadn't before seen his power firsthand.

"We are the masters of shadow, and the arbiters of our own fate. We ask that winter's cold, unyielding grip forge us into a force that none can withstand." After a moment of silence for his sermon to sink in, Werryn lowered his head and lapsed into the ritual chants. Monotone and low, he spoke in a language as ancient as the Low One himself that only the Prelates and a handful of scholars could still understand.

Kael's shadows began to coalesce and writhe, swirling in a dance of ephemeral darkness. Surges of inky-black energy rippled through The Cut. His control was already precarious, teetering just on the edge of chaos. The courtiers, aware of the violent nature of his gifts, looked upon their king with a blend of awe and caution.

Kael dropped his hands to the ground and dug the tips of his fingers into the earth, clawing at the dirt with his fingernails to relieve any fraction of the energy that surged and burned under his skin. His lungs seized and his heart pumped impossibly fast. The Low One was here, beckoning to his shadows from the darkness, stretching and pulling them out of him. Ripping them from his veins.

Mercifully, Kael found some relief by directing his darkness towards the tether. The male cried out sharply as the shadows wrapped around his body, some plunging straight through him. He just needed to last a few more minutes, just to buy Werryn enough time to finish.

But he wasn't as strong as he looked. Too quickly, the male fell silent and slumped forward onto the ground. Kael's shadows retreated from his fading life force and branched out into The Cut, seeking their next target. A deep shudder that wracked Kael's body shot through the ground and zipped up the nearest tree. One large branch crashed to the earth with a loud crack, narrowly missing a cluster of worshippers. Several of the Lesser Prelates stumbled, clutching each other's elbows for balance, but Werryn didn't waver. Steadfast as ever, he continued his invocations. His voice was but a hum in Kael's ears, the steady rhythm of his words all merging into one constant droning sound.

Another crack echoed through the clearing—a whole tree this time, further off, was split clean in half by a constricting shadow. Kael managed to open his eyes long enough to lock them onto Werryn's, and the High Prelate understood by the pain he saw there that he didn't have more than a minute before Kael lost control entirely. Stumbling over his words, Werryn drew the ritual to a premature close.

"In darkness, we find strength. In shadows, we find solace. As winter descends, we find our resolve. It is by the grace of the Low One that we follow our King, our beacon of power; heed His call to arms; and blaze our path to supremacy. Let His reign be eternal." The worshippers echoed the closing statement of the sermon—they knew these words by heart.

Slowly, slowly, Kael called his shadows to withdraw. They slid across the ground and his every nerve fired off in protest as they coiled back into his muscles. His bones. His blood. When the searing pain faded, in its place a hot anger bloomed in Kael's chest. He rose to his feet and approached the tether. The male was barely clinging to life. Kael wedged the toe of his boot under his shoulder and kicked him onto his back. In one smooth motion, he unsheathed the dagger that hung from his hip and drove it into the male's throat, twisting it once for good measure before standing again. He didn't wait to hear the death rattle that forced its way out of the male's mouth.

Kael could hardly remember stalking back to his chamber. Blind with rage, he slammed the heavy door closed and let out a yell so loud and harsh it hurt his own ears. His chest heaved and his body shook. If he thought Werryn wouldn't have stopped him, Kael would have ripped the tether limb from limb, and likely a handful of the worshippers, too. Just picturing the carnage managed to pacify him slightly. The honey wine he poured himself from the bottle on his desk, even more so. Still, his hands shook as he traded the simple ceremonial robes for the ornate set he'd had made for the revelry. Spun from a rich black silk, the edges were trimmed with silver embroidery that swept across the fabric in swirls that closely mimicked the movement of his shadows.

"That was one of your worst performances yet," Werryn said flatly from the doorway. He'd slipped in while the king had still been lost in his own thoughts.

"Do not give your opinions unsolicited," Kael warned. The anger he'd been working hard to quell began creeping back in, so he concentrated on the repetitive motion of sliding his rings onto his fingers one by one.

Werryn ignored the bite in his words. "We must finish the rite. We'll wait a few days for you to recharge, but it cannot be left undone."

"With the way you order me around, it almost seems that you wish to be king." Kael's hands dropped to grip the edge of his dresser. "Tell me, Prelate, do you see yourself fit to rule? Or is it that you consider yourself my superior?" He spoke the words calmly—menacingly so. Usually unafraid of his wrath, his tone now was enough to send a brief chill down Werryn's spine. So he conceded.

"Enjoy your evening, Your Grace." Neither Werryn nor the Lesser Prelates would be in attendance tonight; their part of the Nocturne celebration began and ended with the ritual. For that, at least, Kael was grateful.

He swallowed down another goblet of honey wine and wished for something stronger. The celebration would begin soon, and he had a speech to deliver, but despite his earlier anticipation he wanted nothing more than to sink himself into a drunken oblivion.

Kael chose a delicate crown to wear and settled it atop his head before sweeping his hair away from his left ear. He palmed the earring he'd left sitting out: a long string of white gems, the closest thing to a family heirloom he possessed. Roughly, he pushed its sharp post through his lobe. It had been some years since he'd worn one, and he was meant to wait for Methild to come pierce him properly with a needle, but the brief, bracing pain felt good. It forced him to suck in a deep breath of air.

Settled, dressed, and with the faintest buzz in his veins, the Unseelie King was ready to greet his Court.

6

NOCTURNE, PART II: THE REVELRY

AISLING

The Fae were real: this was a fact that Aisling had been varying degrees of sure of at different times in her life. When she was young, she believed her mother's descriptions of her visits to the Wild with all the blind naïveté of a child. Every word that crossed the woman's lips was gospel, and she wove such fantastic tales—who was Aisling to deny them? Her mother had introduced her to the forest, led her by the hand all the way to the borderlands and drew a line in the dirt there with her finger that Aisling should never, ever cross. In the very deepest reaches of her memory, Aisling was almost positive that her mother had pointed out, only once or twice, some manner of faerie on Brook Isle. A sprite maybe, like the one she'd rescued, or something else similarly small and curious enough to let them approach.

But Aisling grew older, and her confidence faded. She became conscious of the whispers about her mother that often echoed through town, especially during those times when she'd go away, supposedly through a Thin Place. They'd wane while she was gone, for a day or sometimes two, then would pick up again when she came back. The whispers grew into a dull roar when she pulled Aisling out of the island's tiny school to teach her at home from the time she was seven until her tenth birthday, when Aisling threw such a fit that her father finally put his foot down and allowed her to go back. The Fae didn't exist for Aisling anymore then, and the stories her mother told were just that: stories. Aisling squashed that belief down so hard and so deep that she convinced herself that she'd lost it. But even unacknowledged, it remained inside her, the smallest burning ember.

Then her mother was gone. Her stories and sketches were gone. The magic that she brought to the island, and to Aisling's life, was gone. The ember was doused.

And Aisling didn't believe in magic again until, by absolute coincidence, she ran into Rodney at the gas station that night a decade ago. But then, her disbelief was replaced with a cold, cruel, and heavy guilt. Guilt, and regret. It consumed her for years.

Now, she waited for her closest friend to change her into one of the creatures from her mother's accounts and take her to the place she'd demanded Aisling never visit. She'd be the one calling Aisling crazy for this.

"We should go inside. It's going to rain soon." Aisling didn't so much as glance toward the late evening sky, but Rodney peered upward to examine it from where he sat beside her on the steps of his mobile home. It was hazy, but cloudless.

Not ten minutes later, dark clouds had blown in and the first drops of rain began to pelt the roof.

He watched it coming down through the window as Aisling settled on the couch. "I don't know how you always do that."

"In the city I never could. I can't tell you how many times I got caught out without an umbrella. I can always smell it here, though." She shrugged, dropping one hand to scratch Briar's head where he lay on the ground beside her. "Something in the soil maybe, or in the trees."

"Either way, it's impressive." He let the cheap plastic shade fall closed and moved to stand in front of the couch. "We need to get ready."

"It's too early," Aisling complained. She was stalling, and they both knew it.

"It'll take a bit for us to get out there, and I need time to make sure I have the glamour right," Rodney argued.

Aisling sat up and pulled her knees to her chest. "I can't look like me."

"I know."

"*Anything* like me, Rodney," she insisted. There shouldn't be a single trace of her left when he was done—not hair or skin or eye color, build or bone structure.

"*I know*, Ash." He was getting annoyed. He pulled a magazine out of a half-empty moving box on the floor and tossed it at her.

It was two years old; she wasn't quite sure why he still had it. "Pick someone. I need a reference."

She flipped through the pages and pointed at random to a model in a perfume ad insert that had long since lost its scent. "Here, use her."

He tore the page out and studied it for a moment before he folded it into a tiny square to tuck in his pocket. Rodney was already dressed for the occasion in a slim-fitting satin suit, a deep shade of maroon with black lapels. It clashed just enough with his orange hair that the whole look almost seemed to work. He'd seen it in a magazine, too, along with the shiny patent loafers that would more than likely give him blisters by the end of the night.

Rodney returned to the kitchen to attend to the whistling kettle on the stove. Aisling could smell the brew from the couch and wrinkled her nose in disgust. The acrid scent burned her nostrils. Briar, too, huffed in annoyance.

"Christ, that smells," she choked out.

"It'll taste even worse," Rodney promised grimly. He handed Aisling a chipped mug he'd pocketed from a diner on the mainland and she swirled the liquid in it. It was a pale pink, only a few shades darker than completely clear. It looked weaker than it smelled.

"What is it?"

"Quicken tea. Brewed from dried rowan berries." Rodney had pulled the perfume ad back out of his pocket and was examining it closely, memorizing the planes and angles of the model's face. "Drink it all."

With it tipped toward her face, the rising steam made Aisling's eyes water. She screwed them shut tightly and drank the too-hot tea down in three big sips. She had to purse her lips together to keep from gagging. "Why did I drink that?" she rasped once she could speak again.

"To protect you from enchantments." He noticed her alarmed look and tried to placate her: "It's only a precaution. These celebrations sometimes get out of hand. You should be fine, just don't eat or drink anything that I don't give you."

∴

Rodney's glamour felt at first like a heavy down quilt being draped over Aisling's head: both comforting and stifling, a cocoon that prickled over her bare skin. It took several minutes to settle against her form. Once the magic had pressed itself into every dip and curve of her body, the feeling dissipated. Then, at most, it felt like a thin film. The smell of it lingered faintly—the same indescribable scent she'd caught the night he'd turned playing cards to cash.

Aisling's honey-brown hair had darkened to the deepest shade of chestnut, very nearly black, which matched her wide, upturned eyes. The freckles that peppered across her nose and under her eyes had disappeared. Her face was now heart-shaped and angular, with high, sharp cheekbones and rosebud lips. Aisling wasn't large to begin with, but her athletic build had diminished to a much more petite size. Her waist was tiny, and she'd lost about a foot of height. She smiled, satisfied with her newly-elongated digits and viridescent skin that seemed to glow in the moonlight.

"You take entirely too much pleasure in this," Rodney pointed out sardonically.

"Of course I do, look at me." When she twirled, the small wings on her back fluttered in place. "I wish I looked like this all the time."

He scowled. "I like you better as you."

Aisling rolled her eyes. They felt too big for her sockets. "This was your idea." She smoothed her hands over her dress, green as grass and embellished with shining gold stitching that made it look like a patchwork of leaves. It was short, much shorter than anything Aisling owned, but she hadn't been glamoured this way for fun. She needed to look the part that she'd be playing.

Rodney had cast his magic not far from the Thin Place, and the pair made their way there in silence. Aisling was buzzing with nervous energy. She'd turned down Rodney's offer to take a shot or two beforehand, and she was regretting that decision now as they wound through the dark woods.

He'd been overly secretive in the weeks leading up to this night about the location of the Unseelie Thin Place, but now that they were close, Aisling knew exactly where it was. Of course she did—she chided herself for never having guessed. It was perhaps the most obvious place on the island for it to be hidden.

The old lead mine had closed in the 80's, well before Aisling was born, and Brook Isle had never recovered. Though it was never featured in her mother's stories, its black, gaping maw had long given her an uneasy feeling. She'd always chalked it up to the safety presentations the island's fire and rescue squad put on for the school at the beginning of every year: don't get caught out on the mud flats at low tide. Don't throw things off the docks. And never, ever go into the mine. They warned of cave-ins. Toxic fumes. Open chasms one might fall into in the dark that could swallow a grown man whole. All enough to terrify children, sure, but she never outgrew the feeling. When Aisling visited its entrance years ago, on a dare, it wasn't fumes or unstable rock that made her blood run cold. It was the feeling of being watched.

"Shall we?" Rodney was holding his arm out to Aisling. She linked hers through it and rested her hand in the crook of his elbow. She felt steadier with him by her side, but she wished that she had Briar flanking her other hip as well.

As the two entered the mine, Aisling felt compelled to hold her breath, like some sort of dated superstition. They treaded carefully over the rubble, weaving to avoid the stagnant puddles that collected below rivulets of water dripping from the ceiling. To Aisling's great relief, the Thin Place wasn't very deep inside at all. It appeared outwardly as a caved-in tunnel, the stacked boulders blending seamlessly into the rest of the mine. She'd have passed right by if Rodney hadn't stopped and turned her to face it. His mischievous grin was obvious even in the dark as he pulled her forward.

The Veil dragged across Aisling's skin like a sticky cobweb as she passed through, invisible yet palpable enough for her to rub her hands across her face and down her arms as though to wipe it off. She was so preoccupied by the sensation that it took her a few seconds to register that they were standing in a forest of ancient, twisted pines.

When she looked back, there was nothing but darkness. Two small creatures darted out of the tree line nearby, and Rodney urged her to follow them up the stone path ahead.

"Keep your eyes forward," he said in her ear. "You need to look like you've been here before."

She nodded, but it was difficult. She longed to stop and take everything in: the smell of the clean air, the woods, the mountains that she could just barely make out in the distance.

The path led to a structure that was even blacker than the night sky. The moon reflected off its shining surface, and as they entered, Aisling reached out and ran a hand across the wall. It was smooth and cool to the touch. The structure was built from slabs of obsidian, she realized. But inside, the space was small and empty save for a plain throne at the far end.

"Is this it?" she whispered. Rodney nodded towards the faeries, who'd disappeared into a hole in the ground from which a faint warm glow emanated. It was a spiral staircase, wide and worn and lit all the way down by flickering candles. Aisling understood then that the Undercastle was carved into the earth itself, at once both a structure of stone and a labyrinthine cave system. It was disorienting to imagine. The air grew heavier as they descended, laden with the scent of damp stone and soil. Rodney led confidently, but Aisling was quietly glad to have the tinkling laughter of the faeries ahead of them as their guide.

Finally, they grew close enough to hear the sounds of the revelry drifting towards them from a chamber at the end of the hall. Aisling gripped Rodney's elbow a bit tighter; this dreamlike world she'd found herself in was becoming more real by the second and she was unsure of whether she was entirely prepared for the night to come.

The throne room that opened up before them was decorated with boughs of silver pine and great swaths of shimmering black fabric. This time, Aisling couldn't stop herself from gazing around in awe. The cavern was so vast she couldn't even see the ceiling, the sounds of the celebration all echoing up into blackness. Twisted veins of quartz streaked the walls and glittered like stars.

"Welcome to the Unseelie Court, Ash," Rodney said with a wide grin.

The spectacle left her breathless. The revelers, all adorned in strange and opulent attire, moved with an enchanting grace that seemed to defy the laws of nature. Their faces were an array of unearthly beauty, sharp cheekbones and glimmering eyes not dissimilar from those Aisling wore now. Their skin, ranging in shades from alabaster to amethyst to deep midnight blue, shone in the warm candlelight. The air was thick with a heady blend of fragrances—smoky incense, the earthy scent of damp moss, and the sweetness of forbidden fruits. Thin strains of a haunting tune woven by a trio of winged musicians swirled through the cavern, coaxing even the most reserved of guests to join in the dance. Fae of every size and race twirled and spun around each other in giddy circles.

Rodney led her through the crush, aiming for the far side where smaller groups clustered around a banquet table laden with a whole garden's worth of plump, shining fruits. Aisling was keenly aware of the intensity in Rodney's eyes. Even he, the ever-confident Veilwalker, knew to tread lightly here.

"Be careful where you step and to whom you speak," Rodney instructed, his voice barely audible over the clamor of the festivities. "Do not agree to anything and do not ask for names."

He filled them each a heavy goblet with an amber liquid and swept Aisling out of the way of a large being that more closely resembled the trunk of a tree than a living creature. Before she could ask, he passed her the goblet and said, "A spriggan."

"This is safe to drink?" She peered into the goblet. The liquid inside shimmered slightly, a thick, molten gold.

He nodded and took a sip of his own. "Honey wine. You'll like it."

Aisling touched it to her lips, barely. It was sweet, cloyingly so, but by the time she'd licked the taste of it off of her lips she was already craving more. When Rodney's elbow dug into her ribs, she looked towards where he was gesturing subtly with his chalice.

At the head of the cavern on a rough, rocky dais, she could just see the ornate crest of the Unseelie King's throne, carved from black obsidian similar to the structure they'd entered above. The musicians' lilting song was drawing to an end, and the revelers slowed their steps. Despite how hard they'd been dancing, not a single one was out of breath. The male who had been seated on the throne stood and moved to the front of the dais.

The Unseelie King cut an imposing figure, standing tall and broad-shouldered with chiseled features and piercing eyes that swept over the room. Silence rippled outward from the path of his gaze. His silver-white hair fell well past his shoulders and framed a sharp, angular face and heavy brows. His skin, though not colorful like some, was pale, almost translucent. Even from a distance, it seemed to Aisling to radiate a cold aura.

"Tonight, as the dark embrace of winter looms, we gather this Nocturne in the name of the Low One. We stand united before Him as denizens of the night, and we find our strength in its depths. I come to you not as your king, but as His vessel and loyal servant of the shadows." The king's voice, deep and velvet-smooth, rang out clearly as he delivered his speech to a rapt audience. "But tonight, let us pay homage to the power of the shadows that resides within each one of us, a force both violent and beautiful. Let this revelry be a celebration of our resilience, for we have weathered the trials and tribulations of the past.

"The battles ahead loom large and fraught with peril. The Seelie Court seeks to encroach upon our dominions, their insipid light a threat to the delicate balance of our existence. But fear not, for we are the children of darkness, and the shadows are our sanctuary." He paused to let his words sink in. Aisling, too, was gripped by his address. She couldn't tear her eyes from his brooding stare, the cool countenance with which he held himself.

"This winter comes as a harbinger of change—a time to hone our prowess, to sharpen our blades, and to nurture the seeds of cunning and strategy within us all. Our actions will echo through the ages, and our legacy will endure. Let His reign be eternal."

"Let His reign be eternal," echoed the revelers solemnly.

Then the music began again, and the crowd resumed their dance. The Unseelie King sank back into his throne, out of view.

"Bit dramatic, isn't he?" Rodney was looking sideways at Aisling with a smirk that reminded her why they were there in the first place.

She scoffed into her goblet. "You think?"

She had her plan, and she'd seen her target. All she needed to do now was execute.

7

NOCTURNE, PART III: THE MANIPULATION
AISLING

"We need to get you in front of him." Rodney refreshed their goblets. After only one, Aisling could feel heat flooding her veins and warming her cheeks. She wondered idly what color she'd blush under her verdant skin.

Rodney was born for this: the sport, the maneuvering. He was the master in this bout of chess, and he could hardly wait to get the game started. The only way he could have been more excited was if he were on the board himself, rather than instructing Aisling's movements.

"I don't know, this whole thing just feels so...manipulative." Now having seen the king in the flesh, Aisling was losing her nerve. He looked every bit as cruel as he'd been described. Strikingly beautiful, she'd admit, but frightening.

"Well, that's because it is. It has to be. How else are you going to get what you need? Certainly not by asking nicely. And anyway, I gave you three weeks to come up with an alternative plan," he reminded her.

He had, and she hadn't. "I know."

"It could be worse." He shrugged, picking at a large purple plum he'd chosen from the table. "He could look like that." Rodney nodded towards a group of squat, fanged faeries with skin the texture of stone and black tufts of hair down the ridges of their spines. "You're not going to make a move until the party dies down, so relax. We just need to get him to notice you first."

"How are we going to do that?" Amongst the crowd, her tiny form would hardly stand out.

He grinned, then beckoned over a satyr who had been leering at Aisling since the king finished his speech. "You're going to dance."

"No," she pled, eyes wide, when the male took her hand and began to pull. "Rodney, no!" But her words were lost in the noise and the last thing she saw of Rodney was the flash of an encouraging smile before she was spun into the satyr's broad, hairy chest.

He had to lean down to hold her around the waist and his other hand fully enveloped her own. He smelled of all the darkest parts of the forest: the rot, the decay, the mold. She grimaced as he crushed her body against his. But despite his size, he was an agile dancer. On cloven hooves he led Aisling through spin after dizzying spin. As she continued to dance, her nerves slowly gave way to exhilaration. The other dancers blurred into a kaleidoscope of colors and shapes, and she lost herself in the frenzied pace.

Rodney stepped in before the satyr could drop his hand any lower down her back and shooed him off to find a new partner.

"Let me lead you, I'm going to take you closer to the throne," he all but shouted into her ear. He maneuvered them through the crowd deliberately, pausing here and there for several beats to hide their movement in the intricate steps of the dance.

Then, they were front and center to the throne. Aisling kept her eyes on Rodney, on the whirling gowns and wings and braids that brushed against her as they turned, but never let them stray in the king's direction. One song bled into the next and the rhythm rose and dipped like waves crashing on the shoreline. She was giddy and lightheaded and could hardly feel her feet or determine where she ended and the other Fae around her began.

Rodney spun her once more before pulling her firmly out of the throng, back to their quiet corner. She'd been reluctant to abandon the dance, but once she'd stopped, she realized that she could scarcely breathe. Her feet ached and her lungs burned. She would have stayed in there all night if he'd let her.

"Did you feel it?" Rodney asked of the magic that had washed over them with the notes of the music. Aisling nodded—she had. She'd felt so light, she was almost sure she'd been floating.

"I thought the tea was meant to protect me," she said. He handed her a fresh goblet of honey wine and she drank it down thirstily.

"From enchantments. Music, dancing...that's a different magic entirely. It works its way into you until you'd sooner die than stop."

Aisling shivered slightly. Suddenly, she could hear strains of sinister notes underlying the lively tune.

Rodney maintained that they should wait, and so they did, biding their time while the celebration slowly waned. It could have been hours later, or mere minutes, but when the first revelers began to depart, the rest followed. The satyr passed by once in a bid to convince Aisling to leave with him, but the pair managed to avoid further interactions. She could tell that Rodney would have rather been in the center of it all, satiating his Fae proclivities for one night before returning to the human realm, but he refused to leave her side despite her urging.

Those that remained swayed slowly or sat propped against the pillars and walls, halfway to passing out. Certainly by now, no one left was sober enough to pay a pixie any mind.

Aisling grabbed an empty goblet and a bottle off of the banquet table as she passed, pausing briefly to take several long swallows to steady herself. The comfortable drunk she'd been nursing all night had begun to wear off, but the wine quickly brought back a warm buzz as she approached the dais. The role she was playing tonight demanded a level of confidence that she didn't possess on the other side of the Veil. But here in the Wild, she wasn't herself anymore—not really. This Aisling was cool and bold and sure. Ready to act, rather than plan. So she let that wine draw her further into character.

The Unseelie King sat reclined on his dark throne, sharp chin in one hand while his other played over the carved designs of an obsidian arm. He didn't notice her stopping to stand in front of him until she spoke.

"Would Your Highness grant an audience to a humble pixie?" Aisling curtsied deep to the floor, glancing up coyly through her long lashes. She had to concentrate to keep the tremor out of her voice and her limbs as she moved. He slid piercing silver eyes over her before nodding almost imperceptibly. She stepped up onto the platform.

"How can you seem so dissatisfied with such a glorious court?" Aisling turned to take in his view. It would have been enthralling earlier, at the height of the revelry. It was hardly the same now, but still no less impressive. Aisling watched a few waif-like females drifting around a group of very drunk hobs. The king didn't so much as look at them but kept his eyes on Aisling warily.

"What is it that you want?" He rubbed a hand over his face. His diction was intriguing, with the barest hint of a strange accent that Aisling couldn't quite place. Feeling emboldened by the fact that he hadn't ordered her away yet, she sashayed around the back of his throne and leaned around its right side.

"To serve you a drink, My Lord. Honey wine?" She poured the amber liquid into the goblet she'd brought and circled back to the front of the throne to offer it to him. She took a sip from the bottle as she waited with it outstretched.

"You are not supposed to be up here."

"No one has stopped me so far." Aisling raised an eyebrow and looked pointedly at the cup in her hand until Kael sighed heavily and took it. She smiled, satisfied, and took another drink. When she was sure Kael was distracted, she looked for Rodney where he lurked in the shadow of a pillar. He gestured to her to hurry up.

When the king had finished his wine, Aisling shot a hand out and wrapped her long fingers around his wrist. He looked up at her, startled, but his pulse remained steady under his skin. She winked and refilled his goblet. She let go once the liquid reached the brim and sat on the ground beside his throne. After she'd finished the bottle, she tossed it off the dais. Kael watched it roll in a circle on the dusty floor.

"You look bored," she observed.

"Do I?" he said absently into his cup before draining it.

Aisling's heart was beginning to race with the knowledge of what would come next. "We're out of alcohol."

"I believe you've had enough." Kael set his goblet at his feet and leaned back once again.

"I believe you haven't," Aisling countered. Kael glanced back at several empty bottles scattered behind him. Aisling stood, aware suddenly of the slight heaviness of her eyelids. Everything seemed a little softer now. A little hazier. She put her hands on the arm of his throne and moved close.

"Come and play," she said, voice low.

"Excuse me?"

"They won't miss you for an hour or two." Aisling nodded towards two of the king's knights, both flirting with winged females with ruby skin. "Come on."

Kael maintained an expressionless gaze, eyes straight ahead. This had to work—she had to make it work.

In one final bid to convince him, she leaned in close, her lips almost, *almost* touching the very tip of his pointed ear. "Have you ever kissed a pixie?" she whispered.

That got his attention. The intensity of his glare faltered just slightly, and before he could object further Aisling had slipped her hand into his and pulled him to stand. He stopped her before she could lead him off the front of the dais, though, and nodded wordlessly towards a door in the wall behind the throne.

Aisling's blood rushed loudly in her ears as he guided her away from the drunken laughter echoing through the cavern with their fingers intertwined. He led her down a torchlit hallway, far from prying eyes, but stopped midway. The air was thick with anticipation and an electric energy thrummed between them when he turned to face her. Aisling took a step closer, then another, until Kael's back was pressed against the cave wall and there was only an inch of space between their bodies. He was already leaning down, maybe unconsciously. This was coming easier to her than she thought.

Raising herself onto her toes, she tipped her chin to bring her lips close to his. Kael's breath hitched, and she could feel the tension building in him.

"This is a dangerous game you're playing, little pixie," he murmured, his voice low and husky.

Aisling's fingers lightly brushed against the sharp angles of his face, tracing a path down his jawline. "Isn't all of life a game, Highness? Tonight, I thought I might like to play it with you." Her taunting words dared him to take the bait. She'd surprised even herself with her irreverence, but it seemed to be working just as intended.

Kael's restraint wavered and he leaned closer, drawn in by her challenge. His fingers lightly grazed her wings. She couldn't feel them there, but the gesture sent shivers down her spine all the same. Just a breath apart now, he hesitated for a beat. Then another. Then took Aisling's hand again and resumed pulling her down the hallway. She let him.

He led her to the doorway of a chamber, pitch black inside, and Aisling's stomach dropped. The uncertainty of what awaited her past the threshold set alarm bells off in her brain, muted by the wine but still loud enough to bring her pause. *He knows,* she thought. He'd found her out and she'd followed him willingly to her death. Already inside, Kael looked back at her with a smirk playing across his lips, at once both threatening and alluring.

"Are you afraid of the dark?" Now it was his turn to tease.

Aisling set her jaw and met his pale eyes. She wouldn't let him win. "Only when there's something in it to be afraid of."

He seemed satisfied by her answer enough to let her linger in the doorway while he lit a tall, tapered candle and set the silver candlestick on the nightstand. Though the flame did little to illuminate the space, Aisling could make out a simple bed against the far wall. The chamber was small, almost certainly not Kael's, but rather one he saved for occasions such as this, with females such as herself. He turned to retrieve her, letting his hands slide down her waist to rest on her slender hips.

"Better?" Kael asked. His smirk seemed softer now that she knew there was no malice hidden behind it.

"Almost." Aisling stepped inside and closed the heavy wooden door. Then, she reached up to ease the black silken robe from Kael's shoulders. He watched her, studied her, as it slid to the floor and puddled at their feet.

"And now?"

"Getting closer." She took his hand in hers and raised it to her shoulder, guiding it to slip off one of the delicate cap sleeves of her dress. The intensity of his gaze was all over her skin, pins and needles that followed the path of his eyes and left her breathless. Kael's breath, too, caught slightly when his fingers brushed over her.

Aisling slid a hand up around the back of Kael's neck, settling it at his nape beneath his hair, and guided him towards her. He was so much taller than she was in this form, though she thought that even without the glamour the top of her head would only just reach his chin. He let her lead, giving in fully to her direction.

When Kael lightly touched his lips to her pulse, just below her jaw, Aisling's fingers threaded through his hair and she pressed into him. He trailed kisses up, hesitating at the corner of her mouth. He was waiting for her, she realized. To take the lead, to take control, as she had from the beginning. He'd played straight into her trap. Aisling tilted her head and when their lips finally met, the whole chamber was set ablaze.

Kael fell backwards onto the bed, pulling her down on top of him, and the groan he loosed involuntarily raised goosebumps down Aisling's arms. His kisses were raw and wanting and the taste of him was more intoxicating than all the honey wine in the world. His tongue moved against hers with urgent purpose, exploring the contours of her mouth, stoking the fire that had taken the place of every drop of blood in Aisling's veins.

Kael's hands explored her back, bare now after having undone the thin tie that held the fabric around her body, and traced the curve of her spine between her wings. His lips only broke contact with hers once, when a quiet hiss escaped them as her hand brushed over his ear and jostled the earring that dangled from his lobe.

Aisling paused, drawing back to look at him. "Did that hurt?"

"It's nothing." He lifted his head to kiss her neck again but she pushed herself up on his chest.

"Here, let me see." Aisling turned Kael's face to the side and removed the earring back.

"It will close," he protested.

Aisling hushed him and swiftly, gently, pulled the earring from his ear. "There." He gripped her waist when she leaned over and set it on the nightstand before pulling her back down into his embrace.

Each needy touch that followed fanned the flames burning in them both. When he worked his way back up to tangle his fingers in Aisling's hair, gently pulling at the roots, she ground her hips down against his. She felt his hardness there and knew that he'd soon be angling for more, so she backed off. Rodney's words remained clear in her spinning mind: *Leave him wanting more.*

So Aisling sat up. "I believe the game is over for tonight," she teased, out of breath. "I hope you enjoyed the kiss, Highness."

Kael caressed her thighs braced on either side of his hips. Disappointment was obvious on his face, but it was laced with something else, too. Intrigue, she hoped. "What may I call you, pixie?"

She remembered Rodney's warning—one that she'd heard from her mother many times, too—and demurred. If Aisling were truly a pixie, she wouldn't give it so easily. "You can have my name if I decide to see you again."

"It will be your decision alone, then?" His long fingers played across her skin.

She nodded once and echoed his words: "Mine alone."

Aisling pressed one last, chaste kiss to the king's lips then rose off of him. He didn't follow her when she left the chamber, nor did he emerge as she retraced her steps down the hallway. With trembling hands, she tied her dress before reentering the throne room. Save for several faeries passed out splayed on the ground, it was empty.

She'd done it—and she could scarcely believe just how easy it had been. She thought he'd put up a fight, at least, before accompanying a stranger unguarded into a back room. It spoke volumes of his impulsivity, or maybe confidence in his own abilities to defend himself. Aisling shuddered slightly at the thought of what he could have done to her with his strong, lithe warrior's body and fast hands. More than likely, it was she who'd been at risk all along.

As she made her way shakily on tip-toe through the passages, Aisling recalled the tale of the Princess and the Goblin, and how the young girl in the story had been gifted an enchanted thread to guide her back to safety. Aisling wished that she had some such thread now that would lead her out of the winding halls of the Unseelie Court. Though she thought she remembered the way, she made several wrong turns into dead ends before she reached the spiral staircase.

Rodney jumped to his feet from where he'd been resting half-asleep against the trunk of a tree when he heard Aisling's footsteps approaching through the brush. Her hair was wild and she didn't need to see herself to know that her lips were flushed and kiss-swollen.

"What happened?" he demanded. Before answering, Aisling turned and gestured for him to retie the dress that she was holding up with one arm across her chest. She hadn't managed to get it tight enough to stay up on its own. Rodney did so quickly then spun her back to face him. "So?"

"So," Aisling said. "I think we should get home."

He shook her lightly by her shoulders. "Aisling, tell me."

"It was a good plan, Rodney." That was all she wanted to give him for now. Her head was still spinning, her body was still quaking, and her heart hadn't ceased its relentless pounding since the moment she'd locked eyes with the Unseelie King.

Rodney's eyes narrowed. "You enjoyed it," he accused.

She ignored his judgmental look and said simply, "You were right—it could have been worse."

8

THE NIGHT GARDEN

AISLING

Aisling felt like hell. Her head throbbed, her muscles ached, and her mouth tasted foul. But perhaps worst of all, she could still feel the Unseelie King's lips against her skin.

She groaned and pressed the heels of her hands against her forehead. Her skin smelled like pine sap and honey wine and sweat. Though Rodney had removed the glamour as soon as they'd crossed back through the Thin Place, she thought her arms were still tinged a pale shade of mossy green.

The flood of memories, if a bit fuzzy around the edges, sliced at Aisling's conscience like shards of glass. She could recall the thrill of the temptation, the seductive challenge she'd posed to the king. The dangerous gleam in his eyes when he'd accepted. Massaging her temples in vain, Aisling tried to shake off the lingering dizziness from the revelry. She cursed her own foolishness for thinking she could outdance the Fae—or outdrink their king. Now, in the harsh light of day, the whole thing seemed impossibly juvenile.

Still with her palms covering her eyes, Aisling was startled by Briar's low growl. He'd been asleep between her legs but had risen to a crouch over the top of her. His hackles were raised and his lips were drawn back to bare a full mouth of shining teeth, eyes locked on the front door. She reached a hand out to soothe him, but the growl in his throat only grew louder. With some effort, Aisling pushed herself up to sit and lifted one corner of the blinds to see what had spooked him.

Fuck.

Aisling tried to vault up onto her feet, but her legs were tangled in a blanket and the sudden movement sent both her and Briar tumbling off of the couch. Tears sprang to her eyes when her knees cracked hard against the floor. She tripped once more on the length of Rodney's sweats trying to stand before she was able to move, crouching down low, toward the rear of the mobile home. Briar rebounded far quicker and was bearing down on the door.

Aisling threw herself into Rodney's room, where he was splayed out sideways across his bed, mouth hanging open. He hadn't stripped off the glamoured suit, or even removed his shoes. Slipping again on a pile of dirty clothes, Aisling lunged forward and shook Rodney hard.

"Wake up," she said sharply. "*Wake the hell up,* Rodney!"

He moaned, shifted, then rolled over. Aisling was close to tossing a glass of water on him when a harsh rap sounded on the front door and Briar, suddenly discovering a protective instinct that had until now been dormant, let loose a volley of aggressive barks. Rodney swore and sat up, then paled when he saw the panicked look on Aisling's face.

"What is it?" he asked, as though he didn't already suspect the answer.

"He's here."

Rodney was out of bed in a flash, finger combing his hair as he moved. A nervous habit or an attempt to appear presentable, Aisling wasn't sure. She trailed behind him and wrapped her fingers through Briar's collar. Despite tugging with nearly all of her weight, he wouldn't budge.

"Leave him!" Rodney hissed and shooed her to the back of the trailer. She ducked back into his room and pressed tight to the wall. The sound of Rodney opening the door brought dread to pool in her stomach. She could try to climb out a window, she thought, or wedge herself under the bed. But she did neither.

"Majesty," she heard Rodney say curtly. "To what do I owe the pleasure?"

Aisling couldn't hear the king's low response. Ignoring every instinct to stay in Rodney's room, she crept up the hallway. Still hidden, but close enough now to make out both sides of the conversation.

"How did you come to find me?" Rodney asked.

"You aren't difficult to find, changeling, it seems that most recognize you by your hair. An unpleasant man several doors down was kind enough to direct me to your...abode." *Cole*. It had to be Cole.

The disdain in Kael's voice was clear, though its velvet tone brought a blush to Aisling's cheeks. "You carry yourself as a human, púca, but you blend in poorly."

"I belong to no court, and I am not one of your subjects. I cannot be compelled to answer your questions, particularly if you've come to insult me on my own threshold." Rodney matched Kael's derision with his own. When Aisling dared peek her head around the corner, just a sliver, she could see Briar positioned between Rodney's legs. His quiet growl had become a constant hum.

"I have little interest in you or your beast. I've come because you were with a pixie last night." At that, Aisling pulled back quickly and retreated a few steps.

Rodney played it off easily. Casually. Like he was commenting on the morning's weather. "Was I? I can't recall."

"Try." Not an order—a threat, and a thinly veiled one at that. He was growing irritated.

"Has she done something to offend?" Rodney asked. Though his words were measured, Aisling knew him well enough to detect the underlying tension there. Skilled as he was in slippery diplomacy, even he was on edge around the king.

"I seek her name." Kael was slightly louder now as he had moved closer to the open door. It was an ominous demand, particularly after her teasing the night before while she'd straddled his hips.

"She was smart not to give it," Rodney shot back.

"So you know her?"

"Scarcely more than you do, it would seem. We passed through the Veil at the same time and became acquainted over a drink. I know little else." It was odd hearing Rodney speak this way, so stiff and formal. A touch too similar to the courtiers he'd mocked at the revelry.

"Does she come from your island?" Louder still. Kael was likely standing at the top of the steps now, just across the threshold. Toe-to-toe with Rodney.

"I've not seen her before, nor since," he replied simply. "I left before she did."

A long beat of silence, and then the sound of retreating footsteps on gravel and the door slamming shut in the king's wake. Aisling's knees buckled with relief and she slid to the ground where she'd been standing.

"I'd say you caught his attention," Rodney commented when he rounded the corner. He offered Aisling his hand and pulled her to her feet. "Maybe a little too well."

Briar wound his way between them, panting, and pressed his head into her stomach. She steadied herself against his warm body. "Do you think he knows?"

Rodney thought for a minute, replaying the interaction, then shook his head. "He'd have killed me right there in my doorway if he did." He nudged Aisling playfully in the ribs then said, singsong, "I think he likes you."

She looked down at Briar to let her hair fall forward and hide her flushed cheeks. "Do you think I should go back?"

"Not just yet, but we should strike while the iron's hot. Tomorrow."

Tomorrow. The idea sent a faint electric thrill through Aisling. She promised herself that what she felt was fear, and fear alone.

⁘

Aisling was green once again, though this time she insisted on a slightly more modest gown. This one, the blazing orange of autumn leaves. But she couldn't enjoy it. Tonight, the glamour felt uncomfortably tight and binding. Her mind continued to stray back to the king; she couldn't escape the memory of his intense gaze, the confident arch of his brow. His teasing smirk as he led her down that dark hall.

"Try the garden tonight," Rodney advised from his perch on a stump. The sun was setting quickly, and soon it would be time to return to the Unseelie Court.

"How do you know he'll be there?" Still clumsy with her elongated fingers, Aisling raked her hair back from her face and clipped it at the nape of her neck. She was nervous and fidgety and was having trouble standing still. She'd tried to convince Rodney to don a different glamor and accompany her, but he seemed sure that it would be less conspicuous for her to go on her own.

"I don't, but there's a good chance." While Aisling had been astride the Unseelie King, Rodney had been hard at work on the drunken revelers. As it happened, he and Aisling weren't the only pair given to speculate about the king's activities. Often, Rodney had learned, he spent nightfall in the garden. If he wasn't there, he was likely kneeling before the altar in The Cut. Rodney wasn't keen on sending Aisling there just yet.

"And if he's not?"

"If he's not, come back and we'll look someplace else in a couple days. Aisling," he said her name firmly and waited for her to turn and look at him. "Don't go into the Undercastle by yourself."

"You couldn't pay me," she said honestly. She'd navigated those passages once on her own—only just—and wasn't eager to do so again. "What if he asks my name again?"

Rodney shrugged. "Make one up, or give him your own. It doesn't matter much either way. Your name holds no power over you."

"It's too bad we don't know his full name, that would make this a lot easier." *Kael.* Rodney had whispered the king's name just before Nocturne, and ever since she'd rolled it over her tongue. It tasted illicit. She wondered how it would sound in his dulcet voice and barely-there accent.

"Sure, but where would be the fun in that?" He winked. He took far too much pleasure in this. Aisling rolled her eyes.

Rodney's directions to the night garden would take her around the back side of the obsidian structure that concealed the entrance to the Undercastle and over the ridge of a hillock dotted with naked, twisted blackthorn trees. The garden, hidden there, bloomed only in the silver wash of moonlight. Even before she crested the knoll Aisling could smell the flowers, sweeter than anything she expected to encounter in the Unseelie Court.

It was unkempt and overgrown, a darkly wild beauty that drew her down a narrow path that cut through its center. Though not alive, as the Shadowwood Mother's thicket had been, the garden was possessed by a magic of its own. The tiny white petals of night jasmine shone like pearls, and ivory moonflowers unfurled on slender stems that swayed as she passed. Ahead, large, trumpet-shaped flowers hung down from a low tree like pale lanterns in the darkness. The blossoms were veined with intricate patterns that shimmered a soft turquoise. Aisling reached up to stroke one of the petals with her finger, but a hand around her wrist stopped her short.

"I wouldn't." Kael had appeared from out of the darkness, approaching on footfalls lighter and more silent than the vespertine breeze. A trait befitting of a predator. He stood behind Aisling now, chest nearly against her back, and had reached around her to catch her just an inch from the bloom. "Angel's trumpet. Quite poisonous."

Aisling turned to look up at the king, who glowed just as the flowers around them, as regal as he was ethereal. Her breath caught slightly. He heard it. "Thank you."

His moonbeam eyes played over her skin and the corner of his lips pulled up into the barest smirk. "So you've returned."

"So I have," she said, regaining her composure.

He offered her his arm from beneath a cloak of midnight blue. "Walk with me, pixie."

Resting her hand in the crook of his elbow, Aisling let Kael lead her deeper into the garden. He pointed out various flora as they walked, most of them in some way poisonous. The blooms hadn't been maintained for a reason: in the shadows, their dangerous nature was allowed to flourish unchecked, a reflection of the Fae that had planted them. It was a stark reminder to Aisling of why she was there in the first place.

"You enjoyed Nocturne?" he asked.

"Very much. I've not been to such an extravagant celebration in a long time." Aisling imagined that her pixie self would prefer smaller, more intimate affairs.

"I'm pleased it was to your liking." Kael's other arm was outstretched, running his fingers through the leaves of a thick shrub. "Though I know of one satyr who was particularly disappointed in how the night ended."

So he had noticed. Each facet of Rodney's plan had been executed without fail, every outcome predicted flawlessly. He'd be glad to hear it. "I think I made the right choice," she replied.

The night seemed to stretch endlessly around them as they walked. The garden's saccharine smell and the way Kael kept her arm pinned close to his body was nearly enough to make Aisling's head spin.

"Have you come to tell me your name?" The way he asked wasn't prodding or intrusive; rather, it was intimate. Something that he hoped she would share with him. A gift. Kael pulled her to stop beside a crystalline pond and took both of her hands in his own.

"Aisling," she whispered up at him.

He repeated it once, then again, as she had in private with his. "A pretty name for a pretty faerie."

"Will you tell me yours?"

Instead of answering right away, Kael moved his hands to Aisling's hips and walked her backward until she was pressed against the trunk of a tree. Its bark was rough against the pointed blades of her shoulders and would likely have scraped uncomfortably against her wings if she could have felt them, but she hardly noticed. His presence, his magnetism, overwhelmed her. Vaguely aware that she was meant to be the one in control, Aisling considered turning to push him up against the tree, instead.

But there was no harm in letting herself enjoy this position for a moment.

Kael reached up to caress Aisling's cheek softly with cool fingers, a mockery of affection that stilled her heart and halted her breathing for a brief second before she met his gaze and realized the cruel intent that glinted in his eyes. He smiled down at her, a dark, twisted thing that drew a slow-rolling chill up her spine and raised the fine hair at the base of her skull. No longer the seductive, enigmatic King; this was the monster Rodney had warned her of.

Then, quicker than her mind could register, his arm was against her throat, crushing her windpipe and pinning her to the tree. Aisling's skin pulled and burned as he roughly shredded the glamour she wore, leaving her raw and exposed in her own skin, her own clothes. Without that thin layer of protection, she could feel the garden's magic grating against her like sand in the wind.

Aisling gasped for breath, her hands clawing at Kael's forearm in a futile attempt to free herself. He was too strong. Panic surged through her veins as she stared into the unyielding face of the Unseelie King. Waves of hatred rolled off of him, thick and tangible.

"Who are you, human, to think you could make a fool of me?" His words came as a deep, unearthly growl as he lowered himself so that the two were face to face, foreheads nearly touching.

"I'm no one, truly," she rasped. Fear tightened her throat even further beneath his arm.

"Not Aisling?" He spat her name this time, like acid.

"I am Aisling, but I'm no one." She was at a loss for words as she struggled to breathe under the pressure he kept on her windpipe. Her voice came out hoarse and her shallow breaths were noisy and ragged. Her vision was beginning to darken around the edges. Kael held her there for a second longer before he released his hold on her throat and stepped back. Aisling fell to her knees on the soft earth at his feet, gasping wildly with the effort of dragging air back into her lungs.

"You've made a grave error in coming here. Truly unwise, though I'd expect nothing less from a human," he said disdainfully. When Aisling looked up at him, he was staring at her as though she were an insect he would crush under the heel of his boot.

"Send me back," she begged. Desperation was roiling in her stomach, rising in her throat and making her eyes sting with hot tears. "You'll never see me again."

Kael's predatory smirk grew. He was delighted by Aisling's distress. He reveled in it, drank it up as fuel for that vicious fire that burned within his chest. "I think not. It is a pity, really. You were a rather fun plaything."

A deep flush of shame spread across Aisling's cheeks. "Fuck you," she threw back.

"You should have." The smirk faded from Kael's face until he wore a neutral, expressionless mask. "You won't get another chance."

Aisling's eyes darted around the garden, trying to identify a way out that wasn't the path behind him. But she couldn't run. Even if her legs hadn't been violently trembling, even if she managed to slip past Kael, there was little chance she'd even make it as far as the edge of the garden. He moved with all the speed and grace of a practiced warrior and with his long stride, he would be on her in seconds.

She had little choice but to let him take her.

Aisling was unsteady on her feet as Kael led her tripping down the spiral staircase. Several times she stumbled, and each time he waited until she'd almost hit the ground before tightening his iron grip on her elbow and wrenching her back upright. She could already feel bruises blooming over her neck, and she was sure she'd have more where the rings on his fingers dug into her arm.

Rodney would know. When Aisling didn't return through the Thin Place, he would know something had gone wrong. He'd find help, or he'd come himself. She just had to survive until he did.

Wordlessly, they marched through the winding halls of the Undercastle. They were descending still, following the narrowing corridors down and down deeper underground. The air grew colder. Staler. Aisling could feel the stone walls pressing in on them. She thought if she listened hard enough, she might even be able to hear the creaks and groans of rocks settling against each other as the earth shifted around the structure of the tunnels.

Kael kept a steady pace that forced Aisling nearly to jog alongside him to keep up. If she slowed down, she would fall, and she wouldn't put it past him to drag her the rest of the way to wherever he was taking her. In fact, it would likely give him great pleasure to do so. His jaw was set hard and his eyes remained focused straight ahead, unwavering even when Aisling lost her balance or trailed behind. She kept her mouth shut. She wouldn't beg, wouldn't ask questions. She wouldn't cry, despite the harsh tears that threatened to spill from her eyes. She wouldn't give him the satisfaction.

He stopped when they reached a heavy wooden door, guarded by two sentinels—malformed, grotesque redcaps that both raised their lips in a snarl when they saw the pair approach. One had a hand wrapped around a tall spear; the other, a broadsword that he let drag on the ground. Kael threw Aisling to the floor at their feet and she bit back a sob when her hip took the brunt of the impact. The redcap with the spear reached down and roughly hauled her back to stand. He stood only as high as Aisling's shoulder, but was three times as wide, at least. His thick arms hung long, past his knees, and he carried himself as though they were almost too heavy for his frame. He yanked her around by her hair to face the king.

"Who sent you?" Kael demanded. "A Solitary faction? Or perhaps the Seelie Court has become so cowardly as to use their human pets for spies?"

"Neither," Aisling gritted out. "I was curious, I've—" her words were punctuated by a sharp gasp as several strands of hair were torn out at the root. "I've heard stories. I was only curious."

"And just how did you come by such a convincing glamour? The púca?"

She couldn't implicate Rodney in this, not if there was to be any chance of him coming to her aid. "I waited by the Thin Place. I bartered with a sprite for it."

"Curiosity is a poor excuse for deception," Kael hissed. "You will pay for your lies." He signaled to the redcaps with a slight nod of his chin before he turned on his heel and ascended the corridor, cloak sweeping behind him as a silent, trailing shadow.

9

TO FEED THE KING

AISLING

In the bowels of the Undercastle, an overwhelming chill penetrated with piercing fingers to wrap around Aisling's very bones. She rested on a damp floor of hard-packed dirt, which she couldn't see, but could feel when her fingers curled against it.

"You're ours now, girly," the redcap had told her after the Unseelie King left her in their keep. The creature's voice was guttural and his hot breath on Aisling's face reeked of decaying meat and stale blood. "Got the perfect cell for you."

That cell was little more than a hole carved into the stone wall of a longer cavern, scarcely wide enough for Aisling to lie down flat, and several inches too short for her to stand fully upright. Stagnant cave water trickled from the ceiling into a puddle in the corner that her hand found when they tossed her in like a discarded doll. A heavy gate locked behind her—iron, she guessed, by the thick leather gloves one of the sentinels pulled on before swinging it shut. And when they returned to their post at the top of the stairs, closing the wooden door there, she was swallowed by the dark.

It was panic that gripped her first. Though she'd never before been particularly claustrophobic, something about the way that heavy, inky darkness pressed in on her forced her breath to come in short, uneven gasps. She clawed first at the too-tight neck of her sweater, then at the ground as though she might be able to dig her way out beneath the bars. She dug and dug until her fingers ached, and when she realized she hadn't even managed to clear an inch of dirt, Aisling's cries grew more frantic. It was the sound of those cries, ringing starkly off the stone walls, that brought her back into her own head. Slowly, slowly, she settled her breathing. Calmed her racing heart. She'd had her time to panic; it would do little good to indulge in that feeling for much longer.

Aisling was overtaken then by the cold, sinking feeling of acceptance: she'd played the game, and she'd lost. Scratches marred the wall at her back, a haunting calendar that marked the last days of a prisoner held there long before her. There was no real light here, no circulation of air or sounds beyond the steady drip-drip-drip to her left. She worked her jaw back and forth to relieve the pressure that had built in her ears—the dungeon was deep below the surface. Impossibly, hopelessly, oppressively deep.

Everything Aisling did was cautious. Calculated. Risks were weighed, outcomes assessed. But with the king, she'd been impulsive. And it had cost her. She was nothing more than a silly human girl who thought she could play at Fae politics and come out on top. The prophecy, true or not, was a curse. It mattered very little whether she was truly the Red Woman; either way, she was a prisoner. Either way, she was completely at Kael's mercy, and she knew all too well that he had none.

"You're a human." A thin voice snaked out of the shadows, breathy and low. Whether male or female, Aisling couldn't tell, nor could she determine just how close to her they were. She didn't answer. "I can smell you." The speaker dragged out the *s*, making a long hissing sound that preceded the word.

"I am," Aisling responded hesitantly. "What are you?"

"A prisoner," the voice said, "like you. We're all the same down here in the dark."

"Are there more?" Blindly, Aisling ran her hands back and forth across the dirt as she crawled to kneel in front of the iron bars. She held onto them, leaning forward until they pressed against either side of her forehead. Her eyes scanned ahead, but she couldn't discern a single shape or form before her.

A laugh then, bitter and weary. "It's just the two of us, now. What do they call you?"

"Aisling," she offered. She shouldn't have, maybe, but it hardly mattered. In truth, though she was unsure just what she was talking to or what their intentions may be, she took some small comfort in knowing she wasn't completely alone.

"You'd give up your name so easily?" Aisling could hear the surprise in their tone; clearly, this Fae was not well-acquainted with humans.

"My name has no power over me."

"Still," they asserted, "I hope you don't expect the same in return."

Aisling shook her head as though they could see her. Maybe their vision was better than hers. "I don't. Why are you here?"

"Prisoner of war," they said simply. "And yourself? What business might a human have with the Unseelie Court?"

Aisling let the question hang in the air for several minutes, considering how to answer, or if she should answer at all. She didn't trust the owner of the voice—hiding in the murky shadows, it could belong to anyone. They could be a faerie sent by Kael to get information, or something more sinister that lurked here for the sole purpose of toying with his captives.

"I made a mistake attempting to get close to the king. I thought I had control," Aisling admitted carefully. "But I underestimated him."

Her admission earned her another gravelly chuckle. "The Unseelie King has a way of unraveling even the most carefully-spun webs. Count yourself lucky you're still alive."

"I don't feel lucky," Aisling muttered, her fingers tracing the wrought-iron bars.

"Survival is a gift for as long as you can hang onto it," they advised, voice tinged with melancholy. "They'll come for you eventually."

Aisling let her eyes fall closed as her heart sank. When the bars began to hurt her face, she crawled back to her place against the wall and slid her hand out across the stone until it found the rivulet of water. She collected some in her palm, then brought it back to splash across her cheeks. It was undoubtedly dirty, but it felt good all the same.

"What happened to the others?" she asked into the void.

"They were taken to feed the king," the voice responded.

Aisling's blood froze solid in her veins as a dagger of fear plunged through her gut. She hadn't thought she could feel any more afraid, but those words once again sent her heart hammering violently against her ribcage. "What do you mean?"

"Just that." Their tone was dispassionate; they'd long since accepted this as their fate. "His magic is an entity unto itself. It needs to consume. Life—breath, blood, bone—makes it stronger. That's if it doesn't tear you apart first. He was born to carry it, both a blessing and a curse. It hungers, it yearns, and it demands sacrifice."

The weight that had settled on Aisling's chest constricted her lungs once more and her hands balled into tight fists in her lap. The thought of Kael's insatiable magic feeding on the lives of those who crossed his path filled her with dread. No longer could she deny the dangerous predator lurking beneath the king's allure: she was trapped now below the den of a monster both ancient and formidable.

Unable to quiet her racing thoughts or slow her speeding heart, Aisling stared out into the unrelenting abyss. The voice didn't speak again, but neither did Aisling engage it further. She counted the seconds in her head as they passed, a distraction at first from the silence, but as the number crept higher and higher, so too did her anxiety grow. She quit somewhere around four thousand and instead focused on the sound of the water. She kept one hand underneath it, catching each droplet and letting it flow from her palm, concentrating on its coolness. Its steady, consistent rhythm. She willed her pulse to match it. At one point she might have even dozed off for a while, but in that darkness, it was hard to discern when the color behind her eyelids was just as black as it was with her eyes open.

When the door at the top of the stairs opened once again, the barest light that filtered in was very nearly blinding. A figure descended—not one of the redcap guards, but a slight male in a robe that looked several sizes too large. Aisling watched him approach, eyes wide and fearful. Through the bars, careful to avoid touching the metal with his bare skin, he tossed a wad of white cloth towards her.

"Put it on," he ordered. Aisling held it up in front of her. It was a shift dress made of paper-thin cotton, already marked with dirt from where it had landed on the ground at her feet. The male turned his back so that she could change, her movements awkward in the small space. "Remove everything."

A fresh wave of paralyzing fear resigned Aisling to comply. Her cheeks burned with shame as she unhooked her bra and slid down her underwear, utterly exposed beneath the diaphanous fabric. She cupped shaking hands over either breast, shielding herself from the male's gaze when he turned around. But he didn't so much as glance at her; instead, his eyes seemed to look straight through her. He stopped her before she could step out of the cell and shook his head.

"Shoes, too." Aisling kicked off her shoes and balled her socks into them, as though she'd be back. She doubted she'd be back.

"I am sorry, my friend," the reedy voice whispered from the depths as the male led her up out of the dungeon.

Aisling didn't bother attempting to get her bearings as they walked, but she imagined where he could be leading her. The throne room, maybe. There would be a crowd there to watch her execution at the hand of the king. Or would she be eaten? *It hungers, it yearns, it demands sacrifice.* Was she to be the sacrifice? The loose skirt of the dress rippled around her violently trembling body. She thought of her friends. Of Rodney, of Briar. Only Rodney would know what had happened to her, the rest would wonder if she'd returned to the mainland without saying goodbye. Briar would think she'd left him alone. The tears she'd refused to shed in front of the king were unstoppable now, carving new tracks over her dirt-stained cheeks.

The male, who kept a slower pace than Kael had, led Aisling to the foot of the spiral staircase and beckoned for her to climb it ahead of him. The soft swishing of his robes sweeping across the stone behind her was oddly soothing.

Back above ground, it was night—whether again or still, Aisling wasn't sure. But it was frigid, and even though the fresh air was sweet as it filled her lungs, the cold gripped her and intensified her shivering. She hated, *hated* how weak she would appear when she finally stood in front of the king: reduced to a shuddering, tear-soaked mess in a dirty, too-thin garment. More still, she hated how much pleasure it would likely bring him to see her this way—afraid. Afraid of *him*. So Aisling raised her chin. Straightened her spine. Squared her shoulders. There was little she could do about the shivering, but she clenched her jaw shut so hard it throbbed to stop the noisy chattering of her teeth.

The male took the lead again, directing her toward the tree line. Her eyes darted across to where she thought the Thin Place waited, and suddenly she understood why he'd made her remove her shoes. She couldn't outrun him barefoot, not when each stick and jagged stone that dug into her soles made her wince with every step.

He stopped her in a moonlit clearing, where a handful of other males in similar robes stood on a circle carved into the dirt. Thick, snaking tree roots wove under and over the ground around their feet. One of the robed figures was stooped over, lighting candles one by one. At the head of the circle was an altar of sorts—a large triangle formed of branches lashed together with fibrous twine. It was with this altar at her back that Aisling was forced down onto her knees. In front of her, sitting cross-legged amongst the roots in the center of the circle, was the Unseelie King. All the resolve that she'd mustered on the walk over disappeared at once. Aisling dropped her head to study the ground and squeezed fistfuls of the dress against her thighs.

There was a heaviness in the clearing, one that wasn't entirely natural. The air was difficult to breathe in a way that it hadn't been just on the other side of the tree line. Aisling squeezed her eyes shut and tried to force deep breaths into her lungs. Her chest and back ached with the effort.

Then, the silence was broken by a low voice at the altar uttering an invocation in a language entirely unfamiliar to Aisling. It flowed lyrically, the lilting words almost entrancing in the way they were woven together in one long, unbroken phrase. The air grew thicker still, squeezing her from all sides in a suffocating embrace. Against her better judgment, curiosity and dread drove Aisling to raise her head just slightly to take in the scene in front of her.

Kael was dressed simply in black cloth, a contrast to her dress and the silver-white of his hair that flowed loose down his back and framed either side of his face that he kept tipped slightly forward. The expression he wore wavered somewhere between concentration and pain and his knuckles blanched white as his long fingers dug into his knees. His lips moved along with the voice behind Aisling to form the shapes of consonants and vowels, stringing them together voicelessly.

The night around Aisling shifted and flexed with the power of the incantation and a strange dance of shadows began to unfold around Kael—*from* Kael—wisps of darkness that swirled and pulsated like living things. Aisling's breath hitched; this was the magic the voice in the dungeon had warned her of. That insatiable, sentient thing that needed to consume. As the currents reached out to her, she was frozen in place. She felt a scream building in her throat, but no sound escaped her lips.

Tracing the path of his magic as it moved, Kael's frosted eyes met Aisling's and for a second, less than a second, the air stilled. The shadows pouring from his skin slowed their tempestuous dance and hung suspended, frozen, inches from where they had begun to curl towards her arms. The connection between them was ephemeral, yet it sent electricity coursing through Aisling's body. She felt both drawn to and repelled by this unfathomable force that resided within the Unseelie King. His eyes widened, almost imperceptibly, before he dropped them back down. The moment he did, his shadows resumed their aggressive movement.

Aisling, too, lowered her head once more, transfixed by the threads of shadow that now drew roughly across her skin. Her body could scarcely register the power that was ensnaring it, and the touch of the magic felt somehow both searing hot and ice cold. The shadows slid along her bare arms, writhing against her, creeping ever closer to her neck. Aisling squeezed her eyes shut and pursed her lips, imagining the tendrils seeking out a way to burrow into her. To strangle her from the inside out.

A tremor rolled through the clearing and even the roots of the trees seemed to tighten their grip on the earth, grasping for stability. Over the chanting that filled the air around them, calling to the twisting shadows, Kael growled: "Finish it."

Aisling braced herself, but her end never came. The invocation slowed, quieted, then stopped altogether. Though she kept her eyes closed, she could feel the shadows sliding back down her arms, the energy being drawn away from her. The pressure eased and breath flooded back into her lungs in a loud, ragged gasp. Angry red abrasions on her skin oozed blood that dripped down her wrists into the soil. When she dared to open her eyes, she saw that Kael remained hunched over and out of breath. He may have been trembling harder than she was.

"Return the tether to its cell," the leader of the rite commanded as he stepped away from the altar. Without looking at her again, Kael pushed himself to his feet and disappeared from Aisling's narrowing

THE RED WOMAN AND THE WHITE BEAR

field of view. She was dizzy, and when hands grasped her arms to pull her up, her knees buckled beneath her. The male who had delivered her to the clearing waited impatiently for a moment before trying again, this time supporting her around her waist and half-dragging her back to the Undercastle.

It wasn't until they were nearing the dungeons that she could walk without his aid, but all thought of escape had gone out of her mind anyway. All thought of anything, really, besides those sinister shadows that snaked out of Kael as easily and naturally as the blood that flowed from the wounds on her arms. They were all she could see, and the chilling fear they'd suffused into her veins was all she could feel.

Once again behind those thick iron bars, Aisling found an odd sort of solace. While they confined her there in the darkness, she was reassured by her belief—however untrue it may have been—that they might also serve as a shield that would keep Kael's potent magic at bay.

The other prisoner murmured softly then, to no one in particular: "Lucky, indeed."

10

STILLED

KAEL

The ritual had to be completed tonight. The pressure that Kael was under to perform only intensified the wrenching chaos of his magic. Control was well out of reach; the best he could hope for was to maintain some semblance of it while Werryn completed the truncated rites that he'd rewritten for time. They were bare-bones. No sermon, no prayer. No audience tonight, either. The nervous energy of the Lesser Prelates was distracting enough as it was.

Werryn had hardly begun speaking before the shadows tore out of Kael at full force, a caged animal finally set loose. He had felt them in his chest since his failure on Nocturne, waiting coiled, ready to spring. The pain of their leaching from his skin was almost cathartic: he was giving in, giving his magic the freedom it had been craving since he reined it in. He thought he should do so more often.

It pulled towards tonight's tether, the traitorous human girl he'd tossed in his dungeon for just this purpose. A cruel smile tugged at his lips as he raised his head. He was eager to watch his shadows rip her apart, to feel them devour her from the inside out and drain her worthless life force until there was nothing left.

But then their eyes met. And his shadows stilled, along with something else somewhere inside of him. And for the first time in a long time—maybe in the whole of his long, long life—Kael was afraid. And he hated it.

So he dropped his head again and focused his gaze on the earth. On each tiny, individual grain of soil. The stones, the bits of decaying pine needles and the pointed corner of a rune carved there. He urged his shadows ahead to snake across The Cut and he begged silently for the Low One to strengthen them, to bless his court for the coming winter. He compelled his magic to kill that infernal girl, but it was as unwilling as ever to heed his instruction. Instead, when he glanced up again, its tendrils were exploring her. Drawing from her, still, but only very little. Not nearly enough to ground him.

"*Finish it.*" Kael hardly managed to force the words through gritted teeth. Every inch of him burned, pulsing in time with the surges of black energy that shot from his body out to the very tips of the trails.

The next thing Kael saw was the satisfied look on the High Prelate's face, and the slow ebb of his shadows as they retracted towards him. Kael extended his hands to receive them but could scarcely hold his own two arms out in front of himself. His chest heaved and he fell forward, spent.

Kael remained in The Cut long after the others had departed. The simple act of pushing himself up onto his feet had been monumental, so he stayed propped against a tree, watching each candle burn itself out one at a time. He barely had the energy to think straight, but his mind churned all the same.

The fragile balance between his morality and the raw power that coursed through him was a delicate thread to walk upon—and he did not do so well. But tonight, he thought that he felt the faintest flicker of it when he saw his shadows reflected in the girl's wide, terror-filled eyes. Whether it was or not, though, mattered little. Morality wasn't what had halted his magic mid-motion, nor was it what had kept those winding black threads from tearing through her soft flesh. That, Kael had no explanation for. It vexed him to no end. In that split-second, the girl seemed to have more control over his shadows than he did. But was it over his magic that she held some sort of power? Or was it over Kael himself?

When he fixed his eyes on the last flickering flame that danced in the darkness, the wide-open clearing began to close in, suffocating him. Whispers of doubt taunted him with insidious words. Anger, the constant undercurrent to his thoughts, simmered just beneath those venomous barbs. Where he had for so long placed his faith in the Low One, in the belief that he was chosen for greatness by the deity himself, Kael now felt abandoned. The shadow magic he wielded had once made him feel invincible. He had believed that with its power, he could reshape Wyldraíocht as he wished. But instead, it was taking control of him and molding him into something he didn't recognize.

Amidst his choking doubts, Kael questioned whether he was truly blessed by the Low One or merely a pawn in a cruel cosmic game. He dug his nails into his palms and fought back the urge to draw his sword and slash at the altar until it was nothing more than a pile of branches on the ground. His eyes played over the triangular form, its peak in line with the apex of the moon's arc through the sky this time of year. Before he could move towards it, a breeze rustled through the trees overhead and the sound steadied him. His deity had remained there with him, had felt what Kael felt and had heard his every thought, and now those vicious whispers in Kael's head were no longer his own, and no longer as harsh. *A reason,* the Low One intoned sweetly. *I chose you for a reason.*

⁖

The Unseelie King was unaccustomed to being enticed by others; he was usually the one who held the power in such situations. Yet, there was something in the audacious pixie who dared to challenge him that he found intriguing. Something about the way she'd navigated him, guided him, without once making him feel vulnerable. But this human girl, curled in on herself on the dirt floor of his dungeon, wasn't her. This was an imposter, a liar. She'd used him. He'd come to expect such transgressions by now, and he was disturbed that he'd let it happen again so easily.

And yet he would have gone back for more.

The thought of taking her right there in the garden had crossed his mind unbidden when he had her squirming body pinned to that tree, a flash as brief as a strike of lightning, but the idea had repulsed him as quickly as it had come. It did even more so now as he regarded her through the iron bars. His lip curled back from his teeth when he once again felt the ghost of her fingers brushing across his skin.

Someone had left a small cup of water for her, probably all she'd been given in the days since the ritual. She was likely rationing it. Kael slid the toe of his boot between the bars and knocked it onto its side. They both watched the water trickle out, only to be sucked down into the dirt. Her face remained expressionless.

"Tell me what you are," he commanded.

Aisling raised her head from where she'd had it cradled in one of her arms and squinted as though the low light from the lantern he held was blinding. Weak human eyes took so long to adjust. "I don't understand."

"If you truly are a human, then tell me where you came by the magic you used in The Cut." An amulet, perhaps, or some sort of sigil she carried hidden away. She would have bargained for it, and magic that strong would have cost her dearly.

She pushed herself up to sit. "I have no magic."

"You lie," Kael bit back.

"I'm telling you the truth. I didn't do anything." She remained stoic despite his pressing, which only served to heat his blood further.

"You repelled my shadows."

She held out one of her arms to show the abrasions that encircled it, still crusted with dried blood. "Hardly."

"Your fear smells, Highness." A teasing voice curled out of a cell deeper in the cavern and the prisoner there took an exaggerated breath in through their nose. "Like burning leaves."

"Quiet, sylph," Kael growled. He'd forgotten they weren't alone. His fingers twitched where they rested on the hilt of the dagger strapped to his thigh.

"I quite like the idea of the Unseelie King being afraid of a human girl." They were baiting him. It was working. Kael turned on his heel and stalked toward the source of the voice, feeling his shadows tighten in him like a second skin stretched taut beneath his own. The sylph's melodic laughter echoed off the stone walls.

"You dare to mock me, creature?" Kael hissed. He caught a glimpse of the sylph's ethereal form through the darkness, the pointed features and shimmering wings that marked their kind.

The sylph fluttered closer, their mischievous expression undeterred by Kael's hostility. "Why not?" They paused, letting the words sink in before continuing. "Tell me, King of Shadows, do you truly believe you are in control, or are you just the puppet of your beloved god?"

Kael's grip on the dagger tightened until his knuckles turned white. The creature was in his head. The sylph's taunts struck a nerve, stirring the doubts that he had worked hard to suppress since the ritual.

"Quiet!" Kael roared, and his shadows surged into the cell, snatching the sylph out of the air in a fury of inky filaments. The prisoner laughed, teasing Kael even as the shadows pulled them closer. Ignoring the way the iron bars burned his skin through his sleeve, Kael lunged forward and slashed the faerie's throat open with the tip of his dagger. Honey-colored blood leaked out of the gaping wound, but for a brief moment, the sylph's lips twisted into a self-satisfied smirk. They'd goaded him into this—into giving them a quick death. It was clever, really. Kael withdrew his shadows to let the sylph's lifeless body drop to the ground.

In her own cell, Aisling sucked in a ragged gasp. She scrambled back to press herself against the wall when Kael returned to stand before her. "Why did you come here?" he demanded.

"I told you, I've heard stories." Her voice trembled now and her eyes were locked on the dripping dagger still clutched in Kael's hand. "My mother told me stories of your kind since I was young. I wanted to see for myself."

"The púca glamoured you." A statement, not a question. Aisling winced. "His home reeked of quicken tea." Kael left out what he hadn't realized when the girl, as a pixie, had been pressed against his body: that the faint fragrance of rain-soaked earth beneath her lingering pine scent had been that of magic.

"It was my idea, not his." This human was an anomaly—not only knowledgeable to a degree about the Fae, but friendly enough with one to attempt to protect him now.

He hummed, scrutinizing every movement of her hands. The heaving of her chest as she struggled to breathe through her fear. The tone of her voice. He thought she may finally be telling the truth—if not in its entirety, at least the better part of it. But even if she was only a foolish little girl, not a spy or an assassin or a threat to his court, she still held more power than she realized. And that in and of itself was reason enough to keep her locked away.

If Werryn had noticed what had passed between the two in The Cut, he hadn't yet let on. Kael thought that he'd reacted quickly enough to mask the exchange, but surely the High Prelate would have questioned how the tether had survived. They rarely did, if ever. Kael had stayed clear of the dungeon for several days following the ritual to ensure his visit wouldn't raise suspicion, and even then he'd been careful to avoid the eyes of the Prelates when he made his way down. As he exited now, he confirmed with the redcap sentinels that no one had followed. His secret was safe for the time being.

But, as though drawn by Kael's unease, Werryn found him later on in the throne room cleaning splatters of dried sylph blood off of his boot.

"You're troubled," he observed. "Why? We completed the ritual. Can you not feel His blessings?"

Kael gave a curt nod. "I feel them. It will not take two tries next time."

"The human girl played a pivotal role in our success, did she not?" Werryn watched him closely.

Kael's jaw clenched. For a second, his movements with the leather brush became a bit rougher than they should have before he managed to mask his agitation. "A mere tether, Werryn. Nothing more."

The High Prelate raised an inquisitive brow, not entirely convinced by Kael's clipped answer. "Are you telling me she had no effect on the outcome? That her presence was inconsequential?"

"I assure you, her involvement was limited to anchoring the magic," Kael replied firmly, keeping his emotions under strict control. "The same as all the others."

"And yet she lived, unlike all the others."

"Perhaps I needed less grounding to maintain control this time." Having scrubbed his boot mostly clean, Kael uncrossed his legs and lowered his foot to the ground. He sat back in the throne and rested his chin on steepled fingers.

Werryn observed Kael's relaxed pose, at odds with the impatience that flickered across his face. "A good sign, then. You're making progress."

"Thanks almost certainly to your persistent needling," Kael retorted in a tone that bordered on acerbic.

Werryn ignored his sarcasm and repeated, "Almost certainly."

Kael would try again to use the girl—he might have done so tonight in the dungeon had he not been distracted by the impudent sylph. He would try again and this time, he'd make sure she didn't survive.

11

INTO BATTLE

KAEL

"We're standing ready to attack, Your Highness, but scouts have returned describing numbers far greater than we expected." Raif held out a scroll of parchment to Kael that illustrated the disparity in detail. If the scouts had counted correctly, the Third Company was outmanned two to one, at least. The front wasn't far from the Undercastle, just a day's ride, but the Captain of the Guard had made it back in half that to share this news with the king directly.

"All Solitary?" Kael asked as he read over the notes.

"Not all; a group of Seelie warriors arrived yesterday." Raif set his gauntlets down with a noisy clatter before wiping his brow with the back of his hand. His face was streaked with grime from the ride and his dark curls were plastered to his forehead. With a grim expression, he accepted a chalice of honey wine from Kael.

Kael paced the study with long, graceful strides. While he read, he held the edge of his own chalice against his lower lip without drinking. It wasn't until after he'd finished reading that he tipped it up and emptied it in three swallows. Then he poured himself another. "How do they look?"

Raif held a hand over the mouth of his own chalice to abstain from a refill when Kael offered. "Our troops, or theirs?"

"Both."

"May I speak plainly?" Raif set the chalice aside and crossed his arms over his chest plate.

Kael gestured with his full cup. "It's why I made you my captain, Raif. I would expect nothing less."

Raif offered a tight-lipped nod of appreciation before he said, "Your soldiers are tired, Kael. The Solitary are cunning, and with Seelie warriors at their backs, I'm not sure how well they'll fare."

The Third Company was among the Unseelie Court's most elite warriors—for Raif to be concerned about their performance was a very grave thing indeed.

Kael moved to his large desk and unrolled an ancient map of the realm. Reaching across the sheet, he slid over a jar to weigh down one stubborn, curling corner. The sudden movement sent the Luna moth contained inside into a frenzy and it beat its furry body against the glass in a desperate effort to escape its prison. It wouldn't live but a few days more; the others from the eclipse had died quickly, their fragile wings already decaying into the soil of the night garden. Methild had caught this one for Kael, a gift as he prepared for Nocturne. She'd harbored a soft spot for the king since he was a boy.

He ran a long finger up the map to the northeast, where the Third Company awaited their orders on the far border of Lord Somrith's Dominion of Nyctara. To the west, the Fifth Company was returning from securing the Dominion of Astraloris for the Unseelie Court. It had been an easy victory—they may yet have the strength for another battle. If they delayed their return, they could travel north and join the Third Company in a day. Their numbers would put them nearly even with that which the Seelies had amassed.

Watching over the king's shoulder, it was as if Raif knew what he was thinking well before he said it out loud. "I'll send word to Commander Eamon before I ride back."

"I will ride with you." Kael finished his drink then straightened up to his full height. It had been months since he'd seen battle, and his time sitting idle at court left a thirst growing in him that needed quenching.

Raif was openly apprehensive about travelling back with the entire royal caravan in tow. "Your offer is appreciated, Your Highness, but unnecessary."

"I don't believe I was asking for your permission, Raif," Kael shot back at his friend. "I am not one to lead from afar. We'll depart shortly with a small company and reach the front by nightfall. If Commander Eamon's troops arrive in the night, all the better. We'll attack at dawn."

Raif knew better than to question Kael further. An experienced warlord, each and every move the king plotted out on that timeworn map was calculated with near-expert precision. His consultations with Raif were a formality, at best. If he'd made up his mind, this would be the plan they'd execute.

The pair exited the study in opposite directions: Raif, to send the king's message to Commander Eamon; Kael, to prepare for the ride to Nyctara. His leathers and armor were cleaned and polished, ready as always for his retrieval. The leathers he would wear for the ride. The black armor, though light as a feather, would remain packed until it was time to fight. He sent for Werryn, who took one look at Kael's battle-ready costume and the longsword that hung from his hip and nodded solemnly.

"Have you need of me, My Lord?" The High Prelate asked.

"You'll join my company. We leave for the front at Nyctara presently." His words were clipped, but the excitement that underlined them was unmistakable. His hand already itched to palm the hilt of the sword and his magic was clawing at his lungs for freedom.

"And the girl?"

Kael thought for a moment. It would be an opportunity to test the human's limits, to see whether what happened in The Cut had been a chance occurrence or something greater. Either way, his company would be one body lighter on the return ride. Inside the cage of his ribs, his shadows roiled in response. "Might as well," he replied dismissively. "Seems a shame to waste a perfectly good tether."

"Shall we make her walk?" Werryn sneered. Though the image of her tied behind a horse tripping barefoot all the way to their camp brought a smirk to Kael's lips, he shook his head.

"She would only slow us down. Ensure that she is bound properly and assign her a rider."

Not once had the High Prelate thought to offer a tether for battle before. During combat was the only time that Kael was free to set loose his magic to its fullest extent, consequences be damned. So Werryn was suspicious—perhaps Kael hadn't hidden the incident as well as he'd thought. But come morning, it wouldn't make a bit of difference.

⁂

The king's tent stood amidst the sprawling encampment, a solitary dark island in a sea of white canvas. Inside, lanterns hung from cording to light the space. The glow they cast danced wildly as gusts of wind slipped through the tent flaps. The heavy scent of leather and metal filled the air as Kael, with determined precision, fastened on the last plate of his black armor.

Aisling's presence at Werryn's side was an unsettling disruption to his preparations. They stood silent in the corner of the tent, yet to see her there was an anomaly amidst the battle-hardened warriors who filtered in and out around them. Kael had done his best to ignore her since they entered quietly minutes before, but dawn was fast approaching.

Without a word, Kael clasped a gauntleted hand around Aisling's upper arm in an iron grip and dragged her out of the tent towards the battlefront where his warriors stood already in formation. She stumbled on numb feet over each step. The tide of battle was drawing closer, the pounding footsteps of the enemy soldiers echoing in the air. This girl tripping alongside him was a puzzle piece that Kael wasn't sure how to fit into the coming chaos.

Finally, he halted her, positioning her to face him with her back to the distant front where the Seelie and Solitary soldiers were filing into line. She shivered there in front of him in that thin white shift she'd been dressed in for the ritual. It was filthy now, and she was weak and pale from her time in the dungeon. Kael's hold on her arm remained tight and unyielding as his gaze darted to the approaching enemy. Adrenaline surged through his veins when a low horn sounded from behind him, a notice that time was slipping through his fingers like sand.

Kael had hoped, perhaps against reason, that he could find some way to use the power she held over his magic to his advantage. But now, staring down the distant line as they broke into a run, he knew he couldn't afford to rely on chance. The enemy was too many, they were coming too fast, and here Kael stood idly with his charge. Something in the sight of the tips of oncoming spears and swords over her trembling shoulders compelled Kael to toss her aside to where the High Prelate stood ready to call to his shadows in service of the Low One. Maybe there was a way to harness that connection again, but now wasn't the time to explore it. The battleground was no place for experiments or doubts.

"Take her," he ordered harshly. He didn't have time to waste trying to use her. The girl's stumbling form seemed to move in slow motion when he cast her aside into Werryn's grasp, and Kael's gleaming sword was drawn in an instant as the deafening sound of metal against metal commenced on all sides.

Bitter-scented bloodlust charged the air around him as Kael led the offensive toward the far line. His keen eyes quickly parsed through the fray—the Seelies rode on horseback, while the Solitary Fae battled on foot, most wearing too-big armor. They were fierce, but disorganized. Though it would have been a hard-won victory had the Fifth Company not joined, most of these approaching faeries were not fighters. Even from this distance, he could feel the churning dread that rose in their throats the moment they saw the cast of his pewter tresses against black armor. Kael's wrath was known to have been the ruin of entire villages. Scores had fallen to the sharp edge of his blade, and more still to those insidious, snaking shadows that poured from him when they grew so large, coiled in his chest, that he could no longer carry them inside.

His sword was a blur of deadly precision as he cut a path to the center of the field. Raif and two others moved with him, flanking him to the left and right. The ground trembled with the weight of their footsteps and the clash of arms echoed like thunder in the king's ears while he looked for an opening in the violent dance. A pause, just the length of a breath, was all he needed to strip off his gauntlets and bring forth a fury of shadows that surged from his skin. They carved an arc around him and sent a trio of Solitary bodies dropping to the ground in an instant.

Kael's shadows swirled around him, weaving between sparring pairs and tearing through the enemy line. They were opaque, and strong. As savage as their master. In battle, Kael and his shadows shared a common goal: destruction.

A Solitary sidhe, wreathed in silver and wielding a pale blade, engaged Kael in a bid to draw his attention. Their meeting sent shocks of power through the air, visible as shimmering waves of energy warping the breeze. Kael's shadows fought against the sidhe's radiant light with an explosive collision that cracked the earth beneath their feet. A long thread of darkness wrapped around the being's throat and tightened until it sliced clean through the skin, no longer so luminous in death.

But suddenly, he felt it: the tether. His shadows had locked onto something grounding and calm. Kael jerked his head to the left where Werryn had gathered the girl up onto his horse and was clutching her in front of him, presenting her like an offering. Her face was beset by terror and pain as tendrils wound up her legs.

And the Unseelie King was filled with an anger so great and choking that he could scarcely breathe.

With a vicious yell, he wrenched his shadows away from her, back under his tenuous control and sent them ahead. Behind. Outward. He was a vessel filled with rage older than the earth and hotter than the sun. It burned beneath his skin, coursing through his veins with every beat of his cruel heart. It gave him purpose. Drive. His rage allowed him to kill fiercely and indiscriminately. With or without a weapon in his hand, he was a force of nature. For all on the battlefield, Seelie and Solitary and Unseelie alike, he was both terrifying and breathtaking to behold.

He let those hungry currents of magic take and take and take whatever they wanted—and take they did. They rippled outward, ribbons of darkness ensnaring the assaulting forces and pulling them apart in an abyss of inky oblivion. Alternating between vapor and solid, between plunging into chest cavities to strangle organs and slicing through flesh and bone, his magic swept through the enemy ranks. But not just the enemy—his own warriors, too.

Kael was only vaguely aware of the Unseelie soldiers dropping around him as his breath came in sharp, noisy gasps and the sound of rushing wind filled his ears. Distantly, he heard Raif screaming his name. He became aware of Werryn, next, when the High Prelate let out a harsh cry. Kael turned just in time to see a thick coil of darkness plunge into the male's gut, throwing both him and Aisling from his horse. Shockwaves reverberated from the spot where Kael's knees hit the ground as they buckled under the agony of trying to regain control.

In the muted glow of dawn, the battle was over, but the war within Kael continued to rage. There on the battlefield, the quiet stillness of victory was marred by the sounds of the dying in the carnage that had befallen both sides. The air was acrid with the stench of blood and spent magic. An icy numbness settled in his bones, but alongside it simmered the primal satisfaction that his thirst had been sated.

Armor battered and sword stained, Kael blindly found the reins of his mare that had ridden out to her master. She walked with him as he crossed the field. His own soldiers shrank back in fear of the slow-moving ebony serpents that trained across the ground behind their king, still unwilling to be pulled back inside their vessel. Werryn lay writhing on the ground at his feet, but Kael's eyes slid over the Prelate to the girl, huddled against the cold flank of Werryn's fallen mount.

As he drew closer, Kael's shadows reached towards Aisling but hesitated almost in deference when they recognized the presence that had quelled their voracious hunger before. He crouched beside her, the joints of his armor biting into his knees.

Kael's grip on his sword's hilt slackened as he stared at her, a storm of emotions roiling within him. The intoxicating rush of his magic had dulled, replaced by a stark realization of the destruction he had caused. The fragile girl before him now was a mirror that reflected the cost of his unbounded fury. As much as he wanted to, he couldn't look away from what he saw there.

But he had to escape the screaming.

12

A MORE COMFORTABLE PRISON

AISLING

Aisling had been too afraid to speak and too weak to fight back when she was pulled into the midst of a battle ripped straight from the pages of a horrific storybook. But unlike during the ritual, she kept her eyes open this time, for all of it. For every nightmarish, surreal moment. The terrific clash of forces was almost awe-inspiring: the way the lithe Fae warriors fought was as graceful as a choreographed ballet, and as frightening as the attack of a ferocious predator. Amongst them, smaller, stockier faeries barreled into each other with outsized swords and thick wooden shields. There were beings that shot through the air like bullets on wings that fluttered so rapidly they were but a blur, and those that approached on thundering horseback.

And now, she'd witnessed firsthand the devastation that Kael's shadows wrought: on the enemy, on his own men. On the Unseelie King himself. The blackness didn't only shoot outward, but twisted in winding, lightning-like patterns from the tips of his fingers on up into the cuffs at his wrists. When she saw them cresting over the neckline of his armor, crawling towards his jaw, she imagined they had crept all the way up his arms, unseen beneath the leathers and gleaming metal. In her terror, Aisling clung to thoughts of home. Of her life before she was called the Red Woman, when she was content with her apartment above the hardware store and her job at the library, and the most difficult challenge facing her was the decision of whether or not to return to the mainland. When the closest she'd come to the Fae were the afternoons spent lounging on the couch with Rodney flipping through magazines. Before her skin knew the Unseelie King's touch, and before her body knew his magic.

As his shadows seized her, much like before, Aisling was prepared for death. Her mind went blank and her body became paralyzed. She'd already given up. But this time, those midnight-black fingers seemed somehow gentler, the abrasions they left behind less severe. Even still, she felt her energy being drawn into their darkness and her vision grew spotty and clouded. She'd likely have passed out had she not been thrown off the rearing steed—then it was the violent crack of her head against the ground that brought her to unconsciousness.

Aisling awoke not minutes later to the discord of agonized screams. Those who were still alive—just—begged for the sweet release of death. No one moved to give it, though. Not on the enemy side, where there were no survivors left capable of tending to the mortally wounded. Even amongst the ranks of the Unseelie Court, those warriors still standing remained rooted in place watching Kael wrestle his magic into something close to submission. His expression was unreadable, a contradictory mask of triumph and pain. Of pride and disgrace.

She could manage little more than to shrink away as Kael approached alongside a skeletal black warhorse with bone-white eyes. He crouched close to her, studying her pensively before taking her by the waist and hoisting her onto the creature's back. The sudden movement nearly rendered her unconscious all over again. The horse scarcely looked robust enough even to be saddled, yet once Kael had Aisling seated in front of him it carried them both away from the battlefield in a swift gallop with ease.

Every impact of the horse's hooves on the packed dirt sent another arcing shock of pain into the base of Aisling's skull, each one a merciless reminder of the violence her body had endured since she'd returned to the Wild. Wind rushed past, biting at her exposed skin and bringing tears to stream down her cheeks. Her senses felt dull, her thoughts swirling in a haze of pain and confusion. She struggled to keep her eyes open to make sense of the shifting landscape as they rode on.

Despite her own discomfort, Aisling couldn't ignore the tremors that wracked Kael's entire body. Through his armor and against her back, she could feel the convulsions that beset his muscles. His grip around her waist, though tight, was far from steady. If the animal moved with any less grace, she was sure they'd both fall from its back. She clutched its wiry mane to anchor herself.

The journey was a blur of agony that felt both interminable and fleeting as Aisling slipped in and out of consciousness. She wished for Kael to say something, anything, but she didn't know what it might be. She couldn't imagine what she could say to him, either. Would she thank him, or curse him? She'd seen the flash of indecision in his cold eyes before he threw her out of the way. He'd likely saved her life by doing so. It was the High Prelate who'd kept her there, murmuring his quiet incantations.

"Tell me how it feels," he'd demanded when Kael's shadows began winding up her bare legs. "Tell me what you're doing." As if he thought she was calling to them or controlling them in some way. But she wasn't—the only thing Aisling could do was attempt to calm her rising panic.

So the pair rode in silence. Kael's armor was uncomfortable where it dug into her back but if she wasn't braced against it, her head and neck jostled excruciatingly, churning her already-throbbing migraine into a fiery storm.

When the Undercastle came into view in the distance, Aisling's fingers tightened in the beast's hair. On their approach to the obsidian structure, she held onto the faint hope that there would be some respite once they were within its cold stone walls. Yet, even through the fog of pain and the sounds of the battle still ringing in her ears, she recognized where she was being taken once Kael handed her off to a Prelate waiting at the bottom of the spiral staircase.

⁖

THE RED WOMAN AND THE WHITE BEAR

Time didn't exist in the dungeon. In the dark, damp cavern, day and night blended invisibly into one long stretch, impossible to measure. Aisling's body quickly lost its rhythm, sleeping in fits and starts, cycling through hunger and thirst at random. But she couldn't drink, nor could she eat even the plain breadcrust a robed Prelate tossed into her cell periodically. Maybe that was how she could have counted the days passing, but often it was already lying at her feet when she woke. There were three pieces scattered near the bars now, but she had no way of knowing how many times each day they attempted to feed her. It was unlikely they adhered to any sort of schedule at all.

Groaning, she rolled up onto her knees to be sick into the dirt. Despite the roiling in her stomach, the only thing she could manage to bring forth was acidic bile that stung all the way up her raw throat. When Aisling raised her head from the floor, the solemn face of a Lesser Prelate swam before her—the same one who had received her after the battle. He'd quietly let himself into her cell and was kneeling down close. His features were distorted as the dungeon spun around her.

"You are unwell," he said in a voice that nearly sounded kind—a marked contrast to the harshness she had come to expect from the Unseelie Court. Aisling could only nod meekly. She'd had migraines before, but never one such as this. If he had told her that she had an axe in the back of her skull, she wouldn't have been at all surprised. As it was, he reached a hand up to the side of her head and his fingers came away slick with blood. The wound from her fall was still open and was by now caked with dirt and filth.

The male grasped Aisling under her arms and guided her to her feet, supporting her when she swayed unsteadily. A cold shot of fear flooded her veins. Surely, he couldn't be taking her to tether the king's shadows a third time. She wouldn't survive it—she wasn't even sure she'd survive the climb up that spiral staircase.

"Please." The weak word came out softer than a whisper, barely audible over her shaky breath.

"You're in no condition to be kept down here." He began leading her to the open door of her cell. "I am taking you to a chamber where you can rest."

Aisling sagged against his arm in relief and she let him support most of her weight as the pair ascended. The stairs were arduous, but the air at the top was clean and sweet and Aisling dragged in lungful after lungful gratefully. It was far from fresh, but at least not so laden with mildew and humidity as the stale air of the dungeon.

The Prelate was tall, nearly taller than Kael. His arm was slender but strong, all wiry muscle hidden beneath the billowing black robe that hung from his shoulders. His firm guidance kept her trudging forward through the corridors of the Undercastle. Once he had led her out of earshot of the redcaps still standing guard, he lowered his head so he could speak quietly into her ear.

"I'm a friend of the púca," he said.

Aisling stumbled, tripping over her own feet in surprise. "Rodney? Is he here?"

The male chuckled. "*Rodney*," he repeated. "What a remarkably human name. No, he isn't here."

"Oh." The disappointment was crushing. Aisling would have given anything to see her friend's sly smile and that shock of orange hair. Vaguely in the back of her pain-addled mind, Aisling wondered whether this was the acquaintance Rodney had been intent on finding—though she couldn't recall the name he had given her. But the Prelate didn't offer any further insight into his relations with her friend. With the sheer effort it took to keep herself standing, she was unable to formulate a clear thought, much less ask any further questions. For now, she was simply content to be led away from her prison and to trust that the male was telling her the truth.

He led her slowly to a chamber, small and simple, similar to the plain stone room where Aisling had lain with Kael. The bed was a welcome sight, and with the Prelate's support, she sank onto the soft mattress. Her body trembled with exhaustion and pain. The male pulled a tiny vial from a pocket inside of his robe and held it to Aisling's lips.

"Drink," he instructed. Another flare of fire at the base of her skull was enough to override all rational thought, and she did as she was told. The shot of liquid was thick and cloying and almost immediately brought her eyelids to flutter closed. Every sore, knotted muscle in Aisling's body relaxed, the tension dissolving into a warm wave of relief.

The calm didn't last long, though, and once Aisling was alone she grew hot and anxious. With the draught having dulled some of her pain, she felt sure this was her window to escape. She tried to sit up quickly but swore when she found that her body didn't possess the strength. Rolling onto her side, she tried again, more deliberately this time, using her hands and elbows to bear her weight. She had to stop and rest halfway before she could make it fully upright. With one hand still steadying herself on the mattress, she shoved the heavy blankets off her legs and swung them over the edge of the bed. The room pitched and reeled as she struggled to her feet, but her eyes remained focused on the heavy wooden door at the far end. It cracked open just as her knees gave out and she collapsed back onto the mattress.

A slight female bustled in then, slender arms hooked through the handle of an overlarge wicker basket half her size. The faerie was scarcely taller than the doorknob and looked to be nearly as old as the Shadowwood Mother. A hob, Aisling guessed. Her thin nose wrinkled at what was certainly Aisling's own odor: sweat, dirt, and stale blood. Aisling tracked her path as she flitted around the room lighting candles, but her vision couldn't quite keep up with the movements of her head and it blurred around the periphery.

"Methild Nym," the faerie said. That she'd given the entirety of her name so freely to Aisling meant that she was already under the servitude of another, likely a courtier or maybe the Unseelie King himself. "I've been sent to look after you. May I?" Her thin lips curved into a pitying smile and she waited for Aisling's permission before approaching.

It was a welcome surprise, being asked for her consent. Throat still raw from her earlier retching, Aisling managed only a weak nod.

"Your head plagues you," she observed. Aisling's head throbbed as though responding to the mere mention of the pain. The female's touch was cautious as she laid a damp cloth across Aisling's forehead.

She shivered and drew the blankets up around her shoulders. With twig-like fingers, Methild parted Aisling's matted hair and spread a thick salve over the wound there. Aisling winced, expecting some discomfort, but the herb-scented balm brought nothing but relief.

"We're unaccustomed to visitors from your realm," Methild remarked with a touch of wistfulness while she worked the medicine into Aisling's scalp. "You are a rare thing, indeed."

She spent the rest of her time in the chamber working in silence to wipe Aisling down with wet rags, lifting her limbs and turning them this way and that to scrub roughly at the dried mud that had crusted over her skin. If she had any energy left at all, Aisling might have been embarrassed by the intrusion, or at the very least uncomfortable with the attention. She couldn't recall the last time she'd allowed herself to be cared for in this way. Now, she didn't have much choice. In her current state, she could hardly even help the hob by holding up the weight of her own arms.

Methild scurried in and out of the room a handful of times to refresh Aisling's water or reapply the salve, but Aisling hardly registered it. She was adrift in the feverish recesses of her mind, somewhere between home and kaleidoscopic memories of the ethereal Nocturne revelry. It all seemed so much darker in her head: the pointed, leering faces of Fae spinning around her in double-time while somewhere unseen the Shadowwood Mother laughed and laughed at her frantic dancing.

The next time Aisling consciously opened her eyes, though, she felt better. Still weak, but her stomach no longer ached and her skin no longer burned with fever. Her migraine, too, had largely subsided. Her mind felt less like a battleground and more like her own.

When a cool hand pressed against her forehead, her heart leapt into her throat. She hadn't heard the scuffling of Methild's rough slippers on the floor; she thought she'd been alone in the room.

Kael was seated nearby, his form rigidly perched on the edge of a chair. A book was cracked open over his knee where he'd turned it to mark the page when Aisling stirred. His expression was indecipherable in the dim light.

"Your fever has broken." Kael's voice, while far from kind, was unexpectedly soft. Aisling's surprise to see the Unseelie King sitting at her bedside, addressing her in a tone not laced with malice, was obvious on her face. His lips curved in a faint, almost wry smile and his posture shifted as he began to rise.

The king's movement startled her, and with shaky urgency Aisling attempted to sit up. She was more successful in her effort this time, but only made it partway before Kael's hand landed on her shoulder, urging her gently but firmly back against the pillows.

"Let me see your hand," he requested, holding one of his own out to her. It caught her off guard, and reflexively she withdrew it from beneath the blankets and placed it in his. Aisling hadn't noticed before how rough his callused palms were. So distracted by the feeling of Kael's hand on hers, she had no time to react when, in one swift motion, he locked a manacle around her wrist. He leaned down to secure the other end to the bedpost.

Aisling's pulse quickened, a mixture of shock and betrayal knotting her insides. She looked up at him, her eyes searching his face for an explanation. In his gaze, she found an odd sort of blend of pragmatism and something that might have been sympathy. But if it was, she was surely imagining it there. She understood, then, that she was still his captive. Albeit in a more comfortable prison, but still trapped all the same.

"You're stronger now." His explanation, curt and unyielding, arrived like a cold gust of wind. "I will not risk you attempting to escape."

Tears welled up in Aisling's eyes, distorting Kael and the room behind him as sobs of frustration and helplessness shook her shoulders violently.

"Please," she choked. "Please, no, I swear I won't." The words got caught in the grip of her dry throat, constricted by anguish. By panic. She could do nothing but beg.

Kael dropped her hand back onto the mattress. It was an abrupt dismissal, a clear indication that her pleas were heard but would remain unanswered. As he left, the sound of a lock sliding into place on the outside of the door was the final echo of his cruelty.

13

CAGED BIRD

AISLING

Though time passed and her strength returned, the weight of the manacle on Aisling's wrist never lessened. She'd been in the chamber for five days, and was in the dungeon cell for two before that after Kael had ridden her back from the battlefield. She had gleaned this information from Methild, who now informed her first thing upon entering the chamber whether it was morning, noon, evening, or midnight.

There in the Unseelie Court, Aisling learned, most of the Fae rose in the evening to go about their business. In the absence of sunlight in the Undercastle, her body began to slowly grow accustomed to this timetable, too. By the fourth day, when Methild came in for her evening ministrations, Aisling had just risen after sleeping straight through since she'd closed her eyes that morning.

The wizened faerie had with her the basket of wet rags again, but this time Aisling insisted on cleaning herself. Her movements were stiff and slow. Methild stood by with a look of impatience, obviously keen to do it herself in a more efficient manner. After tapping a toe on the ground for several minutes, she instead busied herself dragging Aisling's waste bucket out into the hall to be removed. Aisling tried to ignore the slight female's grunts as she hauled it from the room. Whatever scraps of dignity Aisling had hoped to cling to went out with it.

Methild returned, wiping her hands on a dingy apron, with a Fae soldier in tow. He held a large pail filled to the brim with water that sloshed onto the floor as he walked. Methild shot him dirty looks over her shoulder each time she heard it splash on the stone. He left after he set it down where she indicated, having given little more than a passing glance at Aisling. From her apron pocket, Methild withdrew a small glass bottle.

"Come," she said, "let me help you with your hair." Methild had braided it back, but when Aisling felt along her scalp the strands were stiff with dried blood and the sticky remnants of salve that hadn't soaked in.

The soldier had placed the bucket close enough that Aisling could kneel before it, but only just. She had to extend her arm all the way outward at the end of the length of the thick chain to reach it. The strain made her shoulder ache.

"Can you undo it?" Aisling pleaded with Methild. "Just while you wash my hair? You could even ask the guard to wait by the door."

Methild hummed, lips pursed, then shook her head. "I must follow orders."

Aisling sighed heavily and let the faerie guide her head down into the water. It was cold, nearly freezing, and she sucked in a sharp breath. Methild lifted Aisling's soaking hair and reached down to tap the side of the bucket, and plumes of steam began to rise from the surface of the now-hot water. When Aisling looked up at her, she held one finger to her lips. A secret—likely, the hob wasn't permitted to use her magic. At least, not in the service of a human prisoner. As Methild worked her pointed fingertips through Aisling's tangles, the faerie hummed a melancholy tune in her raspy voice.

Once she was settled back in the bed, wrapped in fresh sheets and draped in a clean cotton shift, Aisling brought the ends of her wet hair to her nose. It smelled of the flowers that bloomed in the night garden, heady and sweet. When it dried, it was soft as silk.

She was still running her fingers through it absentmindedly when the door opened again. This time, Kael leaned against the doorframe. His casual posture made her uneasy—it didn't match the intensity of his gaze or the furrow between his brows. Aisling shifted to sit up straighter against the headboard, everything in her begging to run as he studied her. But she couldn't. She was acutely aware then of just how thin the slip was, the way its sheer fabric barely concealed her body underneath.

But Kael didn't seem to notice. His eyes never left hers, even as Aisling's swept over him, searching for any sign of those misty tendrils reaching out to her. She found none.

"Trying to convince my handservant to set you free, were you?" His voice was cold and dripping with ire. He crossed his arms over his broad chest while he waited for a response.

So it was the king that Methild served, after all. Tension rippled across Aisling's shoulders unbidden. She hadn't been; not at all. She'd simply hoped for some relief from the shackle's weight on her wrist, which was by now raw beneath the metal. But his assumption reignited the defiance in her chest that had been slowly rebuilding with her strength.

"I don't want to be chained like an animal," Aisling shot back, her tone sharp.

Kael sneered. "I believe I preferred you when you were too weak to share your opinions." He pushed himself off the doorway and stalked closer. Despite his obvious disdain, he reached for the wooden chair that Methild had pushed out of the way for Aisling's bath. He dragged it to her bedside and lowered himself onto its edge. His closeness brought an overwhelming disarray of emotions to wash over her—fear, mostly. But curiosity, too. She avoided letting herself look at his hands, now folded in his lap, to spare herself the shameful reminder of the sparks they'd ignited when he'd traced them down her glamoured spine.

"I only meant for a few minutes, just while she washed my hair." Aisling conceded finally. She worked two fingers under the cuff to rub her sore wrist.

"Was your mother Fae?" Kael asked abruptly after observing her silently for a moment.

Frowning, Aisling looked up at him and shook her head. "I've told you, I'm human."

"You mentioned she'd told you about our kind." He leaned back, settling into the chair. It was too small for his height.

Aisling nodded slowly, her hands twisting in the fabric of the blanket that covered her legs. "She used to tell me stories," she began, a faint smile finding its way to her face as memories flooded back—memories which, most of the time, she kept carefully locked away. "About beings like you, places like this. Not quite like this, though. She made the Wild—*Wyldraíocht*—sound brighter. More beautiful."

Kael's eyebrow lifted, a nearly imperceptible shift in his expression to something like amusement. "Do you think my kingdom isn't beautiful?"

"In its own way, I suppose," Aisling admitted thoughtfully. "Like in the way that something sad can have a kind of beauty. But wherever it was that she visited was different. 'Bathed in golden sunlight,' she always said. I wanted to go there with her so badly."

"She never took you?" His tone was softer now, the anger he'd started out with replaced by a hint of curiosity akin to Aisling's own.

"She said Thin Places were too dangerous," Aisling replied. Her words were heavy with longing and regret.

"She was right." Kael's lips twitched into a wistful half-smile, as if to say *she told you so.*

"Methild told me that you rarely see humans here. Do you think she ever came?" In spite of herself, there was the smallest ember of hope burning in her heart.

Kael thought for a moment before answering. "She was likely taken to the Seelie Court. They are far more...eager to host human visitors than we tend to be. Does she speak of it still?"

Aisling traced patterns on the blanket, a distant look in her eyes. Her smile faded, and that tiny ember burned itself out as quickly as it had flared. "The people where I'm from thought she was sick," she said numbly. "They sent her away to a hospital on the mainland. She killed herself there."

"I am sorry." Kael's countenance softened a fraction further. There was an unexpected edge of empathy threading through his apology.

"It was a long time ago now." Aisling shrugged. "I guess I just hoped that I could find some sign of her here." As the thought left her mouth, she realized just how true it was. Though she'd come in pursuit of answers to the riddles posed by the prophecy, she'd been much more easily convinced to do so than her cautious nature should have allowed. It was for this reason—seeking a connection to her mother, and maybe some way to redeem herself for her own disbelief, for letting her be taken away in the first place—that she'd gone along so willingly with Rodney's plan.

"You've validated her stories, is that not a sign?" he mused. Kael's silver eyes held an understanding that seemed almost out of place, but they froze over again when they found their way down to Aisling's wrist. "Though, at what cost?"

She tugged at the chain instinctively. The connection they had shared, however brief, was slipping away before she could hope to take advantage of it. It was as if Kael had pulled up a drawbridge, shutting her out once again. "This cost is artificial. You're the one keeping me here; you could let me go."

"Ah, the brave words of a caged bird. You may have gained Methild's sympathy, but you will not find the same in me."

Aisling swallowed the lump in her throat, determined to hold her ground even as Kael's demeanor shifted. "I'm not asking for your sympathy," she countered angrily. "I'm asking for my freedom."

"You're in no position to be asking for anything at all." He rose and pushed the chair back against the wall with his foot. Then, he reached into his cloak and withdrew a leather-bound book that he tossed onto the bed beside Aisling. "Here," he said brusquely. "To keep you entertained. It would serve you well to learn exactly why humans should not simply wander into Wyldraíocht."

A Historical Record of Fae and Human Relations. Aisling's nostrils flared, her fingers itching to pick up the book and throw it at his retreating back. "You can't keep me locked up forever."

Over his shoulder, he asked: "Can't I?"

The question hung in the air behind him as a veiled threat, lingering even in his absence.

Bitterly, Aisling flipped open the book in her lap and scanned the first few pages. The volume read like a history textbook, a dry retelling of the establishment of Thin Places at the behest of the Unseelie Court. The print was tiny, the subject was dense, and Aisling had precious little patience for the tedious lecture on Fae diplomacy. Throughout the night she'd try several times more, if for nothing else but a distraction from her own thoughts. Each attempt ended with an irritated sigh when she was unable to maintain focus on its contents for more than a page or two.

Her efforts were interrupted when a robed male entered her room—Rodney's acquaintance, the Lesser Prelate who had taken her from the dungeon. *Lyre,* Aisling finally recalled. He hadn't returned since that night, and she'd been both dreading and anticipating their next meeting.

"Feeling better, I see," he remarked. He carried a tray of food that he set down at the foot of the bed. His hair—black as the oil slicks that sometimes coated the water near the docks—was combed back from his angular face so stiffly that it didn't shift as he moved.

Aisling eyed it apprehensively, still wary of anything offered to her here. "Thank you," she replied. "I appreciate your help."

He nodded, glancing around the room before he pulled out Kael's chair and sat down facing her. "How are you finding your accommodations?"

"Better than the dungeon," she replied cautiously, studying his thin face for any indication of what he was thinking. His vertical-slit pupils were wide in the low light. "Though, I'd prefer a bit more freedom." She rattled the chain against the bedpost for effect.

The Lesser Prelate's expression remained neutral. "I'm afraid that's not within my control, Aisling. I do believe that it's best for you to remain here for now."

"Best for whom, *Lyre*?" Aisling emphasized the name, as he had hers. It was a shot in the dark whether this faerie was the one who Rodney had described—one she took hoping he would confirm her assumption. Though he didn't react, that he didn't correct her was validation enough.

He leaned forward slightly and adjusted his robe around his legs. "Sometimes, what's best for one is best for us all."

Aisling's heart sank at his non-committal answer. It was clear he held information he wasn't willing to share, and her attempts to glean any bit of it from him would be unsuccessful.

"What business have you here, you and the púca?" he asked when she didn't respond.

"Surely he explained it to you himself." If he didn't intend to answer her questions, she wouldn't answer his, either. She was unsure of what, if anything, Rodney had explained to Lyre of her purpose. For now, until he revealed more, she would dance around it the best she could. "Does he know that I'm a prisoner?"

"I've told him of your situation."

Aisling's cheeks flushed hot. It had been the last bit of hope she had to hang onto: that when Rodney found out, he'd find a way to help her escape. If Lyre was telling the truth, and Rodney knew what she'd been through, maybe he was less of a friend to her than she thought. "Has he not asked you to get me out?"

He shook his head. "The favor I owe him is far less than that. He knows better than to even ask."

After a beat of silence, Aisling asked, "You seem to know more about my situation than I do. Is there a reason why you're here?"

"Because you're alive," he said simply. His expression remained impassive when he added, "And you shouldn't be."

⁂

"Did you finish it?" Kael nodded at the book he'd brought that was lying closed on the bedside table. He had returned the following evening, like clockwork and as aloof as ever, to deliver Aisling's breakfast and salve instead of Methild. It struck her as odd to see him carrying the tray—the Unseelie King shouldn't be the one serving her.

"Finish it?" Aisling nearly laughed. "I could hardly make it through the first chapter. I thought you said it was meant to entertain me."

"History is as entertaining as it is valuable," he said without a hint of irony.

Aisling rolled her eyes. "We have very different definitions of entertaining."

"Would you prefer a children's book then?" Kael shot back. Though slightly annoyed, his response wasn't particularly unkind.

"I'd prefer to choose a book for myself, if you'd take me to find one?" she tried. It was worth a try. A walk anywhere, even if it was just down the hall and back, sounded better than anything. Her legs hurt from disuse and her back was knotted from sitting against the too-soft pillows.

He didn't buy it. "Next time I will bring options."

"Next time? Why waste time visiting a prisoner at all?"

Kael narrowed his eyes. For a long time he stood still and quiet. Thinking of a response, or maybe deciding whether or not to give one at all. Finally, he spoke: "There are things I wish to learn before others can draw their own conclusions."

Aisling shifted to better face him. "What kind of things?"

"Things that are none of your concern," he said coolly.

"Then why do you look at me like I might have the answers?" she challenged. She'd caught that look in his eyes a handful of times—just brief, blink-and-miss-it flashes of curiosity—and she wanted to know why.

"Because you likely do, but I do not wish to ask you the questions." Kael began moving towards the door. This way, with Aisling chained to the bed as his captive, he maintained control of their conversations. It was infuriating.

"I hate the way you all talk," Aisling snapped. "Why does everything need to be so cryptic?"

He didn't answer. "I will return tomorrow with more books for you to choose from."

Anger overtook the caution that Aisling had been trying hard to maintain and when she spoke again, her tone was biting. "Is it about why I'm still alive?" Kael froze with his back to her, spine and shoulders stiff. She could hear his teeth grinding from across the room. But he hadn't left yet, so she continued: "The sylph said that the other prisoners had died to feed you. I'm assuming I should have, too, that night in the forest."

She didn't mention that Lyre had confirmed the very same during his clandestine visit. Unsurprisingly, Kael left without responding, slamming the door hard enough to rattle the glass of water on the nightstand. If nothing else, she knew how to get a rise out of him.

But he wasn't the only one hoping to learn something. She was frustrated and wasting time—she was meant to be making progress towards unraveling the prophecy. Towards understanding how she, as the Red Woman, was meant to end a war. She'd seen the conflict now firsthand; she understood the Shadowwood Mother's urgency. That the Unseelie warriors had slaughtered the opposing army with such swift, decisive force left a frightening impression. The way Kael's shadows tore through their bodies as though they were nothing, even more so.

14

MIRRORED

KAEL

Kael lurked in the dim corridor, awaiting Methild's exit from Aisling's room. He'd returned twice more before tonight, each time with a stack of books, but she hadn't been at all interested in the choices. He supposed that his own tastes were dissimilar to hers: he preferred dense tomes detailing ancient histories. Books on war, on strategy. It was unlikely that she would be entertained by such things.

"She is better," Methild's croaking voice sounded even before she had fully closed the door. She dragged behind her a basket of damp rags. "Stronger."

The king pushed himself off of the wall where he'd been leaning. "Has she asked you to unchain her again?"

Methild shook her head. "Stubborn, though. Won't hardly let me do anything for her anymore."

Kael hummed. He could have guessed that she would be—stubborn. She'd seemed it from the very first time they'd met, even beneath the heavy glamour.

"How much longer do you wish me to tend to her, Your Highness?" The old faerie pushed her sleeves up over her bony elbows and re-situated her grip on the heavy basket.

"Until I tell you that you may cease." Kael observed her haughtily, vaguely annoyed by the impatience in her tone. When he'd ordered Aisling into Methild's care, she'd agreed to do so without complaint. As she should. Now, it seemed that she was displeased with the ongoing task.

Methild ducked her head. "Yes, Your Highness." She skittered off into the darkness, her basket grating loudly against the rough stone floor.

"Such insolence from your own handservant." The High Prelate swept into view. He was still hunched and bearing his weight on a cane after the injury during the battle, and all the more petulant for it. He'd been bedridden for three days. Three merciful days that had allowed Kael enough distance to quiet his rage. Now, he only considered plunging a blade into the male's sunken chest. If he'd have seen him up and about sooner, he'd have done so without hesitation.

"You have no right to speak of insolence to me, Prelate," Kael snapped. Werryn's willful defiance of the king's orders on the battlefield should have been grounds for execution, had there been another prepared to take his place as High Prelate. As it was, none of the Lesser Prelates were far enough along in their studies to step into the role. By design, Kael was sure. Werryn was no fool.

"Checking on your pretty pet again, are we?" he sneered.

Kael bristled at the implication. Since the uncontrolled eruption of his magic, and the deaths of nine of his own warriors, insidious whispers had begun to spread through the Undercastle like wildfire—no doubt fanned by the High Prelate himself. The tether had survived, yet again, while his own subjects had not. A tether that, when it came down to it, he hadn't wanted to use at all, but that had captured his shadows all the same.

"You forget your place in this court." The words were carried on a low growl as Kael's hand dropped to his side. He wasn't wearing his dagger there, but his fingers curled into a fist where its hilt would have rested. In the span of a breath, he could let his shadows free to finish what they'd started when they'd driven through Werryn's gut. In this moment, nothing would have brought Kael greater pleasure.

"My place is at the foot of the Low One. I serve him before I serve you."

"If your place is at His feet, then mine is at His left hand." Kael drew up to his full height before the High Prelate, straightening his broad shoulders, and hissed, "You serve *me*."

The only acknowledgement Werryn gave was a tight nod that made the hood of his robe slide back onto his shoulders. "I've gathered several members of the assembly in your study to discuss the girl, if you would care to join."

"My *prisoner* is not yours to discuss." Kael was nearly trembling with rage now, unaccustomed to such blatant impudence, even from Werryn.

"Be that as it may," the High Prelate said over his shoulder as he turned to proceed up the corridor, "your display at the Nyctara front concerns us all. Your conviction after we completed the Nocturne ritual that you hadn't needed a tether was clearly false. You're weaker than ever."

Werryn continued speaking as he hobbled away, leaving Kael with little choice but to trail after him, seething. In his mind, he was a small child again, following after a much younger Werryn and listening to the same lecture. *I was chosen,* he repeated again and again in a bid to block out those memories. *The Low One chose me.*

Four Lesser Prelates were waiting on the arrival of the High Prelate and their king just inside the door of Kael's study. Having already been put in a foul mood, Kael's teeth gnashed together at the sight of them uninvited in his space. He shoved through their tight group to take a seat behind his desk. These were the four furthest along in their studies and, incidentally, the four that Werryn kept closest. In their plain black robes, they traveled the halls of the Undercastle like a flock of ravens. They were as sharp and cunning as the bird, too. Lyre, in particular, seemed always to have the High Prelate's ear. It was Lyre who had alerted Werryn to Aisling's state in the dungeon upon his return. Between the two of them, conspiring from Werryn's sick bed, they had arranged her move to the chamber she now occupied.

Installing Methild as her attendant was the simplest way Kael could think of to monitor the situation. She had nursed him back from near-death several times over, surely not with as much tenderness as she now showed the girl, but she was skilled in her caregiving.

Kael tuned out their droning voices, propping his chin on his palm and moving his fingers in idle circles against his scalp. When one grazed his lobe, a slight chill danced across his skin. The girl had been the last one to touch him there. It had been a small kindness—hardly one at all, really—but it had stuck in his mind all the same: the two fingers she'd pressed to his jaw to turn his head to the side. The cool brush of her hands against his hot ear. How gentle she'd been with him.

No one had ever been so gentle with him.

His eyes drifted to the jar on his desk, where the Luna moth lay lifeless and faded at the bottom. It had died by the time he'd ridden back from Nyctara, but he hadn't been able to bring himself to throw it out. Even in death, it was beautiful.

"You've lost control." The accusation directed at the king so flippantly by one of the Lesser Prelates ripped Kael out of his head.

He straightened up in his seat. "I've not lost control." His practiced impassive tone now barely concealed a sharp edge of fury.

"No, he hasn't—he never had control to begin with. Not really." The High Prelate spoke as though Kael wasn't in the room at all. Just as Kael made to protest, he was interrupted.

"Might the girl be the key to his finding it?" Lyre suggested from where he leaned casually against the back of a plush velvet armchair. "He may wish—"

"You will not speak of me as though I am not present, and you will not imply again that a human has any influence over my god-given magic!" In one swift motion, Kael rose and swept his arm out angrily over his desk. The glass jar flew across the room and shattered against a bookshelf. The sudden noise quieted the assembly at once. "You do not know the toll it takes to wield this magic. And yet, here you sit and speak of *control* as though it's a simple matter." His voice was laced with a bitterness that he'd never quite been able to rid himself of.

The room watched cautiously as a paper-thin filament of darkness curled out of Kael's fist. Shuddering, he withdrew it before it could grow larger.

"You cannot deny that there is something that sets her apart, being that she has tethered you twice now and lived, while your own soldiers fell around you." Werryn raised his hands as he tried to placate Kael, who dropped back down into the chair. "We could just try again, if only to be sure. What would be the harm in that?"

"Or perhaps," another Prelate suggested, "it's not control you need, but release."

A derisive, humorless laugh fell from Kael's lips. "Release? You were not in Nyctara, nor have you been present for any other *release* before that. This magic is insatiable. It takes what it wants, and you would have me give it all that remains of myself." His silver eyes slid to Werryn. "Is that how you intend to take my crown?"

"Your Highness, forgive me." Werryn's tone had gone from placating to pleading. "None of us wish to see you lose the throne. Only to fully reach the potential of your power. Is that not what you want, too? I know how hard you've chased it, and what that chase has cost you."

Kael winced slightly. It was true that he had sacrificed almost every bit of himself, but it had never been entirely of his own volition—not when the encouragement of the Prelates bordered on coercion. He may have walked this path on his own, but they had pushed him to its beginning.

It shouldn't have been possible that the presence of a human girl could so easily disrupt the careful balance of chaos Kael maintained. He could end this, as he had intended to on the battlefield: either with her death, or his own success. Given the price her body had paid after two encounters with his shadows, it would likely be the former. The thought twisted something unreachable in Kael's stomach, such that one of his hands moved unconsciously to grip it.

"We need every advantage we can get in this war," Lyre posited.

A muscle ticked in Kael's jaw. The male was right, and he would try again. But not in their presence. This was his riddle alone to solve. "I am still recovering, and so is she. This is a discussion for a later date," he said with cool finality.

Slowly, Werryn nodded and gestured for the Lesser Prelates to disperse. "Very well, Your Grace."

⁘

Just as the girl had appeared before him as a mirror in the aftermath of the battle, he saw it again later that night when he entered her chamber. In her small form, chained to the bedpost, Kael caught a glimpse of his younger self: a figure controlled for the sake of power. And in that same reflection, he found himself no different from the Prelates who had subjected him to a similar fate.

"It snowed today, didn't it?" she asked.

Kael blinked, and the mirror was gone. The girl was just a girl. "Your pardon?"

"I can smell it."

It had, indeed, snowed the previous afternoon. Kael smelled it too when he woke, sharp and clean. He'd found a thin layer of it covering the night garden on his evening walk. But that a human could sense it from this deep underground was puzzling.

"I'd love to see it," she said wistfully, shaking him again from his thoughts.

"You've seen snow before," he said tersely. "It is no different here than it is in your realm."

She shrugged and the chain rattled softly. "I just miss the outside."

"You should have considered that before becoming my prisoner." Kael moved to his chair, which Methild now left in its place for him beside Aisling's bed.

Aisling huffed a short breath through her nose. "You say that as though this was my choice."

"You made the choice to willfully deceive me, knowing that there would be consequences when you were found out." *When, not if.* Though Kael should have determined her false that very first night, he was drunk and his mind had been clouded by his earlier failure in The Cut. But it was only ever a matter of time.

She turned away from him then to fix her gaze on the opposite wall. Cautiously, he studied her. She did look stronger, albeit still pale and thinner than she had been in the night garden. The abrasions encircling her arms were nearly healed, and her hair was no longer matted with blood where she'd split her head open. He noticed, though, that an angry bruise radiated from where she'd tugged against the shackle, rubbing the skin beneath it red and raw.

Kael sighed. He leaned forward and with deft hands unlocked the cuff and let it fall to the mattress beside her. She froze, still facing the far wall, when his touch lingered just a beat longer than it should have on her pulse. Her irritated skin was warm and her wrist felt small in his hand. Small, but not weak. He wouldn't be so foolish as to underestimate her again.

When Aisling turned back to him, her eyes were filled with surprise and uncertainty. They were a captivating mosaic of hazel, blue, and brown, each hue blending seamlessly into the next. He hadn't noticed their color before. She brought her arm to her chest and held her wrist gingerly, as if unsure of how to move it without the weight she'd grown accustomed to feeling there. "Why?"

He ignored her question. "I will have Methild bring something for that."

Aisling glanced down at her wrist and a lock of her hair fell out of the loose braid that the hob had woven. Reacting almost instinctively, Kael reached out and brushed the errant strand aside. The contact was light; tender, even. A touch that felt like a whisper in the silence of the room. A touch for which he had no explanation.

The girl's quiet intake of breath shattered the spell they were both held under and at once a sense of normalcy returned to the chamber. Kael withdrew his hand as if the connection had been severed by an invisible blade.

He cleared his throat and his expression regained its usual calculated composure. He needed to retreat from the closeness that had just enveloped them. Quickly, he rose from the chair. "Rest," he said. His voice betrayed none of the uncertainty that roiled within him. The softness he had allowed himself to reveal was a rare occurrence, and the action left him unsettled as he closed the chamber door behind his back.

"She won't get better this way, languishing in that dark chamber." Lyre's voice came in a sing-song pitch from the alcove where he was perched, waiting for Kael to pass, robes hanging down over the rough cave wall. "She'll atrophy, along with any power you think she might have."

"I do not believe she has any power at all," Kael snapped. He wanted to be alone; he needed to slow the whirlwind of thoughts crowding his mind.

"Perhaps not, but such things are unknowable without exploration," Lyre said, too casually. "You might at the very least try."

That unsettled feeling continued to linger long after he'd left Aisling, a haunting reminder of a connection that had felt far too potent for his liking. Kael was disquieted; he had somehow allowed himself to step outside his carefully delineated boundaries, and it left him feeling exposed in a way he was unaccustomed to. It was much the same feeling that had plagued him after Aisling, as a pixie, left him following their encounter during Nocturne. His fingers found his ear again, where the ghost of her touch persisted. Idly, he wondered whether she could still feel his touch, too.

15

PLAYING THE GAME

AISLING

He'd set her free.

Kael, the vicious king of the Unseelie Court, had released Aisling from that damned manacle and, in his haste to leave her chamber, had failed to lock the door. Aisling held her wrist still cradled against her chest. It ached; the bruise that had bloomed beneath the metal was dark and ugly. But the soft burning there wasn't from the cuff. It matched the subtle trail of fire that had spread from where the tip of Kael's finger grazed her cheek when he had brushed her hair away. She wasn't sure what had possessed him to do so, but that moment captivated her enough that she almost hadn't noticed when she didn't hear the sound of the bolt sliding into place.

Almost.

If he'd gone to fetch Methild to take a look at her wrist, she wouldn't have very much time at all before the hob turned up. If she could just get out into the hallway and find somewhere to hide, she could wait until daybreak and escape back to the Veil while the Unseelie Court slept. Heart pounding, Aisling stood up out of the bed. In the days she'd been kept in the chamber, she'd only taken a few steps to reach the waste bucket or to kneel down and wash her hair over the basin. The floor was cold under her bare feet and she had to keep one hand pressed into the mattress at her side for balance as she moved. When she reached the end of the length of the bed, she wavered. It would only be five or six more steps to the door. Once she made it to the hall, she'd be able to use the wall for balance. Aisling prayed that she wouldn't have to go far to find a hiding place; she was too weak yet to run.

Unsteadily, she crossed the remainder of the room and all but fell against the door. Her hand hesitated on the handle. It could have been a trap—Kael could be waiting just on the other side to catch her. But she couldn't sit idly by anymore. She was tired of feeling helpless and being tended to and lying in bed when she was meant to be gathering information. No matter what awaited her outside of that chamber, she had to at least try. *The Red Woman would try.*

Aisling counted down from five in a whisper before she pulled the heavy door open. The hallway beyond was quiet and dim. There was no sign of anyone passing by, but she felt compelled to hold her breath all the same as she crept out and eased the door closed behind her.

"So you've gotten your freedom, after all." A smooth voice from a shadowy alcove made Aisling jump and fall back against the stone wall. Lyre emerged from the darkness, sweeping his robes behind him dramatically. Aisling rolled her eyes at his unnecessary entrance. Despite the fact that he had gotten her moved out of the dungeon, she still wasn't sure whether he was on her side.

She squared her shoulders and crossed her arms to hide the bruise on her wrist. "I was given half; I'm taking back the rest."

Lyre cocked his head slightly to one side, a subtle move that betrayed a hint of amusement as he studied her. A strand of his oil-slick hair fell from where it was plastered back. "You won't make it far before you're caught again."

"I might," she responded curtly.

"May I make a suggestion?" he asked, taking one step in her direction. When Aisling only eyed him warily, he continued. "Be patient. Stay in your chamber. Let His Highness see that you can be trusted."

"Why do you want to keep me here?" she challenged. It seemed that everyone was bound and determined to ensure that she remained trapped in the Undercastle.

He hummed. "I believe you and I can be mutually beneficial to each other."

"I'm listening." Aisling leaned against the wall, trying to hide from Lyre the fact that the little strength she possessed was rapidly waning. He could likely tell, though, by the way the color was draining from her cheeks.

"You have a clear effect on the king—it may be easier than you think to get the information you seek if you allow him glimpses of what he wants, as well." A sly smirk touched his lips, but his tone remained thoughtful.

"And what is it that he wants?"

He didn't answer, instead offering a thin smile before saying, "Stay, for the time being. I will encourage him to allow you greater freedom; soon enough, it will feel like it was his own idea all along."

When the pair heard a distant noise further along the corridor, Lyre nodded toward the chamber. Aisling looked back at it: her prison cell. She was so close to escaping she could nearly taste the sea salt air of Brook Isle on her tongue, could nearly hear the sounds of gulls crying and waves breaking on the rocky shore. It was possible that she could make it out; she might even make it home in time for breakfast. But Lyre's words gave her pause, as did the persistent, invisible weight that she'd carried on her shoulders since she'd met the Shadowwood Mother. She couldn't return empty-handed, not when this war was spilling out of the Wild into her own realm. Not when the destruction she'd witnessed on the battlefield threatened her home, her friends.

Aisling took the arm Lyre offered and let him help her back to the room. Instead of climbing into the bed, she lowered herself onto Kael's chair. It was uncomfortable, yet still a welcome change.

"Leave it unlocked," she told Lyre as he turned to go, "so he thinks I didn't take the first opportunity I had to run."

He nodded in satisfaction and left her alone once more.

It would be several nights, however, until she'd see the king again. Methild's visits, too, grew shorter and less frequent now that Aisling needed little from her. Aisling spent the time rebuilding her strength, pacing the short length of the chamber back and forth. During the day, she'd venture further down the corridor on tip-toe, hopeful that she'd find something useful in one of the rooms that branched off of it.

Where the Unseelie Court thrived on secrecy and unpredictability, the Undercastle echoed those values identically. Its hallways, winding like a labyrinth, often led to dead-ends or interconnected with each other in perplexing ways. Had she wandered too far, Aisling could have easily lost herself in the endless maze, never finding her way out. She dreamt about that some days: getting turned around and wandering through blackened corridors, chasing after the sound of Briar barking just around the next corner until her legs gave out and her body was broken by thirst.

When Kael at last returned, he didn't seem at all surprised to find that her door was still unlocked. Aisling thought then that maybe he'd done it on purpose. "Your daily exploration of my castle has done you well; the color has returned to your cheeks."

She stiffened. "I don't know what you mean."

"Have you found anything interesting?" he asked, one eyebrow arched.

"I've not left my room," she lied.

"Here." Kael dropped a pair of dark velvet slippers on the ground. "Methild had to guess your size."

They were a perfect fit, and comfortable on Aisling's sore feet—a much-needed barrier between her soles and the rough floor. "Thank you," she said sincerely. Kael ignored her, one hand already pushing open the door.

"Come." A command, not an offer. He turned and proceeded up the hall, leaving the door ajar. Aisling hesitated, torn. Without any indication of where he might be leading her, she envisioned him once again depositing her in a dungeon cell. She could still hear the haunting rhythm of the water steadily dripping there in the darkness. Gathering her courage, she took step after tentative step until she was following in Kael's wake.

They didn't venture far during that first evening. They walked beside one another, Kael with his unreadable gaze fixed ahead, and Aisling with her eyes downcast, focusing on the cadence of their steps. The silence between them was an unspoken agreement. As it was, Aisling thought their walk would be a one-off event. That maybe some sense of guilt or whatever else it had been that drove Kael to remove her manacle still lingered.

But he returned the next night, and again the night after that. Each time, the pair wandered slightly further, deeper into the Undercastle. Kael took her down paths that Aisling hadn't yet taken herself during her daily exploration—and for that reason she suspected he was having her watched. Still, no one had stopped her. Gradually, gradually, the silence between the two was broken. Just by a sentence or two at first, when Kael would point out something down an adjacent corridor or when Aisling would ask about a locked door. Their conversation was cordial and often short-lived, but she would take what progress she could get.

On the fourth night Kael came to walk with Aisling, his cool aura had thawed some. He gave her a choice—a gesture she hadn't expected. The night garden or the library, he offered. Though the spiral staircase was daunting, Aisling's heart quickened at the prospect of fresh air and open spaces. As though he'd anticipated her decision, he'd brought her warmer attire and a heavy cloak of moss green wool that wrapped around her like a shield against the chill.

The night garden was just as stunning as she remembered it; now, with a light dusting of snow, it was maybe even more enchanting. Each branch and petal and blade of grass glittered with magic, turning their downy white covering a glowing blue. Fractals of that same light flitted across the ground where it reflected off of sharp dripping icicles. The sweet smell of the blooms, which seemed determined to thrive despite the frost, permeated even stronger. As the pair retraced their footsteps down the path they'd walked before Aisling had been imprisoned, she tried carefully to avoid returning to the memory of that night.

Without thinking, Aisling reached out for the same flower that Kael had stopped her from touching once before. *Angel's trumpet.* But the way it sparkled called out for her fingers to stroke its soft petals. To brush away the snow and ice so that it could breathe in the night air, too.

Again, Kael caught her before she could do so. "Do you not recall what I told you the last time you were here?" he demanded. His face was stern, but there was a hint of amusement in his eyes at the quickness with which Aisling could be so entranced by the magic of his court.

"It's poisonous," she mumbled.

He clicked his tongue against the roof of his mouth as he looked down at her. "Naïveté suits you, human. Your vulnerability in this realm is almost endearing." His words dripped down her skin like hot wax, melting and coating every inch of her. It burned, but she found herself wanting more. He reached out and plucked a leaf off of her shoulder.

He was truly beautiful in this light, in a haunting, unforgiving sort of way. All sharp angles and harsh lines, the intensity blazing in his silver eyes enough to make her heart skip a beat for fear of the cruelty she knew he harbored there. And yet, still so undeniably beautiful. He drew her in as a moth to a flame. A fly to a spider's gossamer web. She could so easily be ensnared by him.

But maybe she could do the same to him. She had once before, after all, albeit in a different form. Aisling didn't like who she was becoming here, but it seemed she had little choice. If she was going to get what she needed, she had to play the game with all the rest of them.

Averting her gaze, she turned and continued down the path. Kael didn't offer her his arm this time, but he remained close by.

"What do you know about prophecies?" Aisling kept a neutral tone, despite the way her heart raced and her hands trembled where they were balled into fists in the pockets of the cloak.

"Prophecies?" Kael glanced at her sideways. "Why?"

"I saw a line about them in one of your books." She shrugged. It was a lie—and not a good one—but surely he didn't have them all memorized. "I find the idea interesting."

"So you did read them." She could tell he was smirking without even having to look.

"I skimmed." Aisling kept her focus on the ground in front of her feet; it was easier to feel confident in her ability to lie when she wasn't looking at him directly.

"We have ten," he said. "I know them as well as I do my favorite books. They're told to us when we are young like bedtime stories."

Aisling frowned. "Only ten?" Though it increased her odds that someone might know more about her own, it also made her situation feel all the more precarious. She'd been recognized so easily by the sprite when she had been with Briar—with so few prophecies to distract, she stood little chance of keeping her identity hidden here for long.

"When one comes to pass, it is replaced by another. Some have stood for centuries; others, merely decades," Kael mused. He steered their path back to the garden's entrance. She was running out of time.

"And they always do?" Aisling asked. "Come to pass, I mean."

"For better or for worse," he confirmed solemnly. Aisling wondered whether he was thinking about her prophecy, about how the fall of his court seemed written in stone. The possibility of his defeat being predetermined by fate likely bore significant influence on his decisions as king.

"Who writes them?" Though she did her best to sound detached, she worried that he could see straight through her. This was more conversation, more questioning than he'd entertained thus far during their walks. But she could feel her time to find answers tonight coming to a close.

Kael shook his head. "No one knows that. Tomorrow evening I will show you the library; you can pick out your own books on prophecies, or whatever else piques your interest, since apparently history is not to your liking." He swept his arm out in a gesture for Aisling to walk ahead of him down the spiral staircase. She didn't like the sensation that his looming behind her sent snaking down her spine.

16
A TRAITOROUS HEART
AISLING

"Fireflies?" Aisling asked curiously.

Instead of taking her to the library, when Kael came to her door that evening he said cryptically that he had something else he wanted to show her. He led her down and down a narrow, winding passage that opened up into a damp cavern. Lichen covered the ground and crept up the stalagmites towards rivulets of water that dripped from the ceiling. Ahead of them, tiny glowing balls of light drifted lazily. Some alighted near pools of water, while others danced through the still cavern air.

He looked down at her, one eyebrow raised slightly. "Those are wisps."

Aisling peered closer at the floating orbs. She couldn't discern any form beneath their glow. "They're faeries?"

"They are the echoes of faeries, the part of them that is left behind when they move on." As one ventured nearer to the pair, Kael stepped lightly forward and caught it in his hand. Aisling winced, sure he'd crushed it. When he made his way back, he grasped her wrist and drew it towards him then cupped his hand against hers. Aisling saw the faint glow move between their fingers as the wisp passed from Kael's palm into her own.

"Methild will fetch you a jar if you'd like. You can use it to light your room." His hand lingered there for a beat, his skin cool against hers, before he closed her fingers around the orb and let go. It struck her just how gentle the whole exchange had been—she wouldn't have imagined his hands to be so careful, or to be capable of something so delicate. She ignored the way it made something flutter in her chest.

Aisling raised her fist to eye-level and peeked in. The wisp rested on her palm, though she couldn't feel it there at all. The light it produced was warm and golden. She stretched out her arm and uncurled her fingers one by one, until the wisp floated from her grasp and drifted back toward the others.

"They cannot tell the difference, you know. They're not entirely sentient," Kael said from behind her where he was leaning against the wall. "They're little more than remnants of magic."

Aisling watched them for a moment longer before turning back to Kael. "How do you know there's nothing left of the faeries they were before?"

Kael cocked his head slightly to the side, his eyes shifting between Aisling and the wisps. "I suppose there is no way of knowing."

"Then you shouldn't keep them. Living things shouldn't be held captive," she said pointedly.

He smirked, amused. "Are we still discussing the wisps?"

"Partly."

"Did you truly expect to deceive me without consequence?" Kael pushed off of the wall with his shoulder and watched Aisling closely as she carefully stepped over the loose stones.

She ignored his question; she had no good answer for it. Instead, she considered how to redirect the conversation towards something more productive. The first time she'd seen anything other than ice in Kael's eyes, however briefly, was when she told him about her mother. She'd opened up, and he'd let his guard slip a bit. She could do so again, now, while they were alone and she had his attention.

"I used to feel captive on my island," she said. "When I was young, thinking of my mother being able to escape to someplace beautiful. The stories she'd tell me when she came back, the pages and pages of sketches she made of the Fae she encountered...I was jealous of her. Then when I stopped believing, and she died, it felt like even more of a prison."

"Did you leave it?" he asked thoughtfully.

Aisling nodded. "For a while. I was angry and bitter, but I was lonelier in the city. As much as I didn't want to believe in magic, I couldn't help looking for it. I never found any there."

Kael hummed. "Is that why you returned?"

"No. My father got sick; I came back to care for him until he passed. Being back made me wonder whether I should have left in the first place." Aisling looked back once more at the wisps lighting the cavern. She missed her home desperately; talking about it now made her heart ache.

"You cannot grow without leaving behind what is comfortable." There was kindness in his words, a softness to his voice. Hearing it there was satisfying, almost comforting. It warmed her to him. After a moment, Kael began walking again. He kept his pace slow until Aisling caught up.

"Do you ever leave here?" she asked.

Kael nodded once. "On occasion."

"Where do you go?"

"To battlefronts, mostly. To our borders." As though imagining it as he spoke, Kael's fingers toyed with the dagger he carried sheathed at his hip.

His curt, non-committal answers frustrated Aisling. She wanted more from him. She asked a little more forcefully now, "That's how you grow then? War?"

His only response was a darkly grim smile. Aisling didn't look to see whether it reached his eyes. She wished she was better at this—at the game—like Rodney. He'd have come up with ten different ways to drive the conversation in the direction he wanted, and likely at least nine of them would have worked. But Kael hadn't yet hardened to her, so she pressed on.

"Why are you giving me this freedom?" she demanded finally.

Kael glanced at her then cast his gaze back ahead. "You are far from free."

"I'm not in the dungeon, and I'm not chained to a bed or locked in a room." He was right, though. Aisling was a prisoner—of Kael, of the Undercastle. Of the prophecy that had sent her here in the first place.

"Indeed you are not. And yet you've made no attempt to run," Kael observed.

Aisling bristled at the unspoken challenge in his words. He thought her complacent; weak, even. But it was resolve keeping her in the Undercastle, not weakness. If she'd been so weak as he assumed, she'd have fled that very first night he left the door unlocked. She couldn't leave here empty handed, not after everything she'd been through and not with the threat to her home growing with each passing day.

Though, she considered, it may be to her benefit to let him think of her as the frail human he'd seen in his dungeon. As a curiosity, rather than a challenge. Naïve, as he'd called her in the night garden.

"I'm not so stupid as to think I could navigate my way out of there and find the Thin Place without being caught," she lied. "You never answered my question."

"Didn't I?" he said dismissively.

She snapped then, both unwilling and unable to continue to play. She couldn't take one more ambiguous, teasing response. "You answer very few of my questions, actually, though you expect me to answer all of yours. If my company and conversation is so intolerable, why bother wasting your time on me at all? Why don't you just tell me what it is you want and get it over with?"

The pair stopped walking and turned to face each other. Kael's jaw tightened as he regarded Aisling, his eyes once more icy and impenetrable. "If you are so dissatisfied with my responses, then why do you persist?" His tone cut through the air like a blade.

"Because I thought that if I kept trying, I might actually get a real, decent answer out of you instead of more vague, cryptic bullshit!"

Kael's grip tightened unconsciously on the hilt of his dagger. "And what answers do you seek exactly, Aisling? Do you expect me to lay bare my soul to you, to share my every secret?"

"I expect you to make up your mind," she shot back. "Either treat me as a person, or as your prisoner. You can't have this both ways."

He paused, then said coolly, "Your chamber is in that direction." He nodded towards a smaller hallway that branched off the corridor. He'd corralled any hint of anger that had colored his feature seconds before, now hiding it under that neutral mask he so often wore. "You can find your way back on your own. Or you may leave. Do whatever you wish."

Before Aisling could throw a response back at him, he'd turned and stalked off the opposite way, his figure quickly swallowed by the darkness as he retreated. She stood there for a time, staring after him. Wishing she hadn't let her frustration get the better of her. She'd been so sure they were making progress, and now she thought she may have ruined it.

⁂

After their argument, Aisling was surprised when Kael was again at her door the following evening wearing the same stoic expression. "I told you that I'd show you the library," he said before she could ask. "I keep my word."

The library's shelves were carved into the walls of a cavern that glittered, like the throne room, with veins of quartz. It was small, though, and Aisling was dismayed by the selection she found there. Most of the books were similar to those Kael preferred: history lessons, tales of battle and strategy. Mentions of prophecy here and there, but only ones that had transpired centuries before. *There had to be more.*

When Aisling turned to ask Kael if there were other volumes elsewhere in the castle, she found him leaning his weight on one shoulder against a shelf, absorbed in a book he held open in front of him. With his chin tipped down to read, his moonspun tresses hung like a curtain around his face.

"Find something good?" She almost felt guilty interrupting him, but he hardly looked up. Instead of an answer, he just hummed. To see him this engaged in an activity that seemed so utterly *normal* brought a hint of a smile to Aisling's lips unbidden. He wasn't cold or angry or derisive this way; she might even go so far as to call him unguarded.

That was gone in an instant when the High Prelate entered the library and cleared his throat. It was loud in the quiet cavern. Kael snapped his book shut, already irritated before the male even spoke, and slid it back into its place on the shelf.

"Stay here," Kael ordered Aisling before following him out into the corridor.

She did, for a moment. Just long enough to let them round the corner ahead and begin a conversation in hushed tones. Removing her slippers to muffle the sound of her footsteps, she crept as close as she dared. In that short amount of time, their voices had already increased from harsh whispers to louder, biting tones.

"You said you'd try again with her once she was well. She appears well enough to me." The Prelate did not attempt to hide his impatience.

Kael's response was clipped and unyielding. "You misremember, Werryn. I said only that I would consider it." *Werryn,* Aisling pronounced silently. She was mentally cataloging the names of each Fae she encountered there, though she'd yet to learn the full names of any besides Methild.

"How much longer will you toy with her? Taking her for walks as if she were your pet." He spat the word and Aisling winced when the truth of it lanced through her. "You're putting off the inevitable."

"What I do with my prisoner is none of your concern." Kael would be standing defensively at his full height now, towering over the older male, but the Prelate didn't sound at all intimidated.

The words Werryn spoke next knocked the breath out of Aisling's lungs and echoed in her mind like a discordant melody: "She could fundamentally change how you use your magic. Your whole relationship with it. Do you not want that?"

"Of course I want that, but I will explore it my way and in my own time." Although Kael's response held a thread of frustration, the hint of longing beneath it resonated far louder. Aisling dug the tips of her fingers into the rough rocks at her back.

"You are blind to your own potential; you always have been."

"If I have been blind to anything, it's only ever been your lust for power." The pair's harsh exchange concealed layers of subtext that were well beyond Aisling's grasp, but it made her stomach turn all the same.

"Do not act as if you don't feel that same hunger," Werryn challenged.

"And yet I am the only one who bears its consequences. I will use the girl when I see fit and I will inform you after I'm through." Then came the sound of rocks grinding under boots, and footsteps returning in Aisling's direction. Kael's voice, closer now, as if speaking to Werryn over his shoulder: "You are dismissed."

The ground beneath Aisling's feet shifted violently when Lyre's words came back to her: *you're alive, but you shouldn't be.* This was Kael's purpose for visiting her in her chamber, for allowing her this limited freedom. This was the answer he was seeking to the question he had refused to ask her. Aisling's own motivations had been but a single thread in the tangled web of their interactions. He was attempting to grow closer to her in the same way that she was him. They were manipulating each other.

But it was the realization that her own feelings had grown deeper than mere manipulation that struck her with force. Her chest tightened; she was drowning in this ocean of unacknowledged emotions, unable to come up for air without another wave crashing over her head. All along, they'd only been using each other, and once again, she felt like a fool for thinking she could have possibly held the upper hand. She'd not only lost it to Kael, but to her own traitorous heart.

She should run; she needed to run. She could make it back to the library before she was caught. But from somewhere within that choking wash of emotions, anger rose unbidden. Instead of turning to run, Aisling stepped out from the shadows into the king's path.

17
RELEASE

KAEL

"You were meant to remain in the library," Kael growled at the girl now standing before him in the corridor, feet bare and eyes blazing. Already his blood seared with magic, so provoked that he could hardly contain it, and now he had to face down yet another challenger. He ground his teeth together so hard his jaw ached, but it paled in comparison to the pain coursing through the rest of his body.

"I didn't," she said. Then, "So this is what you've been trying to learn? How to use me, like you did during the ritual?"

Kael gave a tight nod; he couldn't lie. She was no longer blind to the truth, though she understood precious little of it. The Prelates had spun her survival as his tether into something of an obsession within his court. As much as he wanted to deny it, the temptation of what Werryn suggested was a siren's call that he couldn't completely ignore. And like the Prelates, Aisling couldn't fathom the weight of responsibility that rested upon his shoulders. That had rested there for centuries.

When he didn't respond, she advanced toward him. "You would kill me—for what? To forge yourself into an even greater weapon? Are you not already capable of enough destruction on your own that you have to pull me into it, too?"

The tension in the space was palpable, crackling between the two as they faced each other down. Aisling's words were like arrows that struck Kael's embattled walls again and again. He clenched his fists at his sides as surges of power pulsed through him.

"You think you know about my magic." The bitterness of his retort felt sharp on his tongue. "You're nothing more than a naïve little girl."

Her humorless laugh was a cold, stinging melody. "And here I thought you found it endearing."

He did. Kael's eyes flickered to her lips, pursed in an expression of stubborn defiance, and he found himself wondering for one fleeting moment what they would feel like pressed against his neck. The thought at once both soothed and frightened him, which only incensed him further.

"You may possess the ability to change the fate of my court, to tip the scales back in our favor. Why should I waste such an opportunity?" Kael demanded. Though the question was directed at the girl, it was his own mind that shot back an answer: *you shouldn't*.

The insistent murmur was a reminder of the relentless ambition that had been instilled in him since boyhood. It was a crown of thorns that he wore willingly, but it was not without its painful punctures. Aisling's presence, and whatever power she held over his magic, seemed a beacon in the darkness.

Yet even as he rationalized the practicality of his intentions, another voice stirred within him—a voice that he had suppressed for too long. It whispered of desires beyond strategy, of a longing for something that defied calculations and tactics. Kael had grown accustomed to viewing his court and its inhabitants as pieces on a vast war table. But Aisling was beyond all of that; she had managed to insinuate herself into the uncharted territory within him. The dissonance was stark in the clash between the role he was expected to uphold and the ache for something raw, untamed, and utterly uncertain.

Aisling didn't flinch, didn't back down. Instead, she continued to hold his gaze with unwavering resolve. "I won't be used to kill," she declared. "You can't control me."

"I must consider what is best for my court," Kael said, his voice tinged with regret he couldn't conceal. His words were a declaration to himself as much as they were to her. "But it is not you who would be controlled."

Aisling's glare softened, just, before she blinked that softness quickly away. "You can be better."

The challenge hung in the air between them, a gauntlet thrown down that Kael couldn't ignore. It was a provocation. Or, perhaps, an invitation. It was his breaking point. And his restraint finally shattered.

Kael didn't think as he stepped forward until there was nothing but a breath of air between their bodies. He didn't think when he reached out for her, either, and cupped her cheek, or when he brought his lips crashing down onto hers in a fierce and fiery collision.

It was a kiss borne of frustration, of anger, of a passion that had long simmered beneath the surface. His feelings for Aisling had grown stronger with each passing night, with each stubborn exchange and silent walk through the Undercastle. They had defied all of his attempts to rein them in.

Aisling responded with equal fervor, her fingers curling into the fabric of his tunic as she pulled him in tighter, closing the distance between defiance and desire. The searing kiss flooded his lungs with air; when she inhaled, he did too. And the world around them faded into absolute insignificance.

This time felt different from the lustful, honey wine-fueled kisses he'd shared with her when she'd been glamoured. This kiss reached out to something deeper inside of Kael, something he'd thought unreachable. She was warm, so warm, at the points where she pressed against him, and that warmth seeped through his skin to settle in his bones. He smothered the hot flare of desire that rose in him when he felt her body so close to his and swallowed back the words he wished he could say.

But Kael could tell by the way she looked up at him with heavy-lidded eyes that she felt it, too.

"Where are your shoes?" he murmured against her soft lips before capturing them again with his own. His hands on her waist itched to move, to explore her body, but he held them still.

She gestured blindly toward the library without breaking their contact.

It was only with great effort that he did so himself, drawing back to hold her at arm's length. When he did, it was only because he heard footsteps down the corridor that brought him back into reality. "Go get them, I want to take you somewhere."

"Where?" The word was just a breath; she looked unsteady on her feet.

"Away from here."

Reeling, Kael waited for her. He braced himself against the wall, focusing on the texture of it beneath his palm, trying to come back down from wherever that kiss had sent him.

Aisling returned quickly, hopping on one foot as she pulled the other slipper on. Once she was back at his side, he faltered. In the time it took her to jog to the library and back, doubt crept in, with hesitation alongside it.

Until she smiled.

"Come with me," Kael said. He almost reached out to take her hand, but stopped himself and balled his instead at his side.

Kael led Aisling quickly through the twisting corridors, down branching side passages so narrow they had to walk single file, and through the vast caverns that opened up around them. The deeper into the Undercastle they went, the more trepidation began to overwhelm his thoughts. He didn't speak, nor did she. The only sound around them was the quiet draft that circulated through the caves.

Though some parts were dark, lit only by ancient torches with struggling flames, Kael knew the way by heart. He moved surefooted over rubble and around stalagmites along the path his feet had carved over hundreds of thousands of trips back and forth. The scrambling sounds of Aisling behind him, though, reminded him to keep his pace slower than he would have alone.

Finally, the pair entered a distant cavern. Small, and lit by moonlight. A little-known way in and out of the Undercastle. Kael went first, lithely climbing to the top of a boulder beneath the opening in two large strides. Then, he turned and offered his hand to Aisling. When she took it, and gripped it tight, his lungs squeezed as though she'd gripped him there as well. This time, he didn't let go.

"It isn't much further," he promised once they had stepped outside. They were in the darkest part of the forest, yet she seemed unafraid. Only a few more minutes of picking through the underbrush and the pair drew to a stop.

"I've not brought another to this place before you." Kael's heart raced in his throat. He remained a few paces behind when Aisling dropped his hand and stepped forward to explore the small forest enclave. Silently, he watched her take it in: the gurgling stream that wound in and out of gnarled roots and reflected the trees above. The ferns sprouting along its bank and the moss carpeting the ground that glowed a soft turquoise, enchanted by the same magic as the plants in the night garden. The rich, dark smell of damp earth.

"None of your other faerie girlfriends?" she teased, glancing back over her shoulder to where he was standing. "You have a reputation, you know. One that you lived up to the night we met."

Kael blew a short breath through his nose in response; he was glad for her humor to ease the tension. "I suppose the púca told you all manner of stories about the dangerous, alluring Unseelie King and his consorts."

"Was he wrong?" The corner of her lips twitched up. When Kael chose not to answer, she turned to the stone ruins, the remnants of what once must have been a grand moon gate. Now, it was barely that, but still strangely devoid of vines or moss or lichen. "What was this place?"

Kael moved to stand beside her, looking up at it too as though seeing it for the first time. It always felt like the first time, even though he'd been visiting it for centuries. "I've never been able to determine its origin. It was here long before I ever found it."

"It feels special," she whispered.

"It comforts me," he admitted. "I come here often."

"Just to sit?" Aisling lowered herself onto the bottommost broken stone step before the arch. Kael did the same.

"To think, to pray. It's quiet; sometimes I can feel the Low One even stronger here than I can before the altar." He spoke about his god without thinking, but realized when he felt Aisling shiver beside him that she likely did not hold such a positive view of the deity after her experience in The Cut. "I have been King for a long while. This is one of very few places where I can escape that."

She hummed, drawing her arms around her waist. "Was your father a good king?"

Kael angled himself so that their knees nearly touched and shook his head. "My father was a lord. Our crown is not passed by bloodline, but by magic. I was born with the ability to wield shadows, as was given to me by our god Himself. A gift."

"You don't seem like you think of it that way," Aisling challenged.

He could feel her studying him with narrowed eyes, so he kept his own focused on the movement of the stream. "I am grateful for it." *At times.*

"And your mother?" She was leaning closer now, curious about a past that Kael hadn't spoken or even thought of in a very long time.

He drew in a breath, then let it out slowly. "She was a vessel for me, just as I am a vessel for this." He'd never known the female who had given her life to birth him.

Aisling was quiet for a moment while his words sunk in. "Who raised you? Methild?"

"I was given over to the Prelates before my mother was cold in her grave," he said, fighting to keep the bitterness out of his voice. "From the moment my magic was discovered, I was theirs to cultivate."

They sat silently then, bathed in the sounds of the forest and of their own steady breathing. It was a still night. Cold, but without the bite of the winter wind, it was tolerable. Kael leaned back and propped his elbows against the step behind him.

From this position, Aisling could see every bit of him, every detail, down to the pale blue veins beneath his skin where the sleeves of his tunic rode up. She studied his arms, those veins and arteries and capillaries that became a spiderweb of inky black from his fingertips on up when his shadows grew too strong. For a half-second, Kael allowed her to trace her finger over one on the inside of his wrist before he pulled away.

"What does your magic feel like?" she asked softly.

"Agony," he said. "Ecstasy."

"Show me," she urged, still in that same soft voice.

Kael sat up and looked at her sharply. "No."

"You want to understand my effect on it, I know you do. So try." Aisling was looking at him insistently. Earnestly. She was offering herself to him. The very thing she'd fought against, she was now asking for. *You can be better*. She said that she didn't want to be used as a weapon, but this wasn't that. This was something else entirely—a chance for him to test his magic away from the Prelates, away from the battlefield. Not in the service of the Low One or of anyone else but himself. And she wanted to give that to him.

Still, he hesitated, indecision warring in his chest. "I won't—"

Aisling interrupted him. "You won't hurt me."

"You don't know that," Kael insisted. He had before, and he would again. It shouldn't matter; he shouldn't care. But it did, and he did.

"Yes I do. Don't tether to me. Just let me be here with you." There was no fear in the girl's voice and no apprehension in her eyes. Kael was unsure where she derived her confidence in him from, but it was misplaced.

Though torn, he nodded tightly. Kael moved to kneel on the soft moss and drew several deep, shaky breaths. Aisling left the step to sit cross-legged before him. Although she was closer than she likely should have been, he couldn't find it in himself to ask for more space. He wanted her there.

The woods around them hushed in anticipation of what was to come. Jaw clenched, Kael lowered his head and closed his eyes and called upon the shadows that had been fighting to emerge since his confrontation with Werryn. They came violently to the surface, those savage currents, in a bid to tear into anything within reach.

When he felt their familiar sting he dropped one hand to the earth, but before he could dig his fingers into the moss Aisling slipped her own hand into it. He felt her other, then, on his cheek. Her palm was soft and cool as her fingers grazed his hairline. Kael tilted his head to lean into it. Her touch was steadying; he focused on it with all that he had.

With Aisling's hand in his, Kael found himself releasing the tight grip he kept on his magic. The shadows, once frenetic and wild, slowed their chaotic dance. Instead of lashing out, their tight coils unwound lazily. The obsidian tendrils drifted from Kael as steam rising off of water, carried on the breeze and swirling in the ebb and flow of the forest's energy. He didn't dare open his eyes for fear of breaking the spell.

He didn't once feel his shadows pull towards Aisling, so he let them explore. Through them, he felt rough tree bark and the ice-cold water of the stream. The prick of pine needles and sticky sap and the impervious stone ruins. Never before had his shadows felt so much like an extension of himself. Even in battle, where he felt the most at peace, they were merely a projection of his rage. This was something different entirely.

Cautiously, slowly, he called them back. As they curled into his skin, he winced. Still uncomfortable, though not quite as painful. Kael opened his eyes to find Aisling's and his breath caught. She'd tamed his magic—she'd tamed him.

The calm he felt was overwhelming. Aisling caught him when he fell forward, guiding his head down to her shoulder and supporting his weight. She snaked her arms around his waist and slid one hand up to pass gentle circles over his back.

Held tight in her arms and wrapped in the sweet, oppressive quiet of the night, Kael wept like a child.

18

UNTETHERED

AISLING

So the Unseelie King had a heart, after all. One that was wrapped in layers of barbs and buried as deep as the Undercastle, but it was there. It was a fractured, blackened, withered thing. Beating, but maybe only out of spite.

As he'd held onto her tightly, Aisling realized that the fear and the darkness that she felt in The Cut and then on the battlefield, as his shadows wound around her limbs, hadn't been hers alone. Those things were inside of him, too. So this time, she forced herself to be calm, and she forced that same calm into Kael. If one was in control, so was the other. It wasn't magic, not really, but it was something that seemed awfully close.

Lyre was right.

You have a connection, he'd told her during his most recent visit, just hours before Kael came to walk with her for the first time. *Explore it; it will bring you closer.* She continued to let that closeness develop and promised herself that it was strictly in pursuit of information about the prophecy. It was a game of manipulation, pure and simple.

He acts as though he feels something for you, Lyre had whispered. *Do not fall for it. Though if he truly does, it would only be to your advantage.*

Aisling thought herself a fool, softening as she had for her cruel captor—until he took her in his arms and swept her into a kiss that sent her world spinning off its axis and derailed her carefully-laid plans. Of course she wanted answers. But more than that, she wanted *him*. So she gave in without hesitation. And when she took his hand and let him use her, she wasn't sure anymore how much of it was manipulation. The line had grown so blurry so quickly that she was left feeling raw and confused as Kael's breathing gradually slowed from the ragged sobs that wracked his body.

His eyes were still glassy when he finally raised his head from where it had rested heavily against her shoulder. Something new glimmered in them now—hope, maybe. Aisling watched as they played down her face to stop at her lips. Kael brought a hand up and brushed her hair back over her shoulder, paused for a beat, then slid it down the side of her neck.

She was rendered breathless by his touch, fierce yet impossibly gentle. His callused hand grazed her skin so softly, but she could tell by the urgency of his movements that he wanted more. He *needed* more. She did, too.

Slowly, he guided Aisling to lie on the plush bed of moss. Her body settling against it sent ripples outward across the glittering turquoise, as if she were a pebble dropped into a pond. She might have been enchanted by it if her attention hadn't already been captured by Kael, his face hovering just above her own. In the next breath, his lips were on hers and her hands were tangled in his hair. The arch in her back pressed their bodies close, so tightly that she couldn't discern whether the wild hammering in her chest was her heart or his. Maybe it was both.

Aisling wrapped one leg around him, digging her heel into the back of his thigh, and Kael loosed a low groan into her mouth. The sound of it resonated in their kiss and made her teeth vibrate. He sat up in one swift motion and brought her along easily to straddle his hips. Aisling fumbled with the hem of his tunic, both of them reluctant to break contact even long enough to strip off their shirts. The cold air against her bare skin brought every single nerve ending to life. It made each trace of his hands down her back, across her chest, and up her arms feel like raw, pulsing electricity.

"I want you." The ardent need in those words he whispered against her neck drew a tightness to coil in Aisling's core. She kissed him again, this time dragging her teeth lightly across his lower lip before taking it between them and biting down. Kael's hips surged upward in response, grinding against her fervently.

When he eased her onto her back again, Aisling felt the hunger in his eyes raking over her body. For the first time since Nocturne,

Aisling's thoughts weren't racing ahead. She wasn't strategizing or manipulating or weighing pros and cons, good and bad. Her focus was singularly fixed on the trail of flames that his lips ignited on her breasts, the weight of his body pressing her into the earth, the searing heat blooming between her thighs.

"I want you," he repeated, growling this time as though angered by the admission. "I am consumed by you, every night. Every hour." Kael was relentless in his ministrations, chasing kiss after feverish kiss to punctuate his words. Where his fingers dug into her hip, she was sure she'd bruise.

But as those fingers slid to the waistband of her pants, Aisling pressed her palm to his chest. He lifted himself off her slightly.

"Kael," she whispered the warning. He leaned in once more, eyes closed, and pressed his forehead against hers.

"You're right," he said. Then a second time, even softer: "You're right."

It was too much, too soon. He was too vulnerable; so was she. Aisling didn't know what to do with all the things she was feeling now: what to name them, where to keep them inside of her. They'd come on so suddenly—or, rather, she'd realized them so suddenly. If she were honest with herself, they'd been growing deep in her chest, the smallest seed, having taken root when he'd brushed his fingers across her cheek for the very first time. Blooming greater and greater with each glimpse of his softness, with each small kindness he showed her. Never large enough for her to acknowledge until now.

Kael rolled off of her and they lay side by side in the moss, sucking in labored breaths that poured from their mouths as thick fog in the night air. They stayed there in silence until Aisling's teeth began to chatter; the sweat that coated her skin did her no favors as the temperature continued to drop around them. Kael redressed her almost reverently, then himself, and pulled her to her feet.

The walk back to Aisling's chamber was loaded with wordless tension. Kael led her back with their fingers interlaced tightly, but when they reached her door he only pressed an earnest kiss to the crown of her head before leaving her alone in the darkness.

Once, and only once, had Aisling's mother confided in her about the allure of the Fae. She'd come home with a stupid, dreamy smile on her face and stars in her eyes and spoke of a faerie who had twisted flowers into her hair. She said he had tasted of overripe berries when they kissed. She'd drawn him, too, but had never shared that sketch with Aisling. Her words, as beautiful as they'd sounded, stuck with Aisling as more of a warning than a promise. She'd been lured away from her family, from her husband. Surely it could only have been the result of sadistic trickery.

But now Aisling wore that same stupid grin and saw those same stars. As she lay in bed, willing herself to sleep, she couldn't help running her fingertips across her lips. Brushing them over the bruises forming on her hip. Those she pressed into, relishing in the slight pain that made her wince. Her mind was a cloudy haze of emotions that swirled lazily, all of them too far out of reach for her to grasp. She let them play as her eyes fluttered closed, though it wasn't long before one filtered through all the rest: anxiety, suffocating and intense.

Sleep remained out of reach, and she spent the day tossing and turning in the bed until she couldn't stand it any longer. In the early evening hours, Aisling bundled into her cloak and pulled on her slippers and left her chamber to roam aimlessly through the halls of the Undercastle.

Preparing for the rest of the court to wake, servants flitted through the corridors like elusive shadows. Hobs, with their spindly limbs and permanent expression of impatience, carried written messages and baskets of linens and tubs full of hot water. Wide-eyed imps with skin the color of raw egg yolk darted from one hidden corner to another with brooms and tiny hand tools. Aisling stuck close to the wall, doing her best to stay out of their way as they rushed past. None paid her any mind—they didn't even seem to notice her there. Or, if they did, they pretended not to.

Beneath the cloak, Aisling's frame trembled. The shakes had beset her mid-afternoon, after she'd woken up for the hundredth time, and she hadn't yet been able to quell them.

She knew now that she'd been granted complete freedom. She could have left. She could have ascended those worn, winding stairs and headed straight for the Thin Place. She wouldn't have even had to run, as it seemed there was no longer anyone monitoring her. Not even Methild, who Aisling suspected had been asked to act as her sentry since Kael began leaving her door unlocked. But now, she was held there by two things: her purpose, and the king. Though in a much different way, she was still his captive.

As she walked, she replayed scenes from the night before in her mind. He had exposed himself to her in such a raw, painful way. He'd allowed himself to be utterly vulnerable, despite the lengths he went to in hiding that side of himself behind layers and layers of bitterness and cruelty. That armor he wore of an unyielding and invincible ruler, however well he'd conformed to it, concealed someone made fragile by years of feeling out of control.

She could relate. Aisling hadn't felt as though she'd had a modicum of control since the moment she'd been pulled into the prophecy, but Kael's surrender made her even more determined to reclaim it. She could be the Red Woman just as much as she could be his.

Having felt nearly invisible since leaving her chamber, Aisling was startled when a hob cornered her and handed her a tightly rolled sheet of parchment. *Join me in my study,* it read in thin, looping script. There was a crude map sketched below showing the way. She was grateful that it was oriented around her chamber and the library or it would have been nearly as useless as the message itself. It was undoubtedly from Kael, though, and the thought of seeing him again—of being alone with him again—brought a flurry of butterflies to take wing in her stomach.

But she was stopped midway by a strong hand that gripped her wrist. Aisling jumped and whirled around to find Lyre. He gave her a wan smile and pulled her hand to rest in the crook of his elbow.

"Let's you and I take a walk," he said. Something under his genial tone made Aisling's skin crawl. The way he kept her arm pinned against his side felt incongruous with his overly friendly demeanor.

"I was on my way to meet Kael," she argued when he began leading her in the opposite direction from the study. "He's expecting me."

"He can wait." When she looked up at him to protest, she noticed for the first time that his eyes seemed to reflect the low light of the torches like mirrors. Like the eyes of a cat.

Lyre led her around the corner and through a door deep in a shadowy alcove. Had Aisling passed it on her own, she never would have known it was there. This chamber felt colder than the corridor. Symbols, and runes like those carved into the forest floor in The Cut, were etched into the stone walls. There was a large painting at the far end of a dark entity, with shadows rising from it similar to Kael's. She recognized it without having to ask: *the Low One.* Aisling shivered. She knew that Kael valued his connection with the deity highly, but the foreboding figure left a sinking feeling in the pit of her stomach.

Once inside, Lyre released her arm and took a seat in a high-backed chair. He gestured to another, and after a moment's hesitation, Aisling sat on its edge. She pulled her cloak tighter around her body as though she could hide her discomfort from his shining, searching eyes.

"I've heard whispers," he began, his voice low and measured. "Whispers that I've found to be...interesting."

Beneath the cloak, Aisling dug her nails into her palms. "Whispers?" she prompted. She was so full of secrets now; he could have learned about any one of them.

Instead of elaborating, he hummed. "You must know that I am quite well connected, not only within this court. I think you'd find my reach to be rather impressive."

"I don't have time for riddles, Lyre." She made to stand, but a sick curiosity held her in place. She wanted to know what he knew.

"I've learned much from my connections over time that I've used to secure my place here. For example, were you aware that Kael's father was merely a lord, and his mother gentry?"

She repeated what Kael had told her the night before: "The crown is passed by magic, not blood."

Lyre nodded his approval. "And how do you think that infant, born in the farthest reaches of our territory in a dominion that has since been claimed by the Seelie Court, was discovered?"

He was bragging now, and Aisling was quickly losing patience. "What does this have to do with me?"

"My connections tend to have a way of illuminating certain things." He rose then, circling behind his chair to pace leisurely. "Things like your true identity."

Ice flooded Aisling's veins and her lungs constricted painfully. Though she had long feared this moment, knowing that her secret was not as concealed as she had hoped, nothing could have prepared her for the sharp terror of hearing the accusation out loud.

Lyre stopped his movement and doubled over at his waist in an elaborate bow. "It is a true honor to make the acquaintance of the Red Woman, in the flesh."

Aisling swallowed hard, unable to choke back the lump forming in her throat. Her mind raced in an attempt to come up with a story to cover her lie. But all rational thought had gone out of her head, along with the ability to string together a coherent sentence. "How?"

"It is a rare thing here, the hatching of Luna moths. Each year, we're blessed with one, maybe two. But this year, they filled the night garden. Every leaf, every stone, every tree was covered in them." He resumed his pacing, running a hand across the spindles of his chair each time he passed. "And then, changes on your side of the Veil. The Shadowwood Mother has been sending sprites to do her dirty work for countless years; it was not difficult to realize that if I kept a close watch over them, one might eventually lead me to something of interest."

"You send hunters after them?"

Lyre narrowed his eyes. "On occasion, if a patrol *happens* to spot one crossing between realms, they may take it upon themselves to follow behind. It is no secret how handsomely I reward those who bring me valuable information. It took a while for me to determine how these events were connected, but all things become clear with time."

"Who else knows?" Aisling pronounced each word carefully, but her efforts to keep her inflection steady were in vain.

Lyre's sly grin widened. "I, more than anyone, understand the value of secrets. I haven't told a soul, and I don't plan to."

"Then why are we having this conversation?" she demanded, slowly forcing her panic into submission. "What do you want?"

He sat back down and crossed one leg over the other. Absolutely at ease with the power he now held over Aisling. "Protection, my dear girl. In this treacherous court, one can never have too many allies. I want your guarantee that when the storm comes, you will ensure my safety."

Silently, Aisling weighed her options. Trusting Lyre was a gamble, but it seemed she had little choice in the matter. As he said—the Unseelie Court was a dangerous place; having an ally, even one as slippery as Lyre, might be her best shot at navigating it. Instead of answering right away, she redirected: "Rodney seemed to think you would be able to help me. What do you know about the prophecy?"

"I study many things, prophecies included. Call it my own attempt to stay one step ahead of fate." He paused and winked. "But of yours—less than I should, truth be told. I know that it has been around for a very, very long time. I also know that Kael ordered all mention of it stricken from our books. Those pages were torn out and burned centuries ago."

Her brow furrowed. "But you know it; you must know something. What do you make of it?"

"That it is you who must be responsible for ending this war and restoring our broken realm, likely only by seeing to the end of our court. Though," he added, "being that you are here, I would imagine you already put that much together."

Kael's face, the trust she'd seen flickering in his eyes as they'd knelt together on the mossy ground, flashed in Aisling's mind. *Where would the end of the Unseelie Court leave its king?* She shook her head sharply to clear the thought.

He chuckled and leaned back in his chair. "But then, prophecies are rarely as straightforward as they seem. One interpretation is as right or as wrong as the next."

Finally, Aisling found it in herself to stand. Trembling still, but at least steady on her feet. She straightened her spine and stared Lyre down. "I promise your safety if you keep my secret. *And* if you continue to use these connections of yours to learn more about the meaning behind the prophecy." Her request was as good as an admission: she still knew nothing about how to fulfill her role. She was as clueless now as she had been from the start.

Lyre rose, too, and opened the heavy door for Aisling to leave the chamber. "You have my word."

19

A SMALL MERCY

AISLING

Aisling sped down the corridor, eager to put as much distance as she could between herself and Lyre and that looming, malevolent painting that had made the hair on the back of her neck stand on end each time she glanced up at it. Her hands still shook despite the way the conversation resolved. It had gone better than she'd imagined it would, yet she was unsure of Lyre's true intentions, of his trustworthiness. Something in his countenance left her feeling uneasy; his cunning grin made her want to take a shower.

She had little time to dwell on it, though, as she drew nearer to Kael's study. Aisling slowed her pace when it came into view and took a steadying breath. She tried to focus instead on the feelings that had filled her the night before, hidden away in the forest with his lips pressed hungrily against hers. His breath in her lungs, and the sounds of his pleasure in her ears. The thought carried her to his half-open door and across the threshold.

"Aisling," he said, looking up from an aged map spread flat on his desk. The way he said her name filled her veins with a million tiny sparks, and the way a furtive smile unexpectedly warmed his face eased the tension she'd been carrying in her shoulders. "I was beginning to think my map hadn't been clear enough."

"This is hardly a map." She brandished the slip of parchment for effect before rolling it back up and tucking it carefully into her pocket. He'd written it just for her; she wanted to keep it.

Aisling paced around the perimeter of Kael's study. There were more books there, organized neatly in a system she couldn't identify. They looked to be older, more valuable perhaps than those in the library. These were all leather-bound with gilded printing on their spines. Some were written in English, and some in the same Fae language she'd seen on the pages that littered the Shadowwood Mother's thicket. She wondered briefly what it would sound like to hear Kael speak it. She imagined it would be beautiful, full of pretty words and lilting tones.

"More history books," he provided. He'd been watching her make her way around the room from his seat.

Aisling hummed. "My favorite." Once she reached his desk, she looked down at the map. It, too, was labeled in the same foreign language. Harsh, jutting mountain ranges cropped up between dense forests. Rivers flowed down from the peaks, and there was a lake somewhere to the west where several of them joined. Dotted borders crisscrossed the terrain. All of the names and locations were hand-written in a script that closely resembled Kael's. She traced a finger over the closest set of markings.

Kael rose from his chair to stand beside her. He kept his eyes on the map as well. "Last night..." When he trailed off, Aisling braced herself for a curt statement of regret. He started again: "Last night was—"

"Magic?" She winced at her own poorly executed attempt at humor. Instead of correcting her, Kael silently slid his hand across the map and placed it over hers. When she spread her fingers in response, he curled his to lace them through the spaces between. The act of intimacy, however subtle, made the ache that had been growing in Aisling's chest flare painfully. She squeezed his hand tightly, squeezed her eyes shut tightly, then pulled away.

Kael looked at her, brow furrowed. "I apologize, I did not mean to make you uncomfortable."

Aisling shook her head and turned sharply back to the books to hide the tears prickling in the corners of her eyes. He had put his trust in her; he had let her see so much of him. The guilt of keeping her secret gnawed at her insides hungrily. Relentlessly.

I can be the Red Woman and I can be his, she thought to herself again. Then again, and a third time still. And even if she couldn't, she needed him to hear it from her. If Lyre reneged on their agreement, Kael would undoubtedly be the first one he'd tell. She needed to take control of her narrative before the Prelate could twist it himself.

"Is something wrong?" The overt concern in Kael's voice only deepened the ache. Aisling circled around to stand in front of his desk, unconsciously using it to enforce the distance between them.

He paused for a moment when he saw the pallor of her face before he stepped around it, too.

He moved with a languid, carefree sort of grace that would have been entrancing had it not been for the threatening flex of his corded muscles. He carried himself this way not just because he was Fae, but because he was a battle-tested warrior—as Aisling well knew. Trepidation tightened her throat and stilled her tongue under the words that were poised there, waiting to be spoken. He could strike her dead quicker than she could blink. But the way he had looked at her—he wouldn't kill her. *He wouldn't.*

Aisling took two steps back and said, "I need to tell you why I'm here." Kael made to speak, but she raised a hand to stop him. If she didn't get it out now, she'd lose whatever nerve she had left. "The real reason. What I told you about my mother, that's all true. But her stories aren't what brought me here." She glanced up at him, but his expression was unreadable.

"Go on," Kael said coolly.

"When I asked you before about prophecies…" She stopped. Cleared her throat. Started again: "I'm here looking for information about a prophecy."

"Which." A statement, not a question. As if she were still just as connected to him as she had been in the forest, she could feel the way his body was becoming tense, the way his heart hammered against his ribcage. The way his shadows smoldered beneath his skin.

Aisling recounted, as she had to Rodney, the story of her meeting with the Shadowwood Mother. She knew it by heart now, which helped her get it out despite the voice in her mind that begged her to stop, to keep mouth shut, to take it back.

Finally, her story ended. Thick, stony silence settled between the two. Minutes passed. When Aisling looked up, Kael's eyes, which since the night before had borne a quiet softness for her, had hardened. He'd drawn himself up to stand tall and rigid, every bit the unyielding king he was promised to be.

"So it is you who would see the downfall of the Unseelie Fae. The destruction of my kingdom."

She shouldn't have expected less. She'd misled him and earned his trust under false pretenses. She was the enemy. Even still, his response lit a small ember of anger in her. It was Kael and his unquenchable bloodlust that kept the battle raging. His insatiable quest for power over the totality of the realm that prevented peace.

"It would seem that you're able to do that just fine without my help." When Kael didn't entertain her comment with a response, she held his gaze for a moment before she added, "And besides that, the resolution of your war is hardly *destruction*."

"The Red Woman is not welcome in my court. I should kill you where you stand." He pronounced the words slowly with lethal calm.

Aisling shook her head, certain. "You won't."

"That's twice now you've betrayed me. You will not be granted a third opportunity." The way his fingers brushed over the hilt of the dagger sheathed at his hip did not go unnoticed. Aisling's confidence dimmed.

"You won't kill me." She wavered, less certain this time.

Far faster than she could comprehend, he lunged across the study. Several books cascaded from the shelf overhead when Aisling's back slammed against it, her head meeting stone with a loud crack. Kael's face was inches from hers, teeth bared in a menacing snarl. His fingers curled around her throat. They twitched once, then again, before he dropped his hand back to his dagger and narrowed his eyes.

"Run."

That word—that singular syllable—sent a cold shot of fear straight to her bones.

So Aisling ran.

Each loud slap of her slippers on the stone floor echoed like a death knell as she ran blindly through the corridors of the Undercastle. She shed her cloak as she went; she'd be faster without it weighing her down. She knew the path to the spiral stairs well enough by now that she didn't have to question where her feet carried her, and soon enough she'd reached its base. But she couldn't slow.

She took the steps two at a time, tripping and cracking her knee on a sharp edge twice on the way up. Warm blood seeped through her pants and collected around her ankle. But she couldn't slow.

Outside, the cold air only tightened her lungs further. If Kael had sent guards in her pursuit, she was unable to hear them over the ragged, heaving gasps that sounded more like sobs than breaths. But she couldn't slow.

Aisling aimed for the tree line and prayed that she would be able to find the Thin Place once she was inside the forest. It was dark, and snow was falling, and everything looked the same no matter which way she turned. She staggered ahead, dizzy and disoriented. Her movement sent a flurry of glowing white orbs spinning from where they had been resting soundly in the low-hanging branches that Aisling carelessly batted out of her way.

They twirled around her, giggling when their tiny fingers caught the hem of her shirt and tore out strands of her hair. One flitted close enough for Aisling to make out a female figure with skin like frosted glass. The light they emitted seemed to come from within their small bodies, and their wings fluttered so rapidly to keep them aloft that Aisling couldn't see them at all. She could hear them, though, as they whizzed past her ears. She swiped at the beings erratically, knocking one from her shoulder and two from where they'd wrapped themselves in her hair. They shrieked—an ugly, grating sound—but eventually fell behind as she continued to run.

It took her far longer than she would have liked to find the Veil, which glimmered faintly inside a hole in the trunk of a giant old pine. Its gnarled roots grasped cruelly at her ankles as she approached and threw herself headlong through that sticky sheen of magic.

And then she was back in the old mine, back in the forest she knew as well in the dark as she did in the light. It was night there, too, though snow hadn't yet fallen on Brook Isle. Aisling stumbled out of the cave, earning another several bruises in the process, and sprinted with renewed speed once she exited its mouth.

This was her world, her woods. It smelled of home: of earth and sea and just faintly of car exhaust and chimney smoke. But now, heart racing and legs burning, the shadows of the towering pines felt oppressive. The keening and cooing of the birds, threatening.

"Here!" they seemed to call as she pushed through the undergrowth, *"She's over here!"* She had to pause every few paces to remind herself to breathe.

Aisling angled her path toward the road. Once her feet hit gravel, she stopped at last. She doubled over, hands on her knees, and retched onto the ground. Her stomach violently expelled the bile she had struggled to keep down since her confrontation with Lyre. Once she was able to stand again, she closed her eyes and strained to hear any sign of chase: twigs snapping, branches cracking, galloping hooves striking the dirt. She'd crossed out of the borderlands, she knew, though it would have hardly made a difference to a soldier acting on his king's orders. As she waited in the dark, she found only the quiet hum of the forest. The birdsong softened; the trees no longer appeared ominous.

She wouldn't be so foolish as to think he hadn't ordered her execution; not after the hatred she'd heard in his voice. *Run.* It haunted her, that cold tone. So different from the kindness that had been there only moments before. But she deserved it. She deserved every ounce of hatred he could find in his heart for her.

Limping, Aisling finally turned away from the trees and headed in the direction of town. Every inch of her hurt. Vaguely, secretly, she thought that it might not be the worst thing if a sentry were to burst from the woods and run her straight through with a spear. Maybe then someone else would be declared the Red Woman, and she'd be free of the ache in her chest that now seemed like it might be permanent.

It would be a small mercy: death.

20

A COLOSSAL, DAMNED MISTAKE

KAEL

He was stuck still, rooted to the ground where he stood. Kael hadn't taken a breath in so long that his body forced him to do so reflexively. When he sucked in a shaky gasp, the air still smelled of her. *The Red Woman.* The very being he had been warned about since he was old enough to read the prophecies for himself had been standing right there in front of him. Worse, he had let her see all of his most vulnerable parts. Let her touch him, touch things so deep he was unaware that they even existed. And he had liked it.

Aisling's empathy had been at once a balm and a torment to Kael. It unnerved him to lay himself bare before her. So he had resisted her, fighting against the flicker of hope that threatened to ignite within him, for as long as he was able. Yet, deep down in some unacknowledged part of himself, he longed for the gentleness she promised, even as he feared it might ruin him.

It had.

Methild entered quietly to receive her taskings for the day, and though Kael could see her thin lips moving, he was unable to hear her words. The sound of blood rushing in his ears blocked out everything else, even as he shouted at her to leave. She scurried out hastily and made to shut the door behind her, but Kael was already halfway across the threshold.

The sense of calm still left in his chest from the night before was torched instantly by blinding hot fury. He'd been foolish to think that the girl could chase it away—she had only swept it into a darkened corner. It had been waiting there for exactly this.

The Red Woman. Those unassuming blue-hazel eyes of hers had lulled him into complacency twice and he had no one to blame for it but himself. He should have killed her right there in the night garden, when his arm was pressed against her throat. He could so easily have crushed her windpipe or snapped her neck. If not then, in The Cut. Though his shadows had been unwilling, he should have tried harder to force them to take from her like they had every other tether before. He should have used her on the battlefield, as he'd intended. *Should, should, should.*

Instead of doing any of those things, he'd fallen for her.

So this time, when he had her pinned by her throat to the wall, he knew as well as she did that he wouldn't kill her. But the things he felt in that moment, with her warm body caged beneath his, pulled and stretched him in opposing directions. He wanted to worship her as much as he wanted to shatter her into pieces. He would burn every broken shard of her and scatter the ashes, and the place where her remains settled would be his new altar.

Kael stormed down the corridor, not bothering to dodge the smaller faeries that skittered out of his way. Several weren't quick enough and caught the toe of his boot against a shin or the back of a knee. As he rounded a corner, he was suddenly struck by another sickening realization. He'd seen it: the White Bear. He'd been mere feet from its snarling maw and he hadn't even recognized it as such. He'd assumed the creature belonged to the púca.

And the Luna moths that hatched in the night garden just nights before she'd first infiltrated his court—it was all beginning to make sense. A twisted, abhorrent sort of sense.

Raif was exactly where Kael expected him to be at this hour: replacing weapons in the armory after early evening drills with the Third Company. The captain took one look at the expression on Kael's face and braced himself for bad news.

"Prepare the Company," Kael ordered, voice clipped. "We'll ride to the Dominion of Ilindor."

Raif frowned. "There is nothing in Ilindor; no enemy to be fought there."

"There is land in Ilindor that is unclaimed, and I want it." Kael ran his fingers over the tip of a blade lying on the table. It was newly sharpened and drew a thin line of blood across the pad of his thumb with only the barest pressure.

"The soldiers are still recovering from our last battle, Highness." Raif made the protest carefully, but his stance was firm. He placed the last of the shields against the wall and straightened his training leathers. "They need—"

Kael interrupted him sharply. "If I am ready, then they must be too. No one on that battlefield suffered more than I," he hissed. "Those that are too weak to fight again can be replaced. That includes their captain."

Raif stiffened at the thinly veiled threat. "We will begin preparations. I can have them ready in a few hours."

"Make it two," Kael shot over his shoulder on his way out.

"I'll make it two," Raif muttered under his breath.

The Undercastle was humming with activity by the time Kael exited his chamber. His armor was polished and packed; his leathers gleamed in the torchlight. His hair was tied back tightly out of his face, though not braided as Methild had wished. She knew; he knew she did by the pity he saw in her eyes when she helped him with his straps, but she also knew better than to speak a word of it.

Faeries bustled back and forth hastily, preparing supplies and readying the horses. It was no mistake that he'd chosen a dominion beyond one of the court's most distant borders. The ride out alone would take three, possibly four days. By the time he returned, the wretched stench of the girl that hung heavy in the air would have gone from his halls.

Kael needed blood on his hands. He craved the wet sound of flesh tearing from bone and the screams of fear and pain when those who dared face him were enveloped in his pitch-dark shadows. He could hear them already echoing in his mind and it eased his temper some.

THE RED WOMAN AND THE WHITE BEAR

But Werryn, drawn always to his torment, was waiting with the reins of Kael's mare in one hand. Lyre was at the High Prelate's side with Kael's longsword. Kael bristled as they approached. Furax, saddled and bridled and feeding already off of her master's energy, trotted ahead. Kael slung himself onto the beast's back to look down at the Prelates.

"Your sword, my king," Lyre said with a performative dip of his head. Kael snatched the weapon from his hands roughly and slid it over his shoulder into the scabbard at his back.

"Do you not have need of a tether, Highness?" Werryn was unsubtle in his approach; he wanted to know whether Kael had yet tried to use his magic with Aisling.

"No." Furax stamped a hoof into the ground dangerously close to the High Prelate's foot, but he didn't flinch.

"I could bring—"

"The girl is gone." Kael's countenance was steely despite the way his throat threatened to seize around the words. "And I will hear nothing more about it."

Werryn fell back a step then, eyes wide and jaw slack. He sputtered incoherently.

"She didn't work as expected, then?" Lyre provided helpfully. Kael regarded him with caution; the male's amused half-smile made him shift uncomfortably in the saddle.

"She was as useless as any other tether, so I sent her away. She either made it back to her realm or was taken by something in the forest." His knuckles ached from his tight grip on the reins. He was grateful that his gloves hid how the blood had drained from them. "Either way, she is no longer any concern of ours."

Still filling Werryn's stunned silence, Lyre bowed his head once more. "I do apologize, truly. I had hoped that she would perhaps be more than she appeared."

Kael narrowed his eyes. There was something off about Lyre, something that had always made him feel just this side of uneasy. He spoke in riddles and subtext, even more so than most Fae tended to naturally. Before he could pursue it further, though, the sound of Raif barking orders caught his attention. When he turned back, Lyre had taken Werryn's arm and was leading him toward the Undercastle.

∴

Camp the second night was cold, wet, and miserable. Kael had driven the Company hard, insisting that they at least reach the base of the mountains before breaking. The range was impossible to summit this time of year, so they'd have to skirt around. But the more time he spent in the saddle, the less opportunity he had to think about anything other than the task ahead. He didn't care that there was no enemy front to face down; there were without a doubt Solitary Fae who would fight to protect their homes. Their efforts would be satisfying enough until a front opened up elsewhere. If Kael had his way, he'd avoid returning to the Undercastle until spring.

Once camp was made, Raif found Kael in his tent. He was halfway through a bottle of honey wine, sharpening his sword idly. When Raif cleared his throat, Kael stood to serve him a glass. Raif held up a hand.

"Not tonight," he said. Kael poured a goblet full to the brim anyway and left it on the folding map table.

Raif stood stiffly when Kael sat back down, hands clasped behind his back. "I am going to be forthright with you, Kael, because I respect you too much to be otherwise. This is a fool's errand. A waste of time and energy. Ilindor is barren; there are no resources to make it a worthy claim."

"Forthright, indeed," Kael muttered into his cup.

Raif sighed and pulled a chair around. "What is this about?"

"Securing more land for my court."

"Why are we here, Kael?" He was insistent; without reprimand, he was not going to let this go.

Kael drained his goblet and poured another, his expression growing darker with each sip. "Because I made a mistake. A colossal, damned mistake."

"Surely nothing so irreparable," Raif said reassuringly. He leaned forward, trying to catch Kael's eyes. "Has this anything to do with a certain prisoner who I saw fleeing into the woods? If I recall, that wasn't more than an hour before you gave our departure orders."

"Aisling," Kael pronounced her name slowly, like a curse. Like a wish. "The Red Woman."

Raif fell back in his chair with a sharp exhale. "You're certain?"

Kael nodded, tracing the rim of his cup absently. His skin felt too tight as it stretched and stretched to hold his magic. It raged within him against the last scrap of control he was fighting to hold over it now. Outwardly, he attempted to maintain a mask of disinterest, but the faint trembling of his hands betrayed him. If Raif noticed, he chose to ignore it.

"And you let her go." Raif was beginning to see the mistake in sharp relief now: Kael had set free the one surefire threat to his kingdom. "Why?"

Kael didn't answer immediately, instead allowing his thoughts to briefly drift back to their encounters, to the intensity of their connection. "She was unlike anything else. She settled me. Never in all my years have I been able to control my magic the way she allowed me to."

"And you were afraid?" Raif guessed.

"She thought I could be something other than what I am." Kael took a breath and clenched his jaw. "I cannot."

They sat in silence for a time, only broken by the sound of more wine flowing into Kael's goblet. Raif studied the king—the way his shoulders caved slightly inward, no longer confident and proud. He'd given something of himself to the girl and she'd run away with it. "Why did you let her live?"

Finally, Kael met his friend's gaze. He found no judgment there, only concern. "Because I could not live with myself if I had done otherwise."

For Kael, this was as good as a confession. To admit to anything more, anything deeper, would be akin to admitting to his court that he'd never possessed true control over his magic until that night with Aisling. He didn't—he knew he didn't—but that was a secret he would take far beyond his earthly grave. A secret that would now be accompanied by another: that the Unseelie King had fallen for the Red Woman.

Before Raif could speak again, he was interrupted by a commotion outside the tent. Bellowing, and the clash of a sword against a sturdy shield. The pair rose simultaneously to their feet and stormed out into the night, both with weapons raised in anticipation of an attack.

The males of the Third Company were standing in a circle around a dying fire, two of them facing off in its center. Bran, one of the Company's oldest males, towered over Cadoc, one of its newest. Bran had not drawn his sword, but parried each of Cadoc's strikes with his shield easily. His face was contorted into a broad, wicked grin. The surrounding soldiers quieted and dispersed quickly once they noticed Kael and their commander approaching. When Cadoc whirled around to defend himself to them, Bran cracked him across the back with the edge of his shield and sent him sprawling to the dirt.

"What is this?" Raif demanded. He hauled Cadoc to his feet roughly by his collar and held him in place. "What in His name are you doing?"

Cadoc mumbled a string of apologies, but Bran held his ground. He looked past Raif to fix his glare on Kael.

"Our brave King," he spat. He was drunk, and his words were slurred, but his conviction was firm. "So eager to risk our lives for such a *valuable* claim as Ilindor. Did you not slaughter enough of us in Nyctara that you felt the need to drag us to the ends of your territory to do it again?"

Raif tossed Cadoc to the side and stepped in front of Bran. "Take a walk, soldier."

Though the others had abandoned Bran to his own actions, Kael could feel them watching him carefully from a distance. Gauging his reaction. He sheathed his sword and clenched his fists at his sides.

"Your power is no longer under your command, is it? Your precious shadow magic seems to have a will all of its own." The way Bran sneered the words—*shadow magic*—set those very shadows roiling under Kael's skin. When he looked down to where his fingernails were sunken into his palms, the first wispy black tendrils were curling out of his veins.

Slamming his eyes shut, Kael locked himself down. His whole body vibrated with the effort of keeping the savage currents inside. He could deal with Bran another way, or let Raif deal with him instead. He'd be sent back to the Undercastle, maybe relegated to patrol the border somewhere equally distant and cold as Ilindor. But such thoughts did little to quell the crashing, crushing waves sucking Kael down, down, down, ever deeper into that vengeful sea inside of him. Because ultimately, Kael knew, Bran was right.

Aisling. If he could only feel a small fraction of her calm, he could tear himself away and he could prove Bran wrong in front of the entire Company. But there was none left.

Kael's thoughts splintered. The agony that beset his body now was unlike any he'd felt in more than a century: a twisting, excruciating fire that consumed him to the marrow. It snaked down the left side of his body in winding trails from scalp to waist, peeling back skin and separating tissue from muscle. The pain tore his heavy glamour to shreds in an instant; he felt it dissipate into the breeze and the air on his uncovered skin was sharp and biting.

The last thing he heard was the chorus of horrified gasps that rippled through the camp as Bran's limbs were ripped from his body by thick ropes of shadow, and the last thing he felt was Raif's arm catching his weight as his knees buckled beneath him.

21

HOMECOMING

AISLING

Despite the numbness that radiated from her heels, up her legs, and over the curve of her spine to settle at the base of her skull, the sight of Rodney's shock of bright orange hair brought Aisling crashing back down to earth in an instant. Briar must have alerted him to her coming—Rodney stepped out onto the porch before her foot landed on the bottom stair.

His eyes were wide, though whether from fear or relief she couldn't tell. She hoped it was fear. "Ash—" he started.

The loud cracking sound and the sharp sting on her palm still weren't enough to temper the hot swell of rage in Aisling's chest when she struck him across the face. She could have done it again, and again, but she refrained. He touched his fingers to the red mark already blooming on his cheek.

"You left me," Aisling accused. "You left me there to die."

"I never would have let you die, Ash," he insisted. It was as good as a confession.

"I nearly did! Twice!" Briar, eager to reach her, pawed at the door Rodney had closed before he could escape. Neither made a move to open it.

Rodney raised his hands, palms towards her as if attempting to appease a feral animal. She felt like one. "You being there was our best chance to get what we needed."

"We?" she snarled. "Don't you dare act like we've been a team this whole time. You left me there alone; you played no part in any of this."

"Lyre would have told me if you were ever in any real danger."

She bit out a harsh laugh that sounded like anything but. Lyre, the smooth-tongued wolf in sheep's clothing. She was hardly surprised that he and Rodney got along, and less still that Lyre had downplayed her predicament. In fact, he had likely done so from the beginning to ensure she remained there, under his thumb, until he could figure out how best to use her. First as a weapon, then as a shield. He'd played his role well, she had to admit.

The Prelate, she could understand. A creature of habit, he knew just how to walk that razor-thin tightrope of the Unseelie Court. He balanced perfectly his station with his own machinations—one in one hand, one in another, to keep himself steady in the middle.

But Rodney's complicity in her imprisonment, in her torment, in all of this—that was far crueler simply because of how insipid it truly was. His only goal was to play the game. Aisling realized then that her best friend still fancied himself the chess master in this match, and that she had the entire time been his willing pawn.

"Please come inside. Let me explain." He reached out to her, but she pulled away.

"No." Aisling crossed her arms tightly over her chest and glared up at him.

"I didn't know you'd been imprisoned, not at first. I'd spoken to Lyre on Nocturne, briefly, and he knew you'd be coming back, but it took me time to track him down again." Rodney raked a hand back through his wild hair. "He isn't easy to find until he wants to be found."

Briar was whining now, and Aisling wanted nothing more than to go to him. She stopped herself; she knew the moment she had him by her side, she would soften. She couldn't let Rodney off so easily.

Stumbling over his words in his haste to get them out before Aisling got it in her head to slap him again, he continued: "He told me about your connection to the king. The next time I saw him, he told me that he'd found a way to get you out of the dungeon. He told me..." he trailed off then, rubbing the back of his neck awkwardly.

"Told you what?" Aisling said through gritted teeth.

"He told me that he thought you were making progress toward your goal of getting closer to Kael." He was paraphrasing, she could tell, but she hardly wanted to know what Lyre had said in detail. Just that summary alone was enough to draw a pink blush over her chest.

"Did he also tell you that he knows who I am? That he planned to bargain with me—my protection for his silence?"

Rodney blanched then. "No, he didn't."

"He figured it out. I didn't trust him to keep the secret, so I..." Her voice broke, thick with tears that she choked down quickly. They surprised her; she didn't think she had any left. "I told the king, and he sent me away."

"Please come inside," Rodney said again. This time, when he reached for Aisling's shoulders, she let him guide her to the door. She hadn't the energy to be angry any longer.

Briar was waiting just inside, calmer now. Like he knew Aisling needed his steadiness. He bristled for a brief moment when he smelled Fae on her, tail halting mid-wag. She dropped to her knees and buried her face in his soft fur, curling her fingers into it. His breath was hot against her neck and his tail resumed its rapid back-and-forth the instant her arms wrapped around him.

"I took good care of him for you," Rodney said softly. "Probably gave him too many treats, though."

She didn't want to laugh—she really didn't—but she couldn't help herself. It felt more like a sob, but Rodney was satisfied enough to call it progress.

Time flowed differently in the Wild—something Aisling hadn't realized when she'd returned from the Nocturne revelry, drunk on honey wine and Kael's scent. But she learned that all of the time she'd just spent in the Unseelie Court, which Rodney estimated to have been somewhere close to a month, had passed as a mere four days on Brook Isle.

As she tried to force down a dry piece of toast, she considered the implications of this for her mother, who would disappear for a day or two at a time. Wherever she'd been in the Fae realm, it would have felt to her much, much longer. Aisling wondered if her mother ever missed home during those periods away. If she ever missed her.

The bread, though bland, left a sour taste behind on Aisling's tongue. She felt sick—sick in her head, her stomach. Her heart. All she'd learned about her prophecy was that it was a subject forbidden from discussion in the Unseelie Court. All she'd learned about the Red Woman was that she was a damned fool.

Tired as she was, Aisling couldn't sit still. She found a set of clothes she'd left in Rodney's laundry weeks before and stuffed the garments Kael had given her into the bottom of the waste bin under the bathroom sink. She wanted to scrub the scent of him off of her, but once the water was spraying hot out of the showerhead, she couldn't bring herself to step underneath it. Instead, she pulled the end of her braid up to her nose and inhaled deeply. Pine, mossy earth, shadows, magic. It would fade soon, but for now, she could savor the last traces of him there.

In the morning, Rodney drove her and Briar into town in his ancient Subaru, but Aisling lingered in the hallway outside of her apartment door. Coming back into her life felt like tugging on a too-small sweater from the back of the closet: once a perfect fit, now uncomfortable and constricting. Her skin itched and the faint smell of oil and paint that seemed always to waft up from the hardware store on the ground level stung her nose. She'd never minded it before. She missed the smell of the Wild.

A note was taped to her door, a message scrawled in Seb's messy handwriting. *Stopped by to check in after the quake - Li gave me your spare key. Cleaned up a couple broken glasses but everything else looked fine. Let's grab dinner when you get back – Seb.*

Another earthquake. Another echo. Aisling balled the note in her hand and drew in a deep breath, pushing down the guilt that rose in her chest. She opened her door just wide enough to reach in and grab a heavier coat and a pair of gloves, then let Briar pull her back downstairs and onto the street. The cold was his favorite weather; he was all too happy to stay out as long as she wanted. Aisling let him take the lead and he meandered in the direction of the harbor.

"Aisling! You're back!" Lida's loud greeting made Aisling's heart skip a beat. She fumbled for words for a moment, then reminded herself of the weak explanation Rodney told her he'd given when her friends had asked after her. *From the city. Back from the city.*

Lida was waving excitedly from the other side of the street. Aisling raised a hand in response. The tight smile she willed to her lips didn't come close to reaching her eyes. "Hey, Li."

Lida hurried across the intersection to meet Aisling at the corner. Briar's favorite of Aisling's friends, he strained against the leash to push his head into her hand. She scratched behind his ears. "Rodney said you went to quit your job. How did that go?"

"Fine." Inwardly, Aisling seethed; he'd left that part out. Of course, they'd probably gone ahead and fired her by now anyway. And after everything she'd been through, the idea of dressing in a suit and tottering into the office on high heels to sit behind a desk was nearly laughable.

As Lida talked, Aisling tried her best to listen. But the way their breath curled into the cold air, ghostly tendrils that swirled lazily on the breeze, resembled all too closely Kael's dancing shadows. Aisling breathed into her gloved hands instead.

"What are you doing right now?" Lida asked. "Are you on your way somewhere?"

Reluctantly, Aisling shook her head. "Just taking a walk."

"Great!" Lida seized her hand and began leading her in the opposite direction. "I'm on my way to Savers; Jackson and I are going for a weekend away in Anacortes and I want a new date night outfit."

Savers, now Dogwood Boutique, was one of very few clothing stores on the island. It had been rebranded a few years back as a consignment store, but despite the new owner's best efforts, no one seemed keen on the changes. Savers was a secondhand staple in town; Dogwood Boutique sounded too pretentious for Brook Isle. The consignment section shrank and shrank until it was relegated to the back corner, and the better part of the store reverted back to thrifted bargain racks.

Briar's entrance earned a sidelong glance from the girl at the counter, but most had come to accept him and Aisling as a package deal. Despite his size, he was quiet and careful and far better behaved than some of the smaller dogs—and most of the children—on the island. He stuck close to Aisling's side.

Lida's happy chatter soon faded into a monotone hum in Aisling's ears as she wandered aimlessly between racks, fingers glancing off of the different materials idly. She felt out of place, and there was a stinging loneliness that scratched at the very edges of her heart. It was so faint she only noticed it when she was paying attention, but it was there. And it was consistent.

She drifted then toward a vintage white nightgown that hung between a yellow sundress and a pair of faded jeans. It was long and plain, with just a smattering of lace around the neckline and sleeves. She rubbed the slippery fabric between her thumb and forefinger absently for several seconds before she realized why she'd been drawn to it from across the store. It looked strikingly similar to that white dress she'd been forced to don prior to the ritual when she'd first been imprisoned. She dropped the hem as though it had given her an electric shock.

"Gross, Ash." Lida looked at the dress, nose wrinkled. "That sack wouldn't do you any favors."

No, she couldn't imagine it would. Nor had the one she'd worn that night. When she turned away from it, her eyes snagged on her figure in a mirror on the wall. Her stomach sank. She knew that face: distant, distracted. Haunted. It was her mother's face. She swore under her breath and blinked the image away.

Instead, she looked over the top of a rack of skirts at her friend. She'd known Lida since elementary school; she and Seb had been among the few kids to support Aisling unconditionally through all of her family's ups and downs. It was Lida and Seb who Aisling told, in hushed tones on the playground, about her mother's stories—back when she'd believed them. Lida had held Aisling's hand at her mother's funeral when her father had been too angry and bitter to stay through the service. Lida's parents had kept them fed for months afterward.

As she watched Lida deliberate over a blouse three sizes too large for her tiny frame, Aisling wondered what she'd say now if she were to confide her own stories. She wouldn't—*couldn't*—but it was a nice thought. Certainly Lida would be a better audience for everything Aisling wished she could say about Kael. She hadn't yet told Rodney about that part of her time in the Unseelie Court, though he likely had some idea based on what Lyre told him.

But none of that mattered now. Kael was through with her. If both were lucky, they'd never see each other again.

Satisfied with her purchases, Lida suggested meeting Jackson and Seb for lunch. Aisling craved the distraction, but exhaustion pulled her towards home.

"Raincheck?" Aisling again held her gloved hand cupped around her mouth to catch the vapor before it could remind her too much of her mistakes. "I don't want to leave Briar tied up."

"Of course; I'll plan something for next week when Jackson and I get back." Lida dropped her shopping bag onto the sidewalk abruptly and seized Aisling in a tight hug. She held her close, patiently waiting for Aisling to reciprocate. Slowly, Aisling melted into it, hooking her arms around Lida's back. She soaked in her friend's warmth and let it thaw that bitter chill that encased her.

"Does this mean you're staying?" When Aisling nodded, Lida tightened her grip further for a few more seconds before dropping her arms and pulling back.

"Thanks, Li." She meant it with her whole heart. And on the walk back to her apartment, her heart felt lighter for it.

22

IVRAN & THE DRYADS

AISLING

"I have someone I want you to meet." Rodney stood outside of Aisling's apartment, bouncing one foot anxiously against the ground. He gingerly grasped two steaming to-go cups that were likely burning through his gloves. Aisling gazed at him for a moment through her peephole. She hadn't forgiven him yet.

"I don't want to meet any more of your so-called *friends*, Rodney," she hissed through the door.

"He isn't like Lyre, Ash. He's Solitary, like me." He stacked one cup atop the other so he could shake the heat out of his hands one at a time.

Aisling scoffed. "Is that supposed to make me feel better? I don't particularly like *you* right now, either."

"Come on," he insisted. "Open up. Your tea's getting cold."

Aisling cracked the door only as far as the chain lock would allow. "You didn't bring them here, did you?" So far, Rodney was the only faerie who knew where she lived, and she hoped to keep it that way. When he shook his head, she shut the door, slid the lock, then pulled it open wide.

"Thanks," he said with a grin. Rodney handed Aisling a cup and followed her inside to the living room where Briar was sprawled on the rug. He regarded Rodney lazily from this position, tail thumping on the ground. "Hello to you, too," Rodney acknowledged dryly.

While Rodney fell back onto Aisling's sofa and stretched out his long legs, she stood still only halfway into the room. "So?"

"*So,*" he emphasized, "come sit down and drink your tea, and I'll tell you what I've been working on."

She did so begrudgingly, unconvinced that some manner of Fae wasn't about to burst through her door or clamber out of the backpack he'd dropped beside his shoes on the mat. Briar rolled over to lay his head on her feet. He'd been stuck to her like glue since she'd returned from the Wild, perfectly content to spend the last two days in bed with her.

Despite her best efforts to get back onto a normal sleep schedule, Aisling's head felt fuzzy and clouded. Between the swirling, vicious thoughts and the constant churning in her stomach, she hadn't yet managed it. She'd lie awake, tossing and turning throughout most of the night, then sleep away most of the day. She'd been able to reclaim her afternoons, if only to walk with Briar down to the shore and listen to the sea. Once, she would have gone to the forest to clear her head. She couldn't even bring herself to look towards the tree line now.

Rodney's eyes shone with excitement. She'd humor him for now. "Fine, I'll bite. What have you been working on?"

"What would you say if I told you that I could get you into the Seelie Court tomorrow?" He took a sip from his cup. The smug expression he wore nearly made Aisling want to slap him all over again.

"I would say, why don't we just go now and get it over with?" It came out harsher than she meant it to, but the sentiment underlying her words wasn't one she could hide. She did want to get this over with—all of it—so that she could return to her life and try to pretend that none of this had ever happened. She could fulfill whatever was needed from her as the subject of the prophecy and move on.

Rodney rolled his eyes. "Aren't you even a little curious what I was doing while you were gone?"

"Besides not trying to get me out?" she shot back. Rodney winced and the hurt in his eyes weakened her resolve. He felt guilty; she knew he did. In a gesture of goodwill, Aisling settled back on the couch and took a sip of her tea. "Tell me."

"I found the way in. It took a while to convince someone to tell me where to find the Thin Place, and I had to make some bargains that I'm...less than proud of." He rubbed his neck. When he caught Aisling's warning glare, he added quickly, "None that will come back on you. I swear. But I managed to work my way down the line to Ivran."

"Ivran?"

"Ivran knows the dryads who watch over their Thin Place. I doubt they are as close as he likes to claim, but I paid a handsome price for him to broker an introduction." Aisling pictured storybooks with illustrations of leafy, treelike women dancing in meadows and groves. That they, too, could be right here on Brook Isle would have seemed unbelievable just weeks ago.

"Where is the Seelie Thin Place?" She remembered this time to ask the question as specifically as she could. Rodney smiled in approval.

"Do you remember that hike Lida dragged us out on a few years back, up to the viewpoint at the top of the hill on the north side of the island? When it rained the whole time?"

"And you slid halfway down the hill in the mud? I remember." It had been the last hike she'd been able to convince him to join her and her friends on. "There was a bench at the top, I think."

He rolled his eyes. "I'd prefer not to revisit that particular part of the memory. But beyond the viewpoint, back up the hill a bit, there were those two old hawthorn trees."

Aisling frowned, trying to imagine them there. She couldn't call them to mind, only the way the ocean looked from that bench on the cliffside. The water was choppy that day, all whitecapped waves and roiling sea foam. "I don't think I noticed them."

"It's just there, between the two. I guess they bank on people being so distracted by the view that they don't wander back there much." He shrugged, then set his empty cup on the floor. "Either way, Ivran said he'd meet us at the overlook tomorrow morning and take you through."

She bristled at that. She wasn't going into the Wild alone; not again. "Take *us* through," she corrected pointedly. "You're sure as hell not getting out of it. You're coming with me."

"I figured you might say that." Rodney stretched, then settled deeper into the cushions. Drawing out Aisling's anticipation to an annoying degree. "I've already requested time off work."

∴

The wind was biting as the pair climbed the trail. There were steps, but they were steep and slick and Rodney complained the entire way up that he hadn't worn the right shoes. Aisling had cautioned him earlier that morning when he picked her up that even his work boots would have been a wiser choice than the flat sneakers he'd settled for, but he'd refused to return to the trailer to make the switch. Evidently, the strenuous hike uphill had faded from his memory.

Briar was as unbothered by the cold as he was by the grade of the trail, so Aisling looped his leash around her waist and let him pull her along. She'd deliberated most of the night about bringing him, but in the end, she hadn't been able to leave him behind. She needed him to be her anchor. She was nervous; more nervous even than she had been entering the Undercastle for the first time on Nocturne. She'd been naïve then. Now, she knew just what kind of trouble could await her through the Veil.

"I'm curious about something," Aisling panted. The wind whipped her hair across her face, prompting her to reach back and secure the end of her ponytail under her jacket collar. "Why did Lyre owe you a favor in the first place?"

Rodney was stopped in the middle of the trail. Bent over, hands on his knees, catching his breath for the tenth time. He looked up at Aisling, squinting against the sea salt that somehow still stung even as high up as they were. "What?"

"I asked him whether you were trying to get me out, and he said that he didn't owe you that big of a favor."

Still breathless, he waved a hand dismissively. "He just likes me to keep my ear to the ground at events like Nocturne and such. In case you hadn't noticed, I'm a bit less conspicuous than he and those other robed zealots."

Aisling's skin prickled uncomfortably when she recalled how Lyre's yellow eyes flashed in the low light. "I'm not sure I like Lyre."

Rodney laughed, finally able to stand upright again. "No one really likes Lyre, Ash, but you can't deny that he's useful. He's a good ally to keep in your corner."

"I thought the same until he blackmailed me. He was using me the entire time." The pair resumed their climb slowly, side by side.

"It's in his nature," he explained simply. "All of our nature, really. And I'd say you took to it rather well yourself."

Aisling ground her teeth but remained silent. Though Lyre had undoubtedly told him of her closeness with Kael, Rodney still believed that she'd been manipulating him all along. Playing the role they'd crafted for her from the very first night. For now, she was content to let him believe it. Having never once seen him so much as glance at any woman or man on the island, she couldn't imagine he'd understand. Even if he did, he'd still think her irrational for it. She certainly did.

Once they made it to the overlook, Rodney fell onto the bench. The weatherworn wood creaked under his weight. Aisling stood closer to the edge to take in the view. It was too foggy to see as far as Waldron Island to the east, and too cold to linger long, but for a moment she savored it: the quickening of her heart as she looked over the cliffside, the turbulent sea surging against the rocks below. It looked the way she felt inside.

When she turned back, her gaze landed on the hawthorn trees. A safe distance off the trail, they stood together to face the battering winds. Despite the winter chill, their branches were still laden with clusters of berries, tiny rubies among blazing golden leaves. They wouldn't last much longer, particularly once the morning frosts arrived, but for now they clung steadfastly to life. She admired them for it: their resilience.

"Ash," Rodney said, dragging her attention away from the trees. "I'd like to introduce you to Ivran."

She understood at once why she hadn't heard the faerie approach: he was small, maybe only as large as a loaf of bread. He was perched on the back of the bench not far from Rodney's shoulder and balanced himself against each gust of wind with long, translucent wings. The membranes that threaded them so delicately caught what little sunlight strayed through the clouds overhead, glittering. An unruly mop of golden curls framed a ruddy, boyish face with pointed features.

But it was the male's lower body that most clearly marked him as Fae. From the waist down, he took on the form of a grasshopper. His two hind legs, thin and spiny, mirrored those of the insect, each bending at a sharp angle near the top.

Aisling approached slowly. She did her best not to stare, but his unusual form was captivating. Thus far, it was the most remarkable she'd seen yet. To his credit, despite being an avid bug chaser, Briar was unaffected.

"Ivran, Aisling. Aisling, Ivran." Rodney gestured between the two. Ivran dipped his upper half in a sort of bow, wavering a bit on his perch.

"A pleasure, miss," he chirped. His voice was exactly as she'd expected it to sound, not terribly far off from the insect's evening song. A sweet, lilting intonation.

Aisling smiled, her first genuine grin in days. The joy that seemed to radiate from the faerie was infectious. "The pleasure's mine, Ivran. We're grateful for your help."

"Don't be too quick to thank me; I haven't gotten you in just yet." He winked and his upturned black eyes sparkled mischievously. "What business does a human and a changeling have with the Seelie Court, anyhow?"

Before Aisling could give an excuse, Rodney said smoothly, "Business that is none of yours."

Ivran raised his hands. "Point taken, my friend. Let's get to it then." He sprang from the bench to the ground, beckoning over his slender shoulder, and Rodney and Aisling followed him towards the trees. His iridescent green exoskeleton shimmered blue and purple as he hopped along. Halfway there, he paused, drawing the group to a stop. Briar halted just short of stepping on one of his limbs. "Wait here."

Ivran bounded ahead and up into one of the trees. If Aisling squinted, she could just see him whispering against its trunk. She blinked, and two females materialized as though they had peeled themselves from the bark. Indeed, their skin resembled the texture of bark, but softer. It bore intricate patterns that mimicked the swirling grain of wood. An earthy scent followed in their wake, reminiscent of freshly turned soil.

As they conversed with Ivran, each ribbon of their cascading ivy hair seemed to sway with a life of its own while the leaves up above did the same on the ocean breeze. Their limbs moved just as fluidly as the branches. They were the hawthorn trees, come to life. Aisling couldn't help staring this time, mesmerized.

When Ivran nodded in their direction, Rodney nudged Aisling and they continued their approach. Aisling kept Briar at her side on a short leash. The dryads acknowledged them silently, each retreating to press her back against her respective tree. Ivran gazed at their lithe, swaying forms, love-struck.

"What was the price you paid for this, exactly?" Aisling asked under her breath.

Rodney smirked. "A glamour. He wanted to be a man for a night, to lay with one of them. Or both, maybe. I didn't ask him to clarify."

Aisling raised her eyebrows, glancing down again at Ivran. "Did he?"

"I filled my half of the bargain; I don't care to know whether or not he followed through."

She felt a twinge of sadness for the tiny faerie, longing for what he couldn't have. If he had gotten his wish, she wondered whether he felt better or worse for it. If she could have, she would have told him that it is far less painful to remain blissfully ignorant than to miss something one might never have again.

The dryads leaned in towards each other, then, to clasp their hands high overhead. By the rustling of the leaves, it appeared that the hemlock trees followed suit. Between them, beneath their long arms, the Veil shimmered into view. Aisling sucked in a breath and pulled Briar in tighter. Rodney took her free hand, steadying her.

"Enjoy your visit," Ivran trilled.

23

THE SEELIE COURT

AISLING

The Veil in the Seelie Thin Place felt less like a sticky, grasping cobweb and more like a smooth sheet of satin that slid over Aisling's skin. They'd emerged between two hawthorn trees, identical to those they just left save for the leaves, which here were dense and green. Immediately, she had to shield her eyes from the bright sun that hung overhead. It was tinged the same angry red as it had been in the human realm. Over Brook Isle, though, it had since returned to normal as the shifting autumn winds pulled the smoke out of the sky. There was no smoke here, but the rays washed everything with a faint hue of dusty pink.

Before her eyes could fully adjust, Aisling felt Rodney's grip on her hand tighten.

"Ash—" he choked out, voice low.

Something cold and harsh pressed against the side of her neck. A blade; she could tell without reaching up to feel it. Though she couldn't see her captor, she could see Rodney's. He, too, was held still by the edge of a dagger. The one against his neck was curved so that its pointed tip dug into his opposite cheek. A firm hand seized the back of Aisling's jacket and Briar, growling, snapped his teeth at another that reached for his collar.

The guards that found them were tall and lean, with bronze skin and eyes as clear blue as the sky above. Their pale armor shone rose gold in this light; the way it conformed to their bodies made it appear less like metal and more like a second skin, delicate yet strong. There were four of them, expressions hard as they took in their catch.

The first to speak was the female holding Aisling. "A girl, a beast, and a..." She sniffed and her voice took on a tone of disdain. "A changeling. What cause have you for entering our realm?"

"We're acquaintances of the dryads; they granted us passage to visit your court." Rodney bowed his head, shooting Aisling a look wordlessly urging her to do the same.

Instead, Aisling straightened her posture as much as the guard's tight grip would allow. "My name is Aisling, and I'm the Red Woman. I've come with the White Bear seeking an audience with your queen. The *púca* is my escort."

She'd practiced saying those words out loud the night before, then again and again in her head as she and Rodney climbed up to the overlook. But she hadn't planned to say them outright—she'd hoped to save them for the right time, the right audience. So when the words formed on her lips seemingly of their own volition, coming out even stronger and surer than she'd rehearsed, both she and Rodney were caught off-guard. He stared at her, eyes wide and mouth agape.

A tense silence fell over the guards for a brief moment, before they began speaking rapidly to each other in a language with a lyrical cadence that was both foreign and strangely captivating. Their words flowed together as melodically as birdsong. Though she couldn't understand the meaning behind the sounds, the beauty of the language itself was undeniable. Rodney looked less than impressed.

By the deferential tone of the other three, Aisling guessed that the faerie still holding a dagger to her throat was in charge of the group. When they quieted, she lowered the dagger. The male behind Rodney followed suit, and he sucked in a ragged gasp as though he'd just been strangled. Aisling had to bite back a smirk; she'd been through far worse in the Unseelie Court, and she'd been alone then. Suddenly, she didn't feel quite so afraid.

She tipped her chin upwards, looking to the sky. Two of the faeries followed her line of sight. "Aethar sent the red sun as one of your signs; the convergence has already come and gone. I'm here now, and I wish to speak with your queen."

The other three stepped back, and the broad-shouldered female began walking away from the group. "Keep up," she called over her shoulder.

The valley before them, lush and green, glowed golden just as Aisling's mother had described. Wildflowers in soft pastels blanketed the ground nearly as thick as the grass, scenting the air with their sweet perfume. A warm breeze whispered across her cheeks and invited her deeper into the Seelie Court. It carried with it soft strains of a tune being played somewhere in the distance. The quiet song pulled at an invisible string woven between Aisling's ribs, calling her to run. To play. To dance. It buoyed her spirit and she shed all of the pain she'd carried with her through the Veil like a sodden cloak. She let it drop to the ground and walked away from it lighter.

Rodney noticed the faraway look in her eyes and elbowed her sharply. "Watch yourself," he cautioned. Aisling shrugged off his warning and glanced down at Briar, who had settled down and now seemed just as enthralled as she was. Had he not been leashed at her side, he would likely have raced off into the tall grass after one of the tiny faeries that rose up and fluttered away as they passed by.

Beads of sweat were beginning to form beneath Aisling's hair; both she and Rodney had to strip off several layers as they walked. The faerie ahead of them was wholly unbothered by the heat, even laden with armor as she was. Her helmet must have been stifling. Aisling wondered about the distance between the Seelie and Unseelie Courts. It had appeared vast on the map in Kael's study, but it must have been even greater than she'd thought for the climates to be so strikingly varied.

The guard's path cut down a low hill toward a small lake. The crystalline blue of the water, only a few shades deeper than the sky, glittered in the sunlight where ripples spread from things darting unseen beneath its surface. Tall, swaying cattails bordered the shoreline. Sprites, similar to the one Aisling had rescued all those weeks ago, clung to the stalks at different heights. They cackled as their perches danced back and forth. The scene made her wish she could draw, or paint, or otherwise capture it in some way as her mother had. Her memory wouldn't do it justice.

There was a figure in the lake, submerged save for the very top of their head. Long tendrils of ebony hair floated in a halo around them, drifting lazily with the currents stirred by their movements through the water. The guard increased her pace to reach the lakeside before Aisling and Rodney. Rodney caught Aisling's wrist and urged her to wait. She was impatient; she had hoped they would be taken straight to the queen.

When the guard removed her helmet, a long auburn braid unfurled and fell down her back. She called out to the figure in the water in their singsong language. Aisling thought she heard her name and listened more closely. The figure hardly acknowledged her words, lifting one hand out of the water to beckon dismissively. The guard shook her head, then twisted up her braid and repositioned her helmet. She turned and gave a sharp nod before retreating in the direction the group had just come from. Aisling watched, confused.

"Should we—" she began, looking over at Rodney and turning to follow the guard. She halted when she noticed his face. Rodney was gazing slack-jawed at the water, eyes wide and glassy, with a vivid blush creeping up into his cheeks.

The figure in the lake had risen to stand, the waterline now just reaching her bare stomach. She pushed her dark hair back from her face, which had all the sharp angles and upturned features Aisling had come to expect in the Fae. She moved languidly towards the shore, each step revealing more of her body. Two gossamer wings followed, trailing behind her like the train of a gown. Droplets of water slid down every curve of her immaculate porcelain skin. They caught the sunlight as they moved: tiny, glittering diamonds that made her luminous complexion even more radiant.

"Stay here." Aisling tapped her fingers under Rodney's chin to close his mouth then led Briar down to the edge of the lake. Wholly unashamed of her nude body, the faerie crossed the last few yards entirely exposed. Aisling remained spellbound by her ethereal features: the elegant curve of her neck, the slender lines of her limbs, the shimmering strands of dark hair that clung to her form like liquid silk. Absolute, unrivaled beauty in its purest form—the kind that inspired songwriters and artists, a muse to their craft.

"The Red Woman," the female marveled. "We've been waiting for you for a very long time."

"You knew I was coming?" As the faerie stood nude before her, Aisling cast her eyes downward. She didn't possess the countenance of a warrior, as Kael did, but of a royal. This was the queen—Aisling could feel it. She wondered briefly whether she should curtsy or bow.

The faerie stopped once they were standing nearly toe-to-toe, then cupped Aisling's cheek with a damp hand to tilt her face upwards. Aisling let her, lifting her gaze along with it to meet the queen's eyes. They were a deep shade of purple, like two flawless amethysts. They stared straight into Aisling—straight into her mind, her soul. If the queen had been able to see all of her deepest, innermost secrets, she wouldn't have been at all surprised. As it was, the queen's violet eyes seemed to hold just as much awe as her own.

"My sweet girl, from the moment our sun rose red, I knew it was only a matter of time before we'd meet. Aisling, is it?" When

Aisling nodded, still held captive by those eyes, she smiled. "I'm Laure. Welcome to my court."

Aisling couldn't help feeling moved by the benevolence in Laure's tone. It carried an almost maternal tenderness, as if she were soothing a wounded fawn. It was enough to make her regret ever setting foot in the Unseelie Court in the first place. Here, she was welcomed. Loved, even. There...she couldn't imagine what Kael must think about her now without bile forcing its way up her throat.

"It's an honor, Your Highness." Aisling dipped her head, careful to look away from the queen's body.

Laure looked down at herself, as if realizing for the first time that she was still nude. She laughed and reached for a light, backless cotton gown that hung from the tip of a cattail. "I suppose this was not the welcome you expected. I'm afraid I've grown rather accustomed to doing as I please here; we all have. Even our visitors tend to embrace it once the shock wears off." She winked at Aisling as she carefully arranged the dress around her wings.

A brief electric thrill zipped up Aisling's spine when she realized for the first time how constricting her own clothes felt against her skin.

"It's beautiful here," Aisling said sincerely.

Laure smiled, smoothing her hands over her bodice. "It is, isn't it?" She looked down then, at Briar. "And am I correct to assume that this is the White Bear?"

Aisling nodded and nudged him to sit. "Briar. White, though not exactly a bear."

A warm laugh again escaped Laure's lips, and Aisling felt a deep sense of satisfaction knowing that she was the one who had brought forth that musical sound.

"Fae prophecies aren't so rigid as they seem; they're quite open to interpretation. In fact, I'm rather glad you didn't show up here with a bear at your side. Come." Reaching out, Laure took Aisling's hand in her own. Her palm was cool and soft; a hand that had never known labor of any kind.

"Go find Rodney," Aisling told Briar. She dropped the leash, and he bounded up the hill to where Rodney was waiting uncomfortably. Aisling gestured to him to wait there, then let Laure lead her to walk around the edge of the lake.

"So, who was it that found you?" Laure asked. Her strides were leisurely. Graceful. Aisling snuck a look back at her wings that swept through the grass behind them.

For what felt like the hundredth time, Aisling recounted her meeting with the Shadowwood Mother.

Laure hummed, the barest hint of irritation underlying her tone. "She chose not to share that with us, last we visited. And you began your search for answers in the Unseelie Court, did you not?"

Aisling's steps faltered momentarily before she regained her composure. "Do you have spies there?"

"Nothing like that." Laure smiled down at her, then shifted her attention back to the meadow of wildflowers that stretched on ahead. "But I had heard rumors of the king's taking a human prisoner. About a sort of...influence you may have possessed. Is it true?"

Aisling remained quiet, choosing not to answer Laure's question. Her connection with Kael's magic, whatever it may have been, had little to do with her being the Red Woman.

Seeming to understand Aisling's silence, Laure nodded knowingly. "Kael Ardhen is a terribly powerful creature. A true monster, the likes of which I've not encountered elsewhere in my lifetime. You would do well to remember that."

Kael Ardhen. Laure had pronounced each syllable slowly. Deliberately. She wanted Aisling to understand the weight of the gift she was giving her—the gift of Kael's full name. The gift of control. Though if Laure had known it for any amount of time, Aisling wondered why she hadn't yet used it to her own advantage.

"And I hope," Laure added, "that the prophecy rings true. That you are the key to his downfall. His subjects deserve to know peace as mine do."

Aisling thought of the Solitary Fae she'd seen in the battle at Nyctara, clad in too-large armor with swords that hadn't seen a whetstone in an age. There was certainly no peace in the Seelie Court for them, either. She kept this opinion to herself, instead lifting a hand to shield her eyes from the sun and casting her gaze towards the mountains.

"What's that place?" High on the mountainside, tucked between sharp peaks, Aisling noticed a large structure, white even under the rays of the red sun. It looked like it was carved from a type of stone; its tall spires glittered in the afternoon light.

"That is Solanthis, our temple of worship." Laure smiled at the image of the temple in the distance, maybe imagining herself inside its sacred walls.

"Is Aethar your god?" Aisling asked. Laure stopped to look up at it as well. They were atop a low rolling hill now, with the lake just below. "The one that was said to have sent the red sun?"

"She is. She has been good to us since the birth of our court. I'd like to take you to see the temple if you're interested; very few humans have ever set foot inside."

Aisling nodded vigorously. There was something about Laure that made Aisling desperately eager to please her. The air she carried about her, maybe, or the way light seemed to be drawn to her like it was caught in some sort of gravitational pull.

"Excellent. You and I will ride out to the temple tomorrow at dawn. It's not nearly as far a journey as it looks, I promise." Laure squeezed her hand. "And I believe I will order a feast in your honor tomorrow evening." She said it thoughtfully, already planning and beginning preparations in her mind.

For just a moment, before Aisling let herself be swept away by the queen's promises, she hesitated. She knew that she might remain there for some time, but she hadn't fully considered it when Rodney had picked her up from her apartment that morning. She hadn't even packed an overnight bag.

Laure left Aisling to explore and promised to send a messenger to take her to the palace once she'd had her fill. She didn't think she ever would; she could stare at that wide open valley for hours and hours and never tire of it.

Careful to walk only on the trodden path to avoid stepping on the flowers or any other manner of living thing, Aisling returned to where Rodney and Briar were sitting in the grass. Rodney cut a harsh contrast against the landscape in his black torn jeans and oil-stained T-shirt. Despite the beauty around them, he wore a scowl on his face. Briar's expression was one of pure bliss, his tongue lolling from his mouth as two sky blue nymphs wove flowers into his fur with nimble fingers. Even standing on their toes, they only just reached his mid-back.

"So?" he asked.

"So, I'm staying. At least for a couple nights." Aisling lowered herself into the grass beside him and plucked a piece to wind around her fingers. The nymphs scampered off, twittering to each other.

"*We*," he corrected, just as she had the day before. Anticipating her protest, he added, "I know you can handle it fine on your own. But I'm not leaving you this time."

Feeling selfish over just how grateful she was for him in that moment, Aisling wordlessly leaned her head against her friend's shoulder. They stayed there for some time, eventually falling onto their backs to watch the clouds drift by overhead.

As the afternoon light shifted into evening, the guard returned for them. Her expression as she beckoned them to follow was as unyielding as before, though she no longer wore her helmet or carried her dagger unsheathed.

"There's something down in that lake." Rodney paused to glance at it warily as they passed by.

Aisling examined its surface, still now without Laure treading water. "What, like fish?"

"I don't think so. Bigger." He shook his head and barely suppressed a shiver. "I don't like it."

"Well no one is making you swim in it. Come on." Aisling took his arm and hauled him away from the shore.

By the time they reached the palace, it was too dark to make out many of its features beyond its general shape silhouetted against the dusky sky. Bright torches illuminated two great stone creatures flanking the large door as sentries. Though they were unmoving, she was almost sure their eyes followed as they passed.

"*Manticores,*" Rodney hissed. "Don't speak to them." The edge of fear in his voice drew a chill down Aisling's arms, raising goosebumps. She drew them tightly across her chest in an effort to give the creatures a wide berth as they walked between their motionless forms.

"The queen is unavailable tonight, but dinner will be sent to your chambers." The guard said the words coolly without glancing back at the trio. "We do not keep the palace lit at night, so do not wander."

Indeed, the interior of the palace was quiet and dark. The guard carried a single candle to light their way, which she left in a candlestick on a table between two steaming plates of food before leaving Aisling, Rodney, and Briar alone.

They dined together quietly in the small room. Rodney had sniffed Aisling's food, peering at it from all angles, looking for any hint of enchantment. Even once he'd deemed it safe, she could do little more than push it around her plate. Briar ate most of it.

Aisling was afraid, the false bravado she'd so skillfully projected having disappeared along with the warmth and the sunlight of the afternoon.

So she didn't bother to argue when Rodney later crept through the door between their adjoined rooms, a pillow tucked under his arm. Didn't tell him to leave when he nudged Briar over and settled in on the far side of the bed, his head by Aisling's feet. Though she knew she should have forced him back through the Veil when she'd decided to stay, as she laid there listening to the sounds of his slow breathing and Briar's soft snores, Aisling could hardly imagine facing this alone.

24

THE BREATH OF LIFE

AISLING

Aisling awoke just as dawn was beginning to break, having slept far more soundly than she'd expected. Briar and Rodney were still fast asleep sprawled on the bed beside her, so she carefully eased herself off the mattress and slipped out of the room before pausing in the hall to pull on her shoes. The palace was beginning to wake around her, and much like evenings in the Undercastle, the halls were filled with sounds of lesser faeries bustling back and forth to ready those they served.

In the light, Aisling was able to take in the Seelie palace more fully. The details that had been hidden by darkness the night before now danced around her. The palace was more opulent than she could have imagined, almost Baroque in its elegance and scale. The crown molding framing each space was hand-carved with swirling filigree patterns, coated in shining gold leaf. Chandeliers dripping with crystals refracted the sun in rainbow patterns across damask wallpaper.

She had to crane her neck to admire the frescoes that adorned the ceilings, all in soft, faded pastel shades depicting scenes of nature and magic intertwined. Marble statues of ethereal beings frozen in time peppered the corridors, tucked into corners and alcoves. Though most of them were missing various body parts, their serene beauty was no less for it. Aisling didn't let her eyes linger on any of them for too long for fear they'd turn to meet her gaze.

The guard had chosen a wing to house Aisling and Rodney that was not too deep into the palace. Aisling had memorized the turns they took from the front door and was able to retrace that path without error. A carryover, she realized, from her time spent memorizing the routes in and out of the different spaces she'd been held in the Undercastle. She would never be that lost, helpless prisoner again.

Laure was waiting on the front path astride a large white stallion. Its mane was woven through with flowers, just as her own long black hair was this morning. She held the reins of a second horse, this one a soft dappled gray.

"Good morning," she greeted Aisling with a kind smile. "I hope that you found your accommodations comfortable. I do apologize that I was unavailable to show them to you myself."

Aisling quickened her pace as she passed between the manticores, then slowed her approach to the horses. They paid her little mind. She turned then, to take in the exterior of the palace. It was just as grandiose as the interior, with scarcely an inch left untouched by ornamental scrollwork and sculpted reliefs. "It's beautiful," Aisling said. It was, in a way, though she found the sum of all its parts to be slightly overwhelming, too.

Laure leaned down to offer her the reins to the gray horse. "Do you know how to ride?"

Aisling's mind briefly flickered to the two times she'd been on horseback: once, with an anonymous soldier cantering out to the Nyctara front, to what she'd been sure would be her death. The second, gripped by a fading Kael racing back to the Undercastle, still not convinced she'd be alive beyond nightfall. She shook her head. "No, but I understand the concept."

She hitched a leg up to wedge the toe of her hiking boot into the stirrup, then hauled herself up into the saddle while Laure kept the horse still. Its back was broad between her legs, much wider than Kael's skeletal mare.

"We'll ride slow; there's no hurry." Laure guided her horse to turn and proceeded at a comfortable pace. Aisling had to do very little beyond remaining upright; her horse followed Laure's and fell into step by its side.

They rode in silence for a time, the quiet of the valley punctuated by lilting birdsong and distant laughter. Aisling wondered when the music would begin, whether it was an everyday occurrence. As swaths of morning fog drifted lazily across the mountainside, Solanthis appeared almost to be floating on the white mist, rather than anchored to the rough stone.

Laure's body moved as one with her horse, graceful and steady. She wore a velvet cloak of sage green clasped at her breastbone that hid her wings and fanned over the animal's hindquarters. Turning in her saddle, Aisling met Laure's sparkling amethyst eyes.

"Why is your Thin Place so heavily guarded?" She'd been curious about the number of sentries posted there; four seemed too many for their relative strength. Certainly for visitors like herself and Rodney, unarmed and wholly unprepared for confrontation.

"The Unseelie Court tends to hide their entrances in places that keep people out on their own. As we choose more pleasing locations for ours, we must use different methods of protection."

"I didn't know that you chose the locations." Aisling's horse huffed in annoyance when she tightened her thighs against it for balance as it trotted through a small stream. "Does that mean you can move them, too?"

Laure nodded. "We can, but rarely have need to. They are simple enough to close, but establishing a new opening is a difficult task."

"Then the one that I came through—it's been there awhile?" Aisling chewed on the inside of her cheek. She pictured her mother making that hike, greeting the dryads, and passing through that thin skein of magic.

"I would imagine so; I don't believe we've moved any in a century or more." Laure answered as though she knew already what Aisling had been waiting to ask.

"My mother came here, I think. It's exactly how she described it." A sad smile played on her lips when she looked across the boundless meadow. *Bathed in golden sunlight.*

"What was your mother's name?" Laure asked.

"Maeve," Aisling said. "Maeve Morrow. She looked a little like me, I think, or rather I look like her. But her hair was redder than mine." She'd always wished growing up that she could trade her honey hair for her mother's auburn waves.

Laure thought for a moment, then shook her head. "Human visitors are more common here than you might assume. I am sorry sweetling, truly."

The quiet that followed was laced with a disappointment palpable enough that Laure reached across the space between the horses to brush her fingertips over Aisling's arm.

∴

As promised, the ride to the base of the mountain peak wasn't nearly as long as it looked. Rather, it seemed that at the same time that they were moving in its direction, it was also drawing closer towards them. The ascent to the temple was a different story.

Stairs—hundreds of them—were carved into the mountainside, guarded on either side by ropes woven from a pliant metal that gleamed silver. It was cool to the touch under Aisling's desperate grip. Her legs protested as she climbed step after step and her breathing became labored as the altitude got the better of her lungs. Laure was entirely unaffected, and graciously continued a short distance ahead to allow Aisling some privacy to struggle her way up.

The view was as breathtaking as the climb.

Too high up to make out each individual flower, the valley of the Seelie territory was a watercolor wash of greens and pinks and purples and blues. Overlooking it all, the white marble columns of Solanthis rose strong and powerful. Above them, three triangular peaks towered up and up and up, each one larger than the last. The spire of the topmost steeple soared to such dizzying heights it disappeared into the bright sun.

"It was constructed here for a purpose," Laure intoned from the cliffside. Her hair and dress billowed behind her in the warm breeze.

Aisling kept a firm hold on the ropes that banked the stairs. Heights had never bothered her before, but this was coming awfully close. "To watch over your land?" she guessed.

Laure turned back and took Aisling's hand, pulling her toward the temple's entrance. "Aethar came to us when our court was born. In a time of great darkness, she brought light. She taught us to hope; she guides us to keep that hope alive no matter what we must face."

Her words echoed off the walls of the vestibule, which were carved into a smooth ribbed pattern. Vaguely, running the tips of her fingers over each wave, Aisling thought it resembled a gaping maw. And Laure was leading her into the belly of the beast.

"She is the air; the Breath of Life that sustains each and every living thing. We built our temple to her here on the mountainside, high up where the air is thinnest." Laure released Aisling's hand to step into the center of the nave, where a circle of light pooled on the pristine floor. Overhead, a colossal dome was left open in the center to allow the sunlight to stream in. "Where She can most easily hear our prayers."

Curling vines cascaded across every surface, laden with sweet-smelling flowers. They poured from great alabaster urns and dripped down over the balustrades of a sweeping staircase further in. Laure touched them as she drifted past, and they seemed to bloom brighter for it.

"It feels peaceful here," Aisling said. She trailed behind Laure, who had paused at a small alcove to light a stick of incense. Its smell was fragrant and heady.

"She's just there, Her likeness. I commissioned it when I took the crown." Laure nodded toward a mural that depicted a being of pure light, almost fluid though the painting remained static. The hues flowed seamlessly between golds, silvers, and an opalescent color Aisling hadn't a name for. The form in the center was only vaguely human in its shape, with great feathered wings rising from her back and arms that reached and reached outward. Tranquil, but undeniably powerful. "The satyr who painted it swore She came to him in a dream."

Aisling hummed, studying the nearly amorphous figure. "She's certainly more pleasing to look at than the Low One."

Laure hissed, reacting viscerally to the Unseelie god's title. "The Unseelie Court's *religion* is little more than a corrupt bastardization. Their god is no god, but some dark entity their zealots encountered long ago and never let die." She did not suppress her shudder, nor did she attempt to mask the revulsion in her tone.

Still, Aisling was curious. So she pressed: "Whatever it is, it seems connected to the king's magic." She was cautious not to say his name, even in her own head.

"Worshiping that twisted idol is little more than an excuse to revere the depraved. To place blame for all of their misdeeds and their failures on the chaotic nature of the unknown." Laure turned away to gaze up at the mural of Aethar and took several breaths to soften the edge of anger that had taken hold of her.

Aisling moved away to allow Laure space, slightly taken aback by how harshly she'd reacted. A conflict between religions felt so utterly human; she hadn't imagined the Fae would concern themselves over something so trivial.

When she felt Laure's hands brush featherlight against the skin of her neck, she jumped.

"For you," she said, all traces of rage gone now. Aisling looked down to where a small weight had settled against her breast. A circular golden pendant hung there from a thin chain. She lifted it to examine the gift more closely, laying it flat on her palm. The pendant was inscribed with letters she couldn't read, and carved with a tiny, simplified likeness of the mural they stood beneath. On the back, it bore an etching of a sort of cross.

"I can't accept this." All the same, Aisling let it fall back down to rest just beneath the collar of her shirt. The metal felt warm against her skin. She looked up at Laure. "What does it say?"

She said the words first in that melodic, dulcet language, then, "Breath of Life. May Aethar bring you blessings; you deserve every one. I don't doubt that you have a difficult road ahead, and I hope you know that I will stand by you the entire way."

Aisling had to quell the urge to throw her arms around the Seelie Queen. This was the support she'd longed to find since the moment she'd left the Shadowwood Mother's thicket. Instead, she offered only a quiet thanks.

The pair was interrupted by a wraithlike sidhe gliding down the staircase, a stack of tomes clutched in her shimmering arms. Aisling peered up towards the landing, but there was only a pale green door.

"I'd like to learn more about my prophecy, if there is anything more to know," she began, and nodded towards the sidhe's retreating figure. "Do you have archives here? Or in your palace?"

Laure nodded. "Of course; all of our texts are kept here in a reading room at the top of the tower. You're welcome to visit whenever you'd like. I will arrange for a keeper to meet you and show you how the manuscripts are catalogued. It's not an easy system to follow," she laughed lightly.

"I'd appreciate that, thanks." Aisling thought she might return with Rodney. He would complain about the trip up, but it would be useful to have a second set of eyes.

Outside the peace of Solanthis, as they made their precarious descent, Aisling's head began to ache sharply. When she drew in a breath of air, the sweetness she'd thought so pleasant the day before now seemed thick and cloying. A film of it coated her tongue, her throat, the membranes of her lungs. She could drown in it, that floral perfume.

Closer to the palace, a thin, wavering voice sang a song Aisling didn't recognize. It grew louder as they rode until they passed a woman, not much older than Aisling and undoubtedly human, standing amidst a circle of faeries. The small group sat on the ground, watching her performance. Another, a sylph, fluttered close by her side. They ran their elongated fingers through her hair in time with the song. She swayed with each stroke, both of them keeping the steady, driving rhythm. Her eyes were dull. Dead. The look on the woman's face made the hair on the back of Aisling's neck stand on end.

"Just a light enchantment," Laure assured in a conspiratorial whisper, herself tapping a toe in her stirrup, enjoying the song. "A bit of harmless fun."

Aisling teetered on the edge between awed and discomforted. There was a heaviness to the magic here that left her feeling just shy of ill at ease, though she couldn't pinpoint why. It wasn't dark or cruel as the Unseelie Court had felt, with its dampness and constant chill, but there was something different that she wasn't entirely sure she preferred.

25

SHATTERED

KAEL

Having now known calm, having now known what it meant to be in control through the release of the very same, Kael's shadows were more unsettled than ever. He'd not lost his grip—his center—in this way in a very long time, and his court was grateful for it. Now, as he hid away in the pitch-dark of his chamber, the pain he bore was unimaginable.

He couldn't eat, couldn't rest. Couldn't think. Every breath was an agonizing endeavor.

Raif tried to talk him down. Methild attempted to care for him. Werryn sought to bring him before the altar, to pray to the Low One to ease his struggle. None were successful.

Their hushed tones carried through his thick doors, murmured prayers and whispered discussions about what could be done as though their king was unable to hear. But he heard everything, felt everything. And he knew there was nothing to be done.

In his solitude, Kael's mind raced, his thoughts an array of shattered fragments. He thought of Aisling, the Red Woman, who had loosened his iron-clad control. How she'd saved him only to damn him. This was her fault.

As his vision blurred, he was once again confronted by his past, the relentless thirst for power that had driven him to this point. This was his fault.

The rub of his clothes against his ruined skin was excruciating. The brush of the damp air, even more so. There was no abiding the pain he was now stricken with. Wracked with torment, it was all he could do not to collapse to his knees and curl up on the floor.

Ever the warrior, he fought against the darkness that threatened to swallow him whole with every fiber of his being. But this time, he thought he might not be pulled back from this familiar precipice. If he was lucky, they'd let him fall. His magic could take what was left of him.

Maybe they'd all be better for it.

26

DINNER

AISLING

Rodney had only ventured as far as the front lawn of the palace, waiting impatiently with his ever-present frown, idly unraveling a series of tiny braids in Briar's long tail. Aisling gracelessly dismounted her horse and passed the reins off to a waiting hob.

"I'm going to reek of flowers for a month," he complained by way of greeting.

She scratched Briar's head, then Rodney's. He swatted her hand away. "You offered to stay," she reminded him.

"How was your field trip?" Rodney gave up on the braid he'd been working on and leaned back on his elbows.

Too sore to sit, Aisling stretched her calves against the base of a statuette of a dancing pixie. "Interesting. I never realized how much religion meant to the Fae." For all of her mother's musings, and all the time spent pouring over books in the Brook Isle library and scrolling through slow-loading pages on the internet, Aisling had never once encountered mention of the Low One, or Aethar, or any other Fae deities.

"We're not all heathens. How did you get all the way up there, anyway?" He cupped his hands over his eyes and looked across the valley toward Solanthis. From this distance, it looked even higher up the mountain than it had felt when Aisling and Laure had been standing at its entrance.

"Steps," Aisling said. "Lots of them. I told you to wear better shoes."

"Why?" The trepidation in his voice was obvious.

"That's where they keep their archives. Laure said we could visit."

Rodney groaned. "For *what?*"

"For research." Aisling gave up on her calves and eased down beside him to rub her aching thighs. "Unless you happened to find out how the Red Woman is meant to stop a centuries-long war, then we need any information we can get."

He groaned again, this time accompanying the sound with a dramatic eye roll. "I was hoping *Her Majesty* would be able to help you with that."

"She didn't seem to know much at all," Aisling said quietly.

Rodney caught her tone. "Your mom?" When Aisling just shook her head, he sighed. "I'm sorry, Ash."

She shrugged. "I wasn't expecting much."

Her attention was caught then by movement amidst a grove of citrus trees a short distance away, where two impossibly thin females in sheer white gowns were leading a plump boy with golden curls in a dizzy sort of dance. One held him by the wrist, spinning him around and around while he giggled and reached out a chubby hand for the other. His cheeks were flushed with pleasure and his laughter was giddy, but his eyes looked similar to the singing woman's: flat and lifeless. Like one of the fish that occasionally washed ashore near the docks, gills clogged with oil.

"A changeling," Rodney supplied. "There're fewer running around here than I expected; likely most were taken by the Solitaries."

"For what?" Aisling couldn't look away from the boy's awkward toddling.

"Dinner," he said salaciously, then backtracked when Aisling's face paled. "Kidding—kind of. Usually they just live amongst them. Faeries find humans remarkably entertaining."

Aisling turned her back to the trio and focused instead on the gentle rise and fall of Briar's chest. When she could only hear the child's laughter, without seeing those dead, dead eyes, she could imagine him as a normal boy enjoying the company of friends. "Do you think he's here somewhere? The real Rodney?"

"I'm more Rodney than he is," her friend said, almost defensive. "But no, likely not. The baby whose place I took was frail and sick; born too early. I was nothing short of a miracle for his parents."

Aisling smiled then, a fraction of the tension she carried falling from her shoulders. "I knew you were one of the good ones."

"Tea?" A pixie, only slightly larger than the statue nearby, had appeared from the palace behind them. On blue-tinged hands she balanced a tray laden with a delicate tea set and piles of fruit. Her iridescent wings refracted flickering rainbows onto the grass around them as they caught the sunlight.

Rodney shook his head as Aisling nodded. "Thank you."

"The queen would like you both washed and prepared for supper by sunfall." She flitted away before Aisling could say anything further.

"She didn't need to specify that we're washed," Rodney muttered. But neither of them had showered or changed since they'd arrived in the Seelie Court, and it showed. Aisling thought she must smell like a horse despite the way the floral scent of the meadow clung to her hair. She poured them each a cup of tea. Rodney swirled several spoonfuls of honey into his, noisily hitting the metal against the porcelain. Aisling winced; the cup felt so fragile in her hand she was sure he'd shatter it.

Taking only one sip, Rodney set the tea aside and reached for a bowl of berries. Aisling leaned back, tipping her chin up to feel the sun on her cheeks. The tea brought a haziness to her mind and a warmth to spread down her limbs. A sort of nostalgia for something she didn't know—something maybe she'd never known—settled over her heart. The discomforted feelings from before faded away. She could stay here.

∴

Someone had left a gown folded on the bench at the foot of Aisling's bed. She'd been afraid to touch the fine silk until she'd showered and scrubbed her skin pink. The different soaps and lotions arranged in a basket beside the tub all smelled the same: wildflowers, honey, sunshine. So much brighter than the heady scent of the Unseelie Court, even amongst the blooms of the night garden.

Finally clean, Aisling let her fingers play over the gossamer fabric. It was cool and slid through her hands like water. A soft shade of sky blue, the skirt was embroidered with tiny silver leaves and beaded pearl flowers. There was a corset stitched with the same pattern that she struggled to lace. As she cinched it closed across her bust, the light fabric conformed to her figure. Almost a perfect fit, if a touch long.

Rodney looked exceedingly uncomfortable in a suit of pale lavender, with a tight waistcoat that bore a matching floral pattern. Even Briar had a new collar made from what looked like the castoff fabric from Aisling's gown.

"I feel ridiculous," he said, tugging at the hem of the waistcoat. He hadn't made any effort to tame his hair; it stuck up at odd angles as though he'd just gotten out of bed.

"You *look* ridiculous," Aisling teased. She reached under her hair to clasp the delicate gold chain of her necklace and adjusted the pendant to hang at the center of her chest. It gleamed in the candlelight, a beacon. Rodney noticed. His brow furrowed in consternation.

"You shouldn't accept gifts from the Fae, Ash," he chided. "You'll never see the strings tied to what you're offered until they're being pulled tight."

Aisling waved him away. "Who am I to tell the queen no?"

"You're the Red Woman; you can tell the queen whatever you want." Rodney flicked a lock of hair off of his forehead, then offered Aisling his arm. "Shall we?"

"Briar, close." He padded to her side and she linked her arm through Rodney's.

The aquamarine pixie who had delivered their tea met the trio in the hallway between their rooms to escort them to the dining hall. Their path was lit by candles—dozens and dozens of them. The flickering golden light cast an eerie glow on the frescos above, and the looming shadows of the marble statues seemed to dance in their alcoves. Distantly, a harp played a haunting, melancholic refrain. Aisling supposed it was meant to sound serene and soothing, but the way it echoed off the high ceilings and cold stone was anything but. She tightened her grip on Rodney's arm and dropped her other hand to the top of Briar's head. He leaned into her touch.

The hallways of the palace seemed to stretch and stretch, dreamlike, as though they'd never reach their end. Though the plush carpet dampened their footfall, Aisling still felt her every movement, every breath, was impossibly loud. The pixie, by contrast, glided forward soundlessly.

Rodney swore under his breath, drawing Aisling's attention up from the swirling patterns underfoot. She followed his gaze to an alcove ahead, at the far end of the hallway, where a statue of a woman stood. She was posed with candles on each shoulder, fresh and hardened wax coating her form from breast to hip. Flawlessly sculpted cloth the same shade as her skin wrapped her body loosely, and her hair—all that same pale, pale gray—was coiled atop her head out of the way of the flames. A blindfold hid her eyes, but her face was carved into a peaceful, neutral expression. The detail of the sculpting, from each individual hair on her scalp to the creases of her bare feet, was unlike anything Aisling had ever seen.

And then she moved.

Aisling's blood froze in her veins. She stopped short, jerking Rodney backwards. Her body refused to move any closer to the figure. Briar halted too, his hackles raised and a low growl rumbling deep in his chest.

"Just keep your head down," Rodney said quietly in her ear.

"What the fuck is that?" Aisling hissed. The statue—woman—shifted again, settling her weight from one foot to the other. Her expression remained that same impassive mask.

"Keep walking." Rodney tugged Aisling's hand and she stumbled into motion alongside him. A cold sweat beaded down the center of her spine and her heart was stuck high in her throat, racing. The woman was still again as they passed. The pixie didn't so much as glance in her direction, but Aisling couldn't tear her gaze away. Her skin was covered in a thin layer of something that looked like stone, but hairline cracks cobwebbed from her joints, highlighting each part of her body that she'd shifted. She'd only moved a fraction of an inch, but that coating was unforgiving. Aisling hoped that it at least provided her some protection from the burn of the melted wax as it dripped.

As they rounded the corner, Aisling's sharp intake of breath echoed audibly off the high ceilings. They'd reached the doorway to a grand and opulent dining room, and the opening was flanked on either side by two more stone-covered humans. Men, this time; both blindfolded. They were on their hands and knees on the cold marble floor, heads lowered, dozens of candles on each of their backs. This wasn't the first time they'd been subjected to such treatment, nor had they only been there for a short time: the candles were anchored in place by mountains of hardened wax. These two were almost nude save for a pair of stone-colored underwear. A rivulet of melted wax dripped down the back of the thigh of the man on the right. Aisling flinched as though she could feel it heating her own leg.

"Our esteemed guests have arrived." Laure was standing at the head of a long table, angling a golden chalice towards Aisling, Rodney, and Briar. A handful of other gentry were seated on either side of the table in high-backed chairs. All were dressed and made up for the occasion, attire slightly more garish than the soft, muted pastels Aisling expected. *Costumes,* she thought. They looked like they were wearing costumes. The females had rouged cheeks and feathers and flowers pinned into their colorful hair. The males wore jackets with tails. One wore only a satin waistcoat to show off rows of porcupine-like quills that jutted from his bare arms.

Rodney nudged Aisling in the ribs then pulled her down into a bow at the waist.

"There's no need for such formalities, my dears." Laure's laugh was rich and warm. "I'd like to introduce you all to the Red Woman, the White Bear, and their púca companion: Aisling, Briar, and Rodney. Please come sit."

The other dinner guests murmured in appreciation and smiled politely. Several raised their own glasses as the trio approached. The seats at Laure's left and right hand were occupied, so Aisling and Rodney took the next two empty chairs across from one another. Briar settled in on the floor, chin on Aisling's feet.

The female guard who had commanded the sentries at the Thin Place sat between Laure and Rodney. She was still clad in armor, but a more formal suit tonight that somehow looked even thinner and more pliant than the last. Beside Aisling was a long-haired male that looked like he could have been the guard's twin: they had the same grass-green eyes, the same translucent, freckled skin, and the same rich auburn hair.

With a flourish of her voluminous skirt, a similar sage green as the velvet cloak she'd worn to Solanthis that morning, Laure sat back down. The guests at the far end of the table resumed their quiet conversation, but Aisling could feel the eager glances they cut in her direction. Her skin prickled at the feeling of their eyes on her, drinking her in. She wondered whether they were disappointed; surely, they'd hoped that their Red Woman would be a warrior or a soldier. Not merely a plain human.

"You have both met the captain of my guard, Niamh." Laure reached for her hand and Niamh accepted the gesture readily, giving Aisling little more than a curt nod before turning her attention back to her queen. "And this is her brother, Tadhg, my artist. He creates wonderful paintings; he's done my portrait more than once."

The male turned to smile at Aisling. His features were softer, more delicate. The look in his eyes far gentler than the searching, accusatory hardness in his sister's. "Wine?" he asked, brandishing a bottle of deep burgundy alcohol. Even his voice was soft. "We make it from summer berries just south of here."

Aisling and Rodney both slid their chalices to him to fill. When his sleeve shifted up as he poured, Aisling noticed several smudges of paint that he hadn't yet scrubbed away.

"Did you make any of the art in Solanthis?" Aisling asked.

Tadhg shook his head, hair swishing over his shoulders. "No, my art has no place in the temple. Someday, maybe."

"Don't be modest," Laure scolded gently. His pale cheeks flushed pink.

The berry wine was sweet, almost sickeningly so, and left a bitterness on the back of Aisling's tongue that was only abated by another swallow. She drained her chalice quickly that way and with very little in her stomach, it went to her head immediately. Still, the pleasant buzzing in her brain and the surrounding conversation wasn't enough to distract her.

Aisling's eyes lingered on the men at the door. Their faces were utterly calm despite the strain their bodies must have been under. Unlike the woman in the hall, she hadn't seen either of these move a muscle. She had to peer closely to even tell whether they were breathing.

"They're not here, you know," Tadhg commented. Before Aisling could ask, he explained: "Physically they are, of course. But their minds are elsewhere; somewhere peaceful and beautiful. Like a sort of trance."

"Why?" Aisling asked cautiously.

"Why not?" Niamh challenged.

Aisling bristled at the defensive edge to her tone. "Are they being punished for something?"

"Of course not. Their minds are dancing through sunlit fields or floating in crystal clear waters." Tadhg was gazing at them almost wistfully. "How could that be considered punishment?"

"They make you uncomfortable," Laure observed. "I will have them removed." She referred to the men so casually—like objects. Nothing more than furniture. Aisling chose to refill her chalice with more wine rather than respond. Silently summoned, the blue pixie entered from the hall. She tapped each man gently on the shoulder, then turned and walked out. Slowly, without snuffing a single candle, the men crawled out after her. They left behind a trail of wax and bits of gray stone that flaked off of their skin as they moved.

"Darling," the quilled male called from the far end of the table, breaking out of the Fae language to speak to Aisling. "You look terribly familiar. Have you visited us before?"

"Her mother," Laure interjected before Aisling could answer. "Maeve, wasn't it?"

Aisling nodded. The male thought for a moment as he drew in a deep drag off a clay pipe. The tendrils of herb-scented smoke he exhaled through his nostrils dropped heavily to blend with a swirl of mist that seemed to cling to his body. Then recognition sparked in his eyes.

"I do remember her." His lips spread into a wide smile, revealing rows of tiny, pointed teeth. "She sang so beautifully for us."

A falling sensation gripped Aisling suddenly, tightening her lungs and turning her stomach. It made sense to her now: the hoarseness of her mother's voice when she'd return after being away for days. The way it rasped in her throat when she'd greet Aisling; the way she'd drink cup after cup of honey-infused tea to ease the soreness. It was a small detail—in the grand scheme of her mother's storytelling, hardly one worth remembering at all—but it jumped out of her memories now loud and unbidden.

"She stopped coming around, didn't she?" He addressed the female seated beside him. His companion, a nymph with deep golden skin and leaves woven into her elaborate braids, stroked his quills idly with spindly fingers. Her features were so sharp they could cut glass.

"A while ago now," the female said.

"Why is that?" When Aisling was silent, focused on keeping her expression from crumbling, the male's smile turned sinister. "Ah," he sighed. "The humans did what humans do best, is that it?"

"Enough," Rodney said harshly.

"Your people are far crueler than ours; you'd do well to remember that. We'd take much better care of you here." The male's voice was like velvet, enchanting despite the chilling implication of his words. He took another puff on his pipe, openly enjoying watching Aisling squirm under his gaze. A loud scraping sound startled them all when Rodney shot to his feet, shoving his chair back from the table.

Laure, who had been watching the scene unfold with an amused half-smile, waved a hand. "Darragh, you're dismissed."

Darragh dipped his head, then he and the nymph rose and exited the dining room without argument. Aisling shuddered when she noticed that his figure didn't cast a shadow.

Rodney, still standing, gestured to Aisling. "We should go, too."

"Nonsense," Laure said. "Sit, please. We've not even eaten yet; there will be no further interruptions. Only pleasant conversation now, yes?" She looked expectantly around the table until each courtier had nodded in agreement.

"It's okay," Aisling whispered to Rodney, and he sank back down into his chair. It wasn't; she had to cross her legs tightly under the table to keep herself from jumping up and running out of the palace, but she swallowed down her discomfort with another mouthful of that bitter wine.

Though the food was fragrant and exquisitely spiced, Aisling could only stomach a few bites. The rest she pushed around the plate with her fork. She was grateful when a hob delivered a bowl of plain boiled meat for Briar—at least one of them would go to bed with a full stomach.

She was exhausted, and her senses were overwhelmed. But as she was conscious of Laure's eyes on her, Aisling feigned a smile and laughed along with the courtiers while they traded stories of their travels and encounters. Laure spoke very little, simply observing and allowing herself to be entertained by her subjects. Niamh, too, was largely silent. They held hands atop the table, Laure's thumb tracing circles over Niamh's knuckles.

The feast stretched on into the night, and it wasn't until they'd run out of bottles of wine that guests began staggering out of the room.

"A pleasure to meet you both," Tadhg said, excusing himself from the table. Before leaving, he leaned down, cupping Laure's cheek gently and kissing her goodnight. Aisling averted her gaze from the tender moment, but she didn't miss the way Niamh's hand tightened on Laure's just slightly.

Once it was only the four of them left, Laure sighed. "I apologize for Darragh; it's in his nature to behave that way. I would not have brought him here tonight had I known he would cause a scene. I hope he hasn't made you think less of us."

"We'd like to visit your archives in the morning," Rodney spoke for Aisling, and she shot him an appreciative smile.

"Of course, I will make sure it is arranged. A keeper will meet you at the steps." She and Niamh stood together, and Aisling and Rodney followed suit, rousing Briar from where he'd fallen asleep beneath the table. "I'd like to sit down with you tomorrow afternoon, Aisling, and discuss plans. This war has gone on long enough. Send for me when you return?"

Aisling only nodded. The company parted ways at the dining room door and Laure and Niamh disappeared down a dark corridor.

The human statues were gone, and the hallways were barely lit as Aisling, Rodney, and Briar navigated back to her chamber to collapse on the bed. Neither had the energy to change, though Aisling shed the uncomfortable corset as soon as they entered the room.

"What is Darragh?" she asked once they'd settled in.

"*Gancanagh,*" Rodney pronounced. "They call them Love Talkers."

"I didn't like him. I didn't like any of them." Aisling pulled the sheet tighter around her shoulders. Mercifully, despite the chill the evening had left in her bones, the wine pulsing warmly through her bloodstream coaxed her to relax. Distantly, she recalled the first book Kael had given her—*A Historical Record of Fae and Human Relations.* She'd thought it propaganda then, the account of the Unseelie Court's demand to establish and guard Thin Places to separate their realms. Maybe it hadn't been, after all.

27

THE ARCHIVES

AISLING

That bone-deep chill lingered on into the next morning; even the sunlight streaming in through the windows did little to chase it away. Aisling was still on edge, even more uncomfortable now after a night of dreams plagued by living statues reaching out to her from behind darkened corners.

Voices and laughter carried in from the front of the palace, loud enough that she could hear it through the closed windows of her chamber. Music, too. A plucky tune that felt light and effervescent. Aisling wrapped a blanket around her shoulders and crossed to peer out through the gauzy curtains. A crowd of Fae had taken to the lawn. They lounged splayed out in the grass, many of them nude, sunning themselves.

There were no human statues now, but several more children of varying ages danced in a circle. They clutched each other's hands, barely able to keep their feet beneath them. The woman she'd seen the day before sang for a small audience, wearing that same dazed look. She was joined by a man who looked equally entranced. His baritone timbre contrasted with her voice stunningly, but Aisling wondered whether either was aware of the other's presence at all.

The Seelie Court was circus-like in its extravagance, a noisy bacchanal of giddy, cruel delights. Under that shining springtime sun, there was no place to hide. And so instead, these sorts of proclivities were embraced. Welcomed. Encouraged. If the Unseelie Court had seemed like a nightmare, this felt to Aisling more akin to a fever dream: beautiful, if unsettling. At once both enticing and horrifying. She didn't want to look, yet she couldn't tear her gaze away.

The bad taste the scene left in her mouth was even worse than the remnants of the wine that coated her tongue and stained her lips purple.

"Ash," Rodney called her name, pulling her out of her head. He held up her clothes, which had been washed, folded, and returned while they'd been away at dinner. "Get changed and let's go."

Aisling left Briar locked in the large bathroom with a bowl of water and another plate of boiled meat that was delivered with their breakfast tray. She left the rest of the food untouched but wrapped a piece of bread and an apple in a napkin to take along in case her appetite returned later in the day. She'd eaten very little since their arrival.

The stable hob was waiting with two horses just beyond the Fae gathering. Aisling made her way through the revelry following close behind Rodney. So focused on keeping her eyes trained on his heels, she nearly tripped over one of the children. The little girl, with black hair and blacker eyes, looked dully up at Aisling.

"Hi," Aisling said. The girl offered no response, instead opening her mouth wide. A large butterfly crawled out of it and fell wetly to the earth before taking flight. Aisling reeled back, revolted. The girl let out a high-pitched giggle and skipped back to the circle. Rodney had turned just in time to see the insect emerge from her mouth; he too wore an expression of pure disgust.

Aisling was eager now to put as much distance between herself and the group as she could. She grasped the reins of her dappled horse and lined herself up at the stirrup to climb on. Rodney sprang into the saddle of a brown mare with surprising grace.

"My life didn't begin on Brook Isle, you know," he teased when he caught Aisling's incredulous look. "I've ridden once or twice."

Having seen the hob whisper to each of the horses before setting them loose, Aisling was confident in their ability to navigate to Solanthis with little direction from their riders. Rodney seemed to enjoy the trip. Again, she was focused mainly on keeping her balance in the saddle.

As they drew further away from the gathering on the lawn and the sounds of singing and laughter became faint, Aisling's discomfort eased. Rodney, however, only became more despondent as the temple steps shimmered into view on the horizon. His face was contorted into a grimace from the first step to the last, and it was only with Aisling's constant urging that he made it to the top at all. Aisling didn't fare much better; her legs were still burning from making that same climb with Laure.

They collapsed at the top, neither able nor willing to appreciate the view. It was hotter today, and the breeze had died down before they'd even reached the halfway mark. But just as it seemed they'd finally caught their breath, they were summoned by a soft voice from inside the mouth of the temple.

The keeper—the sidhe Aisling had noticed during her previous visit—turned once she'd caught their attention and drifted inside. Every inch of her glimmered in the light that streamed into the nave; when she passed through the pool of it beneath the dome she appeared as little more than a thick cloud of glitter.

"The archives are kept in the tower," she said over her shoulder as they followed her up the wide staircase. Her voice was barely stronger than a whisper. "You have access to everything inside. You need not replace the things you've read; I'll take care of that when you're through. But I must ask that your bags remain outside. Nothing but your bodies and minds go in or out of that room." She gestured to a gilded door, tall and narrow. Aisling shrugged off her pack and set it against the wall.

"How long may we stay?" she asked.

"I will retrieve you when your time is up. Hands?" The pair held out their hands. The sidhe examined them closely, checking their palms and under their nails for any trace of dirt. Once she was satisfied they were clean, she stepped forward. She placed both of her palms flat against the door and lowered her head as though she was murmuring to it. The filigree shone for a moment so brightly that Rodney looked away and Aisling closed her eyes tightly against the glare.

As silent as Solanthis felt in the nave, there in the archives the absence of sound was even more stark. It felt different somehow. Comforting. The sidhe, who had remained behind them in the doorway, drew in a reverent breath. Aisling did the same. It smelled of incense and leather and brittle pages. Of knowledge, of history. A sharp pang cracked across her ribs when she thought of Kael's head bent over his own ancient tomes, silver hair hanging down like a curtain.

"Ash?" Rodney was already standing before one of the oak shelves, so laden with books it sagged in the center. He pulled out the first one within reach and thumbed through it. "What are we looking for, exactly?"

She wandered over to stand with her back against his to examine the opposite row of tomes. She peered closely at the titles, pleased to find more written in English than she'd expected. "I'll know it when I see it."

He snorted. "That doesn't help me."

Aisling glanced back toward the doorway to ensure that the sidhe no longer lingered there before she said, "A way out."

"What?" Rodney looked at her, eyes wide.

"A way out, a different interpretation—*something*." Aisling raked her hair back into a rough bun and crouched down to read the titles on a lower shelf.

"Aisling, what are you talking about?" When she didn't answer right away, Rodney grabbed her elbow and pulled her up to face him, then said her name again sternly.

"It isn't right, Rodney. I understand not wanting the Unseelie Court to take full control, but this? *Laure?*" She hadn't realized the strength of her conviction until she spoke the words out loud, but she'd felt the truth of them. They'd been a noisy refrain in her mind from the moment Laure had dismissed the magicked singer as harmless fun. When the banquet she'd planned in their honor was lit by candles anchored to human bodies, she knew for sure.

Laure, as Queen, was aware and tolerant of everything that went on in her court. She would know about the changeling children. She would have known about Maeve Morrow—maybe not by name, but Aisling wasn't entirely sure if that was better or worse. She shook her head and repeated, "It isn't right."

Rodney's frown softened just slightly. "It's the prophecy."

"Is it?" she challenged. "Because I don't recall it explicitly calling out either court by name. Even Laure said herself that Fae prophecies aren't rigid."

"Maybe, but Ash..." Rodney trailed off to rub the back of his neck, looking around once more to ensure their privacy.

"You saw the scene on the lawn this morning; do you really want the whole realm to look like that? What do you think happens to humans if that becomes normal? What if they stop waiting for them to cross the Veil on their own?" There were worse beings in the Wild than Laure's courtiers, and she didn't doubt that the only thing holding them back from indulging their impulses was an outmoded sense of consequence. If the sort of treatment that was acceptable in the Seelie Court became normalized across the realm, including in those darkest corners, that small bit of protection would be eradicated.

"But an Unseelie rule—" Rodney began in protest, but Aisling cut him off.

"Isn't the answer either; I'm not saying that it is. I'm saying that there's got to be another option."

He thought for a moment, studying Aisling's face. The corner of his lips quirked up as he began to appreciate the challenge. "Door number three."

"Exactly." Aisling grinned, then sighed and looked around the space once more. "We just need to find it."

By the time the sidhe returned to retrieve them, Rodney and Aisling had combed through only half of the shelves in the space. Rodney's understanding of the Fae language was useful, but rudimentary and slow as he puzzled over words he couldn't recall. Aisling paged through most of the books in English, and some of those written in obscure languages that neither of them recognized. In those, she focused on the illustrations.

"I'm sorry for the mess," Aisling said to the sidhe when she pulled open the door, interrupting Rodney as he was sounding out yet another complex sentence. Heavy books and scrolls were piled high on the table in the center of the room.

"That's quite alright," she intoned. "Have you found what you were looking for?"

Aisling picked her bag up off the floor and slung a strap over her shoulder. "Would it be possible for us to come back tomorrow?" She ignored Rodney's dramatic huff.

"Certainly; I'd be happy to have you back." The sidhe locked the door the same way she'd opened it: palms pressed flat, and a low whisper against the wood. Aisling knew to face away from the ensuing glow this time.

⁘

"Welcome back." Tadhg was waiting near the palace steps, casually leaning a shoulder against one of the manticore statues guarding the door. The stable hob was hovering nearby and scuttled forward to take the reins and guide the horses away once Aisling and Rodney dismounted. Both of them winced at the soreness that flared in their legs when their feet hit the ground. "Did you enjoy your visit to the archives?"

"We did, thanks. I believe we'll be returning tomorrow." Aisling put a hand on Rodney's shoulder for balance and rolled her stiff ankles.

"Books exist to be read," Tadhg said with a smile. He pushed himself off of the statue and met the pair on the lawn. His hair shone the color of autumn leaves in the low afternoon sun; he'd tied it back with a green ribbon at the nape of his neck.

"Do you know where I might find Laure? She asked to speak when I got back." Aisling glanced around, thankful that the morning's party had moved on in their absence.

"Laure unfortunately has other matters to attend to; she sent me in her stead to entertain you for the evening." Tadhg bowed deeply at the waist and his eyes sparkled good-naturedly. Despite how desperate she'd been for Laure's acceptance when they'd arrived, Tadhg had since become the only member of the Seelie Court Aisling felt remotely comfortable around.

"I'm not sure we need entertaining," Rodney hedged.

When Tadhg smirked, he looked like a sheepish child. "Really, it's purely selfish on my part. I'd quite like to paint your portrait, Aisling. You with the White Bear."

"Oh, I don't think so. I'm not good at sitting still." Aisling felt her cheeks heat as the artist studied her like he was already composing the piece in his mind.

Tadhg laughed off her protests. "Nonsense; you'll do perfectly. We'll drink tea and eat cakes and have a fine time."

Her hand rose self-consciously to the messy bun high on the back of her head, then to the sweater she'd tied around her waist. There was dust on her jeans from the ride. "I should at least bathe. I could change into the gown I wore to dinner if that would be better."

"Absolutely not," Tadhg said firmly. "I can do your hair down if you'd like, but I've no interest in painting the Red Woman dressed as Seelie gentry. I want you just as you are."

Tadhg waited in the palace foyer while Aisling, resigned, hurried to her chamber to retrieve Briar. He'd tugged her towel from where it was draped over the side of the tub to sleep on. His tail thudded heavily against the tile when she cracked open the door and called his name.

"Beautiful." Tadhg beamed and held out his hand for Briar to smell once they'd returned. He did so, apprehensive, at first, then relaxed. "Come, my studio is upstairs. I've already called for tea."

Tadhg's studio was set up in a corner room, with windows spanning across two walls to capture both the morning and afternoon sunlight. He poured three cups of tea, preparing his own with cream. Aisling took hers plain.

Rodney circled the space as Tadhg got Aisling settled on a simple wooden chair beneath one of the windows. She directed Briar to sit at her side. He sat tall with his ears perked, as though he knew he should be posing, too.

"Why have you covered your art?" Rodney was peeking under the corner of a drop cloth at the canvas beneath. Indeed, all of the work around the studio was shrouded in white sheets.

Tadhg smiled mischievously at Aisling. "You are the first clothed subject I've painted in a while. I didn't want you to see my other work and think that was expected of you."

"I appreciate that," she said with a breathy laugh.

"I could use the practice with fabrics anyway. It is tricky, getting the movement and shading just right." He adjusted his easel and began mixing colors on a palette. "Please, drink and eat as much as you like. You needn't be a statue."

The tea—the same she'd had on the lawn the day before—soothed Aisling's aching muscles and troubled thoughts. She sipped it gratefully as Tadhg began to paint with quick, rough strokes. Rodney continued his exploration of the covered art, pulling back each sheet for just long enough to examine the hidden subject before moving on to the next.

"They're all of Laure," he observed.

"She is my muse, after all." Tadhg's smile was wistful. Secretive.

"Are you and Laure..." Though Rodney trailed off, the implication of his unfinished question was as loud as if he'd said the words. Aisling made to scold him, but Tadhg intervened without missing a beat.

"Laure had a great love once, a very long time ago. Since he passed on, she's rather enjoyed...sampling her wares." Tadhg winked and Aisling flushed crimson. "She likes to collect beautiful things. We all do. I, through my art." He flourished his brush, sending droplets of paint to splatter on the covered canvas near his feet.

"Have you known her long?" Rodney asked.

There was that secretive smile again. "Long is relative, I suppose. Niamh has known her for longer than I; she brought me here after she was made captain. Laure saw a painting of mine in her room."

"What was that painting of?" Aisling finished her cup of tea and poured another before settling back into position.

"Our home. Chin down, please." He gestured with his brush. "Taliesin, to the south. Where we make our berry wine."

"I passed through there once, I believe. It was hot if I remember correctly." Rodney finished his examination of each covered canvas and perched on a windowsill nearby.

Tadhg chuckled. "More than likely. Have you lived in the human realm for a very long time?"

"Long is relative." He parroted back Tadhg's words, and Tadhg snorted.

"Where did you live before?"

"Here and there." Rodney hopped off the sill to circle the room again.

Tadhg paused mid-stroke to look over his shoulder at Rodney, eyebrows raised. "A Veilwalker? There are less and less of those."

Rodney hummed. "There's less and less space in the human world for the Fae."

"I've never quite understood the Solitary, to be honest." He returned to his work, gaining more precision with each stroke. "To live untethered like that. No allegiances, no protection."

"No rules," Rodney added.

"I think even that lawlessness has begun to lose its allure. Laure has extended her aid to a handful of Solitary factions for a number of years now, and even more still of late. They've all seemed eager to accept." As Tadhg turned his attention down to his palette, focused intently on mixing several bright colors into a more muted shade, Rodney's eyes flickered to Aisling's. She nodded subtly for him to continue.

"What sort of aid?" He kept his voice cool and disinterested.

"Why?" Tadhg smirked, though he still concentrated on his colors. "Do you want to make a deal?"

Rodney sniffed. "I could be convinced. It depends on what's on offer."

"There's a great deal to be offered." Tadhg held up the palette, looking back and forth between the color he'd created and Aisling's clothes before attacking it again with his brush.

"And what is it that the Seelie Court gains in return?" Rodney was standing at Tadhg's shoulder now, suddenly far more interested in his process than he'd been when the activity was first suggested.

Without hesitation, Tadhg said, "I am the queen's artist, not her advisor. I stay as far away from politics as I am able."

"Does their contribution have anything to do with the war efforts?" Aisling asked. She set her teacup aside and patted Briar's head, though she was not so skilled at seeming impassive as Rodney.

"Of course not," Tadhg scoffed. "They would no sooner fight to protect our court than we would their land."

Aisling thought of those ill-equipped Solitary soldiers at Nyctara, fighting on foot while the Seelie warriors remained above the fray on horseback, dying for a cause that wasn't their own at the ends of swords and wrapped in tendrils of Kael's shadows. Rodney caught her eye again as though reading her mind. His reaction had been one of shock when she'd returned and told him what she'd seen.

"I would think adding their numbers to the Seelie ranks would be rather beneficial in this war," Rodney suggested casually.

Whether or not Tadhg knew the truth, he didn't let on. He never faltered; his expression and the constant movement of his paintbrush across the canvas gave nothing away as he responded, "The Seelie Court fights its own battles."

28

DOOR NUMBER THREE

AISLING

"What did you mean yesterday when you said that there's less space in the human realm for the Fae?" Aisling broke the silence that had settled over the archive. She was seated crossed-legged on the ground amidst stacks of books.

Rodney looked up from the brittle, faded scroll he was attempting to decipher. "Just what I said. Your world is a lot smaller now than it used to be. There's not a lot of room for magic anymore."

"That's sad," she murmured. His lament, whether or not he meant it to be, was heart-wrenching. It made Aisling feel guilty too somehow. As though she alone was responsible for the world's modernization, its ever-expanding cities and the destruction of forests and lakes and glens and everything else that was once wild and untamed. Her jaw clenched involuntarily when she thought of how hard she'd worked to push magic out of her own life once she felt she'd outgrown her mother's stories.

But Rodney only shrugged. "Just means we have to be better at hiding. Have you found anything?"

"No." Aisling brushed a strand of hair from her face and tipped her head back to lean against the shelf. "You?"

"The only thing I've learned is that I'm shit at languages. I thought I'd retained more." He rolled the scroll carefully and set it aside on a pile of others he'd already scanned and discarded.

"For not having spoken it in 29 years, you remember more than I'd have expected."

He huffed a short breath through his nose in response. "How much longer do you want to keep at this, anyway?"

"We should stay until our time is up. I don't want to give up early and wonder later if we'd have found something if we had kept working." Aisling pulled another book into her lap half-heartedly. Her neck was sore and her eyes were tired and her brain was overfull of utterly useless information.

She'd just set another book aside, frustrated, when a series of soft knocks startled them both. Aisling clambered to her feet, toppling over a waist-high tower of books in the process. She angled her body to hide their mess when she pulled the heavy door open.

"Can we have just a bit more time?" Aisling asked the sidhe. A large, ancient tome was nestled against her chest. It had been opened and closed so many times over the years that the black leather of the spine was cracked and split all the way down. She held it as though her arms were all that kept its pages together.

"You have awhile yet. Here." If she was bothered by the array of books and papers scattered around the room, she didn't show it as she placed the volume carefully in Aisling's waiting arms. Then, still with that same serene demeanor, she further lowered her whisper-quiet voice. "You might find it useful; just be gentle with it."

Aisling opened her mouth to ask what she meant, but she'd already pulled the door closed behind her. The click of the lock sounded sure and final.

"What is that?" Rodney leaned back in his chair to peer at the book Aisling now grasped carefully. "It's massive."

"I'm not sure. She said we might find it useful." She returned to her seat on the floor with the book cracked open across her lap.

His face fell. "Shit Ash, you don't think she's heard us do you?"

"I don't want to think about it if she did," Aisling responded sharply. Her palms were sweaty at the mere thought; she didn't need to voice the possibility out loud. *Could that have been why Laure was suddenly unable to meet the day before?* She bit down hard on the inside of her cheek until that concern quieted.

The book in her lap was hand-written in the dense, curling font of the Fae language. When Aisling ran a finger over it, she could feel the indentation of each letter in the paper. She began flipping through page after delicate page in search of illustrations she might be able to understand. There weren't many, and certainly none that she would consider in any way useful.

Just as she began easing the book closed, a swath of heavy black ink caught her attention. She opened it again and carefully teased the loose page from the binding. The illustration, still as sharp and black as it was the day it was drawn, divided the page into equal thirds. At the bottom, indistinguishable forms writhed and lurked in heavy shadows beneath the soil and thick, twisting roots. The middle third depicted figures within the bark of the trees and surrounded by wildflowers in a lush forest clearing. The top of the page was filled in almost completely: the night sky, deep and dark. Beings floated there—whether one or more she couldn't say; it was difficult to tell where one ended and another began. It—they—were cloaked in stars, angled as though they were gazing down at the forest below.

"Rodney?"

He hummed, nodding without glancing up from the book in front of him. Aisling stood, cradling the open tome, and carried it to the table. She laid it atop Rodney's book and he cast her an irritated glare.

"I was in the middle of reading. What is this?" His brow furrowed and he leaned in closer to take in the tiny, intricate details of the illustration.

"I'm not sure exactly." She ran a finger over the dark, star-speckled sky. "Is that meant to be Aethar?"

Rodney shook his head. "Aethar is only ever depicted as a being of light. She'd never be drawn in darkness like this."

"Can you read any of the text?" she asked.

"Give me a minute, I'll do my best." He shooed her away. Impatient, Aisling moved around the table to pace back and forth. "Could you not?" Rodney demanded irritably after she'd made several passes.

Aisling rolled her eyes and instead pushed a stack of books out of the way and sat on the edge of the table. She gave him a minute. Then two. Then three. Finally, as she was about to ask him for a progress report, Rodney swore under his breath.

"What is it?" She hopped off the table and went back to hover at his shoulder.

"There were three courts. Look." He pointed toward the bottom third. "This is the Unseelie Court." He moved his finger up to the center. "This is the Seelie Court. And here at the top is the third court."

"What do you mean? I've never heard of a third court." Aisling was certainly no expert, but even in the human realm she'd been able to find mention of the Seelie and Unseelie Courts. They were few and far between and passed off always as myths, but they existed nonetheless.

"Neither have I," Rodney admitted. "But this," he underlined a bit of text with his thumb, "seems pretty clear."

"What was it called?" She squinted at the letters as though a narrowed field of vision would somehow make them intelligible.

He scratched his head, thinking for a moment. "There aren't really words in English to translate directly. The closest, I think, would be 'the Silver Saints.'"

"The Silver Saints," Aisling repeated. "They're Fae? What else does it say about them?"

"They're Fae, but old. Like *old* old. All this says is that they've not been seen since the early days when the courts were formed." He flipped through several more pages, scanning for their name again, but came up empty.

"There was something the sidhe wanted us to find in there," Aisling nodded at the book.

"It talks about them as though they're legend." Rodney lifted the page from the binding to examine it again, the tip of his nose almost brushing the paper, then said again, "I've never heard of them before."

Aisling sighed, disappointment weighing down her shoulders. "So all we have is a pretty drawing and a Fae folktale."

"Go on back to your pile, Ash. I'll keep reading. We're not out of time." Rodney tried his best to sound upbeat, but he was losing faith and stamina just as quickly.

But they *were* out of time, very nearly. It was difficult to tell how much had passed before the sidhe returned; it felt like she'd only just left Aisling at the door with that ancient text in her arms. This time, Aisling watched the magic flare and fade as the sidhe locked the archives behind them. It stung her eyes, but it was beautiful.

"Have you found what you were looking for?" She asked, the same as she had the day before.

"I'm not sure," Aisling answered truthfully. Dejectedly.

"I'd imagine you have." Something deep and knowing was hidden in her sing-song tone.

"But—" Aisling's protest was cut short when the sidhe left them at the bottom of the stairs in the nave.

Before she ascended, she turned back to say, "There is nothing left here for you to find."

THE RED WOMAN AND THE WHITE BEAR

The way she said it—sparkling eyes boring into Aisling's, the finality in her tone—somehow settled the restlessness in her chest.

※

Wind battered the exterior of the palace, sighing and sighing. The unforeseen storm rolled in quickly; Rodney and Aisling barely made it back in time to avoid the rain that followed the clouds. Aisling had sensed it coming the moment they'd stepped out of Solanthis, the taste of petrichor thick in her mouth, but even she was surprised by its strength. The dark clouds seemed incongruous with the bright flowers and stark white of the palace as they rode up onto the lawn.

"Something has to keep the grass green," Rodney commented. Aisling shivered, but not from the chill of the storm. It was the soft, almost inaudible growl of one of the manticores as they passed between that drew goosebumps down her arms.

Niamh met the pair in the foyer this time and made it clear that Laure was waiting for Aisling alone. Aisling sent Rodney off to take care of Briar and followed Niamh in the opposite direction.

Laure was seated on a plush armchair beside a small drawing table. She toyed with the hem of her lace sleeve idly. The room was full of flowers, some fresh-cut and arranged in vases and some growing out of the walls themselves. Butterflies flitted between them, alighting delicately on petals before taking back to the air. Aisling ran her tongue over her teeth; they itched when she imagined the little girl with the butterfly in her mouth.

A smile warmed Laure's face when Aisling entered. Niamh remained stiffly by the door. "Sit with me, sweetling. I've been watching the storm. It'll likely be the last of the season."

The chair cradled Aisling's sore muscles when she sat and a contented sigh escaped her lips involuntarily. The consistent thrum of fat raindrops slamming against the windowpanes was soothing; if she hadn't been in the company of the Seelie Queen, Aisling could have closed her eyes and fallen asleep easily.

"How did you find our archives?" Laure asked, sitting back in her chair. It was the same soft shade of pink as her rosebud lips and the blush on her cheeks. Her long black waves were loose and hung over one shoulder.

"The books are beautifully kept," Aisling said. "I hardly felt qualified to handle some of them."

"We have some very old texts there. I must admit I haven't read nearly as many as I'd like. Tea?" Laure offered a cup to Aisling, full to the brim and perched on a matching saucer. Aisling politely refused, unwilling to let her mind grow hazy in Laure's presence. The queen was sharp; Aisling needed to be, too.

"You said that you wanted to discuss plans?" she prompted. Aisling watched Laure, her posture regal and commanding even while relaxed. A fire burned in her violet eyes, a determination that bordered on recklessness. It made Aisling uneasy.

"We've been waiting for you for a very long time, Red Woman." Her smile turned conspiratorial. "*I* have been waiting for you. This has all gone on for long enough; it must end now. The Unseelie

Court must be brought down before they can destroy any more of Wyldraíocht than they already have."

Aisling forced herself to return Laure's smile, but the expression felt wrong on her lips. "What do you have in mind?"

"The rumors of your connection with Kael—are they true? You have some sort of influence over that wretched magic of his?"

In a bid to hide her reaction, Aisling leaned forward, stirring honey and cream into the cup of tea Laure had left for her and taking those few seconds to compose herself. To fix her mask. She thought about how Rodney might answer the question, or Kael: they'd dance around an answer without ever giving it forthright. Aisling did her best to respond as they would. "Rumors exaggerate. It's true that his shadows didn't kill me." She straightened up and held the cup in her lap, then added, "But that's where the connection ends. I can no more influence them than he can control them."

Laure hummed. "That sounds at least powerful enough to distract him during battle."

"If he were distracted by that connection, he'd be far easier to remove. Once he falls, his court will follow." Niamh spoke from where she leaned against the doorframe, eyes filled with the same fire as Laure's. Aisling could feel the predatory drive rolling off of her in waves. She wanted that kill for herself.

Aisling hesitated. "Has there not already been enough bloodshed? I can only imagine another battle would be detrimental to your court, as well."

A subtle tension crept into the room. Laure's smile faltered, wavered, then faded away to nothing. "Aisling, love, sometimes destruction is the surest way to creation. The Unseelie Court is a blight on our realm. We can only build the new once we dismantle the old."

"Is there no way to broker peace without more death?" Aisling was pushing her luck. She felt it in the way Niamh's eyes shot daggers into the back of her neck. She saw it in the way Laure's face darkened. Her look of annoyance sharpened into one of anger.

"Diplomacy has failed us for centuries. Kael only understands strength, so we must be the ones to wield it." Laure's outstretched hand rested on the table and she began to drum a finger against it. Where the tip of her finger met the wood, a single vine curled into being. With each impatient tap, it grew, thickening and elongating. Reaching. "It is either him or me, and trust me: I am the one Wyldraíocht needs on the throne. He will drive it to ruin, just as he has his own court."

Drawing in a steadying breath, Aisling willed the smile back to her face. Loosened her grip that had tightened around the handle of the teacup. Then, with what she hoped was a convincing look of acceptance, she nodded. "You know this war better than I do. I'll do whatever I can to help you end it."

"Thank you." Laure nearly glowed with gratitude. "I know this is a challenging world you've been pulled into, but we're going to make it so much better together."

"I hope so," Aisling said. She did her best not to recoil when Laure reached out and brushed the backs of her cool fingers over her cheek.

"I am truly sorry for what happened to your mother. Humans can be so cruel when they are afraid. There is a place for you here in my court, now and when this is all over. We will care for you here; you will be safe to live out the rest of your days amongst friends."

"Thank you, Highness. I can't imagine anything I'd like more." Bile crept up the back of Aisling's throat, bitter and stinging. Quickly, she gestured to the dust that still clung to her jeans from the ride. "If you'll excuse me, I'd like to go get cleaned up."

"Of course. We will leave the strategic planning to Niamh and her council. There's no need for you to dirty your hands with the particulars." Laure rose alongside Aisling and again closed the distance between them to smooth a hand over Aisling's hair. "We are so grateful for you."

29
A FAVOR

AISLING

She'd had enough. She'd heard enough. Aisling hardly made it back to her chamber, rushing straight past Rodney and Briar to drop to her knees before the washbasin and heave up what little was in her stomach. The force of it made her head spin.

"I can't do this, Rodney," she rasped, head still dipped over the basin. She spat bitterly into the water. "I don't want to do this."

Rodney knelt beside her, carefully twisting her hair back out of her face and tucking it into the collar of her shirt. "I know. It'll be okay."

"No, it won't." She sat up and faced him. Her body was shaken and unsteady, but her mind was clear, and her resolve was strong. "I don't want to be a part of this war. It isn't mine. I can't..." her voice broke and she sucked in a breath. "I won't help them kill him."

"Kael?"

She nodded. She still hadn't told him everything that she felt for the Unseelie King, everything that they'd shared, but she knew he could see it now written on her face.

"We have to leave, Rodney. I won't let them use me like this. I don't care about the prophecy, and I don't care about the consequences of ignoring it. I want out." Aisling's stomach turned again and she gagged, but nothing more came up. Trembling from the effort, she leaned against Briar to stay upright.

Rodney left her side momentarily to fill her a glass of water, then crouched down again. "I'm sorry, Ash. You know I would take this off your shoulders if I could."

"I just want to go home. I want this to be over. I can't do it." Hot tears stung in the corners of her eyes, building and building before they spilled down her cheeks. Exhaustion had settled into her bones and the weight of the prophecy was a mantle she desperately wished she could shed.

He squeezed Aisling's shoulder. "I know. We'll go, okay?"

"They're not going to let me." Her voice was rough, her throat sore.

"We'll figure out a way, I promise. But listen, I need to tell you something." Rodney lowered his voice. "Ivran is here."

"What?" Aisling straightened up and wiped her face with her sleeve.

"He's in the other room; he showed up while you were with the queen."

Aisling frowned. She hadn't even noticed the small faerie as she'd blown past into the bathroom. "Why is he here?"

"He came to warn us." Rodney's voice dropped even further, so that Aisling had to lean in to hear what he said next. "He said someone from the Unseelie Court has been by the trailer a few times since we left."

"Lyre?" When Rodney shook his head, Aisling's heart leapt to her throat. For a moment she thought she might vomit again.

"A soldier," Rodney said.

"Then we'll go to my apartment in the city." It was nearly empty since she'd all but moved back to Brook Isle, but Aisling had continued to pay the rent every month as though she'd still someday return to that part of her life. "We can lay low there and let this blow over."

Rodney didn't have the heart to tell her it wouldn't work; she knew he didn't. So he just nodded.

"I can help," Ivran offered from the doorway. His expression was kind, if a touch pitying. "I have a friend here that owes me a favor."

Guilt joined the swirl of emotions sweeping Aisling away in their undertow and she chewed the inside of her cheek. Favors were currency; they'd all spent too much on her already. "I can figure something out."

"Don't you think on it," Ivran assured her. "I'll be back before you know it."

It would be dusk before Ivran returned, hair damp and cheeks flushed. The storm clouds that had hung overhead resumed their steady crawl onward, dragging away the last of the rain and wind in their wake. The sun came back out just in time to set.

Ivran's friend was a young satyr whom Ivran had once led, stumbling and blind drunk, back into the Wild after he'd crossed through the Veil with such enthusiasm that he nearly charged straight over the cliff at the overlook. And so it was the satyr's idea to use his widely-known love of drink and human women to aid in the trio's escape.

From her chamber window, Aisling and Rodney watched the satyr totter on thick, fur covered legs towards the trees. He carried slung over his shoulder a sack with several tightly wrapped bottles of berry wine—one of the very few things disallowed from being passed between realms. Fae wine was to remain in the Fae realm, and human alcohol was expressly forbidden from being carried back in.

"Once he gets a bit closer to the Thin Place, we'll follow. The guards will be distracted thinking he's smuggling out the wine." Ivran was perched on a chair beside the window so that he could see out, too. His back legs rubbed together, the motion creating a soft chirping melody. A nervous habit, Aisling guessed.

"And if they don't?" Rodney asked.

Ivran flashed a mischievous grin. "He's not afraid to cause a scene."

Once the satyr had crested the hill and disappeared down the other side, Ivran sprung out of the window and disappeared into the tall grass, cutting a wide path towards the trees. Aisling pulled her keys and wallet from her backpack and hid them in an inner pocket of her jacket. It would seem too suspicious to carry it with her; there was little left inside, anyway, save for the pendant Laure had given her. She'd torn it from around her throat violently, breaking the delicate chain, and dropped it into the bottom of the bag.

Keeping a steady, almost painfully slow pace, Rodney and Aisling walked with Briar between them through the palace. Rodney chattered on about an upcoming Fae celebration hosted there in the Seelie territory that he was looking forward to attending with Aisling. There would be music, he said. And dancing, and costumes, and plenty of wine. Though she wanted to seem just as casual, the best she could manage was to nod and hum when he paused for her response.

Outside, the scent of wet earth permeated everything, overpowering even the wildflowers' perfume. Aisling drew in lungful after lungful of it gratefully. The smell of rain would always remind her of home, and she was so, so close to making it back. She hoped it would have rained on Brook Isle, too.

Lost in thought, nearly hypnotized, Aisling fell back when Rodney grabbed her arm. At her feet, the once-glassy surface of the lake churned violently as whatever lived in its depths swam back and forth just beneath.

"I told you there was something in there," Rodney muttered, dragging Aisling away by her elbow. She hadn't even realized that she'd been making her way towards the water's edge.

"I don't like it here," she said finally, and it was a relief to say those words out loud. From the moment she'd witnessed the woman magicked into singing, something about the landscape had unsettled her. It lingered beneath her skin like a cold chill, leaving her constantly waiting in fear of something that she couldn't identify, but felt inevitable.

"I've long preferred the Unseelie Court," Rodney said. He kept his voice low and his gaze ahead, swinging his arms nonchalantly. Anyone watching—and Aisling was sure there were several sets of eyes on them now—would think they were merely out for Briar's last evening walk. "They don't hide their intentions there. You know who your enemies are. There's something strangely comforting, I think, in knowing exactly how someone wants to hurt you."

Rodney led Aisling to cut diagonally across the meadow. Ivran was hidden there in the thickening shadows, his chirping song louder and deeper than the rest of the crickets there. It was a slight difference, only obvious to those listening carefully for it, but Rodney had no problem picking it out and orienting them towards the sound.

"Here!" A bush rustled when Ivran raised a thin arm to wave over its branches. Rodney and Aisling crouched behind it alongside the small faerie. Aisling kept both arms looped around Briar's neck for her own comfort more than his.

"How will we know when it's clear?" she whispered. She had to squint now to see more than a few yards ahead. She tightened her grip on Briar.

"The Thin Place is just in that direction." Ivran pointed to their right. "It isn't far. We'll go once we hear one of the bottles break; that's the signal we agreed on."

Rodney snorted. "Classy."

The group waited in silence and painful anticipation. Aisling's knees ached from holding the crouched position and her feet were beginning to tingle, but she was afraid to shift and disrupt the quiet that had settled around them. Ivran and Rodney were both still as statues in the way only Fae could manage. Even beneath his heavy glamour, Rodney could remain motionless for hours, with only the shallow rise and fall of his chest to betray that he was a living thing.

All of them startled when the calm was abruptly shattered by the sound of glass splintering against stone. The raised voices that followed were closer to their hiding spot than Aisling would have liked.

"Let's go," Ivran hissed. Gripping Briar's leash in one hand and a fistful of Rodney's shirt in her other, Aisling let the faeries lead her swiftly through the darkness. The Veil glimmered before them, a swirling sheen of silver-blue magic that eddied and undulated despite the stillness of the night. They were flying now, closing the distance faster and faster and faster until Aisling felt the magic's caress against her cheeks, and then the chill of frost-heavy grass. Only Briar had managed to stay on his feet; Ivran and Rodney, too, were lying on the ground beside her.

Aisling looked up in time to see the dryads drop their arms, closing the Veil and taking with it the soft glow that had illuminated their landing. But she smelled the salt, and she heard the waves. They sounded like a favorite song. She was home.

She stayed like that, on her back in the grass, for a minute longer. It was cold and the melting frost beneath her was soaking through her jacket, but she allowed herself that moment of peace while her pulse slowed and her breathing calmed.

When Ivran let out a triumphant whoop, she raised up onto one elbow. He was vibrating with excitement, eyes wide and limbs jittery.

"That was great fun!" he exclaimed.

Rodney rolled his eyes, but he couldn't hide the smirk that tugged at his lips. He'd enjoyed it too: the rush. "I wouldn't say *great* fun."

"Well next time, you two can go without me. I'm perfectly happy to stay right here." Aisling fell back down into the grass again and stared up at the stars. Familiar stars; her stars. Her sky. It was clear tonight, a deep bruise-dark purple smattered with those tiny, glittering flecks. She could never see enough of them in the city. In the Wild, with no light pollution at all, it seemed like there were almost too many. But here over Brook Isle, the sky held just the right amount.

The trudge back down to Rodney's car, still parked just beyond the trailhead, was wet and slippery and took them far longer than the hike up had. Both still ached from two days of climbing the Solanthis steps. Once they'd settled into their seats and turned on the noisy heater, Rodney dug in his pocket then wordlessly tucked something into Aisling's palm. She had to switch on the overhead light to see that it was a tiny square of folded paper, yellowed and soft with age. Carefully, she unfolded it to find the illustration of the three Fae courts from the book in the archives.

"When did you take this?" she gasped. She laid it out on the dash and pressed it flat, smoothing the creases.

Rodney shrugged and grinned sheepishly. "Before we left. I didn't want you to come away empty-handed."

Throwing off her seatbelt, Aisling launched herself across the center console to throw her arms around Rodney's shoulders. "Thank you," she whispered.

"It's your choice what we do next, Ash. If you want to leave, we'll leave." Rodney held her tightly. Fiercely. He was a life raft cast out into the storm, and she thought that there wasn't nearly enough space inside of her to fit the gratitude she felt for him then.

"For right now, I really just want to go home and take a shower." Aisling shifted back into her seat and reached into the back to dig her fingers into Briar's fur.

"We should probably avoid the trailer," Rodney said, a bit sullen as he put the car in gear and drove in the direction of town. "I have clothes at your apartment, don't I?"

"I think so. And you can take the bed, the sheets are clean." She didn't mind when he didn't argue. Though her couch was comfortable enough, Aisling was sure she was tired enough to fall asleep almost anywhere.

But as they pulled up to the front of her building, a chill slid down her spine, winding around each vertebra like those creeping vines that strangled the columns in Solanthis. She was back on edge, on her guard. The disquietude had followed her from the Seelie Court and now trailed behind her all the way up the stairs and into her apartment. It lessened some once she'd turned on all the lights and ensured that nothing seemed out of place, but the promise of sleep now seemed a bit further off than it had before.

Showered, changed, and fed, Aisling and Rodney battled their exhaustion side by side on the couch. He felt that same lingering unease; she could tell by the way he jerked himself awake each time his head lolled to one side. The first morning ferry wouldn't leave for hours yet, but Aisling already had a bag for herself and a bag for Briar packed and waiting by the front door. At dawn, they'd all three walk down to the dock and make their way to the city. They'd be safe there, Aisling thought. They had to be. And Brook Isle would be fine.

It was Briar who reacted to the sound first, followed close after by Rodney. It took Aisling several seconds to register what they'd heard: soft, furtive footsteps ascending the wooden stairs. Then, a knock on the door.

30
TOO IMPORTANT TO IGNORE
AISLING

"How did you—" The rest of Aisling's words caught in her tightening throat. Briar's low growl tore through the space her silence left as he pressed himself to her hip, but the two males standing before them didn't flinch.

Lyre's lips curled into a sly smile and his yellow eyes glinted. "I told you once about my connections. Did you think that claim false?"

He stood in the hallway outside of her apartment, clad in all black with a cloak that would barely have passed for human attire, especially on Brook Isle. A tall faerie with soft, dark curls and a hard expression stood beside him, who Aisling recognized as Kael's Captain of the Guard. *Raif,* she recalled. He, too, had made a poor attempt to dress in human clothing. She was grateful that they'd shown up in the dead of night.

"Enough, Prelate," Raif hissed, then turned his attention to Aisling. "You are needed at the Undercastle."

When Raif and Lyre moved forward, crossing the threshold into Aisling's apartment, Rodney stepped in front of her. "Leave," he said. His menacing tone was incongruous with his unthreatening appearance. Deliriously tired, Aisling almost laughed at the contrast.

"Quiet, Veilwalker. This does not concern you." Raif's stare never strayed from Aisling even as he snapped at Rodney.

Despite her racing pulse and trembling limbs, Aisling put a hand on Rodney's arm. "Take Briar into the kitchen and get him some food, will you?" Her voice shook, but she did her best to convey enough reassurance to convince him to back down. Rodney studied her face for a moment before nodding stiffly and retreating with a reluctant Briar in tow. He'd be listening, she knew, poised to return the moment he thought the conversation might be taking a turn towards threatening. That knowledge calmed her somewhat.

"You too," Raif said to Lyre. "Wait in the hall."

Once the pair was alone, Aisling crossed her arms tightly over her chest and glared up at the soldier. "Well? Why are you here?"

He glared right back, resolve unwavering. "You need to come back with us."

"So you can brag to your king that you caught the Red Woman? No thanks." Without any visible reaction or discernible emotion other than the anger he'd worn since he arrived, it was clear that Kael had at the very least shared her revelation with Raif. The number of others who held this information remained uncertain, leaving

Aisling to hope desperately that it didn't extend to the entirety of his court.

"This isn't about the prophecy." The hardness in his countenance seemed to melt away then, and he raked a hand through his curls. His look of malice was replaced with one of concern.

"Then what is it about?" Aisling demanded.

Raif clenched his jaw. Unclenched it. Then he sighed heavily and said, "Kael. He's not well."

Her heart seized, but she kept her face carefully neutral. "He wants me dead."

"And yet here you stand." Raif looked her over, gesturing with a wave of his hand. "If Kael wanted you dead, rest assured that would not be the case."

"He sent me away." She wanted to sound angry, but the words instead came out underlined by a barely concealed edge of hurt that twisted in her gut like a knife. In her mind, Aisling saw Kael before her, the final image she had of him before she fled the Undercastle. The pure rage etched into every line of his face, strands of his hair blowing with the short, angry breaths that sliced through his bared teeth. The crush of his fingers curled around her throat.

Raif heard it too, that hurt. "He was afraid."

"He'll do it again." Aisling looked away to hide the way her eyes now shined with tears.

"He won't," Raif countered.

Once she regained control over that tidal wave of sadness, she looked up at him once more. "How do you know that?"

"I've known Kael for a very, very long time. Long enough to know that he regretted his decision the moment he made it." Raif lowered his voice to make the confession, and Aisling realized then that Kael hadn't sent him there at all. He'd come on his own to seek her out: not to serve his king, but to help his friend.

"Is he sick?" she asked.

Raif sighed again, weary. "May we sit? I'd rather not carry on the rest of this conversation in your doorway."

Aisling regarded him for a beat before leading him to the small kitchen table. She nodded to Rodney and he skirted around them, giving the pair a wide berth and disappearing into the living room. Briar was unwilling to be pulled away again and lingered behind. Aisling ushered him to sit at her feet and rubbed one of his ears between her fingers absently.

Raif took a seat in the chair across from her uncomfortably and glanced around the room. Suddenly self-conscious of the bare walls and outdated fixtures, Aisling cleared her throat. Refocused by the sound, he rose again and began to pace.

"What do you know of Kael's injury?" he asked.

Aisling frowned. Though she wasn't surprised he hadn't mentioned it, she'd never noticed him favoring any parts of his body. "He's never talked about one."

"The full story is not mine to tell. He hides it well, and most of the time it remains forgotten, like a fleeting thought of a memory of a feeling." Raif paused as if testing the weight of each word before he spoke. All those he left unsaid hung in the air between them, taunting.

"But?" she prompted.

"But there are times when he hasn't the power to conceal it. The injury, the pain...it comes back around tenfold. When it happens, he locks himself away. He doesn't sleep, barely eats, for days at a time. It's all we can do to keep him from starving himself." A spark of fear glinted in his dark eyes, but his voice didn't falter. His steps continued, steady: three strides to one side of the room, three back to the other.

"How often does it happen? What brings it on?" The image Raif painted of Kael's suffering made her heart ache.

"It's infrequent, and for that I am grateful. We've not been able to determine its cause, but it seems only to come on when he is at his lowest. When he's lost control." Another twist of that sharp dagger in her gut—*she'd* brought it on. She was why Kael had lost control.

"Why are you telling me this?" she asked cautiously. "I can't imagine this is something he'd like shared." *Least of all with the Red Woman.*

Raif stopped mid-stride to face her, shoulders tense and expression tight. "It is not, and you would do well to ensure that it stays between us."

"Of course," Aisling promised.

With a long, heavy exhale, he sank back down onto the chair. "He'll listen to you."

"What do you—" She was cut off mid-question when Rodney stormed back into the room. He knew what was coming; he'd been eavesdropping from the other side of the doorway and clearly anticipated exactly what Raif intended to say next. And he knew, more likely than not, what Aisling's answer would be.

"You need to leave," he said harshly. "Now. This conversation is finished."

Raif stiffened but made no move to reach for the weapon barely concealed at his hip. He shot Rodney a sidelong glare, then turned back to Aisling to say again, "He will listen to you."

"You're not dragging her back to help your *king* who'd sooner see her dead than have her return." Rodney's cheeks reddened as he raised his voice.

"Rodney, stop. No one is dragging me anywhere," she chided. Then, to Raif, she asked, "What do you mean, he'll listen to me?"

"There is a salve. It seems to soothe the pain long enough for him to regain control, but he denies it." Raif kept a wary eye on Rodney, seething in the corner. He looked suddenly tired, as though Kael's affliction had kept him from sleeping, too.

"And you want me to convince him to use it?" Aisling guessed.

Raif nodded solemnly. "Or at least, to try."

It could have been a trick; he could have been there to lure her with his kind words and pleas for help only to bring her straight back to the dungeon. Or worse. But something in Aisling's chest—something woven around her bones and coursing through her veins—was pulling her back towards the Unseelie Court.

And that pull felt too important to ignore.

∴

"This is a fool's errand, Aisling," Rodney warned.

She stood balanced between two rocks, flanked on either side by Rodney and Briar, staring at the shimmering Veil in the old mine. The overlarge bag she'd packed to take with her to the mainland was slung diagonally across her back, even heavier now that she'd added extra food for Briar. Lyre had stepped through the Veil ahead of them, and Raif waited impatiently behind.

"I know," she said. It likely was, and she'd told him as much too when she tried to convince him to stay behind. But he was adamant that he'd remain by her side, and Briar's panicked barking left her little choice but to take him along as well. If there was any lingering doubt about her true identity, it would quickly dissipate once she arrived with the White Bear in tow.

"He'll be angry that you've come back," he added.

Aisling grit her teeth and said again, "I know." He would be; she knew he would be. He would be furious. Raif was wrong to think Kael regretted sending her away. The moment he saw her, he would regret instead not having killed her when he had the chance, if he didn't already.

Yet even still, knowing what likely awaited her on the other side, she tugged Rodney and Briar with her back into the Wild.

31

SALVE

AISLING

The sound of glass exploding against the inside of Kael's chamber doors made Aisling flinch. Raif remained stoic, stone-faced; he was accustomed to such outbursts by now. Werryn slipped out into the hall, cracking open one door just long enough for Aisling to hear Kael bellowing at him from deep inside the darkened room. Werryn's irritated expression deadened when he saw Aisling.

"What in His name is *she* doing here?" He recoiled as though she were a feral animal they'd brought in from the forest. Aisling's temper flared, but she remained silent. She wouldn't give him the satisfaction of reacting. Lyre stepped forward then, ushering Werryn away despite his sputtering protests.

"I don't like this, Ash," Rodney muttered. Briar didn't, either. He'd balked at the top of the spiral stairs, then several times as the group wound their way down through the labyrinth of passageways to Kael's chambers. She had to bribe him with so many treats the bag was now nearly empty.

Aisling waved him off. "Does he know I'm here?" She knew the answer, but she asked anyway. She was stalling for time. Trying to build up the nerve to breach those heavy doors and face the Unseelie King. She'd been sure, *so* sure, that she'd never see him again. And if she did, she thought it would likely be from the sharp end of his sword. *Still a possibility,* she reminded herself.

"No." Raif gestured then to a young female who had been waiting there in the corridor. Dressed in a plain shift of soft gray, her youthful face was framed by golden ringlets. She looked too innocent, too pure to be buried underground here. Her smile was kind as she produced a small glass jar and held it out to Aisling.

"The salve," she explained.

"Elasha is an apothecarist," Raif said. "She developed the formulation after the second onset of Kael's affliction. That was the worst instance of it, but this is not far off."

Aisling stood before the arched doors and took several seconds to quietly brace herself against what she imagined waited on the other side. Holding her breath, she pushed one open just wide enough to slip through, then closed it softly behind her back.

Kael's chamber was almost pitch-dark, lit only by a single glowing candle on the dresser. The air was heavy and stale and smelled sickly sweet from days' worth of food left to sour untouched on the table.

Aisling stayed pressed against the door, surveying the mess and allowing her eyes a moment to adjust. When a dish shattered against the wood just inches above her left shoulder, she nearly turned and fled, but her feet kept her rooted to the spot. Her heart wouldn't let her run this time.

"I told you to get out!" Kael shouted from where he stood facing away, hunched, supporting his weight against the mantle of a cold fireplace.

"It's me," she said cautiously. "It's Aisling."

His entire body stiffened when she said her name.

"Leave," he said, voice low. Though this time he spoke barely above a whisper, his gravelly tone was threatening. Aisling's pulse was loud as thunder in her ears as she took step after cautious step towards him.

"Raif brought me back." Broken glass crunched beneath her feet, louder than both of their voices.

"Get out," Kael growled again. "Now."

Slowly, slowly, she made her way across the room until she was standing behind him. He kept his back to her, hand still gripping the mantle. His silver-white hair hung limp and tangled, its usual iridescence dull. His shoulders were rounded as he struggled to remain standing and they trembled slightly beneath his tunic, though from exhaustion, pain, or anger, she couldn't tell. The pair remained this way for several minutes, the silence only stirred by his ragged, uneven breaths.

Ever carefully, Aisling raised a hand up and placed it on Kael's shoulder. The muscles there tightened, but he didn't pull away. Rather, it felt like he almost—*almost*—leaned into her touch.

"Will you look at me?" Aisling whispered. He stayed still and quiet. She waited a beat longer, then tried again: "Kael. Let me see you."

The sound of his own name crossing her lips so softly drew a violent shiver through his body. Finally, with his eyes shut tight as though to shield himself from the sight of her, Kael turned.

The left side of his face was ravaged, down to the tendons in some places and to the bone in others. The skin around his hairline was singed black, and down his neck snaked angry red scars. She reached up without thinking, almost in a trance, and touched his face. Her fingertips played delicately over the peaks and plains of his wounds, stuck in some torturous limbo between fresh, healing, and scarred. He sagged against the mantle for support, her touch at once both comforting and agonizing. A low hiss slid through his gritted teeth.

"This was not meant for your eyes," he rasped.

"I've seen worse." Aisling fought to sound sincere despite the lump growing in her throat. His ruined skin was hot under her hand when he tipped his head so his cheek rested against her palm. "Will you let me help you?"

He opened his eyes slowly to look down at her standing before him. He studied her, searching her face. Memorizing it. Then he nodded. When she pulled her hand away, both found themselves missing that contact with the other.

Aisling guided Kael to his bed and he sat down heavily on its edge. Moving quickly, she lit several more candles off of the one on the dresser and set them up on his bedside table. Again, in the light now, she regarded him with as neutral an expression as she could manage.

"You came back," Kael murmured. He said it so quietly Aisling wasn't sure she was meant to hear it at all. She thought he'd say something more: to damn her for it or to order her away again. But he didn't. He just stared ahead with a hollow gaze.

"I came back," she said, then moved forward until their knees were close to touching. From inside of her sweatshirt pocket, Aisling withdrew the jar.

Kael recognized it instantly as Elasha's salve and shrank back. He looked afraid now: afraid of the pain, afraid of her touch. Afraid to let her see the full extent of his weakness that showed so starkly on his skin. She could sense his fear, and her expression softened. Aisling set the jar beside the candles and instead knelt before the king.

"It's alright," she soothed. "They told me it would help, but if you don't want it, I won't force you." She waited, watching him patiently. Kael avoided meeting her eye. When she rested a hand on his knee, he nodded.

Gingerly, groaning, he stripped his tunic off over his head. Aisling's breath caught in her throat. This time, she was unable to stifle her reaction as she took in the twisted, winding scars that disfigured the left side of his body from hairline to hip. The sight brought tears to her eyes that she blinked back harshly. She tried to hide it by putting her full concentration on unscrewing the lid of the jar.

An earthy, herbal scent wafted up from the salve. It had a pale blue cast and shimmered purple in the candlelight. When Aisling scooped out a handful, it was cold to the touch. She stood and looked at Kael, searching his skin apprehensively for a place to start. The damage wrapped around his waist and crawled over his shoulder on down his back, where it lightened significantly.

"I'll start on your back, alright?" He made no move to acknowledge her, instead staring ahead at a fixed point on the wall.

Aisling slid onto the bed to sit behind him. His closeness, something she thought she'd never feel again, radiated a warmth that eased her pounding, aching heart. She let it, just for a moment, before she pushed that feeling aside and refocused herself.

The scarring on his back was only skin-deep. Here, the salve, and her hands spreading it, were nearly comforting. Kael closed his eyes and relaxed beneath her gentle ministrations.

"Not too bad?" Aisling asked as she rubbed the medicine into the redness there. She couldn't be sure in the dark, but it appeared to already be fading.

"Not too bad," Kael responded.

"Good." She worked the salve slowly over his back, giving him time to settle into a breathing pattern and allowing both of their nerves to calm.

They both knew she was spending longer there than she had to, but she needed it as much as he did. There was a pit in her stomach when she imagined the pain he'd have to endure once she moved to the front of his body. And worse still, when she thought that she'd be the one inflicting it.

"You know I have to do the rest," Aisling warned, bracing them both. Her hands continued to rub gentle circles across his back and shoulders. The corded muscles that banded down either side of his spine flexed and tightened as he breathed.

"I do," Kael said.

"Are you ready for that now?"

"Yes." Though his voice was still soft, he was resolute.

Aisling stood up off the bed and circled back to stand in front of him. "Would you rather be sitting like this or do you want to lie down?"

One minute passed. Then another. Finally, as if only just processing her question, Kael eased himself back onto the bed to lean against the stack of pillows. He stared straight up at the billowing canopy above, a dark brocade that draped elegantly, if heavily, over the bed and down each of the four posts.

Aisling sat beside him on the edge of the mattress and carefully smoothed the first handful of salve onto the scars that began at his hip, spreading it slowly upwards over the rippling contours of his stomach. With each sweep of her hand, with each shared breath, her compassion for him deepened. She pushed away the memory of the last time she'd seen him like this—the last time she'd touched him like this. A creeping blush mimicked the heat from his skin on her fingers as it spread up her neck and across her cheeks.

She began working it higher then, towards his chest. The scars there were more pronounced, a deeper shade of red and warm enough to melt the salve away almost instantly. Kael shifted uncomfortably, tensing beneath her touch, pain etched obviously into his features. The scarring that mottled his chest was nearly as bad as that on his face and neck. Aisling halted her progress. She was nervous.

"I'll be gentle," she promised. She wasn't sure who she was trying to reassure, herself or the formidable Unseelie King who was now lying vulnerable beside her.

"Just do it," he hissed through gritted teeth. Aisling twisted her hair out of the way and tucked it into the neck of her sweatshirt before she leaned over him, holding herself up with her free hand on the outside of his opposite shoulder. His eyes were squeezed shut; she was thankful that he couldn't see the apprehension in her own.

She could feel the heat radiating off of his chest before her fingers even met his skin and half-expected the salve to sizzle on contact. A low growl emanated from deep in Kael's throat, and Aisling flinched when he pulled away sharply. Knowing that she was only adding to his pain made her unexpectedly nauseous. She had to remind herself, over and over again, that it would make things better.

"Be still," she murmured. Working as quickly as she could with one hand, she massaged the salve into his wounds.

As her fingers moved deftly across his collarbone and up his neck, Kael's eyes flew open and he sucked in a sharp gasp. Those silver eyes had all the wildness of a trapped animal, caught between the desire to escape the pain and the knowledge that it had to be faced. His right hand shot up to grip Aisling's wrist beside his shoulder. His long, slender fingers encircled it completely and he squeezed until his knuckles blanched white. With his left hand, he found the material of her sweatshirt beside his hip and clenched it tightly in his fist. Aisling paused to let him readjust around her. The pressure on her wrist was enough to make her wince, but she wouldn't dare ask him to loosen his grip.

"We're nearly there, catch your breath." She held in place for several seconds, offering him a moment of respite and waiting for his unspoken signal that he was ready for her to continue. She took a deep breath, too, and concentrated on stilling her trembling hand.

Kael turned his head to the side to give her better access to his injuries and to hide his face as it twisted in agony. He was losing what little control he had left; a tremor wracked his body as a guttural sob escaped his lips.

"Breathe," she urged again softly. She pressed on, ensuring the salve was spread across every divot, every exposed muscle fiber, every raw edge. Kael could no longer stop himself from crying out, and his breaths came in short, ragged bursts as sweat beaded on his forehead. Aisling spoke to him quietly as she worked, her words a steady stream of encouragement and calm.

Finally, she set the jar aside. She wiped the last of the salve off on the leg of her pants and laid her palm gently on the uninjured side of Kael's heaving chest. She willed her pounding heart to slow and swallowed back the bile that had crept insistently up the back of her throat. He kept his face turned away, still gripping onto her with both hands.

"Settle down," Aisling said. "Let yourself relax. You're alright." Minute by minute, Kael's breathing deepened and his grip loosened. His body gradually sank into the mattress and the waves of feverish heat that had been rolling off his body eased.

She guessed that by now, *surely* by now, Kael would have gathered his thoughts and regained his composure enough to challenge her return to the Undercastle. To banish her once more, or to order her locked back in the dungeon. And because hearing him say it a second time may have even hurt worse than the first, Aisling decided it would be best for them both if she left before he could try.

"Rest now," she whispered as she rose from the bed, voice already thick with the tears she knew would fall the moment she exited his chamber. But his grip on her wrist, which had only just begun to ease, tightened again suddenly.

"Do not leave," Kael demanded urgently, almost pleading. He turned his head to look at her, unmasked desperation coloring his eyes.

Stunned by the stark difference between his request and what she'd imagined he would say instead, Aisling stilled. His panic tugged at her heart more than she was prepared for.

"Okay," she whispered. She reached down and pushed a few damp strands of hair out of his face. "I'll stay."

Still, he didn't release his grip. He let his eyes fall closed, and Aisling thought that for the very first time since she'd seen him speaking from the dais on Nocturne, his face clearly showed the weight of the lifetimes he had lived—longer than she could fathom.

Once he'd calmed enough to let her slip from his grasp, Aisling pulled a chair around from his desk and sat as close to his bedside as she could manage. He still trembled, and his breathing, though slower, was harsh and labored. She reached out to him once more.

THE RED WOMAN AND THE WHITE BEAR

When he felt her hand come to rest on his arm, he took it in his own and held it tightly against the scars that carved canyons over his heart.

32

AN OLD INJURY

KAEL

Kael had let himself imagine, only once, what he might say if Aisling ever returned. The angry words he'd hurl at this human girl who had fooled him—who had *used* him—not once, but twice. He thought he'd let her go too quickly, too easily. He'd considered it on the second day's ride toward Ilindor, letting different scripted scenarios unfurl in his mind, but none satisfied him. Not one of his imagined insults were biting enough, nor were his invented punishments harsh enough. He'd welcomed the distraction during the ride, but each version had felt hollow and trivial.

It mattered very little, though. He would never see her again, or if he did, it would be from across the battlefield as she marched alongside the Seelie Court in keeping with her prophesied destiny to destroy him.

But when he heard her voice behind him in the darkness of his chamber, the anger he had deliberately stoked inside his heart didn't surge as he expected it would. Then, when she said his name so softly, it dissipated entirely.

Aisling had come back. She'd come back *for him.*

Once around midday, he awoke with a start, sure it had been a dream. Sure *she* had been a dream. So at the sound of quiet breathing by his bedside, his body reacted before his brain registered what he was doing, shadows leaching out painfully through his ruined skin and finding their way towards her exposed throat. But Aisling didn't flinch, didn't startle. She only took a slow breath and in an instant Kael was filled with that overwhelming calm she was somehow able to force into his being. This time, she did it without even touching him. Maybe she'd sent it through the shadows that slid silently from her neck, almost apologetic in their retreat. The raw red circle they left behind was glaring even in the pitch dark.

A part of him still expected her to recoil in disgust after that; longed for her to pull away and leave him be. But she didn't. And instead of becoming angry or fleeing afraid, she just gently replaced her hand on his chest, tracing soothing circles there with her thumb.

Her touch, her voice, her very presence beside him was the lifeline Kael so desperately needed to haul himself out of the darkness. His pain began to recede, slow as the tide. He came back into himself, bit by grueling bit, guided by the press of her palm.

Aisling was still beside him the next time he woke. Fast asleep, her head was cocked to rest against the side of the chair and her features were relaxed save for a tiny furrow between her brows. He reached out to her. With the tip of his finger just a hair's breadth from her skin, he traced the outline of her arm. Her shoulder. Her collarbone. Bolder still, her forehead. Her cheekbone. Her nose. He could have counted every freckle if the room had been brighter. Then, the bow of her lips. His stomach twisted with want.

Before he could break, Kael slid from his bed and retreated silently into his washroom to bathe and change—something he hadn't managed to do for some time.

In the candlelight, he reached out into the magic that hummed always in the air, manipulating and molding it before letting the glamour settle back over his body. It came to rest gently atop his scars, filling and smoothing and concealing. It was imperfect, and thinner than that which he could typically cast and maintain, but it was a significant improvement. Neither the water in the bath nor the fibers of his fresh tunic brought the same chafing, searing pain they had since his collapse. Now, their contact with his skin felt more akin to running a finger through a flame than being bathed in molten heat.

Aisling still hadn't stirred by the time he reemerged, so Kael busied himself quietly disposing of the rotting food and lighting enough candles to illuminate the room with a warm, golden glow. He made his bed. Fluffed and straightened the pillows. Anything to keep his focus off the nervous energy buzzing through him, turning his movements frenetic and graceless.

It was the sound of broken glass grinding beneath his feet that finally woke her.

When the pair noticed each other from across the room, Aisling rose from the chair defensively, seemingly just as prepared to face Kael's anger as he had been to feel it. They stood facing each other down nearly for an eternity before Kael stalked towards her. Aisling stumbled in her haste to clear the chair and backed into the stone wall. Her eyes were wide and fearful.

Kael stopped a foot away despite the insistent tugging feeling inside urging him to move even closer. Though his heart raced, his voice came out steady and sure when he asked, "Why are you here?"

Aisling looked away, fixing her gaze on the lowest burning candle on his dresser. Kael waited and waited for her answer while she appeared to be giving each word great consideration as she pulled them together. His own mind filled her silence unbidden with fresh lies she might tell, or excuses. Perhaps Raif had threatened her to return, and it hadn't been her decision at all.

Finally, she answered: "Because I care about you." She said it simply and quietly and he could hear—could *feel*—the truth of it.

"That is a curse I wouldn't wish on my worst enemy," Kael said wryly as he took another cautious step forward.

"You can't make me leave again." Aisling was looking up at him now. By the stubborn set of her jaw and the defiant tilt of her chin, Kael knew she wasn't likely to yield. She reached out as though to brush her hand over his arm but appeared to think better of it and dropped it back to her side. "I'm not going to leave," she insisted once more.

Something inside of him—that writhing, coiling thing that felt always ready to burst out of his chest, fracturing bones and tearing skin—settled. The vicious heat that seemed to pulse constantly through his veins cooled, just slightly.

"I would not ask you to." Certainly his assurance was no grand declaration, but it was the best he could manage, and he hoped that for now it would be enough.

Aisling nodded, shifting like she was suddenly uncomfortable with their closeness. Kael took a step back and she swept her eyes over his exposed skin. "You look better."

"Thanks to you," Kael supplied. He pulled down the collar of his tunic so she could see that the scarring was almost entirely camouflaged. She once again looked as though she wanted to touch him, and once again pulled herself back. Kael berated himself momentarily for the way his pulse had quickened at the sight of her reaching for him, for the warmth that had crept into his heart uninvited. He had to remind himself to keep his distance.

"Raif told me that it's from an old injury," Aisling said. She paused then to let Kael fill in the rest. With a heavy sigh, he gestured towards the table. He pulled out a chair for Aisling to sit, then took a seat across from her. Golden light danced over her face, softening her features and making her eyes sparkle. For just a moment, Kael let himself appreciate the girl seated across from him. He'd never imagined the Red Woman would be beautiful.

"I told you," he began, "that I was made king because of my magic. I was raised by the Prelates from birth to fulfill this role because of the gift that I was given by the Low One." He tried to keep his mind on the present while he spoke. He didn't want to get lost in the memories of that part of his life.

"A vessel," she recalled.

Kael nodded. "I've been revered as a symbol of unmatched power all my life. The Prelates knew what I was capable of long before I did; they pushed me to my limits, again and again, under the guise of instruction. They—and the Low One—were the only family I ever knew. It was by their teachings that I learned greed."

Aisling leaned in, listening intently. Taking in every word, formulating a clearer image of Kael in her head. He only hoped it wouldn't be too monstrous.

"They were never satisfied, and so neither was I. I wanted more: to improve my power, to expand my kingdom. To overtake Wyldraíocht and see the end of the Seelie Court. I was young, and hot-headed."

"And that's changed?" Aisling teased gently, one eyebrow raised.

"Would you like to know what happened or not?" he chided. He'd missed her quick humor, though. If he had the energy, he may have even laughed.

She held up her hands. "Alright, alright. No more interruptions."

"I was frustrated, as were the Prelates, by my lack of control. I could manage it, but it was inconsistent. I knew that if I could only harness my magic, gain permanent mastery over it, I could be ten times more powerful than even they anticipated. A hundred times more. That greed drove me down a dangerous path." Kael began to bounce his leg beneath the table. Aisling slid one foot forward to rest the toe of her shoe against his boot, and he took a breath.

"You don't have to tell me any of this, Kael. You don't owe me an explanation." Her gaze was sympathetic, devoid of judgement. He let it comfort him.

"I communed with the Low One; begged him for an answer. What he gave, I misinterpreted. I attempted to complete a blood rite to strengthen my control. All magic comes with a price, but *Sangelas* most of all. Its price is costly, and painful. This was how I paid." He looked away from her then, gesturing briefly to the left side of his body.

"I pushed my magic to the very edge of what I could handle, and then beyond that," Kael continued. "And what little control I had even then was stripped away. What I have now is a fraction of what I had before, at most. I regret it." In truth, there were many things Kael regretted. Giving voice to his regret for sending Aisling away only made him realize all of the others that he'd so carefully concealed from himself over the years.

"I'm sorry that you've had to bear all of this alone," Aisling whispered.

He gave only a tight nod. "We do what we must to survive without considering what it will be like to live with those things afterwards."

When she finally, finally reached out to brush her fingers over the back of his hand, the tension fell from his shoulders. There was a secret part of Kael that had wanted Aisling to see him this way; wanted to know that she would still care for him even when she saw every broken, cruel, twisted fragment. The sharp edges that would, and had, hurt her. The blind fury that he wore as armor. To know that she could see through all of the bitter hatred into his core where that centuries-old storm raged, and that she wouldn't fear the tempest that waited there.

And here she sat, undeterred and unafraid. Her empathy was a force of nature.

She smoothed her thumb across his knuckles. "Thank you for telling me. I'm sure it's not easy to talk about."

"You are the only one who's ever known the full story," Kael admitted. The Prelates knew only that he'd tried and failed; Raif knew only that he'd sacrificed a part of himself to become a stronger king. None but Aisling and himself knew of the blinding, hungry greed that had driven him to the ritual. And none but the two of them would ever know of his regret for attempting it.

"And," he added before she could speak again, "you are the only one to have given me the control I've sought all along."

Instead of responding, Aisling sat quietly, watching the candlelight play over their hands. Kael let her process in silence. Her face was unguarded when she was thinking; he could see the wheels turning over in her mind. Sadness flitted across her features, and hurt. Then resolve.

She stood, and Kael mirrored her action. The scrape of the chairs against stone seemed loud after their stillness.

"I should let you rest awhile longer," she said.

Kael offered a tired half-smile. "Would that I could. I have left matters unattended for far too long in my absence. But," he hesitated, letting that smile mask the panic that gripped his heart, "you'll stay?"

Aisling nodded. "If you'll allow it."

"Without question."

She nodded again, already moving toward the door. Over her shoulder, she made to say something more, but Kael had already caught her by the arm and spun her back into his chest.

The bruising kiss he delivered stopped her from speaking further, punishing her for leaving. Punishing himself for making her leave. She froze, then melted. He curled his fingers around her jaw to still her there against him as he deepened the kiss, pushing his tongue between her waiting lips. He'd been starving for her: for the press of her skin against his, for the way she was so gentle with him despite the scrape of his rough edges. She could have been harsh or unkind, as he had been, but that wasn't Aisling.

He felt the shift in Aisling's body as her initial surprise quickly gave way to a surge of longing and she responded to him with a fervor that mirrored his own. Her arms wrapped around his neck as their mouths moved together with an almost desperate intensity, somehow speaking every unspoken word that hung between them. His grip on her tightened just slightly as he tried to anchor himself to this precise moment. Aisling's mouth was warm and demanding; Kael's breath mingled with hers and he kissed her with such hunger it frightened him. It didn't seem to frighten her, though.

It was only with great reluctance that he relaxed his hold on her and let her settle back onto her feet. Her hands slid down to rest on his arms for balance, but he kept his around her waist. He wasn't ready to let her go.

"I'll send for you shortly," Kael promised, pressing his lips to her forehead this time. Cheeks flushed and eyes shining, Aisling could only nod wordlessly before she took her leave.

33

THE WHITE BEAR

AISLING

Briar was on Aisling almost before she managed to pull Kael's door closed behind her. He lunged forward and planted his front paws squarely on her chest, toppling her back several steps until she could balance with his weight. Rodney scowled up at her from where he was seated on the cold ground on the opposite side of the corridor.

"Really, Aisling?" he groused. "You were in there for ages."

Aisling dropped Briar's paws and crossed over to Rodney, kicking one of his feet with hers lightly. "You didn't have to wait out here the whole time."

He scoffed. "You're lucky that's all I did; I should have come in with you."

"I was fine," Aisling insisted. She held out a hand to Rodney and when he took it, she hauled him to his feet.

"What took you so long, anyhow?" Rodney rubbed his backside and rolled his shoulders, wincing at the stiffness there. He began walking up the passageway in the direction they'd entered from the night before. Briar padded alongside Aisling, occasionally working his head under her hand to be scratched.

"I fell asleep." Her lips tingled and her cheeks felt hot and flushed. She was glad that Rodney seemed more focused on finding his way than on her lie.

"Not with *him?*" he pressed. She didn't like his tone or the way he deliberately avoided saying Kael's name. Even addressing him by his formal title would have sounded kinder.

"No, not with *Kael.*" Aisling stressed his name to make her point. "But even if I had, it wouldn't be any of your business at all."

Not far beyond the entrance to Kael's suite of rooms, Rodney showed Aisling into the adjoining chambers that had been prepared for them. He'd taken the liberty of selecting the deeper of the two for Aisling, so that she'd have to cross through both their shared bathroom and his room to exit back into the hall. She had no doubt he'd done so on purpose.

Her bag was on the bed, open. Rodney had pulled Briar's food out, but he'd left the bowl untouched. Now that he was back at Aisling's side, he ate like he hadn't in days.

"As your best friend, I have every right to worry. So when you put yourself at risk, it absolutely is my business." Rodney leaned against the carved doorway and watched Aisling dig in her bag for a fresh set of clothes.

"I wasn't at risk. I thought he'd send me away," Aisling said, sitting on the bench at the foot of the bed, "but I knew he wouldn't hurt me."

"Well," he started, shifting uncomfortably and rubbing his neck. He was blushing now, and making a concerted effort to look anywhere else in the room but at Aisling. "If you ever want to talk about any of...*that*...I can listen. I doubt I can offer any great advice, but—"

Wrinkling her nose, Aisling cut him off quickly. "Gross, no. Thanks, but no thanks."

Rodney blew out a heavy sigh. "Thank fuck. I really didn't want to hear about it."

Aisling rolled her eyes and shooed Rodney back into his side of their suite so that she could bathe and change. Her fingers still trembled as she worked the soap over her body, the emotions that had been building in her chest since her return wearing aggressively on her nerves. And that kiss—that kiss had told her everything she needed to know. He'd missed her. Once, she wouldn't have thought him capable of such a feeling. But Kael was not the monster that everyone made him out to be. That he made himself out to be.

Rodney was sprawled on his bed when she emerged, and she joined him. He nodded toward the table in the corner, now laden with fruit and bread. "A hob dropped that off a minute ago. Eat something."

Aisling, already comfortable amidst the mountain of pillows stacked behind her, let her head fall back against the headboard. "I will in a while."

With an irritable groan, Rodney rolled off of the bed and went to retrieve the tray himself. He set it between them, then tore a roll in two and handed half to Aisling.

"Eat," he ordered. "Now. You've not had any food since we got back to your apartment."

Aisling made a show of taking a bite of bread. Once she had, she realized just how hungry she really was. She filled a plate with fruit then settled back again. Rodney nodded his approval.

"I'm glad you're here," she said to him. She hadn't voiced the sentiment during their visit to the Seelie Court, but she wished that she had. She thought that she should say so much more often. She was lucky to have a friend like Rodney.

He nudged her shoulder with his own. "No place else I'd rather be, Ash."

"Well, I'm not sure that's true, but I'm grateful either way." Aisling bit into a piece of fruit that resembled a peach but tasted closer to an over-sweet watermelon. She devoured it and would have licked the juice that ran down between her fingers had she been alone. Its pit was small; she rolled it over and over her tongue, savoring the last bits of flavor it carried.

"So what now?" Rodney asked.

"I think I need to tell Kael about Door Number Three." She dropped the pit onto her plate and reached hungrily for the only other peach-like stone fruit on the tray before Rodney could take it for himself.

He sat bolt upright then, sending several grapes tumbling to the floor. "Like hell you do."

Aisling winced; she'd expected this reaction. "He needs to know. And we need someone's help; all we have is that picture. We don't even know if they exist."

"Exactly, Ash. We know nothing about them. Why tell him something that isn't a sure thing?" Rodney pressed.

"Because maybe he knows more. There are books here, too." Old ones—not those in the library, but the ones she'd seen organized so carefully on the shelves that lined Kael's study. With his love of history, surely he would have at least heard of the Silver Saints.

"Listen." Rodney shifted on the bed to face Aisling and waited for her to turn towards him to speak again. "I get that you have some sort of *something* going on with him, but that doesn't mean you can just trust him with this."

"I think I can," she argued. She hoped she could, at least.

"What makes you think he will agree that it's even a viable option? This isn't a favorable solution for him, either. It may not be the destruction of his court promised by the prophecy, but it would still see him removed from power."

Aisling raked her fingers back through her damp hair, frustrated. "I don't know, Rodney. Maybe it does, and maybe it doesn't. But I have to tell him. I have to at least try."

"Why?" he demanded.

She chewed the inside of her cheek, hurt blooming in the spaces between her ribs. Kael wasn't the only one with regrets; she had her own to grapple with, too. She wished bitterly that she'd never let herself be talked into this game of manipulation in the first place. Had she known Kael—had she known what he would mean to her—she would have done things differently. She would never have used him as she had.

"Because I can't lie to him again," Aisling said quietly.

"Ash—" Rodney started, but she cut him off.

"No, Rodney. No more secrets. We're doing this my way now."

He huffed, slouching back against the pillows. "Your way isn't strategic."

"Strategy hasn't gotten us anywhere. We're still no closer than we were when I came to you that very first morning after I met the Shadowwood Mother." Aisling bit into the fruit, sucking the sweet nectar that dripped from its flesh.

"It's gotten us to the Silver Saints," he argued.

"*Research,*" she corrected, "has gotten us to a legend of an ancient Fae court that may or may not be able to be called on as a neutral ruling party." It was dismal, really, when she laid it out that way. By the withdrawn silence that Rodney fell into, she knew he was feeling the same sense of frustration that now weighed on her shoulders.

※

When Kael sent for her, Aisling and Rodney were dozing on the bed, Briar stretched out at their feet. It was Methild who delivered the note for Aisling, and she could have sworn she saw kindness warming the old hob's eyes when she handed over the small piece of paper before scurrying off down the corridor.

Rodney rose from the bed, stretching, as Aisling read the note. It wasn't a long message, nor did it say anything particularly fond, but seeing her name in Kael's handwriting brought a smile to her face all the same. His crude map, too. She would fold it up and keep it hidden away with the other. She hadn't been able to bring herself to throw it out.

"I'm coming too." Rodney was pulling on his shoes. Briar noticed, and immediately attached himself to Aisling's hip.

"No, you're not." She slipped her own on, too, and tugged on her jacket.

"Well what am I supposed to do then?" Rodney crossed his arms, dejected, looking awfully similar to a pouting child.

Aisling rolled her eyes and gestured at the open door. "Go do your thing," she suggested.

Rodney raised an eyebrow. "Which is what, exactly?"

"I don't know, Rodney, go mingle. Make connections. I'd rather Lyre not be our only ally down here. Find us some better friends." Aisling ignored Rodney's heavy sighs and instead turned her attention to Briar, sitting now at her feet. His tail swept back and forth across the floor in a wide arc. Then, she pulled his leash from where it was draped over the back of a chair and clipped it to his collar. It was about time Kael met the White Bear.

On her last visit to the Undercastle, once she'd been allowed to wander the halls on her own, Aisling had felt nearly invisible. The flurry of activity bustled around her, uncaring of her presence there. But now, with Briar lumbering by her side, the faeries gave her a wide berth—the hobs, most of all. Briar was unbothered, having been largely desensitized after spending days being doted on by the Seelie Fae. It was unlikely that he'd find a faerie so interested in braiding his fur here, though.

As if he'd been already gripping the handle, poised and waiting for her to arrive, Kael pulled open the door before Aisling's second knock. He stiffened when he saw Briar, who had fallen into a defensive posture as soon as he'd scented the king.

"I was unaware that you brought your beast," Kael acknowledged curtly, falling back a step. Aisling tightened her grip on Briar's leash and tugged him into the study behind her. His hackles were raised, and his teeth bared, but he hadn't yet begun to growl.

"This is Briar," she said. When Kael only eyed him apprehensively, she added, "He's big, but he's harmless. Honest."

"Charming." Kael kept his distance.

Aisling directed Briar to sit, then reached out to Kael. "Come here, let him smell you and he'll settle down."

"I would rather not." Though he maintained a polite, neutral expression, his tone was clipped and his gaze moved sharply over Briar's form, one predator studying another.

"I'd never have guessed that the Unseelie King would be afraid of a dog," Aisling teased, unable to suppress a laugh.

"I am not afraid of anything," Kael shot back. "Least of all the White Bear."

"Then come over here," she insisted, her hand still outstretched to him. "Please. It's important to me."

Not attempting to hide his disdain any longer, Kael crossed the study with hesitant steps. Once he was within reach, Aisling caught his hand and held it still in front of Briar. She could feel Kael's racing pulse beneath her fingers; the muscles in his arm were taught and ready to move to the dagger at his hip at the slightest provocation.

When Briar refused to approach, she knelt down, pulling a reluctant Kael with her. He bent his knees into a crouch. Finally, slowly, Briar sniffed the very tips of Kael's fingers. It was a tense accord, but enough to satisfy her for the time being. The pair sprang apart the moment she let them go. Kael retreated behind his desk.

"Dramatic," she said. "The both of you."

"A warning might have been nice." Still tense, Kael crossed his arms and leaned against the back of his chair. Aisling took a moment to look around. The only other time she'd visited Kael's study had ended in disaster. Her gaze landed on the shelf he'd pinned her to. Once more his face flashed in her mind, the wrath in his eyes that barely concealed the hurt. The violence his hand on her throat had promised before he let her go. Aisling shivered and pressed herself to Briar.

Kael noticed where she was looking, realizing what image had risen to the forefront of her memory. Maybe getting swept away in that same bitter memory himself.

"Shall we take a walk?" he offered. "There are new flowers in the night garden since you last visited."

Gratefully, Aisling nodded. "Fresh air sounds great."

Even now, as winter had befallen the Unseelie Court, the night garden was lusher than ever. The trees hung heavy, so laden with snow and blooms and icicles that their branches brushed the top of Aisling's head where the path narrowed. She kept Briar tight against her outside leg on a short leash to keep him from sniffing the poisonous flowers, but he was too focused on watching Kael to stray.

"When you left here," Kael began, "where did you go?" When Aisling didn't answer right away, he took her hand and placed it on his arm, tucking it in against his chest.

The simple gesture was comforting enough for her to make her admission. "I went to the Seelie Court."

Kael only nodded. "I thought you likely would."

Aisling recounted her visit in brief, glossing over Laure's intentions of using her as a weapon against Kael and instead focusing on the things she'd noticed about the court. Its sinister underpinnings that still lingered with her.

"I don't want to see them rule. They're no better than..." She trailed off without saying what she intended.

"Us?" Kael filled in the blank. "I might have told you that, had you asked."

Aisling shrugged. "I wouldn't have believed you if I hadn't seen it for myself. And even once I was there, I didn't realize it at first." She drew in a breath then, steeling herself for the next revelation. "But I think there could be a third option."

"I'm listening."

Aisling reluctantly withdrew her hand from Kael's arm to fish in her jacket pocket for the folded bit of paper she'd stowed there alongside his note. She unfolded it carefully and handed it to him to examine. The bright moon overhead and the soft, blue glow of the angel's trumpet blooms illuminated the printed page.

"Do you recognize this?" she asked.

"I do; I have the original artwork," Kael mused, then ran his thumb over the ragged edge where Rodney had torn the page from the book. "Where did you come by this print?"

"The Seelie archives," Aisling admitted, somewhat sheepishly. "It shows the first three courts, right? Yours, the Seelie Court, and the Silver Saints?"

Kael stopped walking to look down at her, an amused smile tugging at the corners of his lips. "Is that what you call them?"

"It was the closest translation Rodney could come up with."

"The Silver Saints," he repeated, then said their true name in the Fae tongue. "They came even before the division of our courts and disappeared not long after. They were Tuatha Dé Danann—Light Bringers, the first Fae race. Neither their race nor their magic, has been seen in Wyldraíocht for a very, very long time."

"They were really real?" Aisling wondered. "The book we found made them sound like legend."

"Many claim them to be. The truth about your Silver Saints is difficult to come by." Kael looked again at the page in his hand then passed it back to Aisling. She returned it to her pocket.

"But you know about them?" she asked.

Kael nodded. "There is a book in my collection, one of very few in existence that tells of their involvement in the creation of the courts."

"What if they could be found again? What if they could fix things?" Aisling was aware of how farfetched her words sounded, but she had clung to the hope of this solution so desperately since they'd found the page in the archives that she didn't care.

"You know as well as I that they play no role in this prophecy." There was a wistfulness in Kael's voice that told Aisling maybe he longed to feel that same hope, too.

"The prophecy isn't clear; who's to say it isn't for us to determine what it means?" she argued.

"That is not how prophecies work."

"Says who?" she challenged again. "You don't even know who wrote it, much less the intention behind their words. It's a prophecy, not an instruction manual." She repeated the words the Shadowwood Mother had said to her in the thicket that night—the very words that had so frustrated her now offered the possibility of a different path.

Kael raised an eyebrow. "You're beginning to sound like one of us."

Aisling smiled back, briefly. "I'll consider that a compliment."

Taking her hand again, Kael pulled Aisling to resume their slow, meandering walk through the garden.

"I notice but one flaw in your plan," he said. "And it is not insignificant."

Aisling held her breath. "What is it?"

"You would still see my court lose its autonomy."

"Not necessarily," she insisted quickly. "I envision them as more of a neutral third party. Like an impartial body that could oversee a transition to peace. Surely you wouldn't see this war continue forever just to gain control over dominions you care nothing about?"

"You seem to forget I am a creature born for war." Kael cast her a sidelong glance as his lips pressed into a dry smirk.

"*Raised* for war, maybe. But born for it?" Aisling shook her head solemnly, tightening her grip on his arm. "There's much more to you than that."

Without answering one way or another, or acknowledging even the possibility of her plan, Kael directed their path back to the Undercastle. "It is cold out tonight," he offered by way of explanation. "You need to get warm."

Aisling didn't press further, but she hadn't given up just yet. Though he hadn't agreed to her idea, he hadn't said no, either.

34

LEVERAGE

KAEL

Sweat beaded across Kael's brow as he lunged forward, longsword gripped tightly in his hand. It gleamed when it caught the light. Raif parried the blow easily, letting it glance off his shield.

"Your strikes are slow tonight," he commented, dodging another swipe. "Soften your grip."

"My grip is fine," Kael growled. His hair slipped loose from where he'd tied it at the nape of his neck and stuck to the sweat that dripped from his temple. Finally, he landed a strike on the outside of Raif's thigh, the blade biting into his thick training leathers. The pair had been sparring for nearly an hour, and to Kael's great frustration, he'd only manage to land four hits to Raif's six. He was out of practice, and he was distracted.

"A decent effort for your first time raising a weapon in nearly a month," Raif appraised, hardly winded by their fight. "Your strength will return. It's your focus that concerns me."

Kael, unbuckling his own leathers, cut a harsh glare in Raif's direction. "I do not recall asking for your assessment of my skills, Captain."

"And yet I've given it all the same," Raif shot back, then sighed. "Did I make a mistake?"

"Beating me? Some would say so." Kael reached up to retie his damp hair, pushing strands roughly back off of his skin.

"Bringing the girl, Kael. I shouldn't have done so without your permission." Raif sat down heavily on a bench at the edge of the training ring and dug at a rock stuck in the tread of his boot with his dagger. Kael sat on a bench adjacent. He leaned forward to rest his elbows on his knees.

"You made the right decision. I would still be shut away if you hadn't." It was a difficult thing for Kael to admit out loud, that this human girl had been the one to drag him back from the edge. Raif knew it, too, and kept his eyes on the stone in his boot while Kael spoke.

"She is not what I expected the Red Woman to be," Raif said.

"Far, far from it," Kael agreed. "My imagined version certainly would have been easier to kill."

"She is as brave as I would have expected, though. It took very little convincing to get her to return once I told her of your injury, despite the way you parted." Raif gave up on the rock and began stripping off his leathers. Kael did the same.

"Indeed, she is that." To call Aisling merely brave felt like an understatement, but he couldn't think of a word strong enough to describe her courage. Or, maybe, stupidity, to have returned to help the male who she believed wanted her dead. Whichever it was, he was thankful for it.

"Care to ride with me?" Raif asked, standing now with his leather chest plate tucked under his arm. "I picked up a perimeter post for this morning. If I were to hazard a guess, I'd say you'd be unlikely to sleep if you returned to your chamber now."

"I could use the distraction," Kael agreed.

Once she'd been saddled, Kael mounted Furax fluidly and joined Raif at the tree line. His mare, slightly smaller but no less intimidating, stamped and snorted impatiently.

"You are the captain," Kael said as they began their route. "Why do you continue to take patrols? Especially at this hour. This job is for far greener soldiers."

Raif slashed at a low branch that hung over the trail and his horse kicked it aside when it fell to the snow-covered ground. "A good leader never asks their men to do what they would not themselves. And I like the quiet of the morning. It's good for thinking."

It *was* quiet, save for the birdsong of those which remained behind to winter there. Kael settled into Furax's rhythmic movement and drew in a breath of crisp, cold air. It wasn't often that he was out at this hour—he preferred sunset to sunrise—but there was something peaceful to being awake while the rest of his court retired for the day.

"And what is it that you have to think about?" Kael asked.

"The same as you, more than likely. The war, the future of your court. What the Red Woman means in all of this." Raif scanned the deep woods, though there was no sign of movement. They hadn't faced a threat this close to the Undercastle in years, but still the patrols continued like clockwork.

"What do you think?" Kael reached forward to brush a clump of snow from where it had fallen into Furax's mane, then leaned back in the saddle. He wished for an advisor to tell him what to do, what could be done. Raif was as close as he would get; Aisling's presence was certainly not a matter he would take to Werryn.

"I do not think she wishes to destroy you, as the prophecy would suggest. But," Raif added thoughtfully, "it is a prophecy for a reason."

"Even if she should stay and do nothing at all in its pursuit, it will come to pass regardless. Fate has already set things in motion." Kael did his best to push feeling out of his voice. He was skilled beyond all else at cool rationalization, but his current situation was putting that skill to the test, and he was failing. There was a crack in that dam he'd erected long ago to hold back his emotions, to keep them out of his way, and it seemed only to spread each time he thought of Aisling.

"What will you do?"

Kael sucked in another deep breath of that sharp air. The cold in his lungs soothed him some. "She suggested seeking out the Silver Saints to act as some sort of mediator in a peace negotiation." He pronounced their true name then, slowly, as though the words alone held the power to bring them back. The translation, though perhaps less impressive, felt somehow safer.

"The Silver Saints?" Raif barked out a surprised laugh. "Can it even be done?"

"I am not sure," Kael said truthfully.

"I haven't heard that name in an age. She'd have us return to the early days then? With the Silver Saints ruling over both courts?" Raif steered his horse down a narrower trail. Furax followed without direction from Kael.

"I am not sure," he repeated. "I think that she is naïve and idealistic to believe such a solution could be viable." He wished he could be, too. Seeing the hope shining in Aisling's eyes had nearly broken him; he'd never felt such a thing. But he wanted to. And if there was anyone in the entire realm that might inspire it in him, it would be her.

Raif dug in a saddlebag and withdrew a flask. He took a pull, then offered it to Kael. "Maybe. But it is clear that she wants to protect you."

"She is misguided." Kael accepted the flask gratefully, the honey wine warming his tongue and throat. He stopped himself short of draining it and handed it back to his friend.

"She cares about you." Raif finished it off then tucked the flask away.

"Again, misguided."

The pair rode in silence for a time before Raif spoke again. "If it were possible—if *you* were the one to raise the Silver Saints—it could give you more leverage on the outcome."

Kael looked at Raif. "Go on."

"If you are the one to raise them, they will see you as the cooperative party. It could give you greater pull in negotiations if they believe you wish to see this war end peaceably, rather than the Seelie Court."

Kael thought about this for several minutes, puzzling over the possibilities. Each path played out in his mind's eye, each decision branching off into countless others. The only path he was certain of was the one that saw Aisling by his side.

"If you're right, that could be the simplest way to maintain control of the end result," Kael acknowledged finally. "I could ensure that it is at least somewhat favorable for our court."

"It is far from a sure thing, but it may be the best option we have considered thus far," Raif said, then added: "however naïve and idealistic it may be."

⁂

The book was exactly where Kael remembered it, pinned between two other thick tomes high on the shelf directly behind the desk in his study, where he kept his most valuable manuscripts. These were not his favorites—those were filled with timeworn pages that he returned to again and again over the years. These were the most ancient, the most rare. He scarcely touched these.

It was bound in oxblood leather, unmarred, the spine barely creased. When it had been brought to him as part of a bounty collected after they'd seized some distant dominion, it was merely a loose collection of pages, tied around the middle with twine. He'd gotten it bound and, knowing wear would only lessen its value, had only opened it a handful of times since. Now, he held it against his chest as he walked through the corridors.

He slept well after his conversation with Raif, but he'd been eager for the day to pass and Aisling to wake. He wanted to speak with her again. More than that, he wanted to see her again. It was only with great effort that he'd left her at the door of her suite after they'd walked together through the night garden. If he'd had his way, and if she hadn't brought the White Bear along to chaperone, he'd have asked her back to his own chamber.

She was waiting for him in the throne room late that night, as his note had requested, but his gladness to see her faltered slightly when he noticed she was accompanied by the púca and the White Bear. Both looked as though they wanted to snarl when he entered.

"You brought company," Kael observed curtly.

Aisling threw him an apologetic smile. "They insisted."

"We're a package deal," Rodney said, squaring his shoulders.

"I was not complaining," Kael assured the three, however untrue. "I trust your rooms are satisfactory? And you've been fed?"

"We've been well taken care of, thank you." Aisling smiled again. It warmed him, that smile.

"Nice to see you understand hospitality, after all." Rodney grunted when Aisling drove her elbow into his ribs. Kael ignored the barb.

"Come," he said. "I would like to show you something." He shortened his long strides just enough for Aisling to fall into step beside him as he led the group across to the far side of the throne room.

"How are you feeling?" she asked, loud enough only for Kael's ears while Rodney trudged sullenly several paces behind.

"Well, thank you." Kael's fingers tightened around the edges of the tome he carried, suppressing the urge to reach out and take Aisling's hand, or to sweep away the strand of hair that had fallen across her cheek. "Very well."

He pushed open the door to a vestibule off the throne room. It was a small space, hand-carved into the stone rather than built from a natural cavern as the throne room was. There was a long table in the center, and torches burning on the walls illuminated the sturdy hewn chairs around it.

"I take meetings here on occasion," Kael explained as they filed in. Briar still gave him a wide berth, to his great relief. "With lords, generally, or their guard captains. Those whom I do not wish to give such access to the Undercastle as to see them in my study."

Aisling's eyes had already found the purpose for Kael's tour and she was moving toward the back of the space as though drawn by an invisible force. He and Rodney followed her, stopping before the rear wall and gazing up at the art that hung there.

"This is the original," she murmured. Four times the size of the page that was still folded up in her jacket pocket, the ink drawing that depicted the three courts was even more ornate than the print. Each fine, tiny detail etched there by hand had significance; the artist wasted no space with filler or meaningless imagery. Reaching above

Aisling's head, Kael unhooked it from the wall and turned to lay it flat on the table.

All three leaned in to peer at it closely. Kael seized the opportunity to step another half-inch nearer to Aisling, just enough that their arms touched when she bent forward. He ignored Briar's warning growl as he did so.

"I thought you might like to see it this way." Kael watched Aisling study the artwork, examining every inch of the uppermost segment that depicted the Silver Saints, high above the Seelie and Unseelie Courts. Even the stars that surrounded them, he'd been told, were accurate to their true placement in the sky when the image was drawn.

Once Aisling and Rodney straightened up and stepped away, Kael hung it back on the wall. Still, all three continued to stare up at it.

"I have given your suggestion a great deal of consideration, you know," Kael said. He kept his eyes on the drawing, though he heard Aisling turn to face him.

"Good of you," Rodney muttered.

"Quiet," Aisling hissed at him, then turned back to Kael. "And?"

He looked down at her. There it was again: that hope. It flooded his veins with a comforting heat. "And, despite my earlier apprehension, I believe that it may not be such a bad solution after all."

"Ah," Rodney said sarcastically. "So there's something in it for you, then. What's your angle, Highness?"

Kael's temper flared and his eyes snapped to Rodney's, boring into them fiercely. "Mind your silver tongue, púca, or you'll find it cut out of your head. Your cleverness will not be tolerated here."

"That's enough, both of you. Rodney, take Briar outside for me then make sure he eats." He opened his mouth to protest, but Aisling beat him to it: "Now. Go on."

Kael held his aggressive posture until Rodney had left the room with the White Bear in tow and didn't relax again until he felt Aisling's hand squeeze his arm gently.

"I'm sorry about him."

Kael offered her a tight smile. "Only one of them is your pet to control, and to your credit, he is much better behaved than the changeling."

Aisling's eyebrows shot up and she laughed loudly—a true, honest laugh. Kael would have done or said just about anything to have heard it again once she quieted.

He pulled out a chair for her and drew up one just beside. When he placed the book on the table between them, Aisling turned her body and their legs touched beneath the table. For a moment, Kael was afraid to move, afraid to breathe. If she'd done so on accident, the last thing he wanted to do was shift and alert her to their contact so she'd pull away. But when he finally did, she remained in place, her thigh pressing lightly against his own.

"This is the book you mentioned?" she asked.

"It is." He smoothed his hand over the soft leather of the cover then lifted it. The binding was still stiff enough to crack in protest as he opened it to the first page.

Aisling clicked her tongue. "I don't know why I expected I'd be able to read it."

"I can read it to you," he assured her.

For some time, the pair poured over the text. Every few pages he'd skim, Kael would translate aloud a passage he thought might interest Aisling. He'd have read her the entire thing, cover to cover, if she'd asked.

"The Silver Saints possess the ability of Far Sight, unique from other Tuatha Dé Danann, which permits them to briefly glimpse into the tapestry of fate, seeing each warp and weft, each thread and gap," he recited. "As such, their kind guided the lesser Fae through periods of struggle and unrest and, in time, set them down the path to develop a system of two courts: the Seelie and the Unseelie, the light and the shadow."

"We could use a bit of Far Sight. Does it say where to find them?" Aisling asked, dubiously eyeing the dwindling number of pages they had left.

"They cannot be found. They must be called, I believe." Kael skimmed ahead several more sections.

"Called?"

He hummed. "With a ritual of some sort, I would imagine. They no longer reside in this realm."

"Something like how you call to the Low One?" Aisling shifted, uncomfortable with even the mention of His name.

"Something like that." When she shivered, he pressed his leg a bit tighter against hers, a gesture he hoped would comfort her against the memory of her experience in The Cut.

"But this book doesn't say anything about it?" She watched him turn the next page, then two more after that.

"It may be too old; it could have been written when they were still here," he surmised as he neared the end.

"Oh." The disappointment was as clear in Aisling's voice as it was written across her face.

Desperate to keep that spark of hope burning in her, Kael said quickly, "I still have several other volumes I can look in."

"*We* can look in," she corrected. "We're on the same team now."

No longer able to resist the urge, Kael reached out to tuck that stray hair back from her face, then let his hand drop to grasp hers where it rested on the table. "Indeed we are."

He kept ahold of Aisling's hand as he walked her back to her suite, after she insisted that she check in on Rodney to make sure he hadn't gotten himself tossed in the dungeon.

"After all this is over, will you teach me your language?" she asked thoughtfully as they stood in the passageway in front of her door.

He raised her hand to his lips and brushed a gentle kiss over her knuckles. "I will teach you whatever you would like."

35

RESISTANCE

AISLING

"I'm going for a walk; I'll be back in a little while." Aisling stood in the doorway between Rodney's chamber and their adjoining bathroom. He was lying sideways across his bed, flipping through an old comic he'd tucked into his bag. He'd had several more, along with two paperbacks, when they'd packed to go to Aisling's apartment on the mainland, but left those behind to lighten his load when their plans changed.

He looked up at her from the page quizzically. "A walk?"

"I'm restless," she said. "I haven't been able to fall asleep yet." She had tried, though not for long and not terribly hard.

"And do you always brush your hair before you go for walks?" he challenged.

Aisling reached up defensively to touch the ends of her hair. "I always brush it before I go to bed," she shot back. "But like I said, I couldn't sleep."

Rodney hummed, then rolled onto his back and held the comic up over his face. "I won't wait up."

It took her longer than it should have to reach Kael's chamber, having turned around several times, convinced she was making a mistake. There was a voice in her head, loud and crystal clear, that repeated over and over all the terrible, cruel things she'd expected Kael to say when she returned. It was unkind, that voice, even though he hadn't been. And she thought that she deserved every unkind thing it said.

By the time she stopped outside of his doors, her heart was hammering almost painfully against her ribs and her palms were sticky with sweat. A light shone through the crack beneath the doors, and it flickered and shifted as Kael moved around inside. She wiped both hands on her thighs before knocking softly. In the few seconds it took him to pull one of them open, Aisling prayed he would ignore the disturbance. Or that the movement inside was Methild, cleaning, and Kael wasn't there at all.

"Aisling," he said, surprised. She loved the way her name sounded in his mouth, almost as much as she loved the way his name felt in hers. "Is everything alright?"

"I wanted to apologize again for Rodney's behavior earlier. I talked to him; it won't happen again." All of the more plausible excuses she'd rehearsed on her walk had dried up on her tongue.

"No need," he assured her. "He is only protecting his friend. I might even call it admirable, were it not directed at me."

"Still," she said, "I'm sorry."

Kael moved closer to her, so that she had to tip her chin to look up at him. "Was there anything else?"

Her breath hitched slightly. "Did you find any other books?"

"A handful. If you'd like, we can meet tonight in the library to read through them." His silver eyes were focused so intently on hers that she thought he might set her aflame where she stood. The heat that burned in her cheeks felt awfully close.

"That would be good."

A smirk lit Kael's face. "You came all the way here to discuss Rodney and books?"

"I just came to apologize for him." The tremor in Aisling's voice, and the fact that Kael undoubtedly heard it, only intensified her blush.

Kael leaned against the other door, still keeping that closeness. "So you mentioned."

"Right," Aisling said. The way his shirt subtly outlined his muscles had rendered her nearly speechless. The way his pants hung low around his hips, showing just the barest sliver of skin above the waistline as he settled his weight onto his shoulder, had halted all rational thought.

"Would you like to come in?" he asked, still in that same teasing tone. When she could only nod, Kael stepped aside and pulled the door open wider. His chamber was warmly lit by candles and a fire that burned low on the hearth. He'd been reading; there was a book flipped over the arm of the chair beside the hearth to mark his place.

"May I pour you a drink?" His voice startled her; she'd hardly heard him cross the chamber to where he kept several bottles of honey wine on a small table. Aisling nodded gratefully, already eager for the drink to soothe her nerves. When he handed her a full goblet, she thought his fingertips lingered where they brushed against hers for just a second longer than they should have.

Kael pulled up a second chair so that they could sit side by side before the fire. The hypnotic movement of the flames gave Aisling something to train her eyes on, something to prevent her from looking over to study the Unseelie King.

"I never truly thanked you," he said after a while, breaking the silence that had fallen over them.

Aisling turned in her chair to face him. He was already facing her. "For what?"

"For coming back. For bringing me back." The marked rigidity he usually carried melted away like ice thawing under warm sunlight—those layers of protection he wore so determinedly had fallen away one by one until all that remained before her now was raw and real.

"I'm just glad I could help." It fell short of everything she wanted to express, those words, but none would have done her feelings justice.

Kael finished his wine, then, once Aisling had done the same, took her goblet and set it on the ground beside his. He rose to his feet and extended a hand to her. When she took it and stood, he guided her to stand directly in front of him. He ran the rough pad of his thumb across her cheekbone and the featherlight touch made her shiver involuntarily.

"There are a great many things I have done in my years that I wish I could change," he said low. "I should not have sent you away as I did."

Aisling had to remind herself to breathe, but the exhale felt stuck in her lungs. "Anyone would have done the same. I should have told you sooner."

"You are here now." Kael slid his hand to her neck, then lower, so that calloused thumb was tracing her collarbone. "And you are so beautiful."

Each word that left his lips ticked down her spine, sending sparks through each vertebra one by one. She leaned into his caress, placing her own hand over his to hold it there against her chest.

"You're not afraid of me?" she asked, though she almost didn't want to know the answer.

He smiled ruefully. "There is only one monster between the two of us."

"Stop that," Aisling scolded, tightening her grip on his hand. "You're not. I wouldn't be standing here if you were."

Kael bent down and kissed her once, softly, then again. "What I feel for you is the kindest thing about me. The only kind thing."

Undone by the earnestness of his admission, Aisling rose up onto her toes to capture Kael's lips, far less gentle than he had been. She was feverish in her desire for him, but she found an edge of resistance beneath it all. She could feel it in the way he controlled his movements, in the way he seemed to pull himself back just before giving in fully. She could feel that same resistance in herself, too, though she was reluctant to acknowledge it.

She braced her hands against his hips and made to push back, but his arms around her waist held her in place. Both were breathing hard. Kael tucked his chin and pressed his forehead against hers. They held each other that way for some time, content to wordlessly be in each other's space. For now, it was enough.

⁂

For a week, Kael and Aisling spent their nights in the library. Briar remained by Aisling's side, growing steadily more tolerant of Kael. Rodney joined intermittently, sitting for as long as his attention span would allow before setting off in pursuit of his own agenda. They read through page after page in the tall stack of manuscripts Kael thought might contain something useful until the words swam on the parchment.

But it was their days that Aisling looked forward to the most. Each morning, she'd tiptoe through her and Rodney's adjoining chambers. Briar was easily bribed to keep quiet and Rodney, the heaviest sleeper she'd ever known, made for a poor sentinel. Only twice did he wake as she opened the door, both times grumbling something unintelligible and annoyed before rolling over and going back to sleep.

Kael began leaving his door slightly ajar, an unspoken signal that he was inside waiting for her. They spent hours together learning, exploring the limits of their trust, of their connection to each other. She was addicted to the taste of him, to his pine scent filling her nose, to the brush of his fingers over her bare skin.

So when he finally asked her to stay instead of returning to her own bed to sleep, Aisling didn't have to think about her answer; it was already waiting on her lips.

He had held her close, arms tight around her even as he slept, as though afraid that if he loosened his grip even a fraction she would disappear altogether. She didn't mind, though. Now, she thought, she was the Red Woman and she was his.

"That can't be it," Rodney said apprehensively. Despite the growing sense of despondency that threatened to crush Aisling, the most steadfastly hopeful among them, they had carried on as the pile dwindled to five books, then to three. But when Kael closed the cover on the last and largest tome, still without having found an answer, all three sat in resigned defeat around the library table.

"I'm sorry," Aisling finally said. "I really thought it would work."

Kael leaned over and pressed a kiss to her shoulder. "We will keep looking."

All week, he'd been careful not to show too much affection when they weren't alone. Aisling had avoided it, too. She was surprised by his action, however brief and small, and was unable to hide her smile despite the glare Rodney shot at them.

"Where else would we look?" she asked, glancing around at the library shelves.

"Books are not the only source of knowledge in Wyldraíocht," Kael said.

At this, Rodney perked up slightly. "You think she would know?"

"She may." Kael leaned back in his chair, a thoughtful expression on his face.

Aisling frowned, confused, and looked between the two males. "She?"

Before either could answer, Werryn stormed in from the corridor. His gaunt face was flushed with rage and a dagger was clutched in his shaking hand. Too weak to brandish it effectively, he held it low in front of his waist. Aisling drew back when he came to a stop nearly within striking distance.

"What is the meaning of this?" Kael demanded, rising from his chair and stepping closer to Aisling.

"You are a fool, Kael, to bring this *serpent* into our court. You've damned us all." His eyes were narrowed and angry and fixed on Aisling.

"*My* court," Kael corrected him coolly.

Werryn ignored him. "You have allowed the Red Woman to bed you with no consideration of the destruction she will wreak on everything we have built."

Across the table, Rodney paled. From where she sat, Aisling could see the muscles in Kael's back tense in response to the High Prelate's accusation. Still, his countenance remained aloof. "Have you only just now realized who she is? It's taken you long enough to see what has been right in front of your face."

"It is your arrogance that will be this court's destruction, Red Woman or no." Werryn hissed the words sharply. Spit collected in the corners of his mouth and his robes seemed to vibrate as he shook with rage.

"You are dismissed, Prelate." Kael took another step so that he now stood between Aisling and Werryn. His hands were balled into tight fists at his sides, and from them thin tendrils of shadow were beginning to leach through his skin. Aisling stood quickly and worked one of his fists open to slide her own hand in, lacing her fingers between his and squeezing. She felt the thready shadow writhe once between their palms before it dissipated.

"She will ruin everything, and you would stand by and watch it happen."

"And you will be watching from a dungeon cell if you do not leave," Kael shot back. "Now."

Werryn, now aware of the dark, thickening ribbons reaching for his wrists, backed away. "She will ruin everything, Kael," he repeated before retreating from the room.

Still keeping her grip on his hand, Aisling guided Kael to sit. That same resistance she felt when they kissed, she found now when she tried to send her calm into him as she had before. He was reluctant to let her back in so deeply, to give her back whatever power she held over him and his magic. She reached across his lap and took his other hand, too, and tried to push past the wall he'd built.

"It's alright," she soothed. "Trust me. Let me help you."

Little by little, she coaxed that wall down. She could feel it coming apart; if she closed her eyes, she could almost see it crumbling until finally, finally, there was nothing left of it standing between them. The resistance was gone.

Kael winced as he attempted to pull those swirling currents back in. They retracted slowly, but willingly. He was in control again.

Rodney, who had not yet seen firsthand Aisling's interactions with Kael's magic, watched wide-eyed, somewhere between horrified and awestruck. She wondered what it looked like from the outside, whether he could somehow see everything passing between her and Kael. The feelings exchanged, the trust growing, the calm overtaking the storm.

If it looked anything like it felt, it must have been beautiful.

Not minutes later, Kael stood in the library's doorway, speaking in hushed tones to a guard he'd summoned. Their voices were too low for Aisling's ears, but she could tell by the set of Kael's shoulders and the tight, affirmative nods of the guard that he was delivering harsh orders.

"I never should have sent you here alone," Rodney muttered, more to himself than to Aisling. He was shaken by the encounter with Werryn, and by witnessing Kael's magic and tenuous control over it up close. Reluctantly, Aisling tore her gaze from Kael's back and turned to her friend.

"Rodney," she said, waiting for him to look at her. "I'm fine."

"But you weren't then," he argued.

"Well, I am now. I don't want you carrying this guilt anymore. I could have said no, too." She stood and circled around the table so that she could lean down and drape her arms around Rodney's shoulders. He reached up to hold onto them and tilted his head so it rested against hers.

"You didn't know what you were getting into. I did."

Aisling tightened her hold on him. "Everything worked out how it was supposed to."

"You will not see him again." Kael came back into the library and stood stiffly beside the table. "I've ordered him kept in his chamber; guards will be posted at his door to ensure it.

"You can't have him executed?" Rodney asked, not entirely sarcastically.

Kael shook his head. "I cannot."

By the drawn look on his face and the pained tightness in his voice, Aisling knew that he wanted to. He'd wanted to before—she'd seen it—but he wouldn't. Werryn was as much of a father figure to Kael as an advisor. Though he'd never admit it, Aisling thought he still harbored some childlike fear of the High Prelate.

"Thank you," she said before Rodney could press further. She straightened up, still with her hands on Rodney's shoulders and, in a bid to distract them both, she asked, "Who were you talking about earlier?"

"Sítheach."

"The Diviner." Kael and Rodney both spoke at the same time. Kael shifted uncomfortably at Rodney's casual use of the female's name, having only given her title himself.

"She's been around for a long, long, *long* time. She sees things," Rodney explained. He looked to Kael for confirmation, who nodded.

"Like Far Sight?" Aisling asked. Giving Rodney's shoulders one final squeeze, she returned to her seat.

"Not quite, but similar. Her magic is called *Gweldealain*." Kael said. "She keeps much of our old knowledge, and from it divines things yet to come."

Aisling's pulse quickened as her hope reignited. She'd have traveled anywhere, met with anyone to forge a new way forward. "How do we get to her?"

"It is less than a day's ride, though it can be difficult to secure an audience with her. Most are turned away." Kael began to pace slowly.

Rodney leaned forward to rest his elbows on the table. "Surely she wouldn't turn away the Unseelie King."

"I have tried more than once without success. But," Kael paused, lost somewhere deep in thought, "the Red Woman may have better luck than I."

36
AFFINITY
AISLING

Kael was still on edge that morning as Aisling settled against him in his bed, tucked amongst sheets of dark silk and warm, heavy furs and a mountain of pillows. He'd spent the better part of the evening shut away in his study with the Lesser Prelates and when he'd finally emerged, the tightness of his jaw told Aisling everything she needed to know. So she'd handed him a book—one of his favorites, she remembered from their first visit to the library—and asked him to tell her about it.

Now, as the fire had diminished to embers and several candles around the chamber had burned themselves out, Kael was relaxed beside her, his heartbeat slower where her head lay against his chest. Engrossed in the history of a treatise between distant dominions, he alternated between reading passages out loud and falling silent, immersed in the words he likely knew by heart.

Mid-sentence, Aisling sat up with a start and he looked at her, alarmed.

"Laure knows your full name," she said. Amidst everything that had happened since her return, between Kael's affliction and their search for information about the Silver Saints, she'd forgotten entirely what Laure had so pointedly shared with her that first day.

Kael set the book aside and his expression of concern shifted to one closer to amusement. "Does she?"

"She said it to me when I arrived, she wanted me to know it. I'm sorry, I meant to tell you sooner. I would never use it, I swear." Her words came out in a rush, strung together almost incoherently in a bid to get them out before he could draw any of his own conclusions.

"And what did she tell you it is?" Kael raised an eyebrow, lips twitching up into a smile. When Aisling refused, he found her hand atop the blankets and squeezed. "You can say it."

Aisling looked down, then away. She couldn't look at him when she said it. "Kael Ardhen."

Kael shook his head. "That is not my whole name, though there are several whom I have allowed to believe otherwise."

"Really?" Aisling met his eyes again, relief washing over her. Laure, arrogant as she was, would have no control over him. He was still free.

Kael shook his head again, then leaned in. He brought his face so close to Aisling's own that his lips lightly brushed against hers when he said, "Kael Elethyr Ardhen."

Aisling's lungs seized and she pulled away sharply, eyes wide, shocked by the gift he'd just willingly given her. It didn't feel right; she hadn't earned it. She didn't deserve it. "I didn't mean for you to tell me; I wasn't trying to get it out of you."

"I know." Kael smiled and pulled her back in. This time, his lips captured hers in a gentle kiss. "Say it."

She hesitated. Inside, the wild thrumming of her heart matched exactly the fluttering pace of the butterflies' wings as they made frantic laps around her stomach. He waited patiently, eyes closed, lips again just a hair's breadth from hers.

"Kael Elethyr Ardhen," she repeated.

Smoothly, he lifted her to straddle his hips and leaned back into the pillows, pulling her down with him. Where their bodies connected, a mellow warmth spread through Aisling in waves. "Again."

"Kael Elethyr Ardhen." She whispered it this time, punctuating each word with another kiss. His body shuddered beneath hers.

Aisling dropped her head and murmured his name a third time into the crook of his neck, then captured the sensitive skin there between her teeth. Gently at first, then harder. Kael's mouth fell open and the low growl that escaped from deep in his throat drew a rush of desire, hot as a flame, to Aisling's core. She could have devoured that sound. She bit down once more, just to feel his grip on her waist tighten again before she relented. She sucked lightly on the spot she'd bitten, soothing the marks she left with the tip of her tongue.

Everything outside of the two of them faded and blurred until there was only the softness of Kael's skin under her lips, the taste of it on her tongue, the hard press of his body, the hold he had on her. She ventured further up his neck, exploring still with her tongue and lips and teeth, eliciting another deep growl.

"Stop teasing," he admonished. His words came out as a strangled gasp, but there was no real force behind them. He wanted this, too. He wanted her, too.

"Make me." She whispered the command against the shell of his pointed ear, then nipped softly at his lobe.

Roughly, urgently, Kael ripped open the thin shift Aisling had changed into, shredding the fabric easily between his hands until it fell from her shoulders, then tossed it to the floor. When he flipped her onto her back he was far from gentle, and her mind went blank with surprise at the quick movement, at the sensation that trailed over her skin behind his hand that caressed her breasts, her curves. He pushed himself up off of her then, straightening to kneel between her legs, and tore at his own clothing. Aisling couldn't keep her eyes from roving over his body, studying his form. A predator, a warrior, and now: hers. She wanted to memorize every inch of him.

Kael pinned Aisling beneath him. She was caged in by his muscular arms as he lowered himself down until the arcs of their hips just barely, barely touched. His silver eyes never left hers, that searing gaze raising goosebumps across her skin. She splayed her fingers over his back to explore the ridges of muscle there that flexed and rippled as he moved against her.

He paused for a beat, just long enough to allow them both to savor that delicious tension building between their bodies. The intensity of the anticipation brought the blood roaring to life in Aisling's veins. When he finally dropped his hips the rest of the way and slid into her, filling her, she couldn't stifle the sharp cry that had been waiting in her chest.

She drove her hips up against his hard, channeling all of the frustration and anger and longing and regret she could dig up from within herself that had been growing there for weeks. Kael took all of her emotion and matched it effortlessly with his own.

His kisses were consuming, claiming her, but even in those punishing thrusts she found the same gentleness that he'd shown her in their quiet, solitary moments by brushing back her hair or sweeping a thumb across her cheek. His pleasure and hers wove together in a single tapestry, stunningly vibrant and so delicate that it seemed one wrong move could have torn it to shreds. They were consumed by that brutal pleasure, and for a brief moment the world was still on its axis.

Aisling's body wound tighter and tighter, the flame that Kael ignited burning hotter and hotter still until she came undone and pulled him straight over that edge with her. Her climax tore the air from her lungs, while Kael's pleasured cries grew louder as he rode her through those rolling waves of ecstasy until they were both quaking.

Sweat-soaked and spent, they melted into each other. Kael remained on top of her, pressing her into the mattress, and she languidly threaded her fingers through his moonspun hair in long, smooth strokes. Aisling was afraid to speak and break that spell that they'd both fallen under, so she closed her eyes and committed the moment to memory with every ounce of energy she had left, cataloging every bit of feeling until she drifted into a dreamless sleep.

∴

"Can you ride?" Kael stood beside his great skeletal mare as the sun set that night, turning the fresh snow on the ground a soft shade of lavender to match the darkening sky. Aisling tugged her cloak tighter around her shoulders, the same one she'd shed when she ran from the Undercastle before. Its thick wool was a welcome barrier against the evening breeze.

"Sort of. But not well, and not fast," Aisling answered honestly. Rodney snorted; he'd been plenty amused by her attempts to ride back and forth from Solanthis.

"You will ride with me, then." While Kael adjusted the saddle, Aisling turned away from the mare's unnerving, milky eyes to Rodney.

"Take Briar and go home," she told him. "There's no sense in you waiting here for me."

"You'll only be gone overnight, Ash, I'm sure I can find some way to keep myself entertained," Rodney insisted playfully. "There's plenty of trouble I can get myself into while you're away."

Though she knew she wouldn't be able to convince him otherwise, Aisling felt guilty for him staying. She felt guilty for wanting him to stay. But before she could argue further, Kael was at her side, helping her onto his horse. He mounted behind her, far more gracefully than she had. When he reached for the reins, holding her tightly against him, the press of his body made her blush fiercely.

"Are you sure you wouldn't rather take your own horse?" Raif's mare cantered around them in a wide circle, warming up for the ride. It seemed as eager as Kael's to get moving.

"We will get there quicker this way," Kael said. He pulled Aisling in even closer and purred in her ear, "I prefer this anyhow."

His breath, warm against her icy skin, made her shiver.

The ride was long and the wind harsh and biting as the horses flew northward through the forest. Aisling spent much of it with her chin tucked and eyes closed. When they slowed occasionally to let the horses walk, Kael would sweep his cloak forward to cocoon her inside with him, keeping one hand loose on the reins and the other arm encircling her waist. The rhythmic movement of his hips against hers might have set her blood boiling again if it hadn't been so cold.

As they drew nearer to their destination, Raif rode ahead at a canter while Kael pulled his horse into a more leisurely pace.

"I never asked you whether you learned anything about your mother during your time in the Seelie Court."

Aisling didn't answer right away; instead, she took in their surroundings. The forest had thinned significantly, enough so that the moon, directly above them now, illuminated their path. A lock of Kael's hair had fallen forward onto her shoulder, and its silver cast shone an even brighter shade of white in the moonlight. She had to tamp down the urge to turn in the saddle to take in all of him, glowing this way.

"I don't think they were as kind to her as her memory made her believe," she said finally. Her mother had died defending it: her memory of the Fae. But those memories had all been false, implanted into her mind so that her body could be used to entertain.

"A great many things can be concealed beneath a beautiful exterior," Kael supplied. "I hope that you will not let it tarnish your memory of her."

Aisling considered this for a moment before shaking her head. If anything, it had softened her memory of her mother. She'd been magicked into believing the Fae's illusion, and that same magic had held her there in the Wild. After all of these years, Aisling no longer blamed her mother for willingly leaving her family for days at a time; the will had never truly been hers alone. More than that, if it hadn't been for her mother, Aisling may not have understood as quickly the hidden cruelty of the Seelie Fae. Maybe she'd still be there, preparing with Laure to kill Kael. Maybe the tea and gowns and wildflowers and pretty words would have fooled her, too.

Rather than pushing her to speak further on the topic, Kael let Aisling reflect to herself, merely pressing a kiss to the crown of her head and riding on in silence. She was so deep in her thoughts that she didn't realize when they drew to a stop beside Raif.

"Hello, Red Woman." A familiar voice pulled Aisling out of her head. The Shadowwood Mother stood hunched in the center of the trail, wizened hands bracing her weight against a walking stick taller than her head. "I had hoped you would find your way here eventually.

"And you," she turned her attention to Kael then, who'd slid from the saddle and was standing with his shoulder against Aisling's knee. The Shadowwood Mother looked at him with that same soul-searching gaze she'd fixed on Aisling once before. "You've had quite a journey, as well."

"How are you here?" Aisling breathed. It felt like a lifetime had passed since they'd met. She was almost a different person entirely now—at least, she felt that way. She was braver, maybe. Less willing to be cowed by others. By fate.

"I am not confined to that thicket, girl. I consort with The Diviner often."

"Will she see us?" Kael asked, voice soft and deferential.

The Shadowwood Mother was unmoved by his tone but nodded tersely and countered, "Are you so sure she's not already expecting you?"

Without another word, she turned and hobbled slowly up the trail. Raif split off to take up guard somewhere unseen while Kael led his mare by the reins after the Shadowwood Mother. Aisling dug her fingers into its mane to hide their trembling.

Turning the corner, the Shadowwood Mother led them to a rocky outcropping that would have seemed out of place in this part of the forest, had the giant boulders that formed it not been covered in a thick layer of moss camouflaging it against the trees. There was an opening there, low to the ground, that looked far too small for either of them to pass through. The Shadowwood Mother gestured towards it with her walking stick.

"In you go," she ordered.

Kael helped Aisling down from the saddle and guided her with a hand on the small of her back to the entrance. The steady pressure there steeled her.

Aisling crouched down low, inching forward uncomfortably through the gap between mossy boulders. But just as she braced herself to feel the rocks scrape against her body, she'd already passed through to the other side where it opened into a tunnel.

"Glamoured to look smaller than it is," Kael said from behind her once he emerged, straightening back up to stand at his full height.

Aisling's sarcastic comeback died in her throat as she stepped forward, turning around in a full circle to take in the space. Crystals—hundreds of them, in different sizes and configurations—protruded like spikes from every surface. There was a narrow path down the center, but most of it had been eroded away by a tiny stream that trickled from some unseen source beneath their feet. It ran the length of the tunnel, disappearing around the curve ahead of them. The water glowed a soft white, as pure as the moonlight outside, and that glow lit the cave system as it refracted off of the crystal clusters.

Kael's hand again on her back urged Aisling to move, and so she followed the stream toward the tunnel's curve. A low hum reverberated around them, a quiet chord that Aisling thought might be emanating from within the crystals themselves. And when she touched a finger to the tip of a large formation that rose nearly to hip height, she felt that chord's vibration there. The whole space was singing with magic.

The hum grew louder as they rounded the curve, where the tunnel spilled into a wide cavern. It, too, was covered in those same singing crystals. The stream traversed between them and dumped into a small pool in the center, on the far side of which sat a faerie whose beauty was so pure and blinding Aisling nearly had to look away.

Her hair was a pale shade of teal and hung as a heavy curtain over her shoulders and down to fan over the ground. Her skin was so translucent that Aisling could make out the blue-green veins that spiderwebbed underneath. It shone dimly, as if she'd bathed in the pool and its glow had dried there.

She sat cross-legged amongst the crystals, nestled so tightly between them that it was difficult to tell where they ended and she began. When she shifted slightly and the white silk of her dress moved with her, Aisling noticed that the crystals didn't end where she began, after all—it was as though she was becoming one with them, merging. And when the faerie raised her head to look towards them, Aisling found only crystalline clusters that jutted out at harsh angles from her eye sockets above hollow cheeks.

"Sit," she commanded. Her voice was ancient and resonant in the vast cavern. It had all the sweetness of youth and the callousness of age. Low and gravelly, yet somehow high and melodic, too, as though she were two speaking as one.

Aisling and Kael both sank wordlessly to their knees. They had to press close together to fit side-by-side on the only patch of ground devoid of crystals.

"A human woman and a Fae king," Sítheach observed. "An unlikely pairing, though no weaker for it."

She shifted again, and Aisling had to take a deep breath to settle a passing wave of nausea when her eyes landed on the Diviner's bent leg. A long, opaque crystal as thick as Aisling's arm had grown up through the muscle of her thigh. Its pointed tip emerged just above her knee.

"Thank you for seeing us," Kael said. He spoke to her in that same hushed, reverent tone he'd used with the Shadowwood Mother.

Sítheach dipped her head, then turned those unseeing eyes toward Aisling. "You are a great deal more than you appear, Red Woman."

Aisling wasn't sure how to respond, so she stayed silent.

"You have an affinity for things," Sítheach continued, "for sensing the weather, the emotions of others. For finding your way even through the most unfamiliar territory."

"I have no magic," Aisling argued.

"No, you do not. It is a human trait; one that has all but disappeared over the years as the world has aged and changed and died all around us. Similar to intuition, but more than that. *Deeper* than that. It is useful if you know how to listen to it properly."

"Keeps me dry, at least," Aisling said wryly. Beside her, Kael tucked his chin into his chest, hiding a smirk beneath his hair. Her mother had worked hard to cultivate that in Aisling from an early age, even as Aisling grew older and tried her best to push her and her stories away. She'd done Aisling more favors than she'd ever realized. There on Brook Isle, limited in its modern amenities, Aisling's affinity had flourished. It made sense then why she'd never been able to feel shifting weather patterns the same way in the city.

Sítheach drew a finger up and down the unblemished surface of a crystal beside her, and the humming in the air grew a fraction louder. "It does much more than that."

"Not that I've noticed."

"He might disagree." Sítheach nodded towards Kael. He stiffened slightly when she added, "You have altered the way he wields his magic. Just as you can receive, you can project."

"I didn't know that's what I was doing," Aisling said.

"It takes more than just kind words and a soft touch to calm a tempest as wild as his," Sítheach explained. "But that is not why you have come here. Ask me your question."

Aisling hesitated, steadying her voice. Her breath. One second passed, then another, before she said finally, "Tell us how we raise the Silver Saints."

37

A HEAVY CROWN

KAEL

An affinity. Kael understood, then, how Aisling seemed to effortlessly give him that control that had for so long eluded him. How even from deep within the Undercastle, she'd smelled the snow. He moved one hand slowly to capture Aisling's where it rested on her knee and laced his fingers between hers. He wished in that moment that he could project the things he felt for her, too.

Sítheach regarded the pair for some time while she considered Aisling's request. Still running one finger over the crystal beside her, she dipped her other hand into the pool. The glow it cast rippled across the cavern's ceiling, sending light refractions spinning. The hum of the magic grew louder still.

"You wish for them to end the war between courts," Sítheach said—a statement, not a question.

"I—*we*—hope that they can guide the courts to peace, how they did in the early days." Aisling's voice was steady and sure, and Kael was once more struck by her bravery. Her conviction. He gave her hand a reassuring squeeze.

"The Silver Saints are born of the stars," Sítheach mused, dragging her hand through the water. "A light that can only be seen in darkness."

Aisling's sharp intake of breath beside him caught Kael's attention. Her eyes were wide, focused on Sítheach, and her hand gripped his fiercely.

"Guided by celestial light," she recited breathlessly. "They were in the prophecy all along."

"Take care with such assumptions, child. The strength of our prophecies lies in their interpretation, not in the intent of the originator."

"If we call, will they answer?" Kael asked.

"To call the Silver Saints is a difficult thing, and costly, but it can be done." The Diviner tipped her chin up, catching fractals of light on the crystals that grew from her eyes. She'd been devoured further and further by her power: each glance into time brought forth a new crystal that would grow unabated where it emerged, be it from the cavern or from Sítheach herself. He was all too familiar with that feeling of being consumed by raw magic. The physical manifestation of hers was as horrifying as it was beautiful.

"Has it been done before?" Aisling was leaning forward, mesmerized by the ancient faerie.

"It has not," Sítheach said. "But something that has never been done before is not, by nature, impossible to do."

"A blood rite?" Kael guessed. He knew the answer before she gave it; he'd known the moment she'd called it costly. A pit settled in his stomach, solid and heavy.

Sítheach nodded once. "Only the blood of the powerful might awaken the dormant Saints. As for how the ritual is conducted, I cannot say. That is in the hands of the caller to determine."

"Will it work?" Aisling asked. She seemed less sure now, almost resigned.

Sítheach smiled serenely, withdrawing her hands to fold in her lap. "I do not predict the future, child. I only divine the threads; it is up to you to weave them as you wish."

She turned from them then, a wordless dismissal, and cast her gaze back into the pool before her. The light there, and the light carried by the stream that flowed into it, began to dim. Kael helped Aisling to her feet, eager to leave before they lost their path out.

"Thank you," Aisling said. When Sítheach didn't respond, Kael nudged Aisling on. She stepped gingerly on either side of the stream.

"King," Sítheach called once Aisling had rounded the corner ahead of him. He turned back and was hit at full force with a wall of magic. It pulsed around him, through him, holding him in place.

In his head, in the deepest recesses of his mind, the Diviner whispered to him: *Every trail through this forest, winding though they may be—switching directions, deviating, crossing rivers and glades and traversing mountains—will bring the traveler to the same destination eventually.*

Once she'd released him from that hold, Kael nodded tightly. "I understand. Thank you."

Trailing behind Aisling out of the cavern, he made a conscious effort to loosen his jaw and let his shoulders fall into a more relaxed posture. It took all of his concentration; the ache in his head left by Sítheach's intrusion did him no favors, either. To his great relief, he found the Shadowwood Mother had gone. He strode past Aisling to reach Furax, using the time untethering her from the tree and readjusting her saddle to rid his countenance of the final traces of tension.

Aisling's closeness in the saddle gave Kael everything he needed to regain focus. He kept Furax at a walk to enjoy it a bit longer.

"Well," she said after several minutes of silence, "it was a nice idea, anyway."

Kael frowned; resignation still colored her tone. "You would give up so easily?"

"You heard what she said, Kael. I'd have thought you above anyone else would have put a stop to this the moment she mentioned blood magic." She shivered, as though the very idea of it frightened her. Kael wrapped his cloak tighter around her shoulders.

"Sometimes the outcome is worth the sacrifice." He wished he could offer more reassuring words, but there were none.

"We don't know what that sacrifice is." She'd twisted around so that she could look at him over her shoulder.

"Maybe not, but it remains the best chance we have."

Aisling shook her head then turned back. "I don't like it, Kael."

He felt the shift in Aisling's body and sat forward slightly in the saddle to pull her even closer. She leaned into him, pressing her back against his chest. He hoped that contact steadied her as much as it did him. They rode on in silence and when they met Raif further up the trail, their horses quickly transitioned into a gallop, carrying them at full speed back to the Undercastle.

Kael led them to return on the shortest route, which Raif had been careful to avoid on their way out. He thought even Furax seemed reluctant to do so, but Kael was determined to make it back before sunrise.

"Keep your eyes forward," he said low in Aisling's ear as they approached Talamarís.

"Why?"

The trail curved through the densest part of the forest, where the ancient pines grew higher than all the rest. They towered overhead as silent sentinels, anchored below by thick roots that wound and snaked across the forest floor. Bodies of dead Fae lay cradled amongst them. Kael reached quickly up to cover Aisling's mouth to stifle the shriek before it could escape her lips.

He hushed her, smoothing his thumb across her cheek. "It's alright. Just keep your eyes up."

She trembled violently against him and when he removed his hand from her mouth, he wrapped his arm tightly around her waist.

"What is this place?" Aisling clung to him, her fingertips digging into his forearm.

"This is where our bodies go when we die," Kael explained gently. "We are laid to rest here amidst the trees and left to be reclaimed by the forest. We return to the earth and give it new life."

It was a concept he'd long found beautiful: Kael saw it as a great honor to give back life to the earth that sustained them, to the forest that protected them. But now, as he looked around, all he saw were the faces of the soldiers he'd slaughtered at Nyctara. They were the embodiment of his anger, of his greed and hunger for power. Their skin was mottled gray-blue and beginning to rot away despite the thin layer of frost that covered them, but they were still recognizable. He still knew each one of them by name.

The war for control over Wyldraíocht—and the battle that raged inside of him—would only continue to eat away at his court until there was no one left to rule over. The realization struck him as suddenly and brutally as a sword plunging into his gut. He'd be alone, and the crown he wore would remain just as heavy. Without subjects, could he even be considered a king?

Not far beyond Talamarís, Kael paused as they passed by The Cut. The Low One had been his guide through every trial he'd faced. The old god's voice in his head had steered him steadily forward since he was old enough to venture into the woods on his own. Kael needed to hear that voice now.

"Is everything alright?" Aisling asked, calmer now that they'd left Talamarís behind.

He removed his cloak and fastened it around her before he dismounted and said, "Wait here."

"Do you want me to take her back?" Raif took hold of Furax's reins.

"I will not be long." He needed Aisling nearby. Kael left them on the trail and pushed through the underbrush until he broke free into the clearing. The sky was indigo now, growing lighter by the minute as the sun rose. He placed himself in the center of the circle, dusting snow off several of the runes with the toe of his boot before he faced the altar and closed his eyes.

The Low One would have come to be close to the time of the Silver Saints; Kael was sure He would have an answer. A better solution. Anything other than what the Diviner had offered.

Kael called out to the Low One softly at first, then with greater force. As his shadows began to surge within him, he allowed several thin tendrils to escape his palms, reaching for Him through the darkness. Grasping, searching for any sign that He was listening.

Please, Kael begged. He squeezed his eyes shut tighter, sent his shadows further. He could feel Aisling, that soothing warmth she imbued in him, and he held onto it as his shadows stretched and stretched.

But the Low One was strangely silent. There was nothing with Kael in that clearing tonight. The air never thickened; the atmosphere never grew heavy. The sounds of the forest continued on undeterred. Kael dropped to his knees as he drew his shadows back. There was an emptiness in his chest that he'd never felt there before. He was lost in the forest without a map. Abandoned.

Again, he had to work to regain his composure and coach his face back into a neutral mask. It took greater effort this time, but he managed to tamp down his hurt and frustration well enough to rise to his feet and return to where Raif and Aisling waited. They both looked at him expectantly. Without acknowledging either, he slung himself into the saddle and pulled Furax into a trot.

Two of Kael's guards were waiting outside the entrance to the Undercastle. He could tell even from a distance that they were nervous; both had white-knuckle grips on the hilts of their swords. The light of the dawn glinted off of their dark armor. Raif's feet hit the ground before his mare stopped, and Kael wasn't far behind.

"What is it?" Raif demanded.

"Visitors," the more senior of the guards said. "Waiting in the throne room."

"How many? When did they arrive?" Kael asked. Behind him, he heard Aisling sliding from Furax's back. He took her hand and pulled her close.

"Two, and not long ago." A stable hob appeared to quickly take both horses away.

Kael guided Aisling forward, towards the guards. "See that she makes it safely back to her chambers."

"The visitors are for her, Highness." The younger guard turned his attention to Aisling then, and added, "Your friend is waiting with them, miss."

Aisling set her jaw. "Show me."

"No," Kael said sternly. His pulse was beginning to race, and a sense of foreboding tugged at his warrior instincts. At his magic. Raif felt it, too, and had already drawn his sword. Kael regretted not having brought his own.

"It'll be fine," Aisling insisted. "Take me to them."

The group moved quickly and in tight formation down the spiral staircase, all of them alert and tense save for Aisling. She walked confidently, seemingly unafraid. She'd grown so much bolder since they'd met. She squeezed Kael's hand once, hard, before releasing it and stepping into the throne room ahead of him. It took every bit of restraint he had to let her.

Rodney was leaning casually against a table where someone had laid out an array of bread and tea and honey wine. He was telling a story, gesturing broadly in an effort to hold the attention of the guests. The redheaded male, who looked to be the twin of Laure's guard captain, seemed entertained. The soldier who accompanied him, clad in the gold Seelie armor, appeared less so.

"Our riding party returns," Rodney said when they entered the cavern. His voice was just slightly too loud as it echoed off the stone walls. "Highness, this is Tadhg, and a soldier who has made it very clear he wishes to remain unnamed."

A wide smile spread across Tadhg's face. "Aisling, I'm so relieved to see you unharmed. When we couldn't find you, I feared you'd been taken."

"I wasn't taken. I left." Her tone was hard as steel.

"Surely you didn't return here voluntarily," Tadhg suggested. His grin faltered just slightly.

"I did." Aisling advanced towards him, forcing the Seelie soldier into a defensive posture. Kael and Raif moved in tandem to flank her on either side.

"The queen is prepared to negotiate for your safe return," the soldier said curtly.

"I'm not something she can bargain for," she shot back. Kael could sense her irritation even before the pink flush that bloomed in her cheeks gave it away.

"Please, Aisling, he meant no offense." Tadhg moved closer, hands raised. "Laure only wishes to see you safe. We all do."

Kael began to speak, but Aisling cut him off. "I am safe."

"Let's all sit down and have a drink," Rodney interjected, all forced friendliness. He brandished the bottle of honey wine. "It may be morning, Tadhg, but it's technically time for a nightcap here."

"They're not staying," Kael growled. Rodney backed down.

Aisling reached back and found Kael's hand again. Her movement was deft and sure. She was sending a clear message. Kael's heart stopped beating, just briefly. Raif tensed beside him, mirroring the Seelie soldier's reaction.

Tadhg's eyes dropped to their hands, growing wide enough to see the whites all the way around his bright green irises as the blood drained from his already pale complexion. "Niamh was right," he breathed.

"Disgusting," spat the soldier.

Kael's temper flared; his breaths came short and fast as heat flooded his veins. His magic writhed beneath his skin, but he clenched his jaw, determined to keep his shadows at bay. He tried to pull Aisling behind him, but she stood her ground.

"Leave," she commanded. If he hadn't been so angry, Kael might have been impressed by her fearlessness. As it was, he would have done anything to keep her from speaking again.

"Come back with us," Tadhg insisted, almost begging now. He held a hand out to Aisling.

She slapped it away. "I won't."

"Tadhg has been too kind; this is not a request." The soldier seized Aisling roughly by the elbow and jerked her forward, forcing her hand from Kael's. She fell to the ground at his side. Despite the fierceness that burned in her eyes, she seemed so much smaller, so much more fragile with the soldier's gauntleted hand squeezing her arm.

The rage that overtook Kael was raw and primal, overriding all that remained of his rational thought. When Tadhg stepped forward, reaching out to help Aisling stand, Kael moved in. His shadows were on Tadhg as he helped Aisling to her feet, ripping him away from her. They encircled his slender body, squeezing and squeezing until his ribs collapsed inward with a crunch that was almost deafening.

Heavy silence followed that sound, just for the span of a breath.

The Seelie soldier was the first to recover, letting out a vicious roar and lunging for Kael. Aisling reacted blindly, stepping out to catch the soldier's arm as it swung in a wide arc. His golden dagger, a gleaming extension of his arm, was aimed at Kael's chest, but instead found purchase in Aisling's shoulder. The curved blade bit into the flesh just below her collarbone and her sharp cry finally broke that dam that had been cracking inside of Kael.

He was fury personified, his body unable to fully contain the shadows within that now spilled into the space, devouring the light. Hatred poured out of him as water from the mouth of a river into a greater, deeper ocean of the same. As on the battlefield, Kael and his shadows shared a common goal. But this time, the shadows listened, converging entirely on the subject of his wrath and leaving the others untouched.

When Kael felt the soldier's terror through those dark currents, he smiled.

38

A STUDY IN DICHOTOMY

AISLING

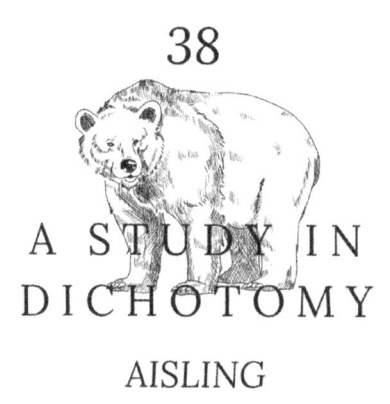

Before the blood began to pool on Aisling's skin, before the pain of the wound even registered, a thick rope of shadow wound around the Seelie soldier's neck and pulled taut in one swift motion, severing his head cleanly. It rolled with dull, wet thuds across the ground and came to rest beside Tadhg's lifeless body. Aisling looked up just in time to see a wicked smirk fading from Kael's face.

She felt the warmth of her blood first. Once she looked down at the stain growing around the frayed edges of fabric where the blade had torn through her sweater, the searing burn brought her to her knees and drew tears to her eyes. Raif and Rodney both caught her on the way down and helped her to sit on the steps leading up to the dais. She pictured it as it was the first time she'd been there, when she'd been glamoured green with a dress of leaves and wings sprouting from her back. How simple she'd thought all of this would be.

"Kael!" Raif barked. Kael turned to them, slowly, like he was waking from a dream. "Find Elasha."

Kael disappeared through the door at the back of the throne room—the very same door he'd pulled her through that night before she'd pressed him up against the wall and lured him in.

"Shit, Ash," Rodney swore. His focus was locked on her wound as Raif tore away her sweater, unable to tear his gaze from it. The color had drained from his cheeks. "Fuck."

"It isn't deep." Raif pressed a cloth over the gash, sending a fresh wave of pain sparking across Aisling's nerve endings. It shot clear down her arm to the tips of her fingers. She bit down on the inside of her cheek hard to stifle a cry.

"Shit," Rodney said again. His skin had turned from paper white to a sickly shade of yellow; his lips pursed in an effort to keep from vomiting.

"Stop looking at it," Aisling scolded weakly once the pain had subsided enough for her to speak.

He swallowed hard and squeezed his eyes shut. "That's a lot of blood."

"It's too bad we can't use it for the ritual," she joked dryly.

Still with his eyes closed, Rodney's brows jumped up, then drew together. "What?"

Kael returned then with Elasha, who shooed Raif out of the way and peeled back the cloth he'd used to examine Aisling's wound. Aisling sucked in a breath and gripped Rodney's hand.

"It isn't deep." Elasha echoed Raif's assessment, her even voice more comforting than his had been.

"She's fine, Kael." Raif had moved to stand beside Kael. He said it quietly, almost too low to make out. Aisling thought she may have been the only one to hear it; Kael didn't acknowledge his friend's words at all. She wanted desperately to reach out to him, to reassure him somehow that she was alright, but he maintained a careful distance and avoided her gaze.

Aisling braced herself when Elasha pulled a jar of thick paste out of the satchel that hung from her shoulder. Its smell was harsh, but it was similarly soothing to the salve Methild had applied to the wound she'd sustained to her head at Nyctara. As she rubbed it into Aisling's skin, the blood congealed and the pain rapidly subsided to a dull, throbbing ache.

"Who was he?" Kael nudged Tadhg's body with the toe of his boot.

"Niamh's brother," Raif answered.

"One of Laure's pets," Rodney added. "Her court artist. He's painted dozens of portraits of her. She'll be furious—Laure and Niamh both."

"You need to take her away from here," Kael ordered Rodney. "Now."

"I'm not going anywhere without you," Aisling said through gritted teeth while Elasha bound the poultice wraps tightly. Despite her protest, he still refused to look at her. He'd angled his body away from hers, only glancing briefly at Rodney to give his order before turning his attention back to the two bodies that lay at his feet.

"It may be wise for you to accompany her—for her protection, and yours. Until we determine what sort of retribution this will bring," Raif posited.

"My presence will hardly do her any good." Kael's jaw was taut and his tone clipped, but the cool detachment he attempted to display was painfully transparent, and Aisling wasn't fooled. She felt that guilt building in his chest, the heaviness of it. The anger he wanted to mask, but couldn't.

With some effort, Aisling worked her way back to standing. Though she felt unsteady on her feet, she ignored the way the room spun around her and walked as surely as she could to step in front of Kael.

"Look at me," she said. Aisling lifted his hand from where it hung by his side. She pried his nails from his palm and ran her thumb across the marks they'd left there. He hesitated, and when he finally dropped his gaze, he didn't look at her, but through her. His jaw was clenched so tightly now she thought his teeth might crack.

"Look at me," she said again, more forcefully this time. "I'm fine."

Finally, he softened a fraction and drew in a shaky breath. Kael's attention slid to the cloth that bound her shoulder, a brief flash of anguish coloring his expression. He lowered his head and pressed a kiss to the bandages just above where the dagger had bitten into her. The light pressure there felt even better than the poultice itself. It was the first time they'd acknowledged each other this way in front of any members of his court, the first time they'd so obviously demonstrated what had grown between them before an audience.

Aisling could feel their eyes on them now, but she couldn't bring herself to pull away from his touch.

"I am sorry," he whispered against that same spot on her shoulder. He kissed it once more before raising his head.

"I'm not leaving here without you. Come with me," Aisling insisted.

Kael nodded. "As you wish."

They moved quickly then, Rodney collecting their bags while Aisling changed into a fresh shirt and leashed Briar. Kael met them at the base of the spiral staircase. He'd changed, too, into a plain shirt and loose black pants that would be passable in the human realm—just. His silver hair was tied back into a bun at the nape of his neck and he'd glamoured away the points of his ears. Still, the tilt of his eyes and the angles of his face would set him apart on the island.

Rodney's car was frosted over when they reached it where he'd left it parked off the side of the road, partially obscured by brush. Kael looked about as comfortable in its backseat as Aisling looked on horseback. She sat close to him so their legs touched; she could feel the tension his body was under. Briar kept a wary eye on him from the passenger seat.

It was evening on Brook Isle, though not nearly as dark as Aisling had hoped it would be to conceal their arrival. As they drove into the trailer park, there were still children playing outside, bundled in heavy winter coats and brightly colored scarves. Rodney pulled up as close to his trailer as he could manage.

"Miss Morrow!" Cole called from behind them.

Aisling groaned and Rodney cringed, swearing under his breath.

"Are...are you hurt? Did this man do something to you?" Cole demanded as he drew closer. Aisling looked down at herself, realizing for the first time that more than a little dried blood was still crusted down her arm and up the side of her neck. "I'll call the police—"

Kael bit off the end of his sentence with a vicious, chilling snarl that stopped Cole in his tracks. Aisling smoothed a hand over the bowstring-tight muscles of his back and urged him on towards the trailer.

"Mind your business, Cole. We're fine here," Aisling assured him.

Inside, Aisling cleaned herself off over the kitchen sink while Rodney moved the coffee table aside to inflate an air mattress on the living room floor. Despite Rodney's offer for she and Kael to share his bed, Kael had insisted that he needed to remain where he could see the door. He took an armful of blankets and pillows from Rodney and made up the couch for Aisling.

She was tired, almost sick with tired, but she couldn't will herself to sleep. Over and over she replayed their conversation with the Diviner. And when she shut her eyes, she saw Tadhg's body lying crushed beside the headless soldier. Frustrated and sore, Aisling rose from the couch well after midnight. She stepped over Briar and tiptoed past Kael to the bathroom.

Stripping down to her bra, she balanced fresh bindings and a jar of salve Elasha had given her on the edge of the sink. The poultice had dried out; the bandages were stiff and tugged uncomfortably at her skin. Aisling peeled them off gingerly, wincing when they stuck in places. The wound underneath had already begun to heal—it looked now to be several days old, rather than just several hours.

"Does it hurt?" Kael appeared in the bathroom doorway. He was leaning against its frame, watching her examine herself in the mirror.

She shot him a rueful smile. "Only when I breathe," she teased.

He approached and swept her hair back over her shoulder to check the wound, long fingers prodding at it gently. She tried not to pull away from the sting. "It will leave a scar," he said.

Aisling grimaced, imagining it already marring her skin. "I know."

"Is that such a bad thing?" He unscrewed the lid of the jar and began spreading the salve over her skin with a tenderness that belied his strength, his rage. The male was a study in dichotomy, capable of unflinching cruelty one moment and such softness the next. Always, always proving himself more than the villain he made himself out to be.

She shrugged. "Most men aren't particularly fond of scars."

"Human men," Kael mused, the barest hint of a smirk touching his lips. She blushed red as the center of the wound he was redressing for her.

"I'm sorry I woke you." Aisling would have been content to watch his hands brushing over her skin for hours, but instead focused on the dripping faucet in front of her.

"I was awake."

"Oh." She hadn't heard him stir; his steady breathing had been as good as a lullaby. "I guess the air mattress isn't the most comfortable."

"Indeed it isn't," he agreed. He tied off the bandage then straightened up. "There."

She missed his touch when he pulled away but thanked him all the same. Finally, she looked up into the mirror and took him in as he stood behind her.

Kael looked so out of place there in Rodney's bathroom, half-glamoured to look human and washed out by the harsh yellow lighting, that she had to laugh. This trailer had been a consequence of her mother's stories, and now here she was with two of them: a púca changeling fast asleep in the bedroom, and the Unseelie King standing barefoot on the blue shag bathmat. He raised an eyebrow quizzically, but she just shook her head. She was too tired to try to explain the absurdity of it.

Rather than return to the couch, Aisling instead went to the kitchen and filled the kettle with fresh water. Kael followed and Briar padded over to lay beside her feet on the linoleum.

"You should sleep. You need rest," he admonished halfheartedly.

"I know." She lit the stove and set the kettle on the burner before pulling down a box from the shelf and holding it up. "Tea?"

When he nodded, Aisling rummaged in the cupboard for mugs. There was only one without chips around the rim: heavy ceramic in a faded shade of emerald and emblazoned with a fox, the Brook Isle High mascot. She set it aside for Kael.

"If you two are going to keep on with all this noise, you might as well pour one for me as well." Rodney turned on the kitchen light, rubbing sleep from his eyes. Briar's tail thumped against the ground, a lazy greeting.

All three sat around the small table quietly for a time, lost in their own thoughts. Rodney toyed idly with the string of his teabag; Kael's hands were folded over the top of his mug. Aisling leaned her elbows on the table and held her mug against her lips, blowing every few seconds while she waited for it to cool.

"Ash?" Rodney broke the silence.

"Hmm?" Swirling steam partially obscured his face as she looked at him over the rim.

"Earlier, what did you mean about the ritual?" he asked.

Aisling cringed; she'd forgotten about her poorly timed quip. She set her mug down on the table and crossed her arms over her chest as tightly as the ache in her shoulder would allow.

"It takes a blood rite to raise the Silver Saints." She turned to Kael then and said, "I've been thinking about the 'blood of the powerful' part. What about Laure?"

Laure was plenty powerful; Aisling had seen it herself. The Seelie Queen could produce plants from nothing, creating and sustaining life with her bare hands. It was pretty magic, and strong. Coupled with her ability to send humans into those enchanted waking dreams, Aisling thought Laure was likely one of the more powerful Fae she'd encountered yet.

Kael looked at her thoughtfully but said nothing in response. Rodney was unconvinced.

"You're talking about killing the Seelie Queen, Aisling? That's impossible," he said. His heavy brows pulled into a tight frown.

Aisling backtracked. Her heart raced at the mere idea, as though Laure might have somehow heard their conversation from deep within the Wild. She recalled the fire that blazed in the queen's violet eyes, the rabid hunger there. "I didn't say anything about killing her. We wouldn't have to kill her, would we?"

"A rite of this magnitude will require an equivalent sacrifice," Kael answered simply. He was stoic: his voice, his expression, his posture. Nothing about him betrayed even the slightest hint of his opinion on the idea, whether he thought it wise or foolish or so far-fetched as to be unworthy of discussion entirely.

Over the fear that had gripped her, a burning sort of resolve flared to life in Aisling. Laure had been keen to use the Red Woman as a means to her preferred end from the moment Aisling set foot in the Seelie Court. Now, here was her chance to reclaim the autonomy she'd been clawing for since she'd learned of the prophecy. Fate was hers to write now.

"Do you know how to perform something like this?" Aisling asked. The sun was just beginning to rise outside the trailer, painting the kitchen in pastels. Kael's hair took on every shade the sunrise threw, iridescent.

He shook his head. "Ordinarily I would turn to Werryn for guidance; he would likely know best how to design the ritual. He understands the old language and is far more practiced in *Rhedelas*—rune casting—than I."

"What about Lyre?" Rodney suggested.

"Possibly." Kael remained impassive. His tea had grown cold, but he kept his hands above the mug as though he could still feel its heat on his palms. Both Aisling and Rodney waited for him to say something more—to say *anything* more—but he lapsed back into silence.

"Can you get him a message without going back in?" Determined to forge ahead with or without Kael's help, Aisling turned to Rodney.

"Sure, but maybe we should think about this a little more first." He rubbed the back of his neck and eyed Kael uneasily, attempting to interpret his silence.

Of course she wanted to think it through. If she had the time, Aisling would have spent days drafting up a roster of advantages and disadvantages to their plan. She'd have spent longer still searching for another avenue to avoid bloodshed and sacrifice altogether. But the luxury of time had faded; now, they had to act.

"Talk to Lyre, Rodney," she directed firmly.

A short while later, as the rest of the trailer park began to wake, Aisling retreated quietly back into Rodney's dark room and curled up in his bed. Her mind was hazy now and her eyelids had grown so, so heavy. At last, sleep was catching up with her. She hoped it would be deep and dreamless.

She didn't hear Kael enter, but shifted over to make space when she felt his weight depress the far side of the mattress. "You're tired," she said, running a hand across the hard muscles of his chest. He leaned into her touch.

"I am." The exhaustion was plain in his voice.

"Have you come to nap with me?" A lazy smile played on her face, eyes half-closed.

Kael pulled a blanket up over their shoulders and wrapped one arm around Aisling's waist. "The púca left. He said he would return later."

"Did he say where he was going?" Aisling lifted her head slightly from the pillow to look up at Kael. She could only just make out his outline; his face was hidden by shadow.

"No," he said. His fingers in her hair eased her head back down and then ran, from root to tip, in smooth, steady strokes.

"Okay."

"You do not trust him," Kael assumed.

"He did leave me in your prison." She was only half-joking.

Kael hummed, moving closer and resting his chin on the crown of her head. "It seems we're both rather accustomed to being used."

Aisling curled into his chest and relaxed as he tightened his arm around her. "I wouldn't use you," she sighed.

39
AS THE MOON DRAWS THE TIDES
KAEL

I wouldn't use you.

Aisling's words echoed in Kael's mind, their soft earnestness prying at his hardened heart and making it ache fiercely. She wouldn't willingly, but the knowledge of what she must do—how he would make her use him—might have been enough to break him right there if he wasn't so skilled at pressing down those sorts of thoughts until they were nearly nothing inside of him. He had this, now: Aisling sleeping soundly beside him, her warm breath gentle as it breezed across his chest. All signs of worry and stress absent from her face. If he could have held her there forever, he would have made any single sacrifice to do so. But that was not the fate written for either of them.

She stirred then and pulled back to look at him with bleary eyes. Even in the dark, the collage of blues and hazels held him captive. "You're still awake."

"Not for much longer." Kael worked his hand underneath her shirt and traced circles on the curve of her lower back with his thumb.

She bumped his thighs gently with one of her knees. When he lifted a leg, she slid hers between them to rest there, pulling herself even nearer, then sighed contentedly.

He smiled. "If you were any closer, you would be under my skin."

"I wouldn't mind." She reached up to smooth her thumb over the crease between his brows. "What are you thinking about?"

A pulse of disquiet surged through Kael, like icy water through his veins, but it took him only a moment to recover. "Only how lovely you look when you sleep," he said.

"Your walls are up." She hadn't believed him; she'd heard that split-second of hesitation before he answered. Her hand moved down to cup his cheek and he leaned into it gratefully. The grounding force of her touch worked its alchemy on his frayed nerves.

"I mislike that you were injured in my defense," Kael tried again. Not a lie this time, but certainly only a fraction of the truth that weighed on his mind. On his heart.

"I'd do it again," Aisling promised solemnly.

"That will not be necessary," Kael assured her.

Her presence beside him an anchor, Kael allowed himself to sleep, too, though it was restless and hard-won. He felt himself constantly dipping in and out of it, never as fully submerged as he wished to be.

He awoke when Rodney cracked open the door, letting in a slant of light. The púca gestured to him. Kael gently extricated himself from Aisling's grip. She groaned, reaching out for him, but he tucked her arm back beneath the blanket.

"Hush," he soothed before running his fingers through her hair once more. "Go back to sleep." She let her head drop back onto the pillow and resumed her steady breathing.

Rodney was waiting for Kael by the front door, so the king straightened his disheveled clothes and followed him onto the porch. The cold mid-morning air was bracing and cleared his head the moment he drew in a deep breath.

"Tell me what you know," Rodney demanded. There was no humor in his voice, nor was there any attempt to manipulate or hide his intentions. He was forthright, for once, and angry.

"I know a great many things," Kael said, "you will have to be more specific." He was goading the púca, he knew he was, but he was unprepared to slide from the knife's edge he balanced on. Once he spoke the truth out loud, there would be no taking it back. The universe would know what he knew.

"There's something more to all of this, and I daresay you're well aware of it, even if Aisling isn't." Rodney stepped forward, seemingly ready to force the truth from Kael if he needed to.

Kael looked skyward, where gray clouds were gathering on the horizon. They were blowing in from the sea; he could smell the salt and taste its tang on the wind. Rodney waited impatiently for his answer, but it took Kael several moments to pull the words from where he'd hidden them in the depths of his heart before he could speak them out loud.

"You mustn't tell her," he finished. "Swear it to me. I know you owe me no allegiance but swear it all the same. For her."

"I swear it." Sobered by Kael's admission, Rodney leaned his elbows onto the porch railing and pushed his hands back through his unruly hair, gripping it at the roots.

"She will need you, after. As reluctant as she will be to admit it." Kael's throat tightened, but he swallowed past that feeling. Pushed all of it back down even deeper than before.

Rodney snorted. "So you've noticed."

"She does not seem overly fond of asking for help." It was Aisling's independence that had endeared her to him from the very beginning, when she'd stepped up on the dais on Nocturne and taken charge. Then, as his prisoner, when she insisted time and again on bathing herself, on walking the halls unguided and unaided. And now, as she seized control over her own fate. But he knew the damage she could do to herself with such a trait. In that way, he saw much of himself in her.

"She's gotten better at it, I think. Either way, I'll be here," Rodney promised.

The púca left then, shaken and likely eager for the excuse to avoid Aisling for a while. When he returned later on with Lyre, both wore the same pale, drawn expression.

"What is it?" Aisling noticed Rodney's face first and sprang up off the couch to greet him. Kael followed close behind, taking care to keep a healthy distance between himself and Briar. It was difficult given the small footprint of the trailer, but he'd managed to keep at least one piece of furniture between them throughout most of the morning.

"Lyre?" Kael demanded.

"The Seelie army is marching on the Undercastle." Lyre's yellow eyes scanned the trailer, cataloging the space and its contents shrewdly. The heavy cloak he wore concealed his robe, but not well enough to avoid a harsh look from Aisling. No doubt she was imagining the possibility that he'd been spotted by any number of Rodney's neighbors, particularly the short, unpleasant man who seemed always to be lurking outside.

Aisling sank into a kitchen chair and Kael moved to stand behind her. "How did they find out already?" she asked.

"They had an additional guard posted outside, waiting," Lyre explained tightly. "He saw the bodies as they were removed."

Kael gripped the back of Aisling's chair, grinding his teeth back and forth until he could speak again without losing his temper over the sheer carelessness with which they'd cleaned up the mess. *His mess.* "How far out are they?"

"Raif has already recalled the Fifth Company; he is readying the others now."

Not far at all, then, if preparations were already underway. And for Raif to have recalled their last company afield meant he anticipated the Seelie army to be moving in at full strength. Kael's mind raced ahead, plotting battle order and strategy. Where the defensive units would be placed, and which of the companies he would reserve for the counter-offensive.

"Is Laure with them?" Aisling's quiet voice pulled him from his thoughts and he looked down at her. She was staring straight ahead at Lyre. Though he couldn't see her face, he could picture the determined expression there.

"The changeling spoke to me about your plan to kill the queen," Lyre said. His mouth curled into a devilish grin. "It would be my honor to assist. I am, as ever, at the service of the Red Woman."

Aisling twisted around in her chair to look up at Kael. The hope he had so missed seeing in her eyes was back for the first time since they'd met with the Diviner. It glowed there, a steady burning ember, and he wished he could have looked away from it.

"This could be our best shot. It would give us more of an advantage to do it in your court, anyway, rather than trying to get into hers." She chewed her lip, anxious for his response.

"You are not wrong," Kael acknowledged. The hope burned brighter. He looked back at Lyre, then, and asked, "You believe you can design the rite?"

"I can design it, build it, and conduct it better than anyone else in your court, Highness. As it was, I have been crafting rituals for the High Prelate for years." He winked at Aisling conspiratorially. Kael was taken aback by this; Werryn had never given the impression that any of the Lesser Prelates were competent enough in Rhedelas to craft anything more than low-level rituals. Certainly, he hadn't ever mentioned that one of them was designing the rites for him entirely.

"What's in it for you?" Rodney challenged. They were two sides of the same coin, Lyre and the púca, though the former more malevolent in his intentions than the latter. Rodney played the game for his own amusement; Lyre did so for personal gain.

Lyre's grin widened further and his catlike eyes flickered over Kael. "The Red Woman has already promised me her protection. What might the Unseelie King have to offer?"

"If you are successful, I will see you made High Prelate," Kael said.

"And Werryn?" Lyre asked, one brow raised.

"Werryn will not protest," Kael shot back without hesitation. The aging male's time had come and gone. Werryn had long overstepped his role, committing acts that would have been grounds for execution if they'd been done by any other courtier. His absolute superiority over the Lesser Prelates had been all that protected him. Now knowing that another could step into his place so easily, Kael would no longer be so tolerant of his insolence.

Kael and Lyre departed the trailer first, cutting across the wide grass field behind it toward the tree line beyond. They moved quickly into the cover of the forest and continued on in the direction of the Thin Place. Though Kael had been reluctant to leave Aisling, he was all too happy to avoid returning in Rodney's vehicle. Rodney and Aisling split off in his car to drive Briar into town, where Aisling had arranged for a friend to watch over him. When Kael left, she'd been on her knees, her arms wrapped around the creature's neck in a fierce hug and her face buried into his voluminous fur.

Silently, he'd sworn to the White Bear that his Red Woman would return, safe and unharmed. Then he'd sworn to himself he'd do everything in his power to see that promise fulfilled.

"May I ask," Lyre began as the pair waited just beyond the Veil for Aisling and Rodney, "why?"

On their walk, Kael had explained to Lyre what he'd learned from Sítheach—what he had told Rodney and hidden from Aisling. Now, as he sat on a fallen log, he looked at the forest around him. It was quiet. Peaceful. Almost as though it was resting before the coming battle.

"Because it is the right thing to do," he said simply.

"Perhaps. But right for whom? And when did you begin concerning yourself with what is right?" Lyre mused. Kael ignored the Prelate's questions then and closed his eyes, listening to the wind rustle through the snow-dusted pines and the deep groans that emanated from their aged trunks as they shifted. *Now,* he thought. He was concerned with it now.

The rush of battle preparations invigorated Kael: the hum of energy that buzzed through the Undercastle, that electric undercurrent of bloodlust, was one that spoke to his basest desires. His mind felt sharper, his orders more certain. This was the role he'd been raised for—not just king, but commander. But Aisling's hand in his as they traversed the bustling passageways towards his study kept him grounded in the knowledge that he had other, greater purposes now. It was a new feeling expanding in his chest, and for once it was not one he feared. Aisling had once promised him he could be better. Now, it was time to be the king she imagined him to be.

"Where will you create the ritual space? Werryn keeps a chamber in the rear caverns for such things, does he not?" Raif asked Lyre. He had met the party at the bottom of the spiral staircase and had received their summary of the plan with grim determination. He, too, was sharpened by the promise of the coming battle.

"No," Kael said before the Prelate could answer. "Angry as she may be, Laure would not be so foolish as to follow me into these halls."

"Perhaps The Cut?" Lyre's mirrored eyes glowed in the firelight of the torch he pulled from the wall to carry outstretched. The shadows of the flames dancing across his face only made him appear more devious and cunning. "I believe I can repurpose many of the runes already carved there to adapt the circle for our purposes."

"There is a great deal of magic there," Kael agreed.

"And it may be strengthened further if you can call to the Low One," Lyre added thoughtfully. Kael nodded. He would not say out loud that the Low One had been silent the last time he'd sought the god's support. Alongside his shadows, blood—fresh and hot and seeping into the earth before the altar—would draw Him out this time, almost certainly.

"Highness?" Eamon and the other company commanders had gathered in Kael's study, awaiting an audience and a chance to strategize over the maps he kept there. Each would undoubtedly have their own idea of how the battle should be executed, of where their company would be best placed in the fray. The males he'd chosen to lead were wise and battle-hardened, but any one of them would cut the others down without hesitation for the chance to claim that victory had hinged on their company alone.

Raif joined the other commanders around the map table, but Kael hesitated on the threshold.

"We three will go to work in The Cut," Lyre said. "The space will be completed by sunup." He turned back the way they'd come and Rodney followed after, allowing Kael a moment alone with Aisling.

"Go on," she said, nodding towards the study. "I'll be fine with them. I don't want to keep you."

Kael raised her hand and pressed a kiss to the inside of her wrist. Her skin was warm beneath his lips and he could feel her heartbeat steady there when he whispered against it, "I would very much like you to keep me."

"Well then hurry back," she said with a smile.

Kael ignored the incredulous stares of his commanders when he entered the study and took his place at the head of the war table.

"You would consort with the Red Woman so freely?" Kharis, Commander of the Sixth Company, challenged dubiously. "As war marches on your court?"

"I am your King. I will consort with whomever I please." The harsh glare Kael gave him would have withered even the strongest trees in the realm, and as he cast it around the table, each commander lowered their eyes in concession.

Raif cleared his throat and leaned over the table to arrange the figurines there. He counted out five opponent pieces and placed them between the Undercastle and the border of the nearest Seelie dominion. He added another three behind those, a rough estimation of the forces following to conduct a second wave of attacks once the primary army had weakened the Unseelie defenses.

On his end, Kael set out the figurines representing each of his companies. He'd already envisioned it all: this strategy was one he'd gamed out time and again with Raif, altering and improving it little by little each year as numbers and strength shifted on both sides. It had only ever been a matter of time before the Undercastle came under siege. What he hadn't ever anticipated, though, was that he would not be leading his army from the center of the frontline. His figurine, a black horse, he removed from the board. The commanders noticed.

"You will look to Raif for your orders," Kael said, preempting their questions. "We developed this strategy jointly, and he has my support in altering it as he sees fit should the need arise."

"And you, my king?" Eamon asked.

"My focus will be on the queen. To that end, even should you have her at the tip of your sword, she is to remain unharmed. Ensure your soldiers are aware of this." When the commanders murmured their assent, Kael added sharply, "She is mine."

⁂

The gentle waves of Aisling's hair felt like silk between Kael's fingers as he toyed with the end of a strand that had fallen forward over her bare shoulder. She looked breathtaking where she lay beneath him atop blankets of fur. She'd wanted to be close to the fire he built for her on the hearth, chilled from working in The Cut, and so he'd layered the blankets into a makeshift bed there on the floor of his chamber.

Her cheeks were flushed now from the fire's warmth, and her lips were pink and swollen from the kisses he'd peppered them with ravenously from the moment his chamber doors closed and they found themselves alone. Kael knelt between her spread thighs, moving his hands to explore her form from the crests of her ribs down over the curves of her waist. She felt so delicate in his grasp.

She was perfect, every bit of her. But instead of telling her as much, Kael said only, "They will likely be here by dawn tomorrow."

"I don't want to talk about that right now." Aisling propped herself up on her elbows, baring her naked chest to him. He made no attempt to hide his perusal of her body, already dewy with perspiration. Those protective instincts that had been ignited to such a dangerous degree in Kael before shifted as he gazed down at her, softening into a different sort of impulse. He traced a callused thumb across her lips. Then, over her collarbone, where Elasha's poultice had already healed her wound into a raised pink scar. A reminder that he'd failed to protect her—and not only that once.

He was hers, he realized, and he felt that realization in his marrow. She had pulled him in as the moon draws the tides: gradually, inch by inch, but with unstoppable force.

Kael dropped forward to blaze a trail of searing kisses across her jawline, down the column of her neck, into the hollow at the base of her throat. He lingered at the notch of her collarbone, where her pulse fluttered just under her skin.

"I have never felt want—never felt need—the way I feel it for you," he purred. Aisling fell onto her back and he settled more of his weight against her, pinning her beneath him. Her lips met his again and parted. Waves of tingling pleasure cascaded through him when her tongue played over his own. The heated tension winding tightly in Kael's abdomen drew lower as he hardened against her.

"Please," Aisling begged, voice trembling, aching for him as he did for her. He'd wanted to savor this, to savor her, for as long as he could. But the hungry look in her eyes pulled a shudder through his muscles and he lifted himself up just enough to allow her to reach down and guide him into her. The way her body responded, tightening around him, was almost too much to bear.

When Aisling opened her legs wider, Kael rolled his hips against hers rhythmically. As they moved together, he tried to stay there with her in the moment and ignore the weight of uncertainty that hung heavy in the air. Yet each touch, each caress, was infused with a bittersweet urgency, a silent fear of what was to come. Neither of them dared speak that fear aloud, though. Not when doing so would make it real.

So they moved together, seeking both comfort and ecstasy in equal measure. Aisling's labored breath kept time with his thrusts and Kael relished the scent of her filling his nostrils, his lungs. She whimpered when he slowed his pace, dipping in and out of her with languid strokes. He wasn't ready for their closeness to end; he was intent on drawing it out for as long as he could, despite the way his every nerve protested for release.

This time, the rapturous climax they shared was a moment of surrender, a collision of two individuals finally, finally acknowledging what bound them.

40

SHADOWS & VINES

KAEL

He felt the shift in the atmosphere even before he awoke to Raif's insistent voice calling his name from the hall—it was subtle, only barely there, but insidious. Kael had ruled over Unseelie territory for long enough that he was very nearly one with it. He knew when something had changed. He could sense when it was under threat.

So he was unsurprised by the hard set of Raif's jaw and the determined gleam in his dark eyes when the male said, "The perimeter guard spotted the Seelie army closing in."

The army's arrival had come far sooner than even Kael predicted, but with their Queen's fury fueling them, it was unlikely that they'd stopped to make camp even once since departing the Seelie dominions. He was out of time.

Behind him, Aisling sat tangled in his fur blankets, clutching one against her bare chest. The fire in the hearth beside her, which had before been raging, had burned down to smoldering embers. Glowing shades of red and orange rippled across her pale skin. When Kael turned to look at her, she was focused straight ahead on the doorway where he stood with Raif. She was so still that he could hardly tell whether she was breathing.

"A moment," Kael told Raif, and closed the door. Then, to Aisling, he said, "It's time."

She shook her head. "It's too soon," she protested.

Kael took several steps towards her, then held out his hand. She took it and he pulled her to her feet. He grasped her chin gently and tipped her face up. "We are ready for this. *You* are ready for this."

"I don't think I am," she argued, her voice a quiet whisper.

"I know that you are. I can see it." Kael tightened his hold on her chin just slightly to keep her there with him. "Fate does not choose the weak, Aisling."

A smile, then—almost as faint as her voice, but it raised the corners of her lips enough that he was satisfied. Kael moved to the chest against the wall and began sifting through the pieces of his armor and battle leathers until he found his chainmail tunic. The cool material moved fluidly between his fingers when he withdrew it and passed it to Aisling.

"Put this on," he said. She pulled it over her head, layering it between a shirt and a heavy sweater. It fell to her thighs, far too big for her frame, but it was light and strong and its protection would give him some comfort while they were apart.

Kael's confidence in their plan grew with each strap he deftly fastened, and once he was finally clad in that black, black armor, he felt sure that they would succeed. His magic roiled and writhed beneath his skin, though not uncomfortably this time. Ready to be unleashed, but not beyond his control. A strength now, rather than a threat.

Lyre and Rodney had joined Raif in the passageway; Kael could hear their voices through the door. He approached Aisling where she stood watching him dress.

"Stay close to Lyre," he told her. Gently, he pulled her hair from where it was stuck beneath the collar of her moss green cloak. His fingers paused when they brushed against her neck, then he slid his hand around to rest at its nape.

"I'm afraid," Aisling admitted. Tears welled in her eyes and spilled down her face when she tried to blink them back.

"It is alright to be afraid." Kael's chest constricted, his heart squeezing as he leaned down and kissed away each falling tear. "You have been brave for long enough; let me have a turn. You've given me all the hope I need to see this through."

"Ready?" Rodney asked, peeking his head into the chamber.

Kael brushed his lips over Aisling's forehead one final time, then nodded and said, "Ready."

"I was thinking," Rodney started as Aisling and Kael stepped into the hall, pausing mid-sentence to draw in a breath. "I was thinking that it would make the most sense if I go with Kael."

Aisling balked visibly. "What? No. I need you with me."

"I'll be there with you for the rite, Ash," he insisted quickly. "But Laure knows you and I are rarely far apart. If she sees me with him, she'll be more likely to follow."

Kael raised an eyebrow, surprising even himself when he conceded, "The púca makes a decent point."

"I liked it better when you two weren't getting along," Aisling muttered. Kael chuckled at this, and with one last gentle squeeze of her hand, he let Lyre take her arm and lead her off down the passageway. He watched until she disappeared around a corner, then turned back to Raif and Rodney.

"You have a weapon?" he asked Rodney. His bright hair flopped when he nodded yes, and he patted a thin sword that hung from his belt. It was undoubtedly one of Raif's, and likely little more than a travel blade, but its size suited the púca's slender frame.

The three males walked quickly in the opposite direction from where Aisling and Lyre had gone. Rodney strayed ahead, but Raif remained in lockstep alongside Kael to update him on each company's position and readiness.

"I changed the positions of the First and Second Companies—there was a gap in the frontline, larger than it seemed on the board. And close to fifty additional foot soldiers arrived in the night from the western villages in Veladryn," Raif said.

Kael's jaw tightened. He would be foolish to deny his army the additional numbers, but these volunteers were untrained and would be underprepared for a battle of this magnitude. He thought of the Solitary Fae conscripted by the Seelie army, how they were sent to the Nyctara front with shoddy weapons and ill-fitting armor. The relative ease with which he and his Unseelie warriors had felled every one of them.

"Position them in the far rear," he commanded tersely. "Their first directive should be to protect the Undercastle unless needed at the front."

"Highness?" Methild called after him, scurrying to catch up from the far end of the corridor where she had likely been on her way to Kael's chamber.

He stopped to wait for her, then said to Rodney and Raif, "Go ahead."

"I've not yet polished your boots or your sword," Methild rasped, breathless by the time she made it to stand in front of Kael. She examined at his feet, dismayed by several faint scuffmarks on the metal.

He shook his head. "That will not be necessary."

"It will take no time at all," she argued. Kael regarded her for a moment. Stooped with age now, she stood only waist high beside him, but she was no less strong than she'd been when he was first brought to the Undercastle and she'd sworn her service to him.

He realized that he'd never once thanked her—it had never even occurred to him to do so. The old hob, who'd served him since he was learning to serve the Prelates and the Low One, had been steadfast in her duties. She'd borne the brunt of his cruelty time and again, and yet had cared for him at his weakest. Had brought him gifts when he was small to soothe his temper, and had continued to do so even now. He thought of the jar with the Luna moth that she'd quietly left for him before Nocturne, knowing the dark place his fear of failure could send him to. She was kind when he hadn't deserved it.

Kael knelt before her and took one of her wizened hands in his. "Thank you, Methild."

"I—" she squeaked, eyes wide with surprise, then cleared her throat. "It is my honor, Your Highness."

Kael rose to his feet. "Gather the other workers and go deeper. The Undercastle will keep you safe." It was true—even if Seelie soldiers managed to gain entry, the labyrinthine tunnels would brook no intrusion much further than the throne room. The twisting, winding passageways would sooner lead the soldiers to madness than to the stronghold of the structure's heart.

⁂

"She'll see us here?" Rodney gazed down from the crest of the knoll, eyes scanning the tree line. He sat astride a dappled mare and toyed with the reins. Ahead, every tall pine shivered with the thunderous footfall of the advancing Seelie forces. Kael settled his weight into Furax's saddle and watched as Raif rode up and down the frontline, making final adjustments to positions and speaking directly with each company commander. As much as Kael wished he was doing the same, he had a greater purpose now. Raif was a fine commander; Kael had no doubt he would lead the Unseelie army with the same unwavering ferocity that Kael would have himself.

"I will be the first target she seeks out," Kael assured Rodney. Only moments after he'd spoken those words, the first Seelie warriors appeared from the verdant darkness of the forest. Their pale golden armor glimmered in the waning moonlight as they approached with the dawn. A low horn sounded then, a call to arms, and the Unseelie warriors drove forward in full force. Kael's hand rose instinctively to the pommel of his longsword and his shadows surged, but he remained still, searching.

Until he found his mark.

Laure entered the battlefield on foot, shoulders back, chin high. Her raven hair billowed out behind her. It cast nearly as stark of a contrast against her golden chainmail as Kael's pale hair did against his black armor. His ribs felt as though they might crack under the growing, insistent pressure of his magic, so he let several tendrils reach from his fingertips. They stretched lazily toward the sounds of battle, only as far as he allowed. They came alive when the first drops of blood were spilled from the stomach of a Solitary pixie that was struck mid-flight by an arrow. She dropped heavily down into the growing fray below.

The next body to fall was an Unseelie warrior, one of Garrick's, from the Fourth Company. It was a swift death, but brutal all the same. The weight of Kael's responsibilities as King—responsibilities that had for so long been overshadowed by his greed and lust for power—bore down on him then, a crushing burden. A torrent of thoughts cascaded through his mind. Fear clawed at him, threatening to strip away the façade of composure he so carefully maintained, eating away at the confidence he'd felt only moments before.

It was the sensation of his magic writhing beneath his skin that brought him back from those thoughts. They could feel her, too, his shadows. They could feel the Seelie Queen's magic, the purest form of creation which she used now to strangle and destroy. Her vines crept forward through her ranks. Her warriors danced around the snaking plants as they reached up, savagely tearing at Kael's soldiers. They struck at the vines with their blades, but no sooner had they severed one than three more grew back in its place.

But Laure's focus wasn't on battle formations or the advancing line; her violet eyes darted back and forth, searching just as Kael had. The fury burning behind them was palpable, and her magic was stronger for it. Niamh remained close by her side, lips pulled back in a vicious snarl.

Before he'd left Raif to ride out with Rodney, Kael had firmly grasped his captain's arm, and Raif had responded in kind. Kael ordered Raif to take Niamh, but no further words were exchanged between the two males. No further words were needed. They were as close as brothers—while Raif didn't know the extent of the plan, he'd surely guessed by now.

"There," Rodney pointed towards Raif, who was now plunging through the clashing soldiers, aiming his warhorse straight for Niamh. She'd noticed him, too, and held her longsword at the ready. Kael drove a heel into Furax's flank and she reared, letting out a sharp bray that echoed across the field and found Laure's keen ears. She turned her attention towards Kael and Rodney and broke into a run in their direction. Distracted now, Niamh paid no attention to her queen's flight. By the time she would turn to look, Laure would be lost amidst the swords and spears and shots of magic.

THE RED WOMAN AND THE WHITE BEAR

Kael and Rodney both pulled their mounts into a swift gallop, first head-on towards Laure before veering off for the tree line. Laure let out a scream as she ran, a guttural war cry. Kael pulled Furax to slow, allowing Rodney the distance to disappear into the forest ahead of him. He would dismount there and continue on foot to join Aisling and Lyre in The Cut, with Kael and Laure just behind.

Kael could hear Laure's vines whispering, curling, reaching for him. His shadows reached back, withering those that drew too close. They were quick, though—a vine as thick as his arm caught one of Furax's hooves and sent the mare careening. Kael reacted reflexively, working his boots from the stirrups before the creature hit the ground. He rolled away from Furax as she struggled back to her feet and used that forward momentum to propel himself into a run.

Laure was still behind him; she roared again when he recovered without faltering. The distance between them was closing rapidly, and when Kael raced into the forest, Laure ran in after him without hesitation. So blinded by her own rage that she could think of nothing but running down the Unseelie King who had slaughtered first her subjects, then her favorite toy.

She was singularly focused; now, Kael knew, she would follow him anywhere.

41

THE RED WOMAN

AISLING

It had been cold as Aisling worked with Rodney and Lyre to prepare The Cut the previous evening. Her numb fingers could scarcely grip the sharp instrument Lyre handed her to etch markings into the frozen dirt before the altar. He crouched beside her, pointing to each empty space and describing the rune she should carve there. Rodney moved ahead of them, clearing snow from the circle with a branch of pine needles he swept back and forth like a broom.

Then, as she stood back with Rodney, watching Lyre continue on with his own preparations, her teeth chattered loudly when she said, "I don't know if I can do this."

"Which part?" he asked dryly. He had his hands tucked beneath his arms and bounced from foot to foot to keep warm.

"Any of it," she'd answered. *All of it.*

Caught up in the moment, she'd been so quick to paint the target on Laure's back that the thought of what she was saying, what she was condemning the Seelie Queen to, had been far from her mind. Now, though, her shoulders were heavy with the burden of a choice she wished she didn't have to make. She was a bystander in a war that wasn't hers, a human ensnared in the tangled affairs of the Fae—and her human heart recoiled at the notion of ending another's life, even for the sacred purpose of raising the Silver Saints.

Laure wasn't innocent; Aisling knew that well enough. Her motives were corrupted by her own virtues, her actions rooted in self-interest and manipulation. Yet, even in acknowledging Laure's misdeeds, the idea of taking her life for the ritual made Aisling's stomach churn.

"You won't be the one to do it, Ash," Rodney had promised. But still, Laure's name had come from Aisling's own lips. Aisling might not be the one to spill the queen's blood herself, but it was she who'd chosen her for the sacrifice.

Was it justifiable, she'd asked herself, to sacrifice one for the benefit of many when that one had no say in the matter? For Aisling, this wasn't merely a question of simple ethics. Her thoughts swirled viciously, torn between a sense of duty to the prophecy and a stubborn moral compass that resisted the idea of spilling blood, even if it might bring peace.

The question haunted her dreams, too, despite having been lulled to sleep by the warmth of Kael's skin against hers and the ebbing flames of ecstasy he'd ignited in her veins. So when she awoke to Raif's low voice at the door, cold dread gripped her lungs so tightly that they felt filled with cement. This was all much, much bigger than she was prepared for, and she felt so small on the threshold of what they were about to do.

There was so much she wished to say to Kael before they parted ways, but the words all stuck in her constricted throat. Even if she had been able to force them out, they would have felt too much like goodbye. And this wasn't that.

Now, waiting, Aisling paced back and forth across The Cut, careful to remain within the bounds of the protective runes Lyre had laid down when they arrived. Beyond the trees, the sound of armored footfalls was thunderous. The forest shook with the might of both armies approaching one another and soon, deafening clangs of metal slamming against metal rent the once-calm air. Shouts followed, deep bellows of anger and anguish. She wondered, briefly, what the echo of this battle looked like on Brook Isle. Whether there would even be a Brook Isle to go back to.

Oblivious, Lyre lounged against the trunk of a tree. Aisling wasn't keen on spending time alone with Lyre on a good day, much less at a moment so fraught as this. Despite her nervous energy, he appeared absolutely at ease as he studied the long scroll of parchment he'd scribbled on. His lips moved as he recited the ritual's words to himself voicelessly so that he would be prepared to utter them in one steady, unbroken refrain when the time came.

Another clash, louder this time, accompanied a pained shriek that shot straight through Aisling's gut. She darted to the far edge of the clearing and retched twice into a tangle of ferns. Her skin felt clammy, drenched in the cold sweat of fear. Her vision warped and spun until she sank to her knees and braced her hands in the dirt. The battle raged all around them, and the smell of spent magic filled the forest with a choking, bitter stench that made Aisling heave again.

With her eyes squeezed shut, she tried to parse through the noise of the fray for a familiar voice: Kael's, or Rodney's, or even Raif's. She strained her ears desperately, but the sound of combat was little more than a discordant roar.

It was an eternity before she finally heard running footsteps crashing through the underbrush. Lyre was on his feet and at her side in an instant, pulling her up roughly by the elbow and tugging her into the camouflaged hiding place they'd constructed behind the altar. Crouching there, Aisling could just see a flash of safety orange bobbing towards them. Rodney skidded into view, scrambling over roots to dive into the concealment beside her. Silently, Aisling seized his hand and gripped it tight.

A second behind, Kael's silver-white hair streamed in the frigid wind as he ran. His footfall was nearly silent in comparison. He halted with his back to them in the center of the circle of runes, both hands free of weapons, waiting. There was hardly any light left to see him by as the setting sun's last golden rays filtered sideways into the clearing.

Laure's approach was preceded by creeping vines: they crawled across the forest floor and wound around tree trunks, tight enough to strangle, a poisonous shade of kelly green. She was stunning in her fury, amethyst eyes aflame and teeth bared as she faced down Kael. Two predators vying for dominance.

"I should have known you would flee to this place to seek protection from your so-called *god*," she snarled, stepping forward. "But Aethar walks with me; your idol is nothing, not even here."

Through the branches that hid them from the circle, Aisling saw the ends of Kael's hair rustle in a soft breeze, the only movement breaking the sudden stillness in the clearing. Laure was wrong—the Low One was there. The queen took another step forward, then one more still, crossing unknowingly into the circle. She was surrounded now by the runic inscriptions they had carved.

When Aisling rose from behind the concealment, Laure faltered for the briefest moment. Then, that burning rage reclaimed her features tenfold.

"You stupid, insolent *child*." She spat the last word bitterly. "You've chosen death and darkness over goodness and peace; you've damned us all."

Aisling moved slowly, slowly, tracing her way around the circle in a bid to draw Laure's attention away from Kael. "The Seelie Court is no more righteous than the Unseelie. Disguising your misdeeds doesn't erase them."

"You've let yourself be blinded, little girl. What the king has done to you is far worse than any of my enchantments." Laure laughed, a harsh, mocking sound. "How do you imagine this ends for you? Happily?"

"It is how this ends for *you* that you should be concerned with," Kael growled. He moved to Aisling's side, briefly brushing the back of his hand against hers before continuing to advance on Laure. Shadows wove around his figure, drawn by the call of their master.

"I see you've improved upon your illusion of control," she shot back. Despite the arrogance in her voice, Aisling thought she noticed a flicker of fear in the queen's eyes as she studied the inky ribbons that rippled from Kael's hands.

Laure jerked her chin upward and the vines that had surrounded The Cut surged forward, sighing and whispering as they moved. When their tapered ends reached the circle, they withered and shrank back. Not a single tendril made it past the edge of the runes. Laure's enraged shriek was ear-splitting. She fumbled to unsheathe a golden dagger from its hilt at her waist, long with a distinctive wavy blade, and lunged.

But Kael was faster.

Her limbs were wrenched out until she was suspended spread-eagle just above the ground. She was held in place by Kael's shadows—shadows over which he had full, unabated control. They danced for him now, did his bidding without protest. Laure was unable to move so much as an inch as he approached her. Her eyes were wide and wild, full lips open in a silent scream.

Having quietly taken his place before the altar, Lyre began his recitation. The foreign words flowed together lyrically, beautiful despite their sinister meaning. This was not the Fae language Kael had spoken to Aisling; this was a dialect far, far older. It was the language spoken during the time of the gods. During the time of the Silver Saints.

Kael reached up and took possession of the dagger Laure still clung to. He turned it over in his hand, then swung. The first slice of the blade split open her palm, sending rivulets of blood streaming down into the dirt. It collected in the runes at her feet. A second slash opened her other hand, adding to the flow.

Two vaporous streams of shadow reached beyond the circle of runes, disappearing into the darkness of the forest. The Low One was with Kael now, Aisling knew. She'd seen his shadows grasp at the presence of his god before, noticed the way they seemed to disappear into the air, pulsing as they connected Kael to the deity.

Then, all Aisling could see of the golden dagger was its hilt protruding from Laure's breastbone. The Seelie Queen's eyes rolled back into her head and her features slackened. When Kael released her from the hold of his magic, she dropped heavily to the ground. It was strange, really—an almost anticlimactic ending for an opponent Aisling had thought to be so powerful. But as she bled out into the earth, Laure appeared just as anyone else. Seelie or Unseelie, powerful or not, they were all the same in death.

Unable to look any longer at her lifeless body, Aisling turned to Lyre. The Prelate continued his invocation, steady and unfazed. His cadence hadn't changed as she would have expected it to as he neared its end. Aisling glanced around, searching the forest for any sign that something had changed. That the ritual had worked.

Lyre's attention was not on the parchment he held, though, but fixed on something else over Aisling's shoulder.

When she wheeled around, Kael was kneeling before her. He gazed at her intently, with so much force that he could have only been etching her face into his mind. Every line, every freckle, every variation of color in her irises. He wanted all of it—he needed all of it. He looked every bit that fearsome warrior who she'd trembled before at Nyctara. Who'd marked her for death not once, but twice. But there was no hint of that cruelty when he looked at her now, no fear or anger in his expression. Only acceptance and love, overwhelming and powerful. In his hand, he held his own dagger. And a cold sort of realization hit Aisling like a punch in the gut.

"How long have you known?" she demanded.

Kael's shadows were but thin filaments now, swirling around him gently. Caressing him. "Awhile."

Aisling fell back a step, shaking her head fervently. "No. I'm not doing this."

"You have no choice. This is the prophecy, Aisling." He was so calm, so sure when he spoke. He'd come to terms with this on his own, without her.

"Fuck your prophecy!" Her voice broke on the word. "I didn't ask for this!"

Kael reached out and took Aisling's hand in his. He held it firmly, calluses scraping across her freezing palm. "Our fates are immutable. We never ask for these things. The futures we are destined for find us, no matter what we do. You cannot escape yours any more than I can mine."

"I won't kill you." She tried to pull away, but he wouldn't let her.

"I don't regret this. Us. I never could, not in a hundred lifetimes. Even while I knew this would be our ending, I would not trade the time we had for anything. And someday, in some other form, we will find our way back to each other. I'm sure of it. But this was never our story—yours and mine—it was only ever yours." He smiled at her softly, sadly, as he slid the hilt of the blade into her hand then gripped it tight under his own and moved it to rest against his throat. "I will do all the hard work. Just close your eyes."

She wanted to. She wanted to clench them shut and picture herself anywhere else, with him, safe. But she couldn't. Instead, Aisling kept her eyes locked on Kael's as he slowly drew the blade from left to right across his throat. Hot blood splattered across her face, shooting from the wound they created together. The spray coated her neck. Her stomach, as his head dropped forward. Her legs, as he fell to the ground. The deep crimson pooled around her feet. But she remained stuck in place, rooted to the ground where she stood. Her vision tunneled around that creeping, expanding puddle.

Besides the movement of the blood, those first few moments after his death felt so unbearably still. She couldn't breathe, couldn't even remember how. Like she had to hold her breath as he drew in his last.

She looked then at the dagger still clutched in her hand. Blood flowed in slow motion from its tip, dripping down into the growing puddle that was spreading past her feet now. She could see it there—see her fingers wrapped around its handle, the hilt resting on the first knuckle of her thumb and her forefinger—but she couldn't feel it. She couldn't feel anything at first.

When the pain finally hit a full minute later, it washed over her as an avalanche: suffocating, all-encompassing. Her entire world was reduced in an instant to the searing, ripping, breathless pain of her heart cleaving in two.

Despite being only a few paces behind her, Lyre's voice seemed infinitely distant as it crescendoed through the rite's final litany. He'd known, too. They all had.

Aisling only vaguely heard Rodney call her name from someplace to her left. As she turned in his direction, unsteady on her feet, he stood still for a moment to take her in.

From the soft rounds of her cheeks to the soles of her shoes, Aisling was stained red with the blood of the Unseelie King. A twisted sort of laugh bubbled up her throat. She understood it now: her title. She thought she could shape the prophecy on her own, to rewrite her fate. Kael's fate. In the end, it was exactly as it had been foretold.

In the end, it was Kael's death that made Aisling the Red Woman.

42

THE SILVER SAINTS

AISLING

A hush seized The Cut as Lyre uttered the last words of the ritual. There was no breeze, no birdsong. Even the distant clashing and shouting ceased, as though the battle had halted altogether. The atmosphere, once heavy with the presence of the Low One, took on a different sort of feel: electric, pulsating, like pins and needles pressed against cold skin.

A downdraft dropped into the clearing then, harsh and violent enough that it sent several large branches crashing to the ground. Aisling was the only one to remain on her feet, so numb to her surroundings that she was barely swayed. Lyre reeled backwards into the altar, destroying it on his way down. Rodney narrowly avoided being pinned beneath a falling limb.

Bright enough to blind, a bolt of white light followed the downdraft. It shot straight into the center of the circle, almost as wide as the trunks of the trees surrounding them. Instead of striking and retracting as lightning, it remained a steady, unbroken stream like a lifeline tethering the vast night sky to the earth below. All around the bright shard, swirling waves of energy surged, rushing upward. A reverse waterfall. The heaviness that magic imbued in the air around them built and built and built, at once both searing hot and ice cold, until finally it exploded in a glaring blast of unharnessed power. The entire clearing was washed with that brilliant white. Aisling had to shield her eyes behind her forearm.

When she looked up, the light had faded to a soft glow. Where the bolt had struck, three figures now stood still as statues. They were nearly identical, save for their stature: the figure in the center stood slightly taller than the other two. The one on the left had arms that seemed almost disproportionately long, and the one on the right was a touch too thin. Their faces were featureless, blank masks without eyes or nostrils or mouths. *Like mannequins,* Aisling thought dully, but they were no less radiant for it. Their luminous, silver-toned skin seemed to glow from within, the embodiment of starlight.

"Child of prophecy, you have given much to bring peace to a world that is not yours." The words emanated from all three figures, echoing ethereally through the clearing. They spoke in a strange sort of harmony, three voices merged as one, projecting the sounds somehow without mouths to move. When the taller of the three stepped forward, their movement was fluid and deliberate. Delicate white gems and incandescent robes blended almost seamlessly with their shimmering complexion.

"You're the Silver Saints," Aisling breathed. She wondered whether she should bow, or curtsy, or avert her gaze. Still in the grip of shock, she did none of those things. Instead, she stood still before the figures, looking into what might have been the eyes of the one closest to her.

"We are Merak," they said, again together.

"You can end this war?" she asked. They nodded serenely, movements in sync.

"The Unseelie King shall be the final victim of this needless conflict. The bloodshed ends with him." All three began to move then, gliding across The Cut in the direction of the battle. The plants on the forest floor parted as they passed, the long trains of their gowns sweeping over the snow and dirt but leaving no trace of their passage. Aisling followed behind numbly on leaden legs. Rodney and Lyre joined her wordlessly, but she was oblivious to anything except the light guiding her out of the forest.

The battlefield was littered with bodies, the snow muddied and stained all shades of crimson. On the frontline, where the two armies had met in fierce and violent combat, the fighting had ceased. Those that were pledged to either court stood entranced, eyes clouded over as the magic of the Silver Saints invaded their minds. Some fell to their knees, others merely halted mid-motion. Most had dropped their weapons. Interspersed amongst them, a handful of Solitary Fae looked around, confused, until they saw the approaching light. Then they, too, lowered themselves down on bended knee. Though their minds remained their own, their reverence was no less profound. Whether or not they believed the Silver Saints to be legend, or lost to bygone history, the entities were here now, walking amidst the dead and wounded.

"Your royals have given their lives for peace," Merak proclaimed. "Their blood was traded in exchange for our awakening."

The warriors stared blankly, slack-jawed, hearing the words in their minds. Aisling and the Solitary Fae only heard them out loud; Merak's voices swirled in the night air such that it sounded like the Silver Saints were speaking from all directions.

"Our awakening marks a turning point in your stories. The cycle of strife will end not with the fall of the courts, but with the rise of unity. Your differences birth strength, but your harmony shall craft your future."

Tears streamed down the faces of many of the soldiers, Seelie and Unseelie and Solitary alike, as the Silver Saints spoke. Aisling felt her own face growing wet with them, cutting rivulets through the blood drying on her cheeks.

"Let our light guide you in this choice: to lay down arms or continue the futile cycle," Merak continued. "The power to shape your destiny lies not in the clash of swords but in the embrace of diplomacy. But choose wisely, for the fabric of your realm hangs on the decisions made from this moment on."

As suddenly as their magic's hold had gripped the fray, the faeries were released. Still, none moved to pick up their discarded weapons. A few staggered to their feet, but many remained in a daze that kept them on their knees.

Aisling's gaze slid to Raif, near the center of the field where the bodies lay thickest. He rose lithely and left his sword where it had pierced through Niamh's stomach and pinned her to the ground. Rodney stepped in front of Aisling, a protective barrier, but there was no malice in Raif's approach. He only stared at her, at the blood that covered her, resigned.

"So it is true, then," he said. "The king is dead." Aisling looked away and nodded, feeling that pain beginning to edge back into her consciousness. She'd have preferred to remain numb; it was a far more tolerable state.

"He gave himself willingly," Rodney hedged.

"I have no doubt." Raif looked towards the Silver Saints then. A distant, haunted expression had settled over his normally impassive face. "Did you not see it?"

"See what?" Rodney asked.

"They showed us our future—Wyldraíocht's future. Just a glimpse, just for a moment, of what it would look like should the war continue." Raif stared at Merak's retreating figures. All three moved in unison away from the carnage back towards the tree line. There, they stopped and returned to their motionless stance.

"And?" Rodney pressed.

"The outcome is not favorable for either side." Lyre had seen it, too, and he wore a similar expression to Raif.

"What happens now?" Aisling croaked. Her throat burned with an unreleased scream of anguish stuck there since Kael had knelt before her. She wasn't sure whether she cared to learn the answer—her part in this was over. She'd done what she was meant to and had paid dearly. There was little left for her in the Wild now.

"Assemblies will be formed, I suppose. Peacemakers from each court who will work alongside the Silver Saints to mend the rift," Raif said. The rest of the battle-weary warriors were beginning to rise all around them. Aisling watched as a spriggan, clad in gold Seelie armor, offered his branchlike arm to an Unseelie Fae struggling to regain her balance on an injured leg.

"You think it will work?" Rodney was watching the pair, too, but still sounded skeptical.

"It has to," Aisling insisted. This couldn't all have been for nothing. Kael's death couldn't be for nothing. She repeated again, more for herself than anyone else, "It has to."

⁘

Both armies worked well into the early morning hours clearing their dead and injured from the battlefield. The losses were steep on both sides, and felt deeply. The Silver Saints watched it all from the tree line, statuesque keepers of a more hopeful future. Aisling thought she could feel their magic lingering over the armies, propagating a sense of peace and calm as she had done for Kael. The pain of the injured was soothed, and the anger of the survivors was curbed.

It did little for Aisling, though, as she sat on the frozen ground amidst the effort. Raif and several company commanders had gone to The Cut to retrieve Kael's body, but she couldn't bring herself to go with them. She couldn't bring herself to do anything, really, beyond mindlessly watching the first rays of sunrise. Rodney sat beside her, one arm around her shoulders. He'd pulled off her bloodstained cloak and replaced it with his own.

"I'm proud of you," he said softly. "Your mother would be, too."

"When did he tell you?" Aisling asked. She was sure he'd known.

"Before we came back. It was something the Diviner said to him. I'm sorry." He tightened his hold around her, but she only nodded. She wanted to be angry—she would be—but for now, Aisling could only feel a hollowness in her chest.

"What happens now?" she asked again, this time about her own uncertain future. Without a prophecy guiding her path, she felt like a ship at sea without a rudder. Without a port. She couldn't remain in the Wild, nor could she imagine returning to her life on the mainland. Even Brook Isle felt distant and foreign.

"Your path is yours again, Ash. What happens now is your decision."

"Is it?" Aisling's question was monotone, without inflection. "It doesn't feel like mine."

Rodney nudged her gently. "Whatever you decide, you've still got me. And you've still got Briar; I think he's probably had enough adventure to last him awhile. I know I have."

Aisling sighed. "Me, too."

43

ELOWAS

AISLING

They'd never said I love you—Aisling hadn't found the courage, and Kael hadn't found the strength. But she whispered it now as she pressed her lips against his cold forehead. Over and over, she murmured those words as a mantra. A plea. Some small part of her thought it might be enough to bring him back. So many other fairytales had been proven true, why not the power of love to wake the dead, as well? But nothing happened. Kael was still dead. Cold and pale and unmoving and dead.

Even in death, he was beautiful.

Kael would lie for three days and three nights before being laid to rest amidst the roots of the trees in Talamarís. The commanders had placed his body on a plain table carved from the same obsidian as his throne. It was the only feature in the cavern, which was vast and dark with a ceiling so high it disappeared into blackness. Two candles were lit, one at his feet and one at his head, but the circle of light they cast hardly expanded more than a foot beyond the edges of the table.

Raif stood guard at the entrance day and night. He was steadfast in his duty: he never sat, never leaned. Never closed his eyes to rest. Inside the cavern, Aisling did the same at Kael's side.

She couldn't fully recall the events leading up to that moment in The Cut, nor could she remember how she'd left that dark place afterwards, as if shock had erased those bookends entirely. She did, however, remember that minute of absolute stillness when Kael had given her his life. The feeling of the blade dragging through his flesh. The way his eyes dulled as the spark of life there faded while he was still on his knees before her. The hot stickiness of his blood coating her body.

She could have used his name, the gift he'd so willingly given her, to stop him from pressing that blade to his throat. But she hadn't—she couldn't—and instead she just watched mutely as he gave himself to the ritual.

Each evening, Methild came to the cavern. She brought with her a basket of clean rags and another of Kael's commanders, Garrik, carried in a steaming bucket of fresh water. Together with the old hob, Aisling washed Kael's body. The first night, it took two buckets and several hours to remove his armor and scrub his skin clean of blood and sweat and dirt. Aisling washed his long, moonbeam hair carefully, somehow still afraid of getting soap in his eyes. They'd dressed him then in a simple set of black robes. They were rough. He'd have hated them.

Before Methild left her alone again, Aisling passed her the strand of gems Kael had worn in his ear on Nocturne. She'd found it atop his desk when she returned to his room to choose the crown he would wear. She held his hand while Methild, stone-faced, pierced his lobe with a long needle and followed it through with the post of the earring.

At some point, Rodney carried in a chair and forced her to sit. She hardly registered his presence, nor did she feel the weight of his hands on her shoulders when he guided her down. She thought her feet should have hurt from standing on hard stone for so long, but the only discomfort Aisling was aware of was the one that lingered in the hollow of her chest. She'd have carved out her heart if she thought it might excise the pain she felt with its every beat. But she knew that as long as she had breath in her lungs, she'd feel the sharp ache of loss there.

On the third night, Aisling clung desperately to Kael's body. His commanders would take him before dawn to Talamarís, where he would rot away. She couldn't bear the thought of him decomposing there, his skin peeling and bones decaying like those other soldiers she'd seen. He wanted to go that way; she knew he did. The customs of the Unseelie Court were as important to Kael as his religion, and he'd consider it his greatest honor to lay with the rest of those faeries who fell for his court during the final battle. Still, it made Aisling sick.

"I love you," she said for what must have been the thousandth time. "I'm not ready to let you go."

Aisling's skin prickled as the atmosphere in the cavern shifted, becoming charged with magic. Merak had filed in behind her, silently and in sync. Their soft white light illuminated the space, reaching into every corner and catching on tiny veins of glittering quartz in the walls. It bathed Kael gently in its glow. When the tallest of the three glided to stand beside her, the gleaming white material of their cloak felt like water where it brushed against her bare arm.

They remained silent for several moments before they said, "You are human; you were born to forget. You will fade, and your memory with you. His face will not linger, nor will this ache inside of you. You will forget him one day and by then you will not even realize what it is you've forgotten."

"That isn't true." She supposed their words were meant to comfort her, but instead only hardened her further against letting him go. She smoothed the ends of Kael's hair that had fallen out of place with the movement of energy the Silver Saints brought in with them. "I won't let it be true."

"You do not have to." The magic around them thickened, the shimmering light pulsing and humming. The other two Silver Saints joined them around the stone table, looking down at Kael. The tallest one remained focused on Aisling.

"I won't," she said again, defiant.

"Then bring him back," Merak said.

Aisling's world stilled.

She recoiled, scrambling to her feet, but she didn't hear the chair clattering to the stone ground. The hum of energy and the dull roar of her own blood rushing in her ears was, for just a moment, loud enough to dampen the ambient sounds of the Undercastle. Finally, she tore her gaze from Kael and looked between Merak's unearthly, featureless faces, searching. They were serene in their plainness, almost angelic. It was no wonder that they inspired such peace, even amongst those Solitary Fae who were untouched by their magic. But that serenity they radiated had little effect on the apprehension and dread that surged in Aisling's chest.

"Bring him back?" she whispered. The words felt wrong, so wrong, in her mouth.

"His *aneiydh*, the basest essence of him—what you might equate to his soul—has been captured. His corporeal flesh must first be released to collect it." Their voice was an echo that rippled through Aisling's fraying consciousness.

She shook her head, hard, trying desperately to clear it. Trying to understand how the finality of loss could somehow be dispelled. "Where is it?"

"Elowas," Merak proclaimed. "The god realm."

In times of crisis, Aisling had long since learned to wrap her empathy in a resilient mantle, a shield against the onslaught of emotions that threatened to engulf her. She reached for that mantle now to steel her, to allow her the clarity of thought to understand the decision she was now faced with. *Bring him back.* She played with Kael's hand rather than look again at his face, tracing the lines on his palm and measuring her own against it as her mind raced.

She could bring him back.

"How?" she demanded.

One at a time, each of the three Silver Saints brushed long, slender fingers over Kael's closed eyelids, then said, "It begins with fire."

PRONUNCIATION GUIDE

Brook Isle

Aisling
ASH-leen

Maeve
MAVE

Unseelie Court

Kael
KAI-ehl

Werryn
WHERE-in

Lyre
LEER

Methild

    MEH-thuld

Seelie Court
 Laure
    LORE
 Niamh
    NEEV
 Tadhg
    TIE-gh
 Darragh
    DA-rah
 Gancanagh
    Ghan-CAW-nah

Solitary
 Sítheach
    SHEE-huh

Misc.
 Wyldraíocht
    WILD-ree-oct
 Gweldealain
    GWELL-dee-ah-len
 Rhedelas
    RED-ell-ahs
 Sangelas
    SAN-jell-ahs

Aneiydh

an-eye-EED

Printed in Great Britain
by Amazon